SWEETER LIFE

SWEETER
LIFE

A NOVEL

TIM
WYNVEEN

Random House Canada

NATIONAL LIBRARY OF CANADA CATALOGUING IN PUBLICATION

Wynveen, Tim
Sweeter life / Tim Wynveen.

ISBN 0-679-31157-2

I. Title.

PS8595.Y595S94 2002   C813'.54   C2002-901709-2
PR9199.3.W97S94 2002

Sweeter Life is a work of fiction. Most names, places, characters, and events are the product of the author's imagination, and any resemblance to actual events, locales, or persons, living or dead, is entirely coincidental. In those few instances when the author mentions real persons and reported events, it is within a similarly fictionalized context and should not be construed as fact.

Jacket Design: Dinnick & Howells
Text Design: Daniel Cullen

www.randomhouse.ca

Printed and bound in the United States of America

10 9 8 7 6 5 4 3 2 1

To Penny and Terry

We talk because we are mortal. —*Octavio Paz*

And because we aren't gods,
or close to gods,
we sing.

> —Donald McKay
> *Another Gravity*

Fling the emptiness out from
    your arms
into the spaces we breathe: maybe the birds will
feel the thinner air with a more inward flight.
    —Rainer Maria Rilke,
      The Duino Elegies

{ SILENCE }

Imagine the scene in Woodstock, New York, on August 29, 1952. John Cage, that most puzzling of American composers, has come to the Maverick Concert Hall for the first public performance of what will become his most famous, and infamous, work. He is forty years old, with angular features and dark hair and a dazzle of laughter in his eyes. He is pretty much unknown outside a small circle of intellectuals, and, even among that select group, some question the value of his work. His *Music of Changes*, for example, based on the random toss of coins, created more confusion than pleasure when it debuted the previous year.

But picture him there at the Maverick in a dark checked suit, with a white shirt open at the collar. He stands serenely backstage, tapping neither his fingers nor his foot as the crowd files into the hall.

They have come on this overcast summer evening to support the Benefit Artists Welfare Fund and are prepared for an evening of challenging music. The performances will vary, with works by Christian Wolff, Morton Feldman, Earle Brown and Pierre Boulez. Cage's newest composition, *4'33"*, will be the second-last selection on the evening's program, followed only by *The Banshee*, written by Henry Cowell. The young pianist David Tudor is the featured performer.

Cage is pleased with the choice of venue. The back of the hall opens on the surrounding forest, and he can feel the humidity of the summer night and hear the occasional breeze sweep through the trees outside. He is so excited by the possibilities that, when the concert begins, he pays little attention. Instead he thinks about sources and directions, where his music has come from and where it is likely to go. He knows he will be asked how he came to write a piece such as *4'33"*, and he wonders how better to explain that time, not pitch, lies at the heart of music, seeping into our consciousness with every pulse of our mothers' blood, and that time, the sad half of Einstein's universe, is what we are born to sing.

When Tudor walks onstage, he is holding Cage's handwritten score and a small stopwatch. He sits behind the grand piano and arranges his music. Grave and graceful, he lowers the fallboard, the double-hinged cover that protects the keys, then clicks the small button of his timepiece. He sits motionless. He makes no sound. After exactly thirty seconds, he clicks the stopwatch and raises the fallboard to reveal once again the eighty-eight keys. He fills his lungs with air. He takes a moment to compose himself.

The second movement begins in the same way, with the lowering of the keyboard cover. This middle movement is much longer and requires Tudor to turn the pages of the score. He pays no attention to the growing uneasiness of the crowd. Again he makes no sound.

A third movement and still he sits, silent as a mime, dark with concentration. The nervous muttering in the hall grows to a howl of outrage by the end of the piece and Tudor's departure from the stage after exactly four minutes and thirty-three seconds of silence. And remember, the audience is comprised of people who cherish the arts, who relish the cutting edge. Even so, they believe, almost without exception, that Cage has gone too far.

The creator hears something quite different that day. Instead of silence, Cage notices the sound of wind in the trees, the complicated rhythms of rain on the roof, the audience chattering like small birds. And he is pleased. It is the embodiment of an idea that came to him a year before.

On a whim, he had dropped by a Harvard lab, their anechoic chamber— what others referred to as "the dead room." It was, he'd been told, a scientific marvel, a chamber of utter stillness. In that muffled womb of sculpted foam and baffles, he hoped to experience a silence both perfect and profound. Instead he heard two distinct sounds that day, one high and one low: the thrumming of his nervous system and blood, he was later told, a lesson that would change his music entirely and lead him to *4'33"*.

Because life knows nothing of silence. Between nerves and blood a song will emerge. Between mind and heart a life will flow. Between words and music a story will unfold.

{ WORDS and MUSIC }

Seagulls huddled in a field, querulous and surreal in the misty morning light. As a tractor approached, they rose into the air in waves, a reluctant cloud of grey and white flecked here and there with yellow beak and black stripe. When they settled moments later on the freshly tilled soil, they knew immediately that something important had passed among them, that the earth beneath their feet had been altered, made new again.

The wind gathered strength off the lake, scattering the last tatters of fog and dancing the branches of the willow where red-winged blackbirds sang of springtime and distant travel. Beneath the tree, near the edge of the irrigation pond, Cyrus Owen sat with his Labrador retriever, Blackie, and waited for the sun to clear the top of the corncrib by the barn. That would be the signal to head back to the house.

Cyrus, a nineteen-year-old farm boy, was lean and muscular from his share of chores. His shoulder-length blond hair danced in every gust of wind, his eyes never straying from the tractor as it crossed the field. There was an edginess about him, a youthful intensity that some might call a sense of purpose.

To watch him as he sat there—really, to see him anywhere, at school, at home—you would never notice that he was born without a ring finger on his left hand. It was not a big deal for him anymore. He had long ago worked out most of his difficulties, both physical and emotional, and seldom gave it a thought. Even so, as a matter of habit, he tended to stand with his left hand in his pocket, or to sit with his fist stuck between his legs. It wasn't a conscious thing on his part, but a residual pose from a more insecure time in his life.

He sat that way now, on a tree stump, his left hand nestled in his lap. He had come to the old place looking for inspiration, a word on the breeze, say, a pattern in the clouds. But there was nothing, or perhaps too much to make sense of. The house had pretty much gone to hell, rented to a meaty-looking biker with a thunderous Harley and a gaunt, freckled girlfriend. The barn was unpainted, showing great gaps in its weathered sides. The coop had burned down years ago. And there was the pain, same as ever, that it wasn't his father but Benny Driscoll working those fields, using that tractor.

Cyrus scratched the dog behind the ear and Blackie leaned his head back, nose pointed to the sky, his tongue lolling. The dog had fetched without fail, marked innumerable trees and fence posts, and sat now with the one who didn't kick him, the one who didn't smack his nose with a rolled newspaper, the one who talked to him and played with him and lifted the edge of the covers at night to let him crawl into bed. Cyrus wished he could be as content as Blackie to sit and let the world roll by. How easy it would be to have no special feeling for the future or the past, to take things as they were and never expect more.

He reached down with his right hand and picked up a large stone, one that covered his entire palm. He squeezed it rhythmically, an exercise he had read about in a magazine (as though it was physical strength he needed just now and not courage). His problem, what had him huddled out here before sunrise, was that he couldn't decide what he wanted to do with his life; or rather, he had decided but didn't know if he had the nerve. He had tallied lists of pros and cons, worked out rough calculations, expenses, elaborate economies of favour and obligation that might see him through a rough spot now and again—but he still hadn't made the leap.

As the tractor reached the far end of the flat, black field and made a wide turn back toward the seagulls, Cyrus got to his feet and, with a grunt of frustration, heaved the rock, watching it smack the muddy bank and then roll below the duckweed and out of sight. Right on cue, Blackie struggled up and padded toward the pond. There, leaning carefully over the bank, the dog lowered its head beneath the surface of the water. Ten, twenty, thirty seconds passed, until the dog began to tremble with the strain, a quiver that gradually became more pronounced and centred itself near the neck and shoulder area.

"Black," he called to the dog, "cut it out now. That's enough, Black."

And when the old Lab lifted its head from the water and backed slowly away from the pond, Cyrus laughed, a single quack. The dog, shuddering like an Olympic weightlifter, had its jaws clamped around the stone, which it carried over and dropped with a thud at Cyrus's feet.

The boy winced at the thought of his own teeth grinding on stone, and said, "You are one stupid dog." Then he pulled up the collar of his faded denim jacket, scant defence against the chill wind, and he and the dog walked slowly across the fields, climbing all the way up to a small orchard on the ridge. From that vantage he turned once again and looked down at the scattering of poor farms along the Marsh Road, with the lake waiting on one side, and on the other the deeper reaches of the marsh itself. Finally, his hands jammed into the pockets of his jeans, he followed the dog along the lane to the large brick farmhouse that was now their home.

Upstairs in his room he picked up his guitar, an old Harmony archtop, and folded himself around it, breathing in the perfume of wood and lemon oil and, above that, the slightly sour tang of the pickup and strings. Quietly he fingered a few of his favourite songs, melodies he could count on to lighten his mood. He should have known better than to go out to the old place. Even at the best of times, it made him feel like a stranger in his own life.

When it was time for school, he found Ruby Mitchell sitting at the kitchen table with tea and toast, not really listening to the CBC. She was still in her housecoat but had her face on, such as it was. She was not his mother but his aunt. Most times that scarcely mattered.

"You were up early," she said.

Cyrus looked at the wall clock and then back out to the rolling rows of apple trees. "Went down to the marsh with Blackie. Needed to do some thinking."

She took a tiny bite of bread, marvelling that he could stand to be outside with a light jacket and nothing but a thin T-shirt underneath. It was April, but the wind still carried the memory of winter.

The voice on the radio rumbled on about Nixon and the Paris Peace Talks, the Calley trial; and Ruby rose slowly and turned the damn thing off. Too depressing, really, an entire history of loss. All those young boys. All that bombing.

"I have to shop," she said. "I could drive you into town."

He made a grumbling sound and stared down at his well-worn Keds. "I'm up. I'll walk. Maybe it'll clear my head." Then he grabbed an apple and moved to the door. But before he could make his escape she touched his shoulder, turning him around until she was looking into his pale blue eyes.

"Whatever it is," she said, "will work out." She slipped a folded piece of paper into the pocket of his T-shirt. Running her hand through the cool silk of his hair, she said, "Isabel's coming for dinner. Try to be on time. I think she wants to give you the benefit of her sisterly wisdom."

They both laughed at that, and he promised to be home for dinner. He was down the steps and halfway across the lawn before he dug the paper from his pocket. It was a blank cheque with her signature. Not from the farm account—those cheques were always calculated to the penny—but from her personal account, her "mad money" as she liked to call it, as if she had ever had an irrational moment in her life. Wrapped around the cheque was a sheet of her memo paper, wildflowers all along the border.

Buy yourself something nice for graduation. Don't want you looking like a farmer.

Love,

Ruby.

He looked at the house and shoved the cheque back into his pocket, trying to imagine himself in a new suit and tie. Then he turned and walked into the wind, his shoulders hunched, his head down.

RUBY WATCHED CYRUS scoot out the door and away. Then she slipped into the laundry room off the kitchen and peered out the low windows to see her husband, Clarence, moving around in the packing shed, looking worn out before the season was even properly underway. A brush with cancer was reason enough to feel tired and anxious, of course; but now he had something else to worry him. He was suddenly convinced that this boy who wasn't his son had decided against a life on the farm.

Ruby had guessed as much the moment she set eyes on Cyrus wriggling in his mother's arms. He was a softy, a cuddler and a dreamer. But Clarence, even with his college education, his history books and fancy magazines, never had a clue. That it had taken him all this time to recognize the fact gave Ruby no satisfaction. She was not one to gloat about such things—her gift for divination, her natural grasp of the heart's varied languages. Rather, these talents made her more understanding of a husband torn by competing terrors: one, that Cyrus would someday soon walk away from the farm; the other, that he, Clarence, out of his love for the land and the solid kind of life it could provide, would say something, do something, to make this boy stay where he didn't belong, deflect him from whatever true path might be revealed to him.

This fear of terrible mistakes, of stepping beyond one's rightful duty, was something Ruby well understood. They had all made enough mistakes for one lifetime. And Clarence would be the first to admit he had made his share. It was laughable, when she thought about it, a man perfectly attuned to the slightest fluctuations in weather, to the rhythms of the agricultural life—and really such a sweet and intelligent man, who nearly every week had a thoughtful letter in *The Wilbury Gazette*—yet so completely out of sync with the nature of his loved ones.

Oh, he tried his best. Ruby had lost count of the times he had come to her seeking forgiveness, guidance, some key to the inner workings of family life. And no question, things had changed for the better. How could they not? They had all been caught flat-footed in the beginning. No time to prepare. No option but to just grab hold of each other and run like heck. In fact, it was only now, with Cyrus nineteen years old, that she and Clarence were becoming the kind of parents they should have been from the beginning. Small consolation for Isabel, who had bolted at the first opportunity. And no help at all for poor Hank.

Just the thought of Cyrus's older brother made Ruby clutch the locket around her neck and close her eyes, remembering the Owens' lopsided house, the barn, the chicken coop that stood partway into the field. She remembered a day she had visited, had to be ten, twelve years ago. Riley was plowing concentric circles around the coop, and Catherine, Ruby's younger sister, a tiny wisp of a thing, stared into the distance and said, "There are times, honest to God, when I could tear down that coop with my bare hands."

It always hurt to see Catherine that way, the stooped shoulders and jittery leg, and Ruby knew very well her brother-in-law was to blame, not the chicken coop. For all his hard work, Riley often went at things in a complicated way. Most men did. It was what made them, at heart, so untrustworthy. And Riley's fixation with that coop was a perfect example, she believed. Oh, no question, men like Clarence and Riley had only the best of intentions, but they too often attached meanings to life that no one else could decipher, causing no end of suffering for those who loved them. Ruby didn't trust ideas or images or even figures of speech. Painting and poetry and philosophy— they all seemed to her a kind of madness, the kind of dizzying distraction that could only lead to trouble. She felt that people had lost their way in a multitude of reflections, when all they needed was to embrace the true and unequivocal love of Jesus Christ our Saviour.

A BONE-WHITE SKY, a high, roaring mountain-bound wind that, inside the wall, they could hear but not feel; out on the court, someone bouncing a ball, *shoop, shoop, shoop*, regular as clockwork; around the yard the syncopated barks and wheezes of massed manhood, the here-and-there commotion of simple roughhouse. A vamp is all, everyone waiting for the note, that single soulful wail that would call them in—a blue note if ever there was one.

And when it came, when the siren sounded, they stopped—grey-suited, grey of face, some of them with grey hair, as if they had inhaled too much dust from this place and were, by degrees, turning to stone—then made their way across the loose gravel of the exercise yard. No one spoke; no one laughed. Some were edgy as blades; some polished to an alabaster sheen. For most of them, it was the saddest part of the day.

A stone archway connected the yard to the main quadrangle. There in the darker shadows, where three weeks before someone had been stabbed to death, Hank watched his man pause a moment to tie his boot, Golden Reynolds acting like he didn't have a care in the world. The others passed by without notice, but Hank angled across the archway until he and Goldie stood facing each other. They jostled a moment, like passing strangers on a busy downtown street, and only the most observant bystander would have noticed Hank pressing fifty dollars into Goldie's palm, receiving in return a small portable radio in black leather, about the size of a Bible, which he tucked under his shirt.

"Batteries?" Hank asked.

And Goldie, a loose-limbed kid as slick as a whip, looked off into the distance and said, "Everything's cool."

Without another word, Hank continued threading his way inside the cold stone fortress, up granite ramps that had been rutted by the footfall of misery, down dank corridors and up three flights of metal stairs to his cell. His heart raced like a getaway car. He was asking for trouble. No music allowed outside of specified hours, and certainly no music allowed in the cells. Nappy Whitlock got himself ten days in solitary for the same thing.

Much later, after lights out, Hank worked up the nerve to take his new possession out of hiding. He crouched on the floor between the toilet and his bed. He uncoiled a thin black wire, at the end of which was a small plastic nub that he nestled in his ear. Then he turned on the radio and extended the long chrome antenna, tilting it this way and that. But all he got was static, undifferentiated mostly, here and there thickening into larger clumps of noise. The stone, he figured. Nothing could penetrate it. Fifty bucks shot to hell.

He tucked the radio inside his mattress where no one would find it. Then he rolled onto the bed and buried his face beneath his pillow. It was the racket he couldn't stand. And the light. After all this time it still bothered him. He'd been a country boy once. He knew quiet. He knew darkness. He knew open ground and arching sky, and it was nothing like this. So after an hour or so of tossing and turning, he walked to his cell door and pressed his face against the metal bars. They felt cool against his skin. He could hear the guards playing gin on the second level. Closer at hand, Nelson Green's whispered prayers for salvation were punctuated by the moans of Moe Fletcher, their primitive duet sung against a ceaseless chorus of coughing and crying and the babble of sleep-talk.

The main cellblock was a perfect square, four storeys high, with twenty cells on each side, on each level. Each cell faced a narrow walkway the guards patrolled, a waist-high railing for safety, and beyond that a vast column of empty space. At any time Hank could see a hundred other cells just like his, with a hundred other stories just as sad. The prison was designed that way, he believed, to remind the inmates that they were nothing special. Like chickens in a pen, he thought. Doomed creatures.

The empty space beyond the railings, a good hundred feet across and four storeys high, magnified every whisper, every moan. Occasionally a prisoner in a lighter mood would test the distance with a paper airplane. Sometimes a bird got in and flew about the space in a panic, and the men would whistle madly, hoping to coax the stupid thing to their cells. About a year ago at morning roll call, Willie Brown, maybe thinking *he* was a bird, stepped out of his cell and said, "Oh, Lord," then vaulted over the railing. It took them weeks to remove his stain from the stone floor below.

Hank wasn't a jumper. Mostly he liked to stand at his door and peer into the middle distance and try to imagine a future for himself. What he'd figured out so far was that if he ever did get out of there, he might like to spend the rest of his days outdoors. A park ranger, maybe. Not too many people to deal with in a job like that, he guessed. Not a lot of stress. The kind of job where they could maybe forgive a man for what he'd done. A park ranger at the Grand Canyon, maybe. That sounded good.

So when he couldn't sleep, this is what he'd do: he'd walk to his cell door and stand with his forehead resting on the iron bars. He'd peer into that open space until he could picture himself in the khakis and tan shirt, the big wide-brimmed hat and leather boots. As clear as something on TV, he would see himself sitting behind the wheel of a jeep, no other people around him, nothing at all except maybe a mountain goat picking its way along the edge to something green.

A SINGLE KILLDEER led Cyrus all the way down to the Bailey bridge near the marina. The wind off the lake had gotten stronger, colder, and he had begun to regret his decision to walk to school. So when Sam Loach came

barrelling down the Marsh Road in his rusted pickup and stopped to offer
a ride, Cyrus accepted.

"Seen Benny out there in your old man's field," Sam said. "Guess he
figures to beat the rains." He laughed, a wheezy sort of chuckle. "Ain't one
of us ever done that. Don't know why he keeps on."

Cyrus kept his opinion to himself. He didn't much like Sam Loach or
any of his family. They went about all things in a half-assed way, and that
included their farm. There was no way Cyrus would criticize anyone in
front of Sam.

The Loaches farmed the same kind of land the Owens had farmed:
reclaimed marsh, dense and black. It wasn't the best soil in the area. For that
you'd have to go north of the ridge to sandy well-drained loam that stood up
to a tractor even a few weeks after spring melt. Some of those farms to the
north already had a few early crops in. By contrast, marshland, even with the
tile beds and the pumps, held the moisture like a sponge. No one in fifty
years had gotten all his crops in before the end of May. And even when you
could get on the land, you were limited in the crops you could grow. The
marsh never generated the kind of heat units you got north of town. It had
never made anyone rich, that's for sure. There wasn't a single family out there
who had ever amounted to a hill of beans.

This year, however, things had been different. The winter had been drier
and the rains later than anyone could remember. A downpour had been predicted every day for more than a week, but so far not a drop had fallen. As a
result, Benny had been on his tractor, getting his hopes up. More power to
him, Cyrus thought.

Sam dropped him off at the main intersection of town. Each corner had
its own bank and, since the centennial celebration three years before, a
sorry-looking maple in a square cement pot. The shopping district stretched
north, south, east and west of the four corners but nowhere near as far as the
eye could see.

Because it was too early yet to head over to the school, Cyrus turned east
onto Talbot Street. He walked past the china shop and hardware store. In
front of the Vogue Theatre he stopped to watch Po Mosely.

Po had been a fixture of Wilbury for as long as Cyrus could remember.

Most adults crossed the street rather than pass him on the sidewalk; most kids spent at least some part of their childhood tormenting him. Not that Po was the kind to get angry or chase. He was a retard, that's all, more funny-looking than ugly. He wore hand-me-down grey suits and battered brogues. Could be the shoes were hand-me-down as well because he had a hotfoot kind of walk, all scrambled and unsteady. He sure did a lot of walking, though. You never saw him when he wasn't cruising the streets in that hoppy hurried gait of his. And if he ever saw a piece of paper on the sidewalk or grass—a gum wrapper, newspaper, bus ticket, anything—he would stoop down without missing a step and try to toss the offending piece of litter onto the road, often having to circle back two or three times before it was properly disposed of in the gutter. That's what he was doing now, making sure the sidewalk in front of the Vogue was free of ticket stubs.

Cyrus liked Po, or rather he liked the idea of Po, that at least one thing in Wilbury was different and off-kilter. When Cyrus imagined New York or Chicago, he pictured a crazy carnival of sight and sound and character—the kind of place where a guy like Po would fit right in, the kind of place that Cyrus couldn't wait to explore.

After a minute or so, Cyrus moved farther along the street to Star Radio, a fusty repair shop for all things electrical—radios, TVs, vacuum cleaners. There in the window, on sale by consignment, was a Les Paul Standard. Cyrus knew it had to be a 1953 or 1954 model because the pickups were black plastic rectangles instead of the later and more common humbucking pickups, which were chrome-plated. It had a Tune-O-Matic bridge and a gold top. Between the pickups someone had stuck a small decal for STP oil treatment. The guitar rested on a rickety metal stand.

Cyrus had been eyeing the Les Paul for nearly a week. He couldn't figure out what it was doing in Wilbury, in Star Radio of all places. Everyone played a Les Paul—Eric Clapton, Keith Richards, Jeff Beck—the Stradivarius of rock-and-roll guitars. Its appearance in town had started him really thinking about what he wanted in life. And the answer, more and more, seemed tangled up with that golden instrument.

While Cyrus stood there, Geordie Jackson came out and smiled at him. Geordie was a great big slab of a man. He coached the local hockey team, the Wilbury Wings. He kept his red hair trimmed in an armed forces buzz cut, the kind of bristly thing you could scrape your boots on.

"Can't help noticin' you got yer eye on that there guitar," Geordie said. "Come and see how she feels. Belongs to the wife's kid brother. Up and joined the navy a while back. Don't think he ever played it much."

Cyrus lifted the instrument from its stand and cradled it in his arms, surprised at the weight of it, as if it were made of pure gold. When he crouched on the floor and started tuning, he noticed a small crack in the head between the first and second tuning pegs of the treble strings. "Look," he said, not critically but softly, like a doctor exploring a wound.

Geordie leaned over and made a farting sound with his lips, a little blooper. "That there's just a little nick, Cy, what we call a surface crack. Happens all the time and such. But you know, between you and me, that's gotta knock the price down some. Reece, that's the wife's brother, he was sayin' how he wanted $170, as high as maybe $200 for the thing, but that seems a bit steep to me. And beings as it's you and a good kid and all, and how I knew your old man real well, I'd say $150 would wrap it up—the case, the cord there, the strap, the whole kit and caboodle. I'd even throw in the stand while we're at it. I got no use for it."

Cyrus stood again and looked out the window as a milk truck rattled past. Then he closed his eyes and pictured Ruby standing in the kitchen. He imagined himself in a suit at graduation. Finally he turned back to Geordie, patted his pocket and said, "You take a cheque?" Ten minutes later he was outside again, holding a case so heavy and solid it made him feel serious and grown-up and real.

School was out of the question now, of course, so he headed straight over to the Three Links Hall where he and his band, Bluestone, had a rehearsal space. Byron Young, Janice's dad, was some grand poohbah in the Oddfellows and for five bucks a month rented them one of the spare rooms upstairs as long as they didn't rehearse on lodge night. It was cool beyond belief to have their own private hangout.

Cyrus fired up his amplifier and blazed away for about an hour, trying every lick he knew. Although the Les Paul felt nothing like his Harmony and would take some getting used to, it was a brilliant instrument. The Harmony was a beginner's axe, something his uncle had bought for him. It certainly had never made him feel like this, like a star, like a pro. He launched into the opening riff of "Born Under a Bad Sign." That's when he noticed Janice standing in the doorway.

"What are you doing here?" he asked. "Get bounced from class again?"

She stepped farther into the room. "Never mind me. What are *you* doing here? And what the hell is that?"

For the hundredth time that morning, Cyrus held the guitar out from his body so he could admire it. "This," he said, "is a sign from God. Totally freaking me out. And you'll never guess where I found it. Star fucking Radio. A hundred and fifty bucks."

"Get out."

"One-fifty. I couldn't believe it. I mean I don't even want to think what it might be worth. It is a sign from God." And they both laughed then and embraced, the guitar wedged between them.

Janice was the band's singer and the closest thing he had to a best friend. Ever since the summer, they had been messing around in private, not like love or anything and, from his point of view, not even like major desire, but just because she wanted to and he didn't mind, because she was soft and sweet and funny and knew him better than he knew himself, because her eyes were so full of mischief and green and sometimes sadness; and even though she was not exactly his physical type—a small-time Janis Joplin was how he thought of her, with her wild halo of red hair, with her freckles and chunky arms and her heavy, mannish way of moving around—the truth was he liked kissing her cheeks, so soft and fragrant, and fumbling around in the dark, and especially the afternoons upstairs in her bed, because, really, when he thought about it, most likely they weren't, either one of them, going to get much else.

Barely able to contain himself, he led her over to the battered sofa in the corner and sat beside her, still holding the guitar. He looked across the room to the plaque on the wall, the motto of the Three Links Fraternity: Friendship, Love and Truth. Then he kissed her lightly on the temple and unburdened himself of his secret plan. "You are the first to know," he said.

HANK SOON REALIZED the radio was not an entire loss. Even the sound of static was preferable to the din of this place—the swearing, the night terrors, the violence, the guards' squeaky shoes as they paced the corridors. Someone had told him once that radio static was the sound of outer space, a pretty cool idea, so he crawled beneath the covers and gave himself up once again to the electronic hiss. More than the universe, it reminded him of the sound of wind in the trees, waves on a distant shore. And what he wouldn't give for the accompanying smells instead of this damp stone and mildew and potato rot, all of it topped off with industrial disinfectant. Even here, way up on the third floor, it always smelled as though he was underground.

He shifted a bit in bed, nestling the radio closer to his body. That small movement brought the antenna to rest against the metal bed frame. Like magic, the clot of static suddenly became a voice, low and jive and full of broken parts.

"Howhowhow, you lis'nin' to the lowdown, brothers and sisters, you lis'nin to the Catfish. Spinnin' the discs that take the risk. Dishin' you all the platters that matter. Catfish got the numbers gonna make you feel right. Catfish got the numbers take you awww through the night. And here's a little number what jus' come in gonna smooth your creases, gonna move your pieces. A little somethin' called 'JimJam' . . ."

Organ, bass and drums vamping quietly in the background. And then a different voice, rich and resonant and full of calm.

> I'd like to tell you a story now, if I may, about a man,
> you know, a man who had all that he wanted,
> not on a golden platter but earned by the sweat of his brow, the luck
> of his draw, the way he looked at the world and turned
> it to his advantage, and how this man, a friend of mine, you know,
> a fellow I'd known all my life like I might know my brother,
> this man, this friend, he comes to me one day pullin' at his hair, his face
> all crazy, his eyes like to pop right out of their sockets
> with grief, and he says to me, "Jimmy, my life is over. It's ashes. Tell me
> what to do now, now that my life is over.
> Tell me, tell me now, tell me: What on earth am I goin' to do?"

The band is right there, loping behind the voice in a rhythm that seems
to have a mind of its own.

Now, you can picture it, right? You can see me, how I stared real hard
at my friend—his fancy suits, his Italian shoes,
the diamond pinkie ring—and placed my hands on his head the way
you've all seen me do before, you know what I'm talkin',
waitin' for the words to come to me, waitin' for the words, searchin' for a way
I could help this friend of mine so filled with sorrow.
And it wasn't easy, let me tell you, but finally, you know, I said
to him: "It matters not what you have done,
but if what you say is true, if this life is indeed over,
then it is time to move on, time to end
this life and somehow, someway, choose another, find that place
you can call your own. And if you can't look forward,
then look back.
                Maybe it's true. Maybe it's true your life
is over. Maybe you don't have no future at all.
But we've all got a past. Look back, I tell you. You gotta, you gotta look back."

Just like that the voice and the music come to an abrupt halt, waiting
through two full bars, though it seems but a minor skip of the heart. Then:

I know what you're all thinkin'. I can hear you in my head.
You're sayin', "Be fair, Jim, you gots to be fair.
You're Jim, you're big, and things have been easy for you 'cause you got talent.
You got the soul and the spirit and the gift of music."
But, oh my my, lookit here, lookit here. Gonna turn in a big wide circle
just like so, and you tell me just what you see.
You see any sign of talent or spirit or soul or musical genius?
Well how could you? 'Cause when you get down to the basic
equation, down to the root of the matter, what I got is Jim.
You see talent? I ain't got talent, got Jim.

You see soul? Well fiddlesticks. I ain't got soul or spirit
or even what some folks'd call e-mag-ination.
Lookit here, ain't got no luck or mojo or black cat bone,
no John the Conqueror root. No friends in high places,
no siree, no nothin' for a rainy day. This right here,
this here what you see is all I got.
Jim is Jim, it's all that I am and all that I ever will be.

A deep breath then, a pause to let the music settle back a notch to a more casual cruising speed. Hank can hear the musicians getting playful, tossing things back and forth, snippets of melody, sketches of groove. Background singers coo softly, "All I'll ever be . . . all I'll ever be . . ."

The voice returns, sounding friendlier somehow, not so strident.

I know what's makin' you scratch your head, what's prickin' your behind.
It's the music you find so hard to swallow, the tunes,
the riffs, the grooves, the holy roar. And don't forget The Solo.

Once again the band starts goosing the groove, the drummer in particular really laying into that snare drum now. Suddenly the rhythm is not so complicated. Hank can tap his foot.

We always come back to The Solo, don't we,
always come back to this same place in time.
We watch where it wanders, see where it ends up,
passin' between us some sweet currency,
ever movin' yet never changin',
perfect, immutable, not of this earth
and yet, and yet. . . .
Here's what I want to make clear to you now,
the single thing you should hold to your heart.
Time runs both ways, backwards and forwards.
Our lives will end and start over again—
oftentimes where you least expect it,

not in death but a new kind of life.
And The Solo itself's neither here nor there.
A joyful noise, yes, that much is certain,
but anythin' more is too hard to make out.
Better to ask yourself: "Where does it come from?
What sets it free? Why does it wind
like a river between us, liftin' us up
where we most want to be?"
                                    And the search for the reason,
the search for the meanin' that has brought you this night
to this tent in the trees has brought us much closer—
it will *bring* us much closer if you step up dear friends
and stand nearer to me. The music is nothin',
a sound still resoundin',,, a spirallin' shell
that still echoes the sea, but you must now forget it.
A whole other lifetime. The meanin' is you
comin' here to see me touchin' you—and all of us
standin' together. You've suffered my children,
now come unto me.

When the song ended, Hank immediately turned off the radio and rolled onto his back. He touched the cool chrome of the antenna to his lips. The music or story or whatever you'd call it was unlike anything he'd ever heard before, and yet it felt familiar to him, like something you were supposed to remember but, for the life of you, couldn't.

CYRUS DIDN'T GET HOME until ten o'clock that night. He and Janice had talked for hours. They got takeout. They worked on tunes. Then he hitched a ride as far as the marina. From there he could see, out along the beach where bonfires dotted the sand, smelt fishermen dragging the silver from the water with their nets. The sky was clear and moonless. Even at Orchard Knoll, he could smell the heady perfume of wood smoke and frying fish and the sweet musk of a dying lake.

He'd been tempted to bring the guitar home with him, afraid to let it out of his sight for even a night; but he knew its presence in the house would bring too many questions, Ruby always quick to notice something different. So he left it at the hall instead, pinching himself all the way home, his heart so light he was barely touching the ground. It was only as he walked up the driveway and saw Izzy's car that he remembered she had been invited for dinner.

"Sor-ry," he called out as he stepped inside. "I forgot."

His aunt and sister were in the living room. They had the look of two people who had run out of things to say years ago. Isabel clutched a handful of red licorice that she flicked into her palm like a cat-o'-nine-tails. She was trying to quit smoking again, but the ashtray beside her held three butts, with lipstick halos around the filters.

"Where's Clarence?" he asked.

His aunt rubbed her eyes. It was past her bedtime. "Where he's supposed to be this hour of night. We didn't hear you come up the drive he was snoring so loud."

"Sorry about dinner, Iz."

"It's all right. We'll talk some other time. Ruby here thinks you need to get something off your chest."

Cyrus took a deep breath and decided to plunge right in. He sat on the couch beside his aunt and patted her leg. "That's the thing," he said. "I figured it all out tonight." He looked from one woman to the other. "I'm quitting school."

Ruby had always prided herself on knowing Cyrus's mind. Not that he'd ever been talkative. When he first came to live with them, he didn't say a word for almost three months, his jaws clenched so tightly she could hear him grinding his teeth at night. And even now, years later, she had to coax from him the tiniest details of his school day. So it wasn't his words that had helped her to understand, but his face. He had always seemed to her a still pool, with everything visible. This announcement, however, had caught her completely by surprise.

"That's impossible," she said. "Quit? It's only three months to graduation. That makes no sense at all."

"But it does, don't you see? I don't need school."

Ruby looked to Isabel for help, and Izzy shook her licorice at him and said, "Look, weirdo, even if you were thinking of working the farm here, Gerry was saying just the other day how with the new machinery and the pricing and the futures market, you're gonna need a college education just to grow soybeans. It's the way of the world."

Cyrus looked at her as though she had started speaking in tongues. "Farming? What are you talking about? Doesn't anyone here know anything about me?"

At that point, Clarence came downstairs in his striped flannel pyjamas and housecoat, his hair tousled. Calm as a sleepwalker, he sat in his favourite armchair and said, "Maybe you need to tell us, boy. Maybe when you spit it out we'll all know more about you."

Cyrus had hoped to avoid a scene like this. He looked to Izzy for help. All his life she'd been his ally. She'd taught him to sing rounds when they did the dishes. She'd taught him to dance and, a few years ago out in the orchard, had told him what girls liked and didn't like. But this was one time when she was no use to him, her expression a mix of pity and rebuke, as though he'd been caught stealing.

Taking a deep breath, he looked Clarence in the eye and said, "I was telling Ruby that, you know, I think it's time I quit school."

Clarence nodded. "I thought that's what I heard you say. Only I couldn't believe my ears. It sounded too much like craziness, and you never struck me as crazy."

"Well, that's the thing, I'm not crazy. The way I look at it, in terms of my life, you know, it makes perfect sense."

"Your life. Goddammit, Cyrus, you'd be throwing away your life. Can't you see that? Get your head out of the clouds and look around."

Ruby gave her husband a warning look. "What your uncle is trying to say, sweetheart, is that it doesn't make sense to us that you'd throw away all your hard work when it's just a matter of a few more months. Then with the summer off, maybe things will seem a little clearer."

"Everything is perfectly clear right now," Cyrus said, his voice taking on an edge of irritation. "I know exactly what I want to do, so I might as well get started."

Clarence closed his eyes and let his chin rest on his breastbone as though he were fast asleep again. He wondered, not for the first time, why raising kids was so much harder than farming. Thirty years he'd wrestled with the Fates—floods and droughts, good markets and bad. He'd learned that each new season brought a fresh chance. With Cyrus, though, he just couldn't separate one year from the next, one incident from another. Every victory came tangled in a mess of defeats, every bit of bad news came trailing a long history of grief and disappointment.

"Get started on what," he said at last, "a life as a high school dropout? Because let me tell you one thing, young man, there are times when it's not about what you want, or your life, or any such thing. It's about family and promises and how sometimes you do what you don't want, for the sake of others. I have to tell you straight out here, Cyrus, I don't think I can let you make such a foolish mistake. Ruby and I, maybe we haven't been all you deserve, but we have fed you and clothed you, done everything we could for you. Now you can do this one little thing for us and stay put."

"You don't understand."

"No, *you* don't understand. Let me tell you a little story, all right? About your father. When he first moved out on the farm there with his folks, people in town called him a marsh rat. You understand? A dirty marsh rat. They lived in that chicken shack out there, with nothing but a pot to piss in, while he helped your grandfather try to build something."

Cyrus rolled his eyes. "What is this, history class?"

Immediately, Clarence jumped to his feet, pointing his finger at Cyrus's face. He had never been one to raise his voice, believing it the sign of an uneducated man. Rather, his words became hushed and precise. "You listen to me, boy. You show some respect. That father of yours, I guess he was just about the best friend I ever had, and when he and your mother died, I made myself a promise, you hear, that no one would *ever* call him or anyone in his family a marsh rat again. You understand? If he was here today, by George, he'd peel a strip off your back something fierce, talking nonsense like that. So let me just make this as plain as I can. There will be no high school dropouts in this house."

Cyrus looked at Ruby, at Isabel, and found no support there. Then, swallowing hard, he said, "Whatever you say, Clarence. Time to go, anyway." And with that, Cyrus walked out the door and down the road.

Ten minutes later, Isabel passed him in her dinged Plymouth Belvedere. Freddie, she called it, the first thing she'd bought when she moved out on her own nine years ago. Gerry had offered to buy her a nicer car after they got married, but she wasn't interested. She loved that car. She'd picked it out herself, haggled her own price and slapped down her own cash. It was a symbol of her passage into being an adult, a talisman for her independence. And though she had a better car now for her work, she still preferred the Plymouth for certain occasions.

A hundred yards down the road she pulled over to wait for Cyrus to catch up. As he approached, she rolled down the window and said, "Go home, dummy. This is no good for anyone."

He leaned both arms on the roof of the car and looked down at her. "What do you know about anything, Iz? You're as bad as they are. You think you know what's good for me?"

Those were hurtful words, and she waited a moment before she said, "I'm your sister. I know more than you think. And I certainly know what this would do to Ruby and Clarence, your leaving this way. I'm pretty sure you know, too." When he didn't respond, she was encouraged. She put the car in gear and said, "Get in. I'll take you back."

Instead he reared away from her and shook his head. "Leave me alone. This is between me and me and no one else."

"Really. How convenient. If you believe that, you're even more of a jerk than I thought you were."

He turned away from her then and continued walking down the road. In response she gunned the engine and sped past, peppering him with loose stone. The damage was done, though. She had planted the seeds of guilt, and he could already feel them swelling inside.

At the Bailey bridge, he hoisted himself onto one of the supports and gazed down at the sluggish flow of Spring Creek. Hank used to bring him here, in the year after Burwash but before Portland. Cyrus would have been about six or seven, Hank about seventeen and looking like a young god. The two of them would shuffle down the bank and under the bridge. Hank called it their clubhouse. He'd take a few drinks from his secret flask, chain-smoking Black Cats all the while, and let Cyrus inspect his tattoos. Mostly they just sat out of the sun and wove their words into the complicated rhythms of the creek. "Kid," Hank said several times a day, "life is a peach."

Six months later Hank would be gone for good. He crossed his own dark bridge and left the rest of them behind to untangle the guilt and recrimination. That, of course, was what Isabel had been talking about—Hank, old heartaches—and the longer Cyrus sat there, the more he felt his conviction ebbing. Ruby and Clarence had been good to him, helping to turn a disaster into something more or less bearable. He hoped they knew that, hoped they understood how much he appreciated all they'd done.

Just then a car approached from the direction of the marsh. From the corner of his eye he could tell it was a big black number, a Caddy, perhaps. He wasn't sure. Unlike other boys his age, he didn't know about cars. He couldn't, from a tail light or grille, tell you the make and model.

When the car stopped behind him, Cyrus didn't bother to turn around. He heard the door open, the deep murmur of the radio like something from the womb. Then a man cleared his throat and said, "I hope you are not contemplating anything so rash as jumping. I am afraid I am not the ablest of swimmers."

It was a soft voice, an accent Cyrus couldn't place, though it seemed faintly regal. He turned around to find a man wearing a dark suit and V-necked sweater. He had brown hair that curled down to his shoulders, and hooded eyes that seemed to glisten in the dark. A diamond sparkled on his pinky.

ISABEL DROVE HOME to an empty house and sat in the darkness of the living room, smoking cigarettes and thinking about Ruby and Clarence and her damned kid brother. Even at the best of times a chat with her aunt and uncle could cause her a sleepless night, stirring up painful memories of departed loved ones; and sometimes she came away from her visits with Ruby feeling ungenerous and spiteful. It was sour grapes, of course, for a perfectly decent woman who had done no wrong in her life, a childless woman who, with the purest of intentions, had swooped down in the midst of a great tragedy and snatched Isabel and Cyrus to her bosom.

At the time, Isabel was just finishing high school and was so bitter about her parents' deaths that she resisted Ruby's attempts to mother her, turning a cold shoulder to the hugs and kisses, the evenings with the church choir. She said hurtful things, did hurtful things and ran off a few months later, leaving her little brother with the Mitchells to somehow pick his way through the wreckage on his own. She married Gerry then and moved out to his farm, built a new life. And although she now had reason to think the future would be a sunnier place—and most of the time felt fine, like a woman in her prime—some nights she sat in the dark and pondered the loss, the guilt, the selfishness and, yes, her resentment of Ruby, who for nearly a decade had sifted the meaning of her life from the ashes of another.

When Gerry came home about midnight, Isabel had settled into one of her moods. He knew well enough the signs of her unhappiness and knew he had caused his share of it. So, without a word, he put out her cigarette and guided her upstairs to the bedroom. Without removing her clothes, he tucked her into bed and carefully crawled in beside her.

There were any number of things he might have been tempted to do just then. He might have pulled her into his arms and crooned softly under his breath, Marty Robbins or Merle Haggard or George Jones, the way he used to when they were first dating. He might even have made love to her, mussing her hair and pawing her flesh like he meant to obliterate the person she was and refashion a newer, happier model. But the only time Gerry ever sang anymore was on the tractor, where no one could hear him. And, really, the sexual act—he was sure that even so much as a kiss would be regarded as selfish and insensitive. So he tiptoed down the single safe path left to him. He began to talk about their life together, their plans for the future.

"Reg Foster was at it again tonight," he said, his voice lazy with drink. "Wants me to come in and work up figures for those new barns I was telling you about."

He waited for her to respond. He wanted this to be a conversation, but sarcasm was all she had to offer. "My, my," she said. "Imagine Reg Foster slumming it at the Wilbury Hotel."

She could hear the scratch and rasp of whiskers as he dragged his hand across his face. When he spoke this time his voice was clearer and more businesslike. "I was at the Gaslight Room. Too many young punks these days at the Wilbury. Anyway, Reg says we're crazy if we don't upgrade now while the rates are low. We could double our production, he figures, and be paid off in seven years. Otherwise we'll fall so far behind we'll never catch up. Everybody's doing it—Fred, Marty, Chet, all in hock up to their eyeballs. Any other time I wouldn't give it another thought. You know how I feel about debt. But these new feeders and such are awful slick . . ."

She rolled onto her back and stared at the ceiling. "I thought you said that kind of thing was too risky. I've heard you say it a hundred times."

"I know what I said, but I'm thinking maybe this is different. Maybe there's times you can play it too safe, when you have to stretch a little for the things you want."

She closed her eyes and could see Reg leaning across his desk to pat Gerry's hand, much as Reg had patted hers all those many years ago. She'd gone to his dark panelled office with Clarence and Ruby and listened as he explained the sorry details of her parents' estate. Two weeks later the bank took possession of the farm.

It was ancient history, but it still hurt. She hugged her knees to her chest and said, "If there's one thing we don't need right now, Gerry, it's new pig barns. That's not going to help a single goddamn thing."

RUBY HUGGED HER HUSBAND FROM BEHIND, her cheek pressed against his broad back. Through his pyjamas she could feel the hard ridge of scar tissue from his operation nine months ago, when they had removed part of his lung. "A touch of cancer" is how he referred to it now. All those sprays he used in the orchard, or the pipe he smoked when she first met him, or just rotten luck—it scarcely mattered. She couldn't think of that scar without shuddering, though it only made sense a body would carry to the grave a reminder of such a deep wound.

She could tell by the sound of Clarence's breathing that he was awake. But neither of them spoke. She simply needed to press against him, to soften the jangled edge of her nerves against his warm body.

She had felt this kind of jittery static before, of course, especially on the weekend Riley and Catherine died. Her sister had called to say there'd been more trouble with Hank, and that they were heading up to Hounslow to fetch him home, if possible. But the temperature was dropping, the wind started to howl off the lake, and somewhere just outside of the city, Riley hit a patch of black ice and ran the pickup into a hydro pole. Ruby was sitting by the phone, waiting on word from her sister when the police called, setting in motion a long, lurid nightmare of blood and metal and unanswerable questions. It wasn't until twenty-four hours later, with Cyrus and Isabel in the spare room down the hall, that Ruby and Clarence finally tumbled into bed; and even then she couldn't sleep, couldn't stop thinking and shivering. The only solace she could find was in the feel of her husband's broad back, needing that physical connection in order to hold herself together. Now, a decade later, she could find small comfort there—it was not the same back. These were not the same times.

A car's headlights swept slowly along the wall, up the ceiling and away. She hugged her husband tighter, wishing he would turn around and hug her, too. But that wasn't likely. Whenever he was worried he drew into himself, as though the answer to every problem was locked inside his head. So she kissed his neck and said, "He's a good boy, Clarence. He knows we love him. I'm sure he'll do the right thing and come home."

"Could be," he said distantly. "Could be. But some people, you know, they just don't do the right thing, least in that family."

"He's part of *our* family."

"You think?"

She got up on one elbow so she could see the side of his face. "Come on now," she said, "he's run off before, remember, and spent the night at the hall. I'll go fetch him in the morning, and we'll have a long talk just the two of us. He'll be fine."

"Well," he said, pulling the blanket closer to his chin, "you suit yourself. Could be I've about had enough of the Owens for one lifetime."

Ronnie Conger took a sip of evaporated milk straight from the can and closed his eyes while the elevator took him up to the seventh floor of the Golden Lion Hotel. He'd been awake for nearly twenty-four hours, but that was nothing new. Before he could lay his head on a pillow, he needed to know that his boys were safe and sound. He had responsibilities, to them and to Jimmy. And one of those responsibilities was the two A.M. head check, almost always his favourite part of the day. He liked to think of it as counting his blessings.

Out on the fast-food strip that stretched north of Ironville, the roar and tumult had dwindled to the odd car now and then, each vehicle a discrete disturbance in the general hush, like a falling star that briefly animates the heavens. Inside the hotel the restaurant had closed, the bar, too, the night staff dawdling over their accounts and fighting off sleep. With the lights dimmed and the dingy corridors all hushed and confidential, the inner workings of the hotel itself became more noticeable: the asthmatic wheeze of the heating vents, the vast gurgling network of twelve floors of plumbing, the hum and thrum of elevator and laundry and how many kilowatts of light bulbs, not to mention the irreverent chatter from the ice and pop machines down the hall, like kids on a sleepover who just can't turn it off. It didn't matter the town or country, every hotel come two in the morning gave Ronnie pretty much the same feeling. If pressed to give that feeling a name, he would have said, "Home."

He knocked on the door of Adrian and Kerry's room. Theirs was always the first stop on his rounds; it was where the lads naturally congregated. And sure enough, the door opened a crack and a cloud of smoke wafted into the hall, followed shortly by Adrian's sweet Welsh tones.

"Oh, aye, it's the warden come to clap us in irons," he said for the benefit of the others in the room, who responded with a bedlam of raspberries and catcalls.

Ronnie stepped through the doorway and looked around. As usual, the whole crew, both roadies and musicians, had drifted down to Adrian and Kerry's room to unwind. They were slumped on the beds, squatting on the floor, perched on every available surface. Like pirates, he thought, in the belly of a ship. There were bottles of Jim Beam and Jameson Irish whiskey. There were six-packs of Canadian beer, American beer, mickeys of vodka and rum and rye. Everyone was smoking, or so it seemed. It was story time, each of them chipping in with a tale of wicked wonders, wild characters, other worlds.

Adrian, all hairy and dwarfish, a battered tweed cap on his head, was making tea and passing around biscuits he had found in a little shop that specialized in British imports. "Just like me mum's," he said, offering the plate to Ronnie, who took a chocolate digestive.

Kerry was rolling joints and passing them out. He, too, was from Wales. With his sallow face, the pale scar on his cheek only half obscured by stubble, he looked to Ronnie like someone a half step from the grave when in fact he was a tireless worker, the most dependable of anyone on the crew. The least dependable, the person Ronnie most wanted to keep tabs on, was Cal Hudson, a smart-talking bass player from Philadelphia. Cal had a few problems that marked him as a high-maintenance pain in the ass, and a quick glance around the room revealed that Cal was the only one who had not made it to Adrian and Kerry's for a nightcap.

Ronnie took another sip of his tinned milk and scanned the room a second time for the halo of frizzy hair. "I don't see Cal," he said. "You were meant to keep that sorry pisser in your sights. Was he on the bus?"

Adrian paused with his china cup half-raised. "Looked a bit naff, Arsey. Went straight to his room. Something up?"

But Ronnie had already turned and was walking down the hall to Cal's, a sick pressure building in his stomach. Cal didn't do well on his own. Left alone for even a short while, he tended to make a hash of things. As a result, Ronnie had found that the best strategy was to keep him busy with work or play. Give the guy an idle moment and he was lost.

Ronnie listened at Cal's door and could hear the radio playing softly, "A Whiter Shade of Pale." He knocked a few times but got no response; he fetched another key from the front desk and opened the door, but the chain was on. So he walked back to Adrian's, grabbed Tommy MacIntosh by the arm and dragged him down the hall to Cal's room. Tom and Ronnie went way back, all the way to Glasgow, in fact. More important now, Tom was a bull, easily the strongest man on the crew. Ronnie said, "Give us your shoulder, will you? Cal isn't responding to my summons."

Tom scarcely seemed to move, yet the chain was ripped neatly off the frame. Ronnie handed him the half-empty tin of milk. "I'll handle the rest," he said. "Go back to your party." Then he closed the door behind him and moved into the room.

It was Cream playing now, the free-for-all of "Crossroads." The only light came from a small blue flame on the bedside table, the kind of burner you might find in a chemistry set. Cal was propped against the headboard, the needle still in his arm. His eyes were open and unblinking. When Ronnie touched the hand, already cold and grey and unresponsive, he knew intuitively what to do. He put out the flame, locked the room and walked down the hall to rejoin the others. "Don't know where that boy could be," he said as he retrieved his milk, fixing Tom with a pointed look.

Not long after that, Adrian and Kerry began to drop hints that it might be time for bed. When everyone but Tom had shuffled off to their rooms, Ronnie waved the three of them closer and said, "I need your help, lads. And your discretion. Our Cal is dead."

He laid out the facts as best he could and suggested what he felt was the wisest course of action. They would smuggle the body into the elevator and down to the parking garage in the basement. There would place the corpse in the trunk of Ronnie's Cadillac for a long drive into the countryside somewhere. The best thing might be for some farmer to happen across the body and report it to the proper authorities.

Adrian poured the dregs from the teapot into his cup and downed it in a gulp. "I don't follow," he said. "Why not call the police ourselves? There's no one guilty here but Cal."

Ronnie dragged his hand through the lank curls of his long brown hair. "You forget Jim," he said, his voice low and solemn. "You forget guilt by association. Above all, we must protect Jim and, in turn, ourselves from this stain. We have important work to do. I believe even Cal would have wanted it so. Remember how we found him? Hard to believe it was just five short months ago. I think even the harshest judge would forgive us this small transgression when you consider what is at stake."

Ronnie bowed his head, remembering the young man he had spotted one night in downtown Philadelphia. A dreary November drizzle had given the city an electric shine; and Cal, high as a kite, was parading shirtless along the street behind the YMCA. When Ronnie pulled the car to the curb, Cal sauntered over with all the wrong ideas and started his filthy come-on. But Ronnie could see the sweet damaged boy beneath all that chemical jive and pretense. "Why don't you get in the car for a minute?" Ronnie had said. "Seems a bit of a chilly night to be dressed like that." When Cal slid onto the front seat, Ronnie clasped his hands together as though in prayer. "Tell me," he said, "have you ever thought you might like to be in show business?"

Ronnie shook the memory away and stared grimly at his tour mates. "What do you think, lads?" he said. "Will you help me with this? We are on the cusp of great things, I believe. Our first record is getting airplay. Can we four do the right thing here? I will take full responsibility. You can deny everything. But for now, I need your strong arms and determination."

They were not easily persuaded, but in the end they agreed and went tiptoeing down the hall to Cal's room. By four-thirty they had the body and all of Cal's personal belongings stowed in the trunk of the Cadillac. They hadn't seen a soul.

"What about his gear?" Kerry asked. "Not many musicians go off with their dirty laundry and leave their axe behind."

For a moment, Ronnie was stymied. But then he smiled and said, "You forget that no one but us knows he ever played an instrument. No long-lost relative is going to come calling for something like that. In fact, we bought the equipment so, strictly speaking, it's ours. And as far as a band member getting suspicious, they know better than anyone that our Cal was not a musician. They experienced that sorry fact every night. It will make perfect sense to them that he left his gear behind and went off in search of an easier high."

Then Ronnie got behind the wheel of his Cadillac and fired up the engine. As he rolled down the window, he said, "I'm certain you three can handle everything on this end. Don't forget receipts. I must have receipts. Tell everyone that Cal has cleared out and that I've gone to find a new bass player. Sonny can figure out something for tomorrow, I'm sure. He's done it before." Then he pulled out of the parking space and drove into the night.

Tom looked at the two Welshmen and said, "Itsa fuckin' mucky weddled."

SO THERE HE WAS, Ronnie Conger, back in his car for maybe the hundredth time that day, only this time he was heading miles away from his crew. Nowhere in particular, you understand, but somewhere far, somewhere that felt right. And before long it wasn't highways anymore but gravel roads, and it wasn't nighttime but daylight, and then this long lonely concession road, the straightest road he had ever been on, through the squarest and flattest fields he had ever seen. And he had the radio off and the windows open, even though it was early spring and the air was freezing. The speedometer sat solidly on sixty, the speed limit. He was using his turn signals, too, steering straight and true, because the last thing he wanted was to get stopped by the cops with a dead body in his car, the body of a friend, no less, which was wrapped in a floral bedspread and pumped full of heroin and quite unceremoniously shoved in the trunk.

And it was only then, with the sun up over those wide black fields, and people heading to work, that he realized there was no way he could dump the body in broad daylight—Ronnie Conger stomping through some farmer's field in his expensive suit and shoes and dragging a corpse behind him? No, a stopover was key, a bit of shut-eye, because he was starting to feel punchy. A motel, maybe, some dismal place where no one in his right mind would stop. A little rest, a bite of food. Rome wasn't built in a day.

Up ahead, he spotted flickering neon: Lakeview Motel. Weathered clapboard that had once been painted baby blue. Shutters hanging cockeyed. Mossy roof, weedy parking lot. Vacancy.

Ronnie wheeled into the parking spot farthest from the office and walked over to inquire about a room. The air off the lake was cold and rank and fishy, and he nodded with satisfaction. Just the sort of camouflage Cal might need. Ten minutes later Ronnie was sitting in a room that smelled of mothballs, wringing his hands and wondering how he had gotten himself in this sorry predicament. He was so far away from where he was meant to be, so far from kith and kin.

His father, the Reverend Archibald Conger of the Baptist Church in East Kilbride, a stolid and proper man who spoke in perfectly formed sentences and believed that thought was God's greatest gift to mankind, had scrimped and saved on his paltry wages in order to send Ronnie to a decent school and, when the need was greatest, swallowed his pride and pulled whatever strings he could to get his son, a bright but indifferent student, accepted into the divinity program at Regent College, Oxford, where Archie himself had taken his degree. Unfortunately, Archie's great sacrifice left Ronnie's doubts and desires entirely out of the equation. Had Archie quizzed his son more fully, he might not have wasted his hard-earned money in paving a dead-end path to paradise. But then, how could he have known that Ronnie would have an epiphany four short months into his second year at Oxford?

It happened around the time of the winter solstice, as so many epiphanies do. Ronnie and a few of the more serious students in his college had walked across the Isis to the Fife and Drum, having just handed in their final essays before Christmas break. The idea was to treat themselves to a pint and a steak-and-kidney pie, and to say farewell until the new year. But one pint became two, and as Ronnie neared the bottom of his third ale, Colin McDermid put a coin in the jukebox. Minor chords swelled to fill the room. A brooding, sultry beat, a twangy American voice:

Keep on ridin' with the herd,
Runnin' with the pack,
Flappin' with the birds,
But honey—don't look back.

A pop tune like something you might get from Gene Pitney or Bobby
Rydell. Catchy, in a mindless sort of way, and Ronnie at first was only half-
listening. Then, after the second plaintive chorus, the room was filled with a
sound as stirring as Gabriel's trumpet, only it wasn't any kind of instrument
Ronnie had ever heard, or any kind of musicianship he could understand. In
fact, it was so otherworldly, so large and joyful and confusing, that the minute
the solo ended he couldn't remember a single note of it, couldn't think of a
way to even describe it to himself or name the effect it had had on him.

He handed Colin another coin. "Play it again," he demanded.

The song, he discovered, was called "Don't Look Back," by a singer
named Gil Gannon. On second listening, the lyrics and melody seemed
inane, simple sentiments given an anxious treatment. Ronnie was about to
turn away from the jukebox disheartened, as though the whole thing had
been a momentary aberration, but then the solo started and he stood transfixed, struggling to understand just what it was he was hearing. A keyboard
of some sort, he was certain, but no keyboard he had ever heard before, and
played in a fashion that was unfamiliar to him. Nothing like the church
music he had heard all his life. And when the solo ended, his sense of it
evaporated completely.

He put another coin in the machine and chose the song again. This time
he returned to the table and had everyone pay attention. After the solo had
sounded a third time, he looked at his friends and said, "What is that? What
am I listening to?"

They laughed as though it was the alcohol talking. "Top 40," Colin
mocked. "Nothing to get fussed about. You want to try Brubeck sometime."

"But did you ever hear the likes of it?" Ronnie persisted, waiting for
one of the others to agree with him. "The shapes, I mean. It's almost
frightening, isn't it?"

"Give it up, Conger, you're pickled."

"I'm not . . . I'm stunned. I didn't know, not really. This is brilliant. It's magic."

No one else could hear it; and the more he proclaimed the solo's special virtues, the more they laughed. "No more ale for Conger," they hooted. And when he got up to play the song a fourth time, they threatened him with violence, so he bid them farewell and went back to his room to contemplate his newfound knowledge.

Next morning, Ronnie, who until that weekend had shown no special affinity for music, who in fact had tuned it out whenever possible in favour of philosophy and football, bought himself a record player and a copy of "Don't Look Back," which he played twenty or thirty times without stopping. And still he could find no path into the heart of the mystery.

He memorized the rhythms, gave the solo a phonetic structure that allowed him to scat along with the record, and then, better still, to himself as he walked along the street.

Dwee, dohdweedoh-doodle,
Dwee, dohdweedoh-doodle,
Dwee.
Scoodely-oodelly-oodelly-oodelly
Oodelly-oodelly-oodelly.
Dwee, dohdweedoh-doodle,
Dwee, dohdweedoh-doo-dle-dum.
Bal-lum-pum-pum-pum-pum-pum-pum-pum-pum.

The next afternoon, with snowflakes drifting softly around him, he walked down High Street to do a bit of Christmas shopping. And that's when it occurred to him that if one song on the pub's jukebox held this kind of transcendent magic, then surely others might as well, that "Don't Look Back" and its deliciously maddening solo might be but a pale intimation of the greater wonders that awaited. It was this possibility that made him take his train fare, and the money he had set aside for presents, and spend it all on singles and LPs: pop, gospel, country and western, rhythm and blues, jazz. He called his father that night to explain that he had decided to remain in Oxford for the holidays—to study.

From that point on he was a goner. Six weeks into the new semester he had sold all his books, liquidated his assets, cleaned out his bank account (most of which was owed to the university), and taken the train to London, where he found himself a small flat near Ladbroke Grove. It was 1963.

For the better part of a year he bounced through a series of low-paying jobs—stacking shelves at record stores, clearing tables at clubs, anything that would put him in touch with music and the people who loved it, people who could stand around for hours and testify to the majesty of Lonnie Donegan and Doc Watson, Louis Armstrong and Billie Holiday, Elvis and Big Bill Broonzy and, of course, Jimmy Waters, whose brilliant solo had made "Don't Look Back" a heavenly thing. More often than not, Ronnie's new friends were just like him, with no musical training, no ear, people who had been caught unaware by the ineffable delights of music and had none of the tools required to make sense of it. Words failed them. Hand gestures failed them. In the end they could only say, "Listen, listen," knowing that as often as not the truth would fall upon deaf ears.

Ronnie wasn't stupid. He saw that he had exchanged one religion for another, that he and the others, the testifiers, approached their subject with a kind of evangelical zeal. Yet in contrast to his father's religion, which seemed cold and commercial, with its tit for tat, its various exchange rates for salvation, music, or that evanescent glory he had discovered inside of music, was a pure and purifying thrill.

That second summer in London, the manic fever of Beatlemania beginning to spill across the globe, he travelled north to attend his brother Kenny's wedding in Glasgow. Ronnie now had sharp clothes and long hair, and his father could not bring himself to look at him, which promised to make the occasion as dark and dour as the black brooding stone of the city. But on the day before his brother's wedding, as Ronnie was standing in the pub near Kenny's flat and agonizing over the speech he was expected to give as best man, he felt a massive paw clamp down on his shoulder. "Eh, yew. Gie-us an eighty, will ye? Me throat's a wee bit dry."

Ronnie wheeled around and laughed. "If it isn't Tommy Mac . . ."

"Aye, mate, still kickin'. And lookatcha, ya fuckin' tossel. I dinna reconize ya with a pint in yer hand. Naughty boy. Dinna falla yer old man there, didjiz."

Tommy Mac, even at the age of twelve, had been more man than boy, with thick wrists and fingers, a massive neck and chest, short stumpy legs and a forehead like an anvil, hard and flat and punishing. Ronnie had seen several noses broken by that forehead and, although he well knew the higher standards expected of him as a minister's son, had managed to spend time each summer in Tom's boisterous company. When Tom left home at the age of sixteen, lured into the darker side of Glasgow with Alec Walker and his gang of thugs, Ronnie grieved like a brother.

The afternoon of their reunion they worked through several pints, calling up old haunts, old faces. And the more they talked, the more they discovered it was not just the past they had in common. They were also reunited by a love of soul music. ("Aye, Ronnie, it's trew, the Scots are the nignogs a Europe. Lift tha' barge. Tote tha' fuckin' bale.")

After their fifth pint they hatched a plan: they would rent the banquet hall of the East Kilbride Benevolent Society and put on a concert. Ronnie would handle all the paperwork and the promotion. Tom and a few of his mates would provide the heavy lifting and security. From there it was concerts in Glasgow and Edinburgh. A year went by in a blink, with the two making more money than they had ever made before. Then Bobby Mason, the manager of Scot Free, approached Ronnie with a proposition.

"We're off to America," Bobby said. "Crazy about us over there, it seems. Dates from coast to coast. Disneyland, *American Bandstand.* We could use a road manager with your kind of smarts, mate. A fixer."

Ronnie agreed on the spot. It put an end to the successful operation he and Tom had going, but that was a small price to pay for a pilgrimage to the holy sites of one's belief—New York, New Orleans, Chicago, Detroit, Philadelphia, Los Angeles. When Scot Free returned to Glasgow at the end of the tour, Ronnie stayed behind to live the dream. Working out of New York, he hitched up with other tours and made a name for himself.

But late in the winter of 1968, on the road in Western Canada with Aaron Maxx, the dream began to unravel. The tour had been a fiasco, as Ronnie had predicted it would be when Aaron insisted on using the

Belko Brothers, a pair of local promoters who normally booked wrestling extravaganzas in mid-size cowtowns. They ran ads on the wrong radio stations, put posters in the wrong places, greased the palms of the wrong people. Worst of all, they booked Aaron into towns so far apart, in the dead of winter, that it was physically impossible to make it to the gigs on time, even if the crew packed up right after a show and drove all night.

Two concerts had already been cancelled, and in Staghorn, Alberta, after driving through a blizzard, they arrived at the arena at eleven at night, three hours after showtime and a good hour and a half after the last person had claimed a refund. The hall was dark, the parking lot empty save for a black Mercedes idling by the side door. Inside the car were the Belkos, large men with large voices. When they spoke, only their heads were visible through the open window. In the clearest possible terms they indicated that this was their last warning: one more screw-up and they would sue Aaron and impound the bus and gear. For emphasis, their bodyguard, an ex-wrestler by the name of Bull Bodine, swaggered around the parking lot in a menacing fashion.

Aaron, looking ridiculous in velvet pants and a white fur coat, pointed his finger at Ronnie and said, "I knew we should have used an American tour manager. This never would have happened with someone who knew about these things."

Something inside Ronnie snapped. It didn't matter that the Belkos and all the crew and all the musicians were watching. He grabbed Aaron by his furry lapels and slammed him against the side of the bus, which was covered with oil and slush. And when Ronnie had him lined up for a massive head butt, a Mackie special, he just backed away, dusted off his hands and walked toward town. It was time for a change.

He spent three nights in Staghorn, in a seedy little room at the Queen's Hotel, wondering how to get back to New York. He had no suitcase, no coat and less than a hundred dollars in his wallet. But those concerns would soon fade to nothing. He was on the verge of his fateful meeting with Jimmy Waters, which now, almost three years later, had led to another fleabag room in the middle of nowhere, this time with a dead body in his trunk.

He got to his feet and walked to the window, gazing out at the parking lot. No other cars in sight. No traffic on the road. Even so, he hoped to God that Cal didn't start to reek before nightfall. And with that sour thought, he tried to sleep.

At sunset, he drove three miles to the nearest town and bought himself several small tins of evaporated milk. He called Adrian from a pay phone and asked how everything was going.

"Fine, Arsey. Tickety-boo. The drive to Campenola was a bit of a lark, you know. It's not often we have a full day off."

"About Cal, Ade. How are the lads taking it?"

"Relieved, I'd say, that poor Cal has moved on—though I'm sure they might feel different if they knew exactly where he had moved on to." He laughed at his own witticism, and Ronnie could hear Kerry's harsh cackle in the background. Like a couple of old hens, he thought.

"Of course," Adrian continued, "Sonny's been in a right ugly mood all day. Thinks we should cancel tomorrow's show. But he'll be all right. How's everything there, Arsey?"

"Fine. I plan to be in Campenola before showtime, with or without a bass player. How's Jim taking it?"

"Touch and go there for a while. Got tears in his eyes like he'd lost his best mate. But I made him a pot of tea and asked Eura to look in on him. When she left his trailer, she said he was sleeping like a baby."

"Good man, Ade. See you tomorrow."

By the time Ronnie returned to the motel, it was dark, so he took the opportunity to open his trunk and grab Cal's suitcase. In the room, he went through the boy's belongings one more time and found nothing that could tie the corpse to Jim. There was no driver's licence or birth certificate, no identification at all. The only personal item in Cal's wallet was a high school photo. Nor would there be any record of him with Customs and Immigration, even though they had crossed into Canada several weeks ago. The border guard had smiled kindly when he saw the name on the side of the bus—The Jimmy Waters Revival—and when Ronnie showed him their itinerary, playing to church groups across Ontario, the guard just waved them into the country without a second thought.

Satisfied that everything was in order, Ronnie hauled the luggage out to the car and did a final sniff check. Two hours later, a pale moon on the horizon, he set off in search of a likely spot for Cal's resting place. Around eleven o'clock he found the perfect location. There wasn't a house in sight. Just in case, he pulled to the side of the road and sat there for ten minutes with the lights off, nursing a can of Carnation. Not a soul passed by.

Finally, his features scrunched with distaste, he dragged Cal's body out of the trunk and along a narrow path that led to a small shack. On the door of the building was a sign, "Pump Station #1." Ronnie propped the body against the rear of the shack, facing away from the road, and returned to the car for Cal's belongings, which he set around the body just as Cal might have arranged them. Then he carried the towel and the bedspread back to the car and sat behind the wheel, shivering. After a few bleak moments he started driving slowly past wide black fields, weedy ditches and the occasional dwelling. The road then climbed a steep ridge, and as he approached a more settled area, with farms on either side of him, he began to feel even more nervous. If people spotted his Caddy, they might tie the two things together when they discovered Cal.

Just then a car pulled out of a driveway a hundred yards ahead and sped down the road away from him. Ronnie slowed his car to a crawl and stopped. To his right, where the car had come from, stood a two-storey farmhouse, large barns and outbuildings, and acres of fruit trees. In the silvery glow of moonlight, everything seemed so neatly arranged, so lovingly tended, he could scarcely imagine the kind of people who might live there. Geniuses, perhaps, adepts at the art of living, whose time on the planet displayed a wholesome perfection that made his own life, and the lives of those with whom he travelled, seem a blighted, shadowy existence.

After pausing there a few minutes, he put his car into gear once more and crept past the farmhouse, slowly picking up speed as he went. Turning a wide curve in the road, he saw a bridge up ahead of him, and on the bridge, a young man sitting on the supports, as though he were preparing to jump. That image spoke to him as clearly as any he had ever seen in a painting. He thought: The boy is troubled. The boy is the answer to my problems.

It was always this way. Like boxing or soccer, like the circus even, Ronnie saw the music business as a way out, a bridge across, a road up from whatever dead-end, broken-down, hard-luck life you might have been born to. With quick feet or quick hands, with tricks or licks or derring-do, one could make a bright new shiny life for oneself without the blessing of family or fortune or a fine education. These were natural callings for the downtrodden, the oppressed, the ostracized. And this boy looked very much in need of an open door.

Ronnie was playing a dangerous hunch in making himself visible, but he brought the car to a halt in the middle of the bridge and stepped out. Then he cleared his throat and said, "I hope you are not contemplating anything so rash as jumping. I am afraid I am not the ablest of swimmers."

The boy looked over his shoulder, and with a weak smile said, "Don't worry. I'm just sitting here thinking. Besides, I'd break my neck before I drowned. There's only six inches of water down there."

Ronnie closed the door and folded both arms across the roof of the car. "Seems a chilly spot to be sitting on a night like this. Surely there are more comfortable places to ponder the mysteries of life. Is there somewhere I can drop you?"

"Chicago's what I'd like. But I guess I should just head home."

"Ah," Ronnie said, "home. It's funny, but you rather had the look of a young man with another destination. I spotted you from a fair piece down the road there, and the moment I set eyes on you, I had the sense—don't ask me why—that you were saying a goodbye of some sort. And I suppose it reminded me of myself at your age, taking my last fond look at home before I headed down to London."

The boy snorted good-naturedly and swung his legs over the bridge to face him. "You're from England?"

"Scotland, in fact, but everywhere really, Scotland, England, Ireland, New York. The world, as they say, is my playground." He paused a moment to consider once again the wisdom of what he was doing. Then he stepped around his car and offered his hand. "My name is Ronnie," he said, "Ronnie Conger. And you are . . ."

"Cyrus Owen."

"Owen," he repeated. "That sounds like a good strong Anglo-Saxon name. And Cyrus, let me guess, you are what, eighteen?"

"I just turned nineteen."

"Yes, and wondering what the future holds. I remember well what that feels like, let me tell you." He smiled kindly, noticing for the first time the deformed hand that rested in the boy's lap. And in that moment Ronnie knew he had found his needy soul. He clapped him on the shoulder and said, "But never mind my boring story. Tell me this, Cyrus, have you ever thought you might like to be in show business?"

THEY STOPPED AT THE THREE LINKS HALL just long enough to fetch Cyrus's gear and pile it in the trunk. ("Just there on that old bedspread, my dear boy.") The moment they got back in the car, however, Cyrus started to have second thoughts. He had no idea where he was going. He had about ten bucks in his pocket. Worse, this guy could be a pervert for all he knew. As the car turned onto the eastbound freeway, he felt his spirits sink further. After a few minutes of deepening anxiety, he said, "What kind of show did you say it was again?"

"Well, I don't think I ever said in so many words. Are you familiar with Jimmy Waters?"

Cyrus shook his head uncertainly.

"No, I thought not. Before your time, perhaps. What do you listen to, Cyrus, Jefferson Airplane? Grateful Dead? Rolling Stones?"

"Anything really. I like it all as long as it's good."

Ronnie laughed. "As long as it's good, yes, I know what you mean. You like the music you like. Very well put. And you know, I'm sure Jimmy's music will speak to you. The first time I heard it I was mesmerized. I tell you—and this is no exaggeration—when I heard his solo on the recording of 'Don't Look Back,' my life was changed forever. Does that make sense to you?"

Cyrus looked out the side window at the nighttime scenery flashing by. He knew the song, of course. Who didn't? A golden oldie, one of the countless crappy pop tunes that clogged the airwaves before the British Invasion. And although he wasn't a fan of the music, he was excited by the prospect of playing with a recording star, even a faded one. This Ronnie Conger didn't seem so bad, either. Cyrus had never met an adult who talked about music this way. He looked across the seat and said, "For me, it was the Animals, 'House of the Rising Sun.' I bought the single and played it a thousand times.

Something about it, I don't know, it scared me. It was like—and this is weird—but when I was a kid, I went camping with a friend and we heard wolves. Just plain scary, but good scary. Scary the way it was meant to be, like it's a lesson or something."

Ronnie laughed again, this time with real feeling. "Cyrus, my boy, you are a poet. That is exactly what I mean: music that is a lesson, a pure and sometimes frightening communication." And with that he howled like a wolf.

Years later, Cyrus would marvel that he had driven off with Ronnie that way. How many young people hopped into strangers' cars and were never seen again? How many people accepted the kindness of others and ended up shilling for Reverend Moon or L. Ron Hubbard, or getting caught in the nightmare of someone like Jim Jones? And while some might label the music business itself a kind of cult, demanding similar sacrifices, promising similar rewards, it never felt that way to Cyrus. All his life there'd been a place inside him he needed to reach, a power inside him he needed to tap, a story inside him he needed to learn. That night, as he cruised through the darkness in Ronnie's Cadillac, he sensed for the first time that all those things might be possible.

Isabel sat on the sunporch nursing a coffee and staring vacantly across the front yard to the dirt road that ran past their farm. It was the first warm day of April, and the flies, stupid and fat and not long for this world, were swarming the house again. They made a sound like corn popping as they bumped against the walls and windows, not a welcome noise by any means; it heralded another terrible season of pig reek. By June she wouldn't be able to open her windows and doors. The air conditioning would run non-stop. Even if she changed the filters every week, the smell of her clothes would make her gag.

Gerry never minded as much; but then, after the lung-scorching stench of the barns themselves, ammonia so dense it made her eyes run, the rest of their property probably came as a breath of fresh air. On summer nights, he often sat outside on the lawn and drank a beer or two. She'd seen him take his pie and coffee out to the picnic table under the maple and eat it with a hundred flies buzzing around his head.

When they were first married, she assumed she would get used to everything, but in fact it seemed to get worse with time. Every year from April to November, Isabel felt sick to her stomach; and now, with the warm weather on its way, she would begin again to dread Gerry's coming to bed at night, settling his long frame on their cheap Sears mattress set, the one they had bought before they were married and that now dipped so badly she had to cling to the edge to keep from rolling into him. Even after a shower, the smell of him, the prickle of his leg hair, and especially those crazy tufts on his back, were too much for her. She tried not to think it, but more and more often the picture came to her that she was lying in the dark with a hog, and she felt stricken in her heart that she could ever think such things about the man she had married.

Lord knew she wasn't perfect. She had never been a beauty, twiggy as a brush pile. She knew that people talked about her, too. They would say she wore too much perfume. They'd wonder who she was trying to impress—the new clothes always, the beauty parlour once a week. And they would think it curious that she insisted on having a job when Gerry needed her there on the farm to do all the things a farmwife does. They'd feel sorry for Gerry, and she was pretty sure he would agree with them (though he would never let on).

But Isabel didn't care about any of that. She was proud she had graduated top of her class from the real estate course at St. Clair College. She enjoyed painting her nails. She loved her new cream pantsuit, and the older red and blue ones she had bought last summer at Dainty Miss. She loved her brief-case with its rich leather and brassy clasps, and loved how it felt to get behind the wheel of the big new Buick she leased from Rollie Marks to chauffeur clients around. She was thrilled most of all to have a job at Demeter Real Estate and to get away from the damn pigs. It seemed to her such a sensible decision. At last. At last she was moving in the right direction. And while she understood that you couldn't turn back the clock, she felt you could at least make up for lost time, which was just what she planned to do.

After she had finished her coffee, she lit her first cigarette, the only guilt-free smoke of the day. Then she headed upstairs to get ready for work. She had just finished putting on her makeup when she heard Gerry clomp upstairs and stand in the hallway. He pushed open the bathroom door with the toe of his boot and stood watching her awhile, his arms across his chest.

"Be late tonight?" he asked.

She brushed off the front of her blouse, then double-checked to see if she could do anything more with her face. At last she turned to him and said, "No, I don't think so. No appointments. I thought we could have baked chicken and Rice-A-Roni."

He nodded, his mind not on dinner or her job. "About Reg Foster. . . ."

She tossed her cosmetics into her little zippered bag. Without turning, she said, "I thought we'd been over this. You always said we'd never use the home farm for collateral."

"I know what I said. But maybe this is different."

"Gerry, the only thing different is Foster. Five years ago he wouldn't give you the time of day, remember? Now he's trying to rope you into a big loan you don't want and don't need."

"Or maybe," he said, his face darkening, "maybe *you* don't know anymore what I want or need." Then he pounded down the stairs and out across the yard to the barn.

JANICE OPENED HER EYES to find her mother leaning over her. It was morning; but judging from the colour of the walls, it was too early to get up for school. Her mother was still wearing her housecoat, and the look on her face jolted Janice wide awake.

"It's Mrs. Mitchell," her mother whispered. "Cy's aunt. She's in the front hall. She wants to talk to you."

Janice threw on some clothes and followed her mother down. Sure enough, Ruby Mitchell was standing by the front door in her brown cloth coat. She looked so tired and wired that Janice knew immediately that something terrible had happened.

Ruby's face brightened with hope the moment she set eyes on her. "Cyrus," she said, "have you seen him?"

Janice turned to her mother, and then back to Ruby, but it was Cyrus's face she saw, outside the Three Links Hall last night. He was smiling like an idiot, drunk on his own good fortune. She had asked him to be careful. Like a lot of guys, he got stupid when he was happy.

"I haven't seen him since yesterday, Mrs. Mitchell. We met at the hall after school and had a pizza. I came home about ten, I guess."

"Well, I was just at the hall. I thought he had maybe slept there last night. He does that sometimes when—well, you know, he was a little upset—and so I went there and the door was locked, and I called his name and pounded on the door like I sometimes do, but he didn't come down, and I started wondering if he was okay, or maybe he was hurt or sick or—" Ruby covered her mouth with a liver-spotted hand and took a deep breath. "I was wondering if maybe you had a key I could borrow . . ."

"I'll come with you," Janice said.

To a stranger, the change at the rehearsal space would not be apparent. It was a dusty room filled with drums, microphones, amplifiers and a threadbare collection of flea-market furniture. But Janice and Ruby understood right away. Cy's equipment was gone. They walked together to the spot where his amplifier usually stood, and they stared at the bare wooden floor, which showed a clean rectangle the size of his Fender Dual Showman, outlined in dustballs and picks and broken strings, candy wrappers and crumpled set lists and song lyrics. It was like his gear had been vaporized, leaving only its shadow behind.

Janice turned in a circle to see if perhaps Cyrus had moved his amp to another spot. Beside her, speaking in a dream voice, Ruby said, "His amplifier, his little suitcase for his cords. It's all gone."

Janice walked to the window and looked out on the street. It was a sunny day, as fresh and clean as the morning after a storm. She and Cyrus had talked for hours last night about his quitting school and heading off soon to find a full-time band, maybe in Hounslow or even Toronto to start with, one day making a name for himself. But she never imagined he meant so soon. It didn't seem possible. A part of her found it hard to believe he'd even been serious. He was good, probably the best musician in Wilbury; but there were any number of guitarists in Hounslow who could play circles around him, and Hounslow was as far away from the big time as you could get. Did he really believe he would become a star?

She turned to Ruby and said, "The amp weighs a ton. I know. I've helped him carry it. So he couldn't get very far without wheels. He must be at someone's house. You know, Seth has a car . . ."

Ruby felt a wave of relief. How could she have been so stupid? Cyrus had stormed out of the house, followed moments later by Isabel. Mystery solved. Izzy had picked him up and offered to let him stay at her place. Then they came to get his gear. What else could it be?

Ronnie couldn't sleep. He had tucked the boy into bed, gone to check on the rest of the crew and come tiptoeing back to the room just as the sun was beginning to paint the sky pink. But as exhausted as he felt, he still couldn't close his eyes. It saddened him to see the boy sleeping there so fitfully. The twisted sheets and the grinding teeth reminded Ronnie of another hotel room in another town, and the night he met Jimmy Waters, one of the world's anxious sleepers.

Back then, Ronnie had anxieties of his own. He had walked out on the Aaron Maxx tour in Staghorn, Alberta, and was renting a room in the Queen's Hotel, a room that smelled of smoke and stale beer, and throbbed all night with the red glow of neon. He was also running desperately low on cash and wondering what to do with the rest of his life now that he had more or less tossed his career down the dumper. Then one morning he flipped on the black-and-white television bolted to the wall and, there amid the snow and flickers, he saw Dick Clark: the sharp suit, the slicked-back hair, the youthful good looks. Just the sight of him—not to mention those fresh-faced Californian kids with the white smiles and crisp clothes and wholesome energy—made the day seem a little brighter. Better still, Dick was talking to Gil Gannon and sharing a good laugh.

Gil was short, a little heavy and not nearly as handsome as Dick, but he had all the swagger and self-assurance you'd expect of a major star, even though he hadn't had a hit in years. He had massive gold rings on his fingers. When he laughed, he shook from head to toe.

Dick waggled the microphone playfully and said, "What say we talk to the animals in the band." Immediately the musicians began to mug for the camera, cutting up like teenagers, even though they had to be thirty or older. They were dressed in identical black suits with narrow collars, white shirts and skinny ties, way behind the fashion curve for 1968. They had short greasy hair.

The drummer held his sticks to the top of his head, like Martian antennae, and Dick laughed and said, "I guess we know why they call you Moonman." That got a rise out of the girls in the audience. Then Dick angled closer to the keyboard player, a pale, slouching giant whose solemn attitude was entirely at odds with the rest of the band. He had a neatly trimmed beard, black hair and beady eyes. Dick sat beside him on the piano bench and said, "James Waters, I presume."

"That's right, Dick. But you can call me Jimmy."

"Welcome back to *American Bandstand,* Jimmy. What's it like being voted the best keyboard player of the decade by *Songmaker Magazine*?"

"It's all right, Dick. An honour, I guess."

"I bet it is. And well deserved. That solo of yours on 'Don't Look Back'? Wow. You've been playing how long?"

"All my life, Dick."

Dick was getting frustrated with the mopey one-note answers. He moved in close, really working, and said, "You fellas have been on the road non-stop, what, going on three years now. Japan, Europe, Australia—I don't imagine there's anyplace you guys haven't seen. What's it been like?"

A nearly unbearable silence built as everyone waited for Jim to respond. The guys in the band grew watchful. Though Gil was still jiving and posing, his eyes had lost their playful spark. And Jim just sat there shaking his head as if he were in pain.

Dick, the consummate pro, laughed like it was all some kind of gag. He nudged Jim with his elbow and said, "Seriously, now, how's it going?"

And something strange happened then. Jimmy Waters, the man who had brought music into Ronnie's life, this sad-faced giant with the bad posture, grabbed the microphone, stumbled from behind his keyboard and edged up to the camera, his face nearly pressed to the lens. And in the hushed smoky voice of an all-night DJ, he said, "It's going great, Dick. In fact, it's all gone. I'm done. I'm history." Then he dropped the microphone to the floor and shuffled through the stage curtains and away.

Ronnie watched the entire scene with a breathless fascination: to finally see the man, the author of his joy, the genius of his time, and to know he really existed; then to watch helplessly as he self-destructed before the eyes of the world. And that much was clear just watching the show; Jimmy had been virtually quivering onscreen.

A few days later Ronnie found a brief article in the entertainment section of the newspaper, describing how Jimmy Waters had walked off the set of *American Bandstand* and disappeared without a trace. Two concerts had been cancelled so far, and the rest of the U.S. tour was in jeopardy if he didn't show up soon.

That was all the news Ronnie needed to shake off his dark mood. If ever there was a purpose in his life, a meaning to be grasped, this was it. Maybe there was nothing he could do, but he had to try. At the very least he had to one day tell Jimmy Waters to his face what a difference his playing had made in one man's life.

Next day Ronnie set off for New York. He thumbed a ride as far as Winnipeg and, with his last few dollars, caught a bus to New York. After one night in his apartment in Brooklyn, he cashed a small bond he'd put aside for emergencies and hit the road again. His first move was to contact Gil Gannon's booking agent, Nate Wroxeter.

"That bastard is costing me a fortune!" Nate shouted into the phone.

"I understand," Ronnie said. "That was my thinking exactly. If there was anyone who wanted a piece of Jimmy's hide, it would be you. And that's why I called. I thought we could assist each other. I plan to spend the next few weeks tracking him down. It would help to know who else is interested should I find him, and just how interested they are."

Nate was two-hundred-dollars interested and gave Ronnie all the information he had on Jimmy: born in Port Swaggart, Pennsylvania, on the south shore of Lake Erie; last known address, Bleecker Street in New York.

It was easy enough to check out the address in the Village. Ronnie spoke to the landlord and found that Jimmy hadn't lived there for a few years and still owed six months rent. He heard, too, about a wife and kid who had grown tired of waiting for him to return and had gone off in search of a new life.

A week later, with spring just beginning to stir, Ronnie headed for Erie, and then west along the lakeshore, where he discovered that the town of Port Swaggart no longer existed and hadn't for years, swallowed in America's post-war sprawl and boom. As he drove along the Industrial Parkway (what used to be Lakeside Drive) he came upon a stretch of shoreline that had once been home to fishing boats and sandy beaches and was now a bleak stretch of toxic industry. About five miles further on, between an oil refinery and an abandoned tire factory, stood a small clapboard motel, all tumbledown and spooky, like something from a horror movie. Ronnie wouldn't have given it a second glance if not for the sign out front: Waters Inn.

He pulled into the parking lot, which had become a dumping ground for plastic garbage bags, bald tires, threadbare furniture and grimy household appliances. Careful not to brush against anything, he threaded his way toward the motel office where a wooden slammer, completely off its hinges and missing all but a few tatters of screen, leaned against the wall.

Ronnie called through the open doorway and got no answer. Inside he found more trash, and human excrement, but he held his nose and pressed farther into the office, past the front desk. There, a creaky stairway led to a second-floor apartment; and in the front bedroom overlooking the bay, or what remained of the bay, Jimmy Waters lay curled asleep on a bare, stained mattress, his eyes clamped shut, his jaws clenched, his face twitching to the manic rhythm of his dreams.

All that afternoon Jimmy tossed and turned. When he finally opened his eyes, the sun had begun to fade. He looked straight at Ronnie and then sat up slowly, calmly, as if all along he'd been expecting a stranger to appear.

Ronnie offered his hand in greeting. "I can't tell you what an honour it is to meet you at last," he said. "Your playing has made an enduring impression on me, that much is certain. Would you believe me if I said you had changed my life?"

Jimmy leaned forward over his knees, his hands gripping the edge of the mattress. He was dressed in the same clothes he had worn on *American Bandstand,* and they had seen much better days. His beard had grown shaggy, his hair a riot of intentions. "You're not an American," he said.

"No, you are right about that, but I love your country more than my own, and I love American music more than anything I can think of. And your solo—"

"Man, I don't want to hear this. . . ."

Those words startled Ronnie. "What I mean is your music, your solos, they lift us up, don't they? They show us the better side of our nature."

Jim slumped to his side, his head resting on the mattress again, and groaned as if he might be sick to his stomach. But Ronnie pressed on. "Do you . . . I mean, surely you believe your music has made a difference."

"Difference? I don't know what in hell you're talkin' about." Then he turned toward the wall and was soon asleep again.

Ronnie found a small wooden chair that had somehow been overlooked in the general fouling of the place, and he sat for hours and watched Jimmy sleep. Sometime before dawn, he slipped away to an all-night convenience store and bought plastic-wrapped sandwiches and beer. He brought in his suitcase and covered Jim with a sweater.

Next morning Jim accepted a sandwich and seemed genuinely pleased when Ronnie handed him a quart of Schlitz. But he still wasn't talking much. About noon, Ronnie tried another approach. "You're originally from around here, aren't you?"

Jim's only answer was to take a bite of sandwich. Then, with a grunt, he struggled to his feet and walked to the window that overlooked the bay. He leaned against the frame and touched his index finger to the jagged spikes of the broken panes, one by one. Finally he said, "My daddy moved us here from Arkansas. Got hisself a little fishin' boat. Back then, we rented a cottage not too far down the shore from here. Hardly remember it myself. So long ago it's like a dream. Trouble was he never could make the payments on the boat and he lost it to the bank. Bit of a drinkin' problem. Drifted around some. Ended up on the docks down in Erie. Wasn't a big man, you understand, not what you'd think of as a longshoreman, but he was stronger 'n a team of mules. I guess that's how I remember him best, like Marlon Brando in that movie there. *You* know . . ." He turned to fix Ronnie with a questioning look.

"*On the Waterfront,* you mean?"

"That's the one, *On the Waterfront,* that was my daddy. Coulda been a contendah . . ." He laughed darkly and then turned away from the window. "Where you from, if you're not American?"

Ronnie was in a space and time that seemed to vibrate with unseen possibilities. He cleared his throat and said, "I was born in Scotland, but even when I lived there it never really felt like my home."

Jimmy snorted, a grudging acknowledgement that he, too, had known the feeling of rootlessness. "Where does, then?"

"Feel like home? I don't know. Maybe nowhere. But I always thought I'd know when I found it. Maybe I haven't been paying attention."

They continued to talk throughout the afternoon, continued drinking. Jim seemed most interested in reminiscing, his stories jumping all over the place so it was hard to follow. In return, Ronnie told Jim about his early days in Glasgow and the way he had dashed his father's dream that they would both one day be men of the church. When he described that pivotal evening in Oxford and hearing the solo on the jukebox, Jim grunted in disbelief. "You're some kind of fool," he said.

Maybe it was the air of decay that hung about the place and the quantity of beer he had consumed, but as the day wore on, Ronnie began to agree with Jim's assessment. It *was* foolish to have come all this way to rescue Jimmy Waters when his own life was a complete shambles. Walking out on a tour the way he had, nearly throttling the star of the show, these were things that would not be forgiven. All things considered, it was unlikely he would ever land himself another gig.

At one point the darkness overcame him. He touched his forehead and said, "I don't know what I was thinking, coming here. I don't know what got into me. I suppose I had some half-formed notion I might be able to help you through your current troubles. But the sorry truth, my friend, is that I am in trouble enough myself. Everything is ashes. I don't know what on earth I'm going to do."

Jimmy, who had been slumped against the wall, opened his eyes and stared at him a long while without blinking. Then he slowly got to his feet and placed his hands on Ronnie's head, his fingers tapping out a familiar but crazy rhythm on his skull. He said, "If your life is over, then start again. If you've lost your strength, use your weakness. If you can't find your way, then it's time to get lost. If you can't look forward, look back, look back. If you can't look forward, look back."

Jim stopped talking then, stopped tapping, and wandered over to the window where he stared into the darkness. But Ronnie knew immediately that he had glimpsed the first vague outlines of something glorious, possibly the grandest thing he had ever conceived of: The Jimmy Waters Revival.

THE IDEA WAS REALLY VERY SIMPLE. He wanted to hear Jimmy play The Solo one more time, that was all. It didn't have to be with Gil Gannon. It didn't have to be anywhere special. But just once Ronnie wanted to hear that magic played live. Just once and he could die happy.

Jimmy was resistant to the idea, even though he had never stopped playing The Solo in a way, had even tapped it out on Ronnie's skull that day. In the weeks that followed, he played it on kitchen counters and car dashboards and just about any surface he touched. Even so, it took Ronnie more than a month of browbeating to get him in the same room with a keyboard. They had made their way back to New York by then, back to Ronnie's apartment. One day, Ronnie asked him to play something, and Jim became agitated.

"Who, me? I've done my time, I've reached the end."

"Easy now."

"It's not easy, it's hard. It's over and I can't do it no more so don't be talkin' like that. Me? You're outta your mind you think I'm goin' near that shit again."

The more he was pushed, the more Jimmy resisted, so Ronnie tried a different tack. It was easy enough to find musicians who might be interested in jamming with Jimmy Waters—he was still a big name, a respected star— so night after night Ronnie invited drummers and bass players and guitarists around to the apartment to see if he could find some chemistry that worked.

Jimmy ignored these strangers, hiding in his room or treating them like riff-raff. But then, on a whim, Ronnie invited a keyboard player to drop by on his own, a grizzled veteran. Rumour was he had been a hotshot at one time but had stopped getting calls. Bad attitude was the rap, not exactly a team player. But this guy, Sonny Redmond, sat down at the battered Heintzman and played "Rainy Night in Georgia," even managed a bit of vocal in a raspy echo of Brook Benton, and Jimmy seemed to perk right up. He eased out of his bedroom and stood in the doorway, rocking to the rhythm. And when Sonny shifted into a mournful blues tune, Jimmy moved away from the doorway and into the middle of the room. He stood there with eyes closed, fingers twitching, until finally he opened his arms and, in the deep, warm voice of a preacher, said, "I'd like to tell you a story now, if I may, about a man . . ."

It was such a surprising thing to do that Sonny stopped playing and turned around to listen. But as soon as the music stopped, the spell was broken, and Jimmy hurried back into his bedroom and refused to budge.

Next night, Sonny dropped by the apartment again. The first song he played was "Stormy Monday," and right away Jim moved to the centre of the room, his fingers going a mile a minute, his head thrown back. Just like before, the words began to spill out. "I'd like to tell you a story now, if I may, about a man, you know . . ."

This time it was Ronnie who fouled up. He misunderstood those dancing fingers and tried to guide Jimmy closer to the piano. With an almost frightening power, Jimmy knocked Ronnie sprawling on the floor and then fled to the bedroom.

On the third night, Sonny shuffled into the apartment and sat at the piano bench, cracking his knuckles. "So what's the deal, professor? Is there a gig or what? I ain't doin' this for my health."

Ronnie sat beside him on the bench and explained as briefly as possible what he had in mind.

Sonny squinted at him. "You want me to put together a band, and we'll jam every night for your freaky friend here in case he maybe decides to play again?"

"I was rather hoping it wouldn't take very long. Once he hears the right music, I am willing to wager that he won't be able to resist. If you leave an attractive space, I am certain he will rush forward to fill it."

Sonny looked at him dubiously. "I hate to be the fly in your ointment, pal, but just one obvious question: Who's going to be picking up the tab? I ain't the Welcome Wagon."

Ronnie laughed. "I can appreciate that, Mr. Redmond. No, I have some cash set aside for this purpose. I would appreciate it, however, if you could assemble a duo for now."

One week later, Sonny arrived with a drummer named Chuck Ray. They set up their gear in the apartment. Ronnie had rented a small Farfisa organ, too, and had it all ready to go in the centre of the room, just in case Jimmy got inspired.

To warm up, Sonny and Chuck slid easily into some highly syncopated funk. When they got bored with that, they ran through a few jazz standards. After an hour or so, Ronnie was pacing up and down the apartment. Jimmy had yet to leave his room.

"Any requests?" Sonny asked.

Ronnie shrugged and said, "Why not try the magic number?"

Without a moment's hesitation, they kicked into a souped-up version of "Don't Look Back." And just as quickly a blood-curdling scream came from Jimmy's bedroom.

Next night they set up again, but this time Ronnie discussed with Sonny what they might play. "We are dealing with a delicate sensibility here, my friend, so please do not take this as a reflection on your musicianship. I, for one, thought your performance last night was sublime. However, it did not do the trick. Now, whatever it was you played those first nights on your own seemed to be more in the right direction, did it not? You were able to coax him from his room at least."

Sonny nodded and settled into a slow gospel tune. There was nothing fancy to it at all, just blocking out the chords, riding the soothing groove. But right on cue, Jimmy walked out of the room and over to the Farfisa, his fingers alive, his eyes rolled back. In a deep, rich voice, he said, "I'd like to tell you a story now, if I may, about a time when I was not much older than five or six . . ."

They played all night, and Jimmy never once stopped talking. Sonny and Chuck clued in to the challenge right away, matching their music to the rhythm and tone of Jim's stories. That meant opening up and listening hard, to not only hear what was going on in that moment but to feel what would happen in the next. By the end of the night they were all exhausted. But twelve hours later they were right back at it, working on grooves that were more R&B this time. And Jimmy came out and told a different batch of stories.

That night as Sonny and Chuck were packing up to go, they were laughing and shaking their heads. They didn't really understand what was going on, but they were kind of digging it, too. After Ronnie handed them an envelope containing their evening's pay, he jammed his hands into his pockets and said, "Here is the sad part, my friends. I believe we are witnessing something special here. I am sure you feel it, too. Alas, I have run rather short of discretionary funds. In short, I am broke and may not be able to afford another night like this for quite some time."

Sonny said, "Yeah, well, we've all got problems, right?"

"You are indeed correct, my keyboarding friend. But I was hoping you and your associate here might be able to assist me with mine. Perhaps, if you thought about it, you might know of a suitable venue where we could showcase this little performance of ours. Surely others would find it as entrancing as we do. A paying audience would allow us to keep body and soul together while we wait for our man to come back to his calling."

Sonny looked at Chuck, and then back at Ronnie. "You're crazier than I thought."

"Just think about it, my friend. That is all I ask."

Sonny did think about it and arranged a test gig at the Ithaca Tavern, just to see if Jimmy would do his thing in public—which he did. Then Sonny suggested they book the Dunes, a smallish roller-skating pavilion down by Coney Island with hardwood floors, a soda fountain up front and glittering stars painted on the ceiling.

Ronnie thought it was a splendid idea. He drew on all the talents he had developed back in Scotland, arranging the publicity, the posters, the tickets (not an easy thing to do without signalling Nate Wroxeter and the musicians union), and managed to fill the Dunes for three nights.

He still didn't know what to make of the performance, and neither did the audience; but each night he watched with satisfaction as Jim stepped further out of his shell, the trickle of words becoming a flow, and by the third gig, a flood. And while Jim had yet to play a single note on his keyboard, Ronnie was willing to wait for that—they were at least making a little money. Two weeks later they took their show out of town with the idea that they would ride that fading name as far as it would take them and maybe, if they were lucky, witness a miracle.

Cyrus opened his eyes with a blink and stared at a white pebbled ceiling where sinuous cobwebs danced on currents of air. Early-morning sunlight spilled in through sliding glass doors that led onto a concrete balcony. He sat up warily, gazed about the room—paint-by-number art and Swedish-style furniture, a colour television and mini-bar, a Gideon Bible on the night table beside him—and was relieved to see his clothing and guitar sitting where he had left them. In that moment, his presence in the room seemed a mistake so vast and complex he could not even begin to grasp its enormity. He was wondering if he should grab his gear and split, when Ronnie came out of the bathroom, a towel wrapped around him.

"Ah, my friend," he said, "I hate to disturb you after only a few hours sleep, but we are in for a busy day, I fear. Before I go down for breakfast, perhaps we should discuss a few of the particulars we neglected last night."

Ronnie slid into the bathroom again and emerged a minute later wearing dark slacks and a black knit pullover with a triangle of white T-shirt showing above the collar. He sat across from Cyrus and pulled on socks and a pair of black high-heeled boots. When he noticed they were spattered with mud, he wiped them with the edge of a blanket until they were polished to his satisfaction. He said, "I am sure you must be curious how much you will be paid, that sort of thing." He raised an eyebrow and reached across to pat Cyrus's hand. "Worry not on that point, young man. We pay a fair wage—one hundred American dollars a week, whether you have been with us a decade or a day. In addition we pay your hotel accommodation plus breakfast. Dinners are provided backstage after sound check. We offer lunch to the crew during set-up, naturally, and you are welcome to partake if you care to show up for it. Mostly the musicians don't—sound checks are not until four or five. In that case, lunch is your own responsibility, as are phone calls, meals on non-show days and dry cleaning. We will pay to keep your gear in order. New tubes if you need them, repairs when necessary. Strings are your domain. Clear?"

Cyrus nodded, relief spreading through him like a drug. This was sounding more like the real thing all the time.

"There is one small proviso," Ronnie continued. "You may earn a hundred a week, but you will receive only seventy-five. The rest is held in reserve. Enforced savings, if you will. A little something for a rainy day. If you need extra cash for an emergency, we can discuss some temporary arrangement to cover your expenses. I am sure I don't need to tell you, my boy, that life on the road is full of temptations, with plenty of time to indulge them. Money is just the nudge that can set so many people down the wrong road. So naturally we do our best to nip that sort of thing in the bud."

Of all the gigs Cyrus had played with Janice and the others—at the high school, the Purple Pad—the whole band had never made more than thirty bucks. A hundred a week plus expenses, while nothing like the big time, still sounded like a step in the right direction. And this Ronnie character seemed pretty cool. He reminded Cyrus of the manager the Beatles had, what's his face, Brian Epstein. Sharp dresser. Fancy boots. Proper, too. Kind of dignified.

Sitting up straighter, Cyrus rubbed his eyes and said, "You're talking about crews and shows and sound checks, and I still don't know what kind of show you put on."

Ronnie laughed, which seemed to be his standard response to Cyrus. "Isn't that crazy?" he said, shaking his head with disbelief. "I am sorry. I keep assuming that everyone has heard of the Jimmy Waters Revival."

"So it's like what, an oldies show?"

"Oldies, yes, I like that. In a manner of speaking, that is exactly what it is. But so much more. I quite frankly don't know how to explain, other than to say there has never been a show quite like ours, so that makes comparisons difficult. You will just have to see for yourself. I can promise you one thing, however: you have never played with better musicians."

Ronnie got to his feet and slid into a dark jacket. "Now," he said, "it is past my breakfast hour. If I were you, I would think about a little nourishment as well. And if you need to call someone, you know, so they don't worry, you can charge it to my room. Considering our rather impromptu meeting and departure, I think that would be wise."

After Ronnie left the room, Cyrus sat in stunned silence. Finally he picked up the phone and called home. Ruby answered on the first ring.

"Cyrus? Honey, where are you? We've been worried sick. I thought you had gone to the hall to sleep the way you've done before, but when I went there this morning it was locked, and I was so worried, I went over to see Janice, and she came back to the hall with me, and all your equipment was gone. And then, well, then we figured you had maybe stayed with Isabel, you know, but when I phoned, of course, she didn't know, and then this morning I heard about this business over there by the pumping station and I didn't know what to think and—"

"Ruby, I'm fine. Don't worry, okay?"

"Well, I don't know what that would be like, not worrying. What with all we've been through, I don't think we could ever spend another day, any one of us, without worrying . . ."

Cyrus took a deep breath and let it out slowly. In a calm, measured tone, he said, "I'm not Hank, okay? I'll be fine. I promise."

"But where are you?"

It was the hurt in her voice, the soft quaver, that brought the necessary tenderness back to his words. "I'm working, Ruby. I'm in Campenola. I got a job as a musician. So don't worry, okay? Everything's fine."

"Oh, Cyrus."

"Come on, cheer up. I have to run now, but I'll call again." Then he quickly hung up and fell back on the bed. When he had regained his composure, he dialled Izzy's office number.

"Where the hell are you?" she scolded.

"Hey, lighten up. I'm in Campenola a few days."

"Campenola? That's 250 miles. What are you doing there?"

"I got a gig with a band, Iz, a lucky break. I can't believe it, really, it's so cool. But look, that's not why I called. I want you to go see Ruby and calm her down a bit. She seems pretty upset."

"I wonder why. It's funny how men have a talent for getting people all excited, and it's women who have to calm them down."

"It's not like I wanted to upset everyone. Anyway, I'm nineteen, Iz, an adult. Why's she have to make such a big deal? This is good news."

In a softer tone, she said, "Seems to me she's got good reason to be upset. That scene last night was almost word for word the kind of shit we used to hear from Hank."

"I'm not Hank."

"Okay. But you still disappeared into thin air."

"Twelve hours. You'd think she'd be used to that by now."

"Come on. You weren't at the hall. You weren't with friends. And there's that weirdness out by the pump."

"What weirdness? Ruby said the same thing."

"This morning Ernie Hicks found some kid dead as a doornail. According to Ernie, they found some drug paraphernalia and a suitcase. Could be an overdose, they think, but nobody knows this guy from Adam or how he got there. It's so close to the house, and with you disappearing, Ruby got spooked. Who wouldn't?"

Cyrus closed his eyes a moment. "Look," he said, "I'm sorry. The last thing I wanted was to worry anyone."

"Well here's the thing, dummy. It doesn't matter what you want. It's what you do."

RUBY WATCHED ISABEL PARK beside the garage then dawdle over to the house. At the door she pulled her niece into her arms and said, "Here I am worrying about myself, and look at you, poor girl."

"Poor nothing," she said, suffering the embrace for her aunt's sake. Ruby had always shown far more affection than any of the Owens could return.

The hugs and sympathy felt as sticky as flypaper to Isabel.

Ruby stepped back then and ran her hand along the sleeve of Isabel's jacket. "Did you see Clarence? Maybe you could tell him his coffee will be ready. There's *kuchen,* too."

Isabel walked across the back lawn, her arms folded across the front of her cream suit as if that might help her hold on to her patience. (First Gerry, then Cyrus and now this—it was already past noon and she hadn't managed a single bit of work yet, her "little job," as Ruby called it.) She passed beneath the clothesline and walked over to the packing shed, with its conveyor belt and hoppers and stacks and stacks of corrugated cardboard. Everything was quiet now and covered with a fine layer of dust. No sign of her uncle on the packing floor or in the big walk-in cooler, so she headed over to the barn, the biggest building on the farm. Made of concrete blocks and a corrugated metal roof, almost two storeys high and 120 feet long, you might almost mistake it for a hockey rink. It had huge double doors along the south end, and at least three-quarters of it served as a garage for her uncle's equipment: the tractors, the wagons, the sprayers, a couple of Model T's he'd converted to flatbeds and used out in the orchard to carry the pickers and their baskets, their harnesses and their funny three-legged ladders.

At the other end of the building, on the west side facing the house, there was another large sliding door that led to her uncle's workshop. It was where he spent a good part of his winter welding, greasing, rebuilding, and sometimes doing nothing more important than feeding apple wood into the pot-bellied stove. There was a workbench and tools and a turquoise plastic radio as old as her memories. Beside the bench stood a vintage pop machine and a sofa with half the stuffing ripped out by mice. As a young girl, she used to sit there on summer nights, the crickets kicking up a fuss outside, the ball game on low, and listen to her father and uncle talk about weather and prices and what damn fools they had in the government. She loved the sound of those sloppy southern voices on the radio, like so much corn on the cob, and the three of them—father, daughter, uncle—lounging in the shed and sipping Coca-Cola.

No sign of Clarence in the barn. She called his name and got no answer. Then she noticed him standing motionless on the far side of the house, inspecting the tree there. She crossed the yard again and moved up beside him. "You okay?" she asked, touching his shoulder.

He turned slowly to look at her, his face drained of life. In a weary voice, he said, "Right as rain, Bel." After a moment, he added, "This thing never did bear the way I hoped it would."

She knew what he was doing, what he was thinking. "Come on," she said. "Ruby's got coffee. She made *kuchen*."

He shook his head, remembering a skinny girl full of piss and vinegar, and a sad beautiful young boy, and how the three of them had walked to the back of the property that first winter together and cut shoots off a wild apple tree growing near the creek there. The fruit was of no commercial value, but he preferred it to a Mac or an Empire, the flesh soft and spicy, staining blood-red with each bite through the skin. They stored the shoots in the cooler all through that winter, safe and sound. And come spring they went out beside the house, knelt in the dirt, and he showed them how to graft those fragile buds onto the sturdy root stock. The delicate incision of the bark. The careful placement of the scion into the opening. The proper use of rubber tape and grafting compound. Izzy ran off a few weeks after that but didn't run far, landing in the arms of an ignorant pig farmer. The whole thing left Clarence bitter—her wilfulness, Ruby's sorrow, his own heartache that a pretty girl like that would waste herself on the likes of Gerry Muehlenburg.

He glanced at her now, still a young woman but looking much older than her years. He tucked her arm under his and turned to look down the road. His voice hushed and full of distance, he said, "I know with Hank it was never easy, but your mother and father, well the times were different, they didn't know. They were just so young, what did they know? Not like any of us were any help, either, my God. And then with you and the business with Gerry . . ."

"The business?"

"You know, getting married like that and how we thought you weren't ready, when really it was most likely us, we weren't ready. But you understood that, Bel. You always had a good head on your shoulders. A good heart. And heck, I know you've never had much use for me and Ruby, but at least you were never one to make folks pay for their mistakes."

"Come on, Clarence, you're talking nonsense."

"Am I? I guess what I mean is I've always wanted . . . what I always thought was your folks maybe went at this family thing too early, and we came at it so late, and if only, if only me and Ruby and your folks, if only we had known, any of us, what in hell we were doing . . ."

She tugged on his arm and said, "Come on, let's go in."

He looked over to the barn, where swallows swooped in and out of the open doorway. Then he followed her dutifully around the corner to the porch.

Isabel seldom ate sweets, but the smell of the apple *kuchen,* Cyrus's favourite dessert, was irresistible. She cut three generous pieces and carried them to the table, where her aunt and uncle sat, looking as feeble and stricken as the folks at the seniors home where she volunteered two nights a week. She ate her cake without making a sound, watching the two of them mired in stunned silence. And with each bite of her dessert, she got more peeved. When she had finished, she pushed her empty plate to the side, took a scalding sip of coffee and said, "You're acting like he's dead. You're acting like this is some horrible tragedy. Killed in a car accident, maimed for life. You should be thrilled. He actually sounded happy, you know that? This isn't history repeating. It has nothing to do with Hank or me. He's happy. You should be thrilled."

"Really," Ruby said. "We should celebrate this? Look at your uncle. Are you happy to see him this way?"

"No, I'm disappointed. Seems to me you're both being selfish."

If there was one thing Ruby couldn't abide, it was hearing someone criticize her husband. She primly folded her hands in front of her. "Is that what it is, selfish? I was wondering what this feeling was, Isabel. Here I was thinking we were heartbroken, and all along we've just been selfish. But I suppose you know all about that, don't you, dear—being selfish, I mean—with your little job and fancy clothes and that poor husband of yours dragging himself to the Hilltop six days a week so he can get himself a hot lunch—"

Ruby stopped dead, as if she'd been pierced by her own words. She actually covered her mouth with her hand to prevent any more venom from escaping. Clarence shook his head and looked down into his lap. And Isabel rose without a sound and walked out of the house. She realized well enough that her aunt and uncle had been through an awful lot these past few months. The operation and the never-ending worries. The way every little twinge and sniffle would take on significance. And now, on top of everything, they had Cyrus's foolishness to deal with. So it wasn't Ruby's outburst that bothered her (that was already forgiven) but the very real sense that they were all fragments of a vessel that had once been whole and that no amount of fussing could ever mend.

B y the time Cyrus made it down to breakfast, another anxiety had taken hold of him. He sat opposite Ronnie and said, "Mr. Conger, I've been thinking."

Ronnie, who had been scribbling in a day planner, put down his pen and smiled. "Yes? What about, my friend? And please call me Ronnie. Everyone does."

"Well, the thing is, I've been wondering about an advance. I kind of left town unprepared. I need clothes, toothbrush, basically everything."

Ronnie didn't miss a beat. He pulled his wallet from his jacket pocket and placed two hundred dollars on the table. When Cyrus didn't take it, Ronnie raised an eyebrow and said, "Is that not sufficient?"

"The thing is, Mr. Conger—"

"Ronnie."

"Well the thing is I'm not sure. I mean, I'm sure it's enough money, I'm just not sure about everything else. No one has heard me play, and I'd hate to start spending money I can't pay back."

Ronnie bit his lip to keep from laughing. "You are a piece of work, young man. The fact is I stopped lending money to musicians long ago because a musician has never once paid me a penny in return. Over the years they have consumed my beer and whiskey and coffee without once offering to buy a round. They have read my newspapers and magazines. They have gobbled my mints and toffees. If I had a wife, I could be fairly certain that they would have had her any number of ways by now. So, no, do not by any means give thought to repayment. Think of this as a signing bonus, or danger pay or a retainer, if you will. That seems a fair return for your inconvenience if things do not work out. But if things do work out, as I'm sure they will, then for two months I won't invest any money for you. All right? An advance. Is that fair?"

With that, Ronnie pushed the money toward Cyrus's side of the table. "Take it, my boy, go on a shopping spree and be back at twelve o'clock sharp. Sound checks are normally scheduled between four-thirty and six, but I've told Sonny and his troupe to show up at noon. That should be plenty of time for a rehearsal."

Ronnie rose to his feet and glided from the dining room. The sight of him striding away with his day planner clutched to his chest, all decked out in black save for the little white triangle of his T-shirt, made Cyrus think of a priest. Father Conger.

THE CAMPENOLA ARMOURY and Agricultural Centre, shaped like an inverted water trough, was bounded on one side by the Canadian National freight yard and on the other by a harness-racing track. It was like a hundred other places in a hundred other towns across Ontario, Wilbury included, and Cyrus immediately felt more at ease.

Ronnie pulled the Cadillac to the rear of the building, beside a dented Airstream trailer that looked like a silver dirigible losing gas. The trailer was hitched to a rusty Ford Fairlane. Beside the trailer stood a two-ton truck and a retooled school bus painted robin's egg blue, flecks of the original orange showing through. An unsteady hand had painted "The Jimmy Waters Revival" on the sides.

Outside the armoury, a man wearing cowboy boots was tossing a foot-ball into the air and catching it. Nearby, a brown-haired woman sat on a blanket, brushing a yappy little Pekingese. When she saw the Caddy, she waved. The man said, "Just in time, Arsey. Sonny's having a shit-fit."

Ronnie hurried into the hall, and Cyrus followed him. Immediately his spirits sank. He had played his share of high school dances and small local clubs, and this didn't seem much more elaborate than that. It was certainly nothing like the concerts he had been to in Hounslow, or the Grande Ballroom in Detroit.

Out on the floor, pimply-faced kids in white shirts and grey flannel pants were busy setting up folding chairs. A stage—little more than a boxing ring without the ropes and turnbuckles and corner posts—had been set up at one end of the hall. A single roadie was up there connecting cords and cables, and each time he took a step, the spring in the canvas threatened to knock things over like so many dominoes. Meanwhile another man in a tweed cap worked down on the floor setting up a series of small speaker columns at each side of the stage. A bunch of curtains served as a backdrop, and at the front of the stage, two metal T-bars each held a few lights. Also at the front, pointing back toward the curtain, was a small spotlight with a tricoloured rotating disc. That's where Ronnie stood, shouting orders and waving his arms about. Finally he turned to two guys off to the side of the hall—they looked to Cyrus like bouncers or bikers—and cupped his hands like a bull-horn. "Sonny, your new musician has arrived. Time to get to work." Then he pointed at Cyrus, who tried to act cool when everyone looked in his direction.

The two men sauntered across the hall and gave Cyrus the once-over. In the lead was a heavy-set man in his early fifties, wearing baggy jeans and a rumpled black sweatshirt with a Jack Daniel's logo. The flab around his belly nearly obscured his belt buckle, and his eyes were more than a little bleary. The man—Cyrus assumed rightly that this was Sonny—shook his head and, without a hint of kindness, said, "Jesus wept. What did I tell you? He's done it again. Conger doesn't know his dick from his dry cleaning."

Cyrus extended his right hand. "My name is Cyrus Owen. My gear's out in the car . . ." He dropped his hand to his side when no one responded.

Sonny was more concerned with Cyrus's left hand and was making no effort to hide his incredulity. "Do you know anything about music?" he asked with a weary exasperation.

"Well," Cyrus replied, uncertain how much was expected of him, "maybe not as much as you do, but I'd like to give it a try."

"Give it a try? This ain't amateur hour, baby doll. You'd better be one shit-hot bass player or your ass is grass, and Conger's, too. Now drag your gear in here and we'll run through a few tunes while the crew is setting up. Hop to it."

Cyrus cast a nervous glance in Ronnie's direction. "The thing is—"

"Look, there's no 'thing.' Just do what you're told and we'll all be happy as pigs in shit."

"But there is a thing. I'm a guitar player. Mr. Conger didn't say anything about playing bass."

Sonny slumped. "Oh, Jesus Murphy. *Con-ger!*"

Ronnie was already halfway over to them. "Good, good, good," he called out. "You've all met. This is wonderful, is it not? I so love new beginnings."

Sonny laid his hand lightly on Ronnie's shoulder. In the sing-song voice of feigned civility, he said, "Are you a total idiot? Cal was a bass player. What the hell am I supposed to do with this dickweed?"

Ronnie smiled broadly and nodded his head. "I understand your consternation, Sonny, but you know, I see this as a tremendous opportunity for all of us, a chance to learn some flexibility in the face of life's uncertainties. And let's face it, the group had gotten a bit stale. You said yourself that the band would sound a hundred percent better without Cal, and you were right—he was a dear boy but admittedly a weak link. So now you've got your wish and more. You can cover the bass lines, just like you wanted all along. You won't have Cal messing things up. And now we have young Cyrus here, who plays guitar like an angel. This is a step in the right direction, you can't deny it."

Sonny spit on the floor, turned sharply on his heel and marched back across the hall with his entourage. If Cyrus had been nervous before, he was on the verge of tears now, petrified he would make a fool of himself.

Ronnie clapped him on the shoulder and said, "That went better than I thought it would. And don't worry about Sonny. His bark is worse than his bite." Then he guided Cyrus over to a dolly beside the stage. Handing him the keys to the Caddy, he said, "I wouldn't keep him waiting. He's a stickler for punctuality."

Cyrus dragged the dolly outside, opened the trunk and hauled out his gear. When he turned around again, he saw a face staring at him from the

Airstream. A moment later the door opened and a hulking man stepped uncertainly down from the trailer. He had long, unnaturally black hair swept back like a lion's mane, a glistening black goatee, and eyes that were Robin Hood green. He wore a rumpled white linen suit. His feet were bare. He was holding the Pekingese Cyrus had seen earlier.

"The new musician?" The man offered his free hand, which Cyrus promptly accepted. "Always a pleasure, you know, to have a new face remind us what we're all about. The spirit, yes? The vital energy like a river that refreshes us and carries us to a higher place . . ."

The man had a voice like a canyon, deep and reverberating. "You believe in signs, young man?"

"Well—"

"Of course you do. Who doesn't? When your stomach growls, isn't that a sign? When you yawn, when you're thirsty—these, too, are signs. You follow stop signs and pay attention to the first sign of a cold. You head for the exit when there's a fire and follow the highway signs to your favourite fast-food restaurant. Don't tell me you don't believe in signs."

"Well," Cyrus conceded, "I guess I kind of do."

"Mmm-hmm. God gave us signs, too, rules to guide us in our life. Honour thy father and mother. I know your momma and your daddy have rules, and these are things we all must obey. As musicians we follow key signatures and notations, and what are these but signs to the glories that dwell in our hearts. Young Cal followed signs that led him away from us, just as you have now followed signs that have brought you into our circle, which is a very awkward way to say welcome to our little family. My name is Jimmy Waters, and I want you to know that whatever is your problem is my problem. Whatever is your fear is my fear. Do not hesitate to come to me. I am at your service. Our stories are here and forever more entwined."

They were standing so close together that the man's sheer bulk was intimidating. Heat radiated from him, the air musky with perspiration and hair oil and black licorice. He nuzzled his chin into the dog's fur, then looked off into the distance and said, "I remember, Lord, I still remember how it felt to stand where you are standin' now, just there on the verge of mighty things, with all your music before you. Youth is what I mean, your age." He shook his head at the wonder of it all. "Have you ever noticed that music is a one-way street? The first note of any song can lead us anywhere, you know, but only ever forward. Have you noticed that? Into the future. It is a young man's game, you see. Ever forward, the young man's game. Play a single note, any note, and no matter what it is, you will never wonder what may have preceded it but only what comes next. Play a note and you begin to hear the next one before it can even be shaped, already you are movin' forward, ever forward."

Cyrus finally succeeded in pulling free of Jimmy's clutches. He wiped his palm against his pant leg and said, "It's nice to meet you. But the others. I should go inside. They're waiting . . ." Then, backing sheepishly away, he dragged the dolly into the hall.

Sonny, who was standing at the door of the dressing room, waved him in, but not before he took a good look at Cyrus's equipment. "Your gear's not half bad," he muttered. "Let's hope you know how to use it."

As Cyrus set up his amplifier and effects, he realized he'd have to keep his volume down. The keyboard was plugged into a tiny practice amp. The drummer had a snare drum wedged between his knees.

Sonny made the introductions. He pointed to the guy who'd been tossing the football outside and said, "That's Tony Two Poops. He sings some, plays percussion some. He thinks he knows how to play harmonica but he doesn't. And whatever you do, don't play cards with him. He'll skin you alive. Beside him there is D.C."

"Europa," the woman corrected, her voice deep and smoky and heavily accented. "Europa Del Conte. But you can call me Eura."

It was the woman he'd seen earlier with the dog. Up close, he noticed she had a tattoo along one side of her neck, showing just above the collar of her sweater. It was a vine with bright red berries and tiny purple flowers with yellow centres.

"Like I said," Sonny continued brusquely, "that's D.C. Mostly she sucks cock—"

"Sonny!"

"—but she's been known to sing a tune or two. Doesn't have much talent either way, though."

Eura reached into the nearby ice bucket and threw a can of beer at Sonny's head, not at all playfully. He caught it in mid-air, popped the top and tossed back a mouthful. He flashed her a toothy grin.

"Our drummer," he continued, "is Chuck Ray. I'm on keyboards. And you, it seems, are our guitar player." He mouthed the last words with a sour look on his face. Then he put the beer aside and said, "Let's see what kind of trouble we're in."

Chuck winked at Cyrus. "Don't let Sonny rattle your cage. He's only a prick till you get to know him. After that he's just an asshole like the rest of us." Then he launched into a half-time shuffle.

Sonny moved behind a Fender Rhodes electric piano, setting up a loping bass line and framing the occasional chord of a simple blues jam. All the while he kept his eyes on Cyrus, who let a whole twelve bars go by as he fiddled with his knobs and adjusted the strap on his shoulder. He still wasn't familiar with the new guitar, but he was aching to blast away, to feel the power and exaltation.

He cut loose when the band moved into the second verse, a flurry of notes building quickly to a blizzard, his hand racing about the fingerboard and fitting most of his favourite licks into a twelve-bar section. He wanted to show that, even minus a finger, he could blaze away with the best of them. When he finished, Sonny took a turn.

If Cyrus's solo was manic and unmannered, Sonny's was a lazy Southern drawl full of wit and wisdom. There were more spaces than notes, and each phrase had a face and a voice of its own, each voice telling a story, each story leading to the next, a graceful tale of life and humanity.

When the song stumbled to an end, everyone nodded approvingly— everyone but Sonny. He winced as if he was in pain and said, "Listen kid, we don't get paid by the note, you know." Then he left the room and returned a minute later with a rickety music stand and a leather satchel. He pulled out a handful of sheet music and placed it on the stand in front of Cyrus.

"Ah," Cyrus said, "that could be a problem."

"It'll do for now. We'll get you a better stand for the show."

"No," Cyrus explained, "I mean the music. I guess I wasn't very clear with Mr. Conger."

"I don't follow you, kid."

Everyone heard the wariness in Sonny's voice. No one moved. No one breathed. Cyrus touched the stand and said, "I don't read music."

"Tell me you're joking."

"I'm afraid not."

"But chord charts, right? You can read those at least."

Cyrus dragged a hand through his hair and said, "Look, I usually pick things up real fast. I'm sure it won't be a problem."

"Problem?" Sonny suddenly towered over him. "You don't know the first fucking thing about problems, pal. Don't talk to me about problems." He began to pace the room. "So let me get this straight. You don't read. And it's clear you don't know how to play your instrument. You're sure as hell not good-looking. So what's your excuse for living?"

"Sonny," Eura said, "this is just a boy."

"He's a dull fuck who's jerking me around here. Jesus." For emphasis, he kicked out his cowboy boot and sent the music stand cartwheeling across the floor, sheet music flying every which way. Then he turned on Cyrus and aimed his finger like a gun. "Jim likes to have a lot of bodies onstage, so you're gonna stand up there with us even if your amp's turned off. The three of us can cover the rhythm and the chords all right. See if you can stick in a few notes without screwing up the whole thing."

Clarence sat on a stump at the edge of the orchard and gazed down the long ridge where Cyrus had tobogganed every winter. He could see clear over to the next concession, and the next, all the way to the Owens' old place, those big black fields, the fluorescent green of the irrigation pond, the writhing forms of the willows.

Clarence couldn't stand to be around the house just now. It pained him to see Ruby suffering for the boy, pained him, too, that he could do nothing about it and was maybe even to blame. Below all that, haunting his every waking moment, was the question of whether they had caught all the cancer. He felt so tired, and he was afraid that they'd have to go back in and remove more and more of him until there was nothing left. He didn't feel like working and had never had much use for play, so he had wandered out in the April sunlight to think about happier times, which led him back to the day he first set eyes on Riley Owen.

Clarence was sixteen, had just gotten his driver's licence and was barrelling down the Second Concession in his father's Ford pickup when he saw a kid standing in the middle of the road and heaving stones, regular as clockwork, at a fence post fifty feet away. The kid looked to be about ten, and he wore blue overalls and nothing much else—no T-shirt underneath, no shoes on his feet, his blond hair standing straight up like a shock of wheat. A good-looking boy but poor as could be.

Clarence pulled up beside him and leaned out the window. "Hey there, sport," he said, "what's your name?"

"Dizzy," he replied, never breaking his rhythm, "Dizzy Dean."

"Hey that's funny. My name is Babe Ruth."

The kid kept tossing a stone every five seconds. If he threw twenty at the post, fifteen hit their target. Clarence said, "You're pretty good at that. Got any other tricks?"

He stopped throwing and edged over by the truck. "I'm saving up to buy me a ball and glove. Gonna be in the big leagues."

Clarence had half a mind to tell him he'd be better off buying some clothes. Instead he said, "While you're dreaming, why don't you dream me up a million bucks and a gal with big knockers."

The kid gave him a dark look and then grabbed another handful of stones from the side of the road. "That's our place over there," he said, whipping stone after stone into the middle of the black mucky field in front of them. "Jake Owen and son. My real name's Riley."

Clarence leaned farther out the window to get a better look. Settling back into the truck again, he said, "Don't know what place you're talking about, Riley. All I see's an empty field."

The boy scowled at Clarence, then started throwing at the fence post again. "Ain't built yet," he said. "Pa and me'll build it ourselves."

Something about Riley, the certainty, the bravado, made Clarence smile. He'd never had a brother or sister, and the sight of this kid made him ache for one. He wanted to tease him but hug him, too. He stuck his arm out the window and offered his hand. "Pleased to meet you, Riley Owen. Name's Clarence Mitchell. If you ever need anything, that's our place up thataways—Orchard Knoll." Then he stepped on the gas and left Riley standing in a cloud of dust.

The summer of 1931, the Owens managed to build a small barn and a chicken coop. Jake was practical that way, or impractical, depending on your point of view. The house would come eventually, and until it did, they would make do. The important thing was to be productive, he felt. Food was scarce;

most things were. That winter they would live in the coop.

Riley had a hard time those first months of school, getting into a dust-up almost daily, often with older boys who teased him about his threadbare clothing. But with the first snowfall and first snowball fight, things began to change. The boys of Lakeview School soon realized that no one could match Riley's arm and accuracy. By the second week of winter, the taunting had stopped. By the new year, the smarter boys were enlisting Riley's services. Come summer and the baseball season, he had earned their grudging respect.

Some friendships flow in a single direction, with one person taking on most of the maintenance. That's how it was with Riley and Clarence, only not the way you might expect. Riley was younger, poorer, more needful in every way. It would be natural for him to seek out Clarence who had so much to share. But Riley was naturally a loner, and maybe he just couldn't imagine that he had anything to offer in return. Whatever the reason, it was always Clarence who suggested they get together. Not that they were best friends or anything. There were six years between them; they went to different schools. But Clarence, a straight-A student, helped Riley with his homework. He offered him rides around town. And it was Clarence who gave him his first ball glove.

"Here," he said one day, handing the fielder's mitt out the window of the truck. "Never had much use for this. You might as well have it."

Riley turned it over, studying the intricate lacing of the web and fingers. He held it to his face and breathed in the aroma of good leather. Then he handed it back. "Don't think I better."

"Why's that?"

"Ain't mine, is it?"

Clarence studied the glove a moment, then held it out the window again. "Then maybe you could do me a favour, Riley, and break it in for me. The leather's awful stiff."

Riley jammed his hands into the pockets of his overalls. "Could do," he said, his eyes darting from Clarence to the glove and back again. Finally he reached out and took the mitt. He put it on his left hand and pounded the leather with his right. "When you need it back?"

Clarence looked into the distance like he was doing some heavy figuring.

"Hard to say, Riley. Maybe next week, the week after. See if you can whip it into shape, will you?"

It became one of the signatures of their friendship. Once a month to start with, less often as the years went by, but continuing even after they were grown men with their own farms, Riley would ask, "You want that glove back yet?" And Clarence would shake his head and say, "No, not yet. You keep it awhile longer. Needs a bit more seasoning."

And of all the pictures that Clarence had seen in his fifty-six years—the babies, the weddings, the birthday parties and graduations—none had brought him more joy than the photograph Riley sent him the spring of 1940. Clarence had just graduated from the agricultural college in Guelph, and Riley was a tall muscular farm boy who could throw a baseball through the eye of a needle and near a hundred miles an hour. In the picture, he was kneeling on the grass of Briggs Stadium in Detroit, home of his favourite team, the Tigers. On his right was Hank Greenberg, and on his left, Charlie Gehringer. Riley was grinning from ear to ear, having just signed a minor league contract. Soon he would be heading south to play with the Toledo Mud Hens, but for that golden moment in the photo, he was a Tiger. And there in front of him on the grass was the glove.

Clarence got to his feet and began to walk through the orchard toward the house. He'd heard it said more than once that Riley Owen had been born with a pure talent for baseball. But Clarence had his doubts about that. To his mind, talent was like faith—it only showed itself after a lot of practice. Hard work uncovered the nugget of one's talent, and the same hard work expressed it.

Equally untrue, at least by Clarence's reckoning, was the idea that talent was always such a good thing. What if all your hard work uncovered the wrong kind of talent, the sort that could twist your life out of shape and make you unfit for the workaday world? What if, like Riley, you were born with a talent for play—not quite enough to make a go of it, but enough to ruin your taste for honest labour? What then? And how would Riley, in light of his own mistakes, have instructed his son about the future?

According to Isabel, and even a few people in town, Cyrus had some musical ability (though no one, to his knowledge, had ever suggested it was anything more than a passable talent). And while there was nothing inherently wrong with the boy's desire to be a musician, it made Clarence ache with sadness, the thought of all the disappointments he was sure to face. After all, if Riley hadn't made it with pure talent and a full set of tools, what chance did Cyrus have? That's why Clarence had been grooming the boy to work in the orchard.

Of course Clarence couldn't imagine how it felt to reach so far beyond one's grasp. Unlike Riley or Cyrus, he had been born into a life he loved, a job he relished, a world that pleased him daily. All his life he had known who he was and where he was going; and though his talents were much the same as his father's and grandfather's and were applied in the same daily routines of farm life, it was a great source of comfort, he felt, to have his talent and his life in agreement.

For Riley, every day had meant trouble of some sort. In time it had knocked the stuffing out of him and made him a sorry man. Clarence could only hope that Cyrus would be spared that grief.

RUBY LOOKED OUT THE WINDOW to the apple shed. Still no sign of Clarence. She wandered to the back door and looked down the driveway. Her car was just where she'd left it, beside the pickup. No traffic on the road at all. The school bus had rumbled past long ago.

She had work to do but couldn't face it, so she drifted through the house, touching this, straightening that. In the bathroom she took Cyrus's deodorant from the medicine cabinet and inhaled the brisk athletic scent. She smelled his shaving cream, which he used about once a week to scrape off the fuzz. She lifted his toothbrush from its holder and then put it back, a lump catching in her throat.

Upstairs, she worked her way down the hall, poking her head into each room. At the sight of her big queen-size bed she remembered Cyrus sleeping among the coats that one Christmas, could have been the last time they were all together, all the Owens, all the Mitchells. She remembered, too, how he used to come visiting with his mother, before he was old enough for school; and as Ruby and Catherine chatted over tea, he'd dress up in Clarence's jacket and dress shoes, looking so adorable she had wanted to squeeze the living daylights out of him.

His room was just the way he had left it. His guitar was in its case under the bed. His stereo was immaculate, his records neatly arranged. Ruby had always hoped he would do more with the room. Wouldn't another boy have put up baseball pennants or pin-ups or something? Wouldn't there be a street sign maybe, or a notice on the door warning everyone to keep out? With Cyrus it was like he was just visiting. Well-mannered, polite, but not really committed. No calendar on his desk, no doodles on his blotter, no clutter, no photos. There were a few books on a shelf above his bed, things Isabel had bought for him. There was a compass, too. A gyroscope. And a cardboard tube full of Pick-Up sticks.

Without thinking, she grabbed the tube and shook it like a rattle. Ruby had never been one for games, and most especially that one. For some reason, it had always made her feel sad. But Cyrus loved it, even as a teenager. You wouldn't think there would be much to get excited about.

She returned to the kitchen and made tea. When the phone rang, her heart skipped a beat. But it wasn't Cyrus, it was Janice Young.

"Hello, Mrs. Mitchell, any word?"

"Not much. He called to let us know he was safe. Campenola, I think he said. But that's all we know. No school today?"

"Well, yeah, but I was thinking I could come out there this afternoon. I don't want to bother you or anything. I just thought we could talk."

"About what, dear?"

"About Cy."

Ruby felt a secret thrill at the thought of the two of them playing hooky. "Why don't I come and get you?" she said. "We could go for a drive or a walk or a cup of tea. Whatever you like."

They met at the Three Links Hall a little before noon and drove to the town pier for a hot chocolate. For the first while, Janice looked out the side window, not interested in her drink. Finally she said, "I woke up this morning and realized my whole life had changed. I lost my best friend. The band is dead. I don't care about school or summer vacation or anything, not even my folks. How does that happen?"

Ruby squeezed her hand. "You'll be fine, dear."

"I know," she said. "But what I mean is, you think your life is pretty cool, everything pretty much the way you want it, and if somebody asked you to point to the coolest part, the part that makes all the other parts cool, you couldn't do it, could you? Because it's all just your life, one thing, like I see a pair of jeans here and not a million threads. You know?"

"I think I do."

"So how can it be that there *is* one thing, one thread, and you pull on it and the whole fabric comes apart? How could we not know our lives depend on something like that? Shouldn't they teach us that at school?"

"They teach us that at church, dear." Ruby reached out to run her hand across the girl's lovely red hair, wishing she could do more to help her through this pain. "Why don't you come with me this Sunday? You might enjoy it."

"Church? We've never been a religious family."

"That hardly matters, does it? Lots of people aren't. But that doesn't mean you can't still attend the service. And if you don't find religion, maybe you'll find something else."

"Like what?"

"Well, I'm not sure. I know sometimes I just like to get up on a Sunday morning, put on a nice outfit and fix my hair. I'll talk Clarence into coming along but usually he can't be bothered. And it feels so good to be there at the church, whether I listen to the sermon or not, as if I was doing the best possible thing I could ever do."

Ruby felt foolish, talking to a young girl this way. After a long moment, she said, "You're about as thirsty as I am. Shall we walk along the pier?"

They strolled arm-in-arm, the air tangy with fish and fuel and creosote. As they walked, Janice told Ruby everything she knew about Cyrus's plan, how he had taken the cheque and bought the new guitar, how he had intended to put up a few signs in the music stores announcing his availability. But he had said nothing about leaving Wilbury so soon. She had thought he would wait until summer.

"Yes," Ruby said, "but that was before we had our argument. Who knows what we've driven him to? Campenola is hundreds of miles away. Hounslow would seem like just around the corner."

Janice turned to face Ruby. "I've known Cy a long time," she said, "and if you ask me, there's no driving him to anything unless he's already made up his mind. He can be awful stubborn."

"Cyrus? He was always such a sweetheart."

Janice laughed at that. "You've never been in a band with him. When it's something he really cares about, he's like a bulldog."

This was a side of the boy Ruby had never seen. "But he was always so sweet and considerate. He talked to me. We were close."

The obvious response, though unspoken, hung between them nonetheless. What mattered to him was music, and he had kept Ruby in the dark about that. How close could they have been?

WHEN CLARENCE CAME IN FROM THE ORCHARD, Ruby's car was gone. He fixed himself a sandwich and called Frank Pentangeles and asked him if he could help out awhile. Frank, who was older than Clarence and had worked at Orchard Knoll for more than forty years, was supposed to be retired. But he jumped at the opportunity, and they made plans to start next day setting up the sprayers. Then Clarence walked out to the shed and turned on the radio. He had it tuned to the mellow sounds of WJR in Detroit, but he wasn't really listening. He was remembering when he was ten years old, the day he and Frank first learned how to prune.

Frank's dad, Domenic, who had worked at Orchard Knoll for as long as he'd been in Canada, showed them the proper technique. He led them through the orchard until he found a suitably overgrown tree, then quietly began to prune. He didn't go at it like a barber, standing on the outside and trimming here and there; he got right in to the trunk, right into the thick of things, and cut his way out. When he was finished, he turned to them and said, "This is good. Like so." He moved his hand through the gaps he had created with his saw and shears. "So a bird can fly."

The dressing room of the Campenola Armoury had seen more prize fighters than musicians. The apple-green walls were speckled with bloodstains; the air was rich with mildew and sweat and the overpowering sweetness of urinal pucks. But Cyrus noticed none of that. He was staring at his hands. His first show with the Jimmy Waters Revival had been a nightmare, and if not for the people milling about, doing their best to ignore him, he probably would have cried.

Right from the opening vamp he'd been off balance, both literally and figuratively. The stage, displaying the kind of bounce you might expect of a boxing canvas, set up a complicated wave form that threatened to knock over the amplifiers the moment anyone so much as tapped his foot. Cyrus didn't get his sea legs until a good ten minutes into the performance; and musically, he never found his balance. Just when he started to think that everything might be fine, the song would mysteriously shift key and tempo. Or Jimmy would start one of his vocal riffs—not singing really, hard to know what to call it—lumbering here and there along the front of the stage and shouting to the audience, waving his arms while the lights flashed and the music crashed. And all the while the audience sat as stiff as could be, like folks who had walked into the wrong movie or wrong funeral even and couldn't quite work up the gumption to walk out again. Then right near the end of the show, Jim did this thing, this truly weird thing: he climbed down from the stage and wandered into the crowd, over to a grey-haired lady and, what, it was almost like he was massaging her scalp, his fingers flying a mile a minute, his eyes rolled back, as the lady swatted his arms and chest, and howled disapproval.

With all that going on, Cyrus messed up so often that, by the end of the show, Eura was the only one who would look at him—and her sympathetic smile was worse than nothing at all. He had half a mind to grab his gear and go home and save himself further humiliation. But before he could do that, Ronnie walked into the dressing room and sat beside him.

"I have heard music in my day," he said, "but I have to tell you, that was a truly remarkable spectacle. Such feeling. Such abandon. The audience was not all I had hoped it would be, I confess. This is our first time in Campenola, and I fear our show is a bit of an acquired taste. But I can tell you without reservation that I was transported, young man. And you?"

"It couldn't have been worse."

"Well, I wouldn't worry about the finer points. Opening-night jitters and all. These things happen to a novice. But the overall direction, the energy, the vision—Jim was very impressed."

Cyrus snorted in disbelief.

"Truly. He told me himself. 'That boy is a keeper.' So, there you have it. Basically, it's the same thing tomorrow, back here at the Armoury. Sound check at four-thirty." He clapped Cyrus on the shoulder. "You will do better, my musical friend. I have no doubt about that. Besides, we can't break in a new guitar player every night, can we? Oh, and by the way—" he handed Cyrus a hotel key "—you will bunk with Sonny for the time being." At Cyrus's look of despair, Ronnie laughed and said, "Believe me, he is a pussycat when you get to know him."

Ronnie walked off then to speak to one of the caretakers of the hall and make sure everything was set for the show the next day. Cyrus slumped miserably against the wall. He was convinced his golden future had become a bad dream. When he looked up again, he and Eura were alone in the dressing room, and he took the opportunity to study her more closely.

That afternoon beside the bus, he had thought she was attractive; but that had been more inclination than perception—he'd always been drawn to the company of women. Now he realized she wasn't very pretty at all. For one thing, her tattoo was a little creepy. And her face made him think of those police sketches you see on TV, a composite of normal-looking features that would require imagination to make sense of. Judging from the way she carried herself—erect, graceful—he figured she was beyond the age when bad posture might be considered cool. He guessed thirty, maybe even thirty-five. It was her eyes that gave her away, their message dark and complicated, even when she smiled.

Without looking at him, she said, "You need a ride."

Those four words cast a spell in the room. She was old enough to be his mother, she wasn't pretty in any conventional sense, and yet his whole body was on alert. Parts that were normally dry had suddenly grown damp. Parts that were normally moist were dry as dust.

When he stammered something unintelligible, she got to her feet in a nearly liquid motion and moved toward him, tilting her head from side to side like she was trying to understand a painting. She said, "Everyone now is back at the hotel. The bus, the truck, the trailer . . . they are in such a hurry always. But Ronnie has more work to do here yet, so," she stood before him now, one hand resting on his shoulder, "he has asked me to take you in his car back to the hotel. Or to some place you like." Before he could say a word, she grabbed his guitar case and headed for the door. "Come along, Mr. Guitar Player," she said, "this train is leaving."

Five minutes later he was in the Cadillac again. But now, in the darkness outside the hotel, breathing in Eura's perfume, it felt a whole lot different. The engine was ticking, and she turned in the seat and said, "You must not let Sonny bother you. He is this way with all of us sometimes. You will get used to it. He is a good guy. You will see."

Cyrus shrugged, his gaze fixed on her mouth. He found if he focused on a single aspect—her lips or her eyes or her nose—it was better than trying to take in her entire face at one time. Her mouth, looked at in this way, to the exclusion of every other part of her face, was quite pleasant. So he watched her lips and her tongue and the shimmer of slightly crooked teeth in the darkness. And if her youth was a memory, her charms too complicated to absorb in a single viewing, wasn't that attractive in its own way?

He was tempted to kiss her, but before he could do anything about it, she nudged his shoulder. "You must go now," she said. "It is late for talking. Ronnie will finish at the hall soon and need his car."

He dragged his Les Paul from the back seat and watched her drive away, the cooler air feeling to him like relief. Then he turned and noticed the Airstream parked at the end of the lot. Jim, dressed now in blue flannel pyjamas and pissing against one of the tires, looked over his shoulder and said, "Ah, Cyrus, one moment." He wiped his hands on the front of his pyjama top and opened the door of the trailer. "Allow me to extend a bit of old-fashioned hospitality."

The floor was littered with books and newspapers and magazines, fast-food cartons grown rank with age, and here and there an empty bottle or a dog bone. Every step was a misstep, made all the more likely by the yappy Pekingese lunging at Cyrus's legs.

Jim followed him in and with one hand scooped up the dog and tossed it like a stuffed animal toward the rear of the trailer. Then he took two dirty glasses from the kitchen counter, rinsed them briefly under the tap and dried them with the very same pyjama top. He stopped abruptly when he caught the look in Cyrus's eye and swept his arm in an arc. "You are wonderin' how I can live like this, I imagine."

When Cyrus began to protest, Jim silenced him with a raised finger. "Fact is I have always preferred the edge of things: the lakefront, the forest clearin', this journey of ours from town to town. It's where good things happen, young fella. Life, I mean, yours and mine, it's where it happens, on the border between two worlds. Before and after, cradle and grave. We trace a musical line between whole-note rests."

Jimmy smiled then, tickled by his own words, and waved Cyrus onto the bench in the dining nook. After a cursory inspection of the glasses, he slapped them on the table and grabbed a bottle of Jim Beam from the cupboard. He opened the freezer but found no ice cubes. From the refrigerator he retrieved a box of cold french fries, covered with dried, sticky-looking ketchup, and placed it on the table. With a critical sniff, he said, "Not the feast I had hoped it'd be."

They sat then, neither of them touching their bourbon, until Cyrus said, "I'm sorry about tonight. I really messed up."

"Did you? I can't say I noticed. I thought we put on a fine show. And that woman out front, my God, her story was like electricity runnin' up my arms. I'm sure I won't sleep tonight. I felt such grief there, such anger. It brings tears to my eyes even now."

Cyrus stared at his guitar case, which he had set on the floor beside him. He was as confused by this conversation as he'd been by the music. Searching for a more suitable topic, he said, "Mr. Conger told me you are the absolute best musician he's ever heard."

"Mmm-hmm, well, Ronnie may be our guidin' light, but he is, you'll find, wrong about many things. And this is one of them. I was never very good. Well, I was *sometimes* very good and once absolutely perfect. But believe me, I could never hold a candle to our Sonny Redmond."

"I'd still like to hear you play," Cyrus said. "I'm sure I'd learn a lot."

"Ah, but you never will," Jim replied. He waited a beat before adding, "I've taken a vow of musical silence."

"Why?"

Jim held his palms up, a confession of his own helplessness. "Who knows why we do anythin'? Love maybe. Or faith."

"But what have you got against playing?"

"Oh, Lord, nothin' at all. I love to hear everyone play, especially Sonny. His music reaches out to me in ways I don't understand. And I look forward to the music that will one day come from your corner, boy. I predict great things for you."

Cyrus shook his head. "I could never stop playing. Music is everything to me."

"Believe me, it was not as easy as I make it sound. I suffered some until Ronnie came along. He helped me understand what I had to do."

"The show, you mean."

"The *words,* Cyrus, the meanin', this feelin' that I am gettin' somewhere, that we are all of us *on* to somethin', our very own Genesis and Leviticus and Deuteronomy . . ."

Those words hung in the air for a long while, like some heavenly static charge that shuts down communication links and short-circuits transformers and relay stations. Jim reached down to the clutter on the floor and picked up a dog-eared paperback, *It Came Out of the Void*. He studied the garish cover a moment, then waved the novel in the air like it was an important piece of evidence in a trial.

"The world is filled with words, Cyrus. Some nights, walking Fifi, I come back with plastic bags filled with books and papers and magazines that people have thrown out." He dragged a hand through his inky mane and said, "You might not think it to look at me but when I was a boy I was sickly. I searched for truth between the covers of books. Worlds opened up to me and I followed. Now the words themselves have opened up to me. After all this time, they are callin' me back. After all this time I have begun to hear the connections like a melody. But I still have so much work to do. . . ."

They fell into another, heavier silence, Jim drifting into deep thought and Cyrus staring into his glass. He understood the meaning of every single word Jim had spoken; no dictionary was required. What he didn't understand was the way those words had been put together, with an entirely different grammar, it seemed. And sitting in that dog-smelly trailer, twirling around a smudged glass of whiskey, Cyrus realized that Jimmy Waters would be a source of more questions than answers. As soon as he could excuse himself, he gulped down his bourbon, grabbed his guitar and headed for the room he would share with Sonny.

To his relief, there was no sign of his new roommate other than the untidy sprawl of his belongings, so he showered quickly and jumped into bed. But try as he might, he could not sleep, and for the first time since he'd left home, he wished he could sit with Janice and ask her advice.

She was so smart. The first time they went out for coffee she talked for an hour about this school in England called Summerhill. He didn't really get it, but he liked the idea that she was interested in that kind of weird shit. When he listened to her talk about politics and architecture and art, he figured it was like listening to jazz, something he didn't understand and didn't want to understand just yet, but knew one day he would and would look back and say, "Janice was all over that, way back when." No question, she would know what to make of this situation now. She would have it sussed. Tomorrow he would call her. Or the next day. She would freak when he told her about the Jimmy Waters Revival.

He was still awake at four in the morning when he heard the door to the room open, heard the drunken stumbling, the grunts, the curses. The light came on then, and the racket died down. After a minute or so of silence, Cyrus opened one eye. Sonny was staring right at him.

"If it isn't Django fucking Reinhardt. How ya doin'?"

Cyrus rolled onto his back and shielded his eyes. "Look, I'm real sorry about tonight . . ."

Sonny fell heavily onto his own bed and kicked off his boots. "Water under the bridge, kid. Life's too short to worry about things that can't be changed. Anyway, believe it or not, you're a step up from Cal. He couldn't play, either, but at least you have the sense to feel bad about it. He thought he was a genius."

Cyrus flinched at those comments. He wanted to shout that he did know how to play. Instead he bit his tongue and let Sonny continue.

"Truth is," he said, "I'm the one should apologize, leaving you at the gig by yourself. Wasn't the cool thing to do. Forgot about D.C. You'll want to keep your distance from that one."

"Oh," Cyrus stammered, "no problem, she just drove me back to the hotel."

"Yeah, well, maybe." He pulled the covers over him, not bothering to take off his clothes. "My last piece of advice is this. If you ever hope to come out of this in one piece, drop by Adrian and Kerry's after a gig. There's nothing like a good cup of tea to straighten you around."

NINE

Demeter Real Estate had three agents—Sheldon Demeter, Lawrence Bell and Isabel Muehlenburg—with three desks aligned by seniority. That meant Shel's desk was near the front door. The middle of the room was Larry's domain, smelling always of breath mints and Aqua Velva. Izzy's desk was at the back by the filing cabinets, an area seldom graced by walk-in clients. Any business that came her way had to be self-generated. As Shel put it, "Startin' out, you gotta be hungry."

Her routine every morning was to drive in about nine, pick up the new listings, have a coffee and chit-chat with Shel, and then start going door-to-door with her complimentary calendar, maybe hit an open house or two if she could swing it. If she came back by one, the guys would be out at lunch and she could do some cold calling for an hour. But she was late this morning and didn't make it downtown until nearly eleven. By that time it was drizzling rain, and both Shel and Larry were out of the office.

It felt good to sit a few minutes and let the noise settle out of her head. In front of her was a picture of a little bungalow on Orange Street that Larry had listed the week before: two bedrooms, a beautiful kitchen, hardwood floors and a yard full of roses. It reminded her of a gingerbread house, and she had set the picture aside to show Ruby. With Clarence's recent health problems, Isabel thought it was time those two considered retirement and moving off the farm. Ruby in particular had to start thinking of how she would manage on her own. With this little bungalow, a simple twist of a key and she could get the hell out of here and spend her winters in Florida.

Shel came in before Isabel could get down to work. He hung his trench coat in the front closet and walked over to her desk. "Deadly dull these days," he said.

She watched him carefully, uncertain whether he was complaining about her production or his own. "Well," she said, "it seems pretty much the same everywhere. Not just us."

"No," he agreed, "not much you can do about a market like this one but wait it out and try to stay sane. It's good, something like this. Works the riff raff out of the system." He looked out the front window and then back at her. "How about we go up to Hounslow? We could have lunch at the racetrack. My treat."

Isabel felt the blood rise to her cheeks and she looked away. She had heard both Shel and Larry talking in whispers about the "girls" they escorted to the racetrack—some of them married women from around town—and the afternoons of drinking and laughter, often followed by a few frantic hours at the Airport Inn. She felt stupid and ashamed that she hadn't seen this coming.

When she was under control again, she said, "I don't think I could, Shel. I'm just a marsh girl. We kind of take our marriages seriously."

He studied her as she spoke. Then he leaned forward, his smoky breath making her blink. "You better make sure everyone's playing by the same rule book," he said.

"What are you talking about?" Her voice had an edge to it, causing him to step back and jam his hands into his suit pockets, moving his shoulders in a kind of defensive swagger.

"I'm talking about Gerry. I'm assuming you know it's not the draft beer that has him living at the Gaslight Room these days."

And of course she knew, or she would have if she had just stopped to think about it a moment. The faint whiff of perfume lately, his switching to the Gaslight Room when all his life his hangout had been the Wilbury Hotel. The barmaid there, Ginny Maxwell, the chippy bit of trash who'd had her eyes on Gerry going all the way back to high school. That funny voice of his when he answered the phone sometimes. The matchbook from the Riverside Motel in LaSalle that she'd found in his jacket about a year ago. Of course she knew. You'd have to be a fool not to.

Swallowing the lump in her throat, she rose unsteadily to her feet and said, "Your invitation . . . I guess I should be flattered." She traced a pattern on the surface of her desk with a red fingernail, then grabbed her purse and coat and walked out the door.

She sat outside in her Buick for several minutes, surprised by her self-control. No tears, no tantrums. It was a powerful feeling, maybe even liberating. What struck her most was how light she felt, how clear. She saw time stretch ahead in precise, practical steps: the selling of the farm, the splitting of assets. She imagined herself standing in a cozy house of her own, pulling aside the drapes to let in the light and a view of roses.

When she turned on the windshield wipers she noticed that girl, Janice, looking all limp and forlorn, and walking along the other side of the street under a paisley umbrella. Isabel rolled down the window and asked her if she wanted a ride somewhere.

Janice stood a moment thinking, then crossed over. "I was just wandering around," she said. "Wasn't in the mood for lunch today."

Isabel took a deep breath and let it out noisily. "We heard from Cyrus. He's in Campenola of all places."

"Mrs. Mitchell told me. How'd he sound?"

Isabel stared into the distance and then back at this young girl. "You know what? He sounded happy. Excited. And that's great. Good for him. Stay too long in this town and you can rot."

Janice nodded, but not with any enthusiasm. She'd been hoping Cy was miserable and would soon be home.

"I'll tell you what," Izzy said, touching the girl's hand reassuringly, "as soon as we get a phone number or something, I'll give it to you. Maybe you can find out what's really going on."

Janice smiled thinly and watched the Buick disappear down the street. She'd always been put off by the cloud of perfume, the smear of makeup and the nearly audible static of Izzy's synthetic suits. From a distance she appeared to be a jittery, brittle and profoundly unhappy woman, the archetype of all that Janice hoped to avoid in life. But Cyrus spoke fondly of his sister. He said she was the only softness that had survived a hard and stupid family. And maybe she was. Janice was surprised to hear her talking of Cy's departure as something positive. It made Janice think that her own re-action was selfish, that maybe Cy was better off leaving town. He'd cer-tainly talked enough about it. For as long as she'd known him he'd been dreaming about the world outside of Wilbury. Everyone did that, of course, grouse about their rotten luck to be stuck in this hick town so far away from all that was cool. But with Cyrus it was different. It wasn't that he hated Wilbury, it was that he wanted more, of everything. She liked that about him. He wasn't envious or bitter. He was hungry, excited, and it showed in everything he did, the manic exhilaration of his playing, the lip-smacking gusto at the table, the joyous abandon in her bed.

She started walking again, past the Carnegie Library, past the Royal Bank and the four corners. She had planned to hang around the rehearsal space for the rest of the day, but decided that that would just make her feel miserable. So on the spur of the moment, she ducked into the Abbey, the only store in town that had cool clothing. Tricked out with wooden pews and bevelled mirrors with oak frames, the Abbey was an oasis of modern fashion in the land that time forgot.

Gwen Morrow, who owned the store with her husband, helped Janice pick out a dark paisley skirt, and a white cotton blouse from the Andes. "Very nice," she said when Janice tried them on. "Is this for graduation?"

Janice turned in a circle so the skirt unfurled like a matador's cape. And she smiled, only now thinking it through. "No," she said, "not for graduation. For church, I guess."

GERRY ATE HIS LUNCH at the main counter of the Hilltop, the better to make wisecracks to Barb Dutton, who'd been working there for as long as he could remember. It had started to rain since he'd come in, thick grey clouds blowing in from the lake, and Gerry had just tucked into a second slice of blueberry pie when Vince Ragulli slapped him on the back and straddled the stool beside him, a smart-ass sparkle in his eye.

"Drove by your place just now, Muehlenburg. Looks like you might want to get over there. The wife's making a statement."

Gerry nodded and, without a word, finished his pie and coffee in no particular hurry. When he got back to the farm, he parked out at the gate rather than drive up to the house. He sat there with the windows closed, the wipers working, and sucked at his teeth.

Izzy had dumped his clothes on the driveway. His luggage, too. His bowling ball, still in its leather case, was under the tree, beside his fishing rod and tackle box. His sporting magazines—*Field & Stream, Rod and Gun*—sat in neat piles by the porch, the top pages flapping in the wind.

As he sat watching, she drifted serenely out of the house, his golf bag over one shoulder. There, in the middle of the lawn, in the pouring rain, she took out his putter and sent it flying. She did the same with his irons, his woods, looking so cool and methodical it was like she had been practising her entire life. One by one she lobbed his new golf balls to every point of the compass. Then she went inside.

Gerry didn't need to see any more. He understood well enough. He turned the truck around and drove back to town. He'd have to see Peppy Bascombe at the Wilbury Hotel about getting a special rate on a room. And all the way into town, he kept thinking he could kiss those new pig barns goodbye.

People who make a living on the road—baseball players, musicians, travelling salesmen—all struggle with the same illusion: the more distance you cover, the easier it is to believe you're getting somewhere. In reality, nothing could be further from the truth, and Cyrus was beginning to understand that.

Over the span of two weeks they had travelled to ten different towns, each one as faceless and forgettable as the next; they had stayed in ten different hotels, equally without character or charm, and had played to nearly indistinguishable audiences that, without exception, could not have cared less about the Jimmy Waters Revival. That Ronnie was able to fill halls in town after town and charge admission was a great mystery to Cyrus. As near as he could tell, there hadn't been a single person at any of the shows who had appreciated what Jim was doing. Mostly there was bafflement.

Cyrus had problems of his own that darkened each day, chief among them his loneliness. He had hoped to get better acquainted with Eura. He had imagined the two of them chatting pleasantly through all the dull hours on the bus. Unfortunately, she travelled with Jim in the Airstream. And Adrian and Kerry, the most approachable members of the crew, drove the Fairlane and the truck. Ronnie pretty much lived out of his Cadillac, either staying behind to work the phone or going ahead to firm up arrangements. So, by default, Cyrus spent the bulk of his time with the other members of the band, who stumbled onto the bus each morning still half-drunk or stoned from the night before and who, without the slightest greeting or pleasantry, slumped in their seats and started snoring.

Mid-afternoon each day, he made his way over to sound check, after which there was a quick dinner and the gig. And although every night after the show someone asked him to come to Adrian's for a cup of tea, he never accepted the offer, because every night he seemed to play worse than the night before and, much like Clarence, he preferred to suffer in private.

He couldn't understand why, with all his practising and dedication, he had made so little progress. He kept bumping against the same brick wall, unable to find the doorway or even so much as a chink in the mortar that would let him into the heart of Jim's music. And with that in mind, he decided to walk over to the Meckling Auditorium a few hours early. He still wasn't comfortable with the new guitar and figured he needed some extra practice through his amplifier.

Meckling was a town of ten thousand people, a few bars, a few banks, one movie theatre and not much else worth noticing, the sort of place, like Wilbury, where you were viewed as suspicious if you didn't own a car and a house. Taking taxis and renting apartments marked you out as a loser. And walking, Cyrus's preferred mode of transport, was viewed by most as a sign of mental instability. The only folks you ever saw wandering about Wilbury usually had a screw loose, like Po Mosely.

The auditorium stood north of town, beside the Kinsmen Pool, and when Cyrus walked around back he was surprised to find Sonny behind the wheel of the bus, absently picking his teeth with a matchbook cover. Sonny swung open the door and said, "If it ain't the Gee-tar Man."

Cyrus stepped onto the bus. He was already sick to death of the thing. The vinyl seats were torn and stained. A couple of the windows had cracks. A chemical toilet at the back filled the bus with the sweet taint of morgues and undertakers. He couldn't imagine why anyone would want to sit there if they didn't have to.

He balanced the guitar case in front of him and said, "I thought I'd play through my amp a bit. While I'm at it, maybe I could grab those charts and get a little more familiar with the tunes. I'm missing a lot."

Sonny raised an eyebrow. "You don't read, remember?"

"I can read. A little. Just not fast enough to play."

Sonny thought a moment and pulled a folder of sheet music from a brief-case on the seat behind him. "Just so's you know," he said, "these will only get you so far. We maybe start out the way it says, but we don't often end up where we're supposed to. They're kind of like a compass. You ever use a compass? The place you want to go may be due north, but you can't get there from here. There's rivers and ridges and miles of bog, so you go east a ways, and west a ways, and if you're lucky you end up close to where you meant to be. You know what I mean?"

"Kind of, I guess."

"Well it's like this, baby doll: don't go thinkin' any of this here is gospel. Only scribbles on a page."

Then Sonny reached into his bag again and pulled out a reel-to-reel tape. "Tell Ade you want to listen to this," he said. "But it doesn't leave your sight, and you bring it back to me soon as you're finished."

Cyrus nodded his thanks and said, "Sound check isn't for a few hours. What are you doing here?"

Sonny propped his boots on the dashboard. "Gonna jam a bit, the others ever get back from the liquor store."

Cyrus found Adrian easily enough. He was making himself a cup of tea beside the stage. When Cyrus showed him the tape— "JJ2" was written on the cover—Adrian smiled knowingly and led him over to a beat-up Revox by the mixing console. He threaded the tape for him and pointed out a pair of headphones he could use. Then he winked and went back to his teapot.

To Cyrus's surprise, it appeared to be a tape of Jim talking, the back-ground music barely audible. He fiddled with the knobs, thinking one of the channels was turned down, but nothing seemed to help. Noticing Sonny at the edge of the stage, he put the machine on Pause and said, "What am I supposed to do with this? I don't get it."

Sonny shrugged. "What can I say? Either you do or you don't. Maybe you're better off working with the charts."

Cyrus ignored that and started the tape rolling again, Jimmy's voice warm and soothing:

> I'd like to tell you a story now if I may,
> about a time when I was not much older than five or six.
> We had a little house, down at the lake
> in Erie, Pennsylvania, a few years after my daddy lost
> his fishin' boat. And though this little house,
> the one we had in Erie, Pennsylvania, wasn't much
> by any standard—junky tarpaper shack,
> screen door bangin' somethin' awful in the wind—it was ours.
> And from our porch I could see the big old freighters,
> and the cranes and trucks and gulls—
> > everythin' a boy could want of life.

The voice paused, and Cyrus could hear the music much clearer. On the surface, it sounded like a slow, loping blues, but it wasn't. He tried counting it out and got lost. It sure wasn't any kind of metre he was aware of. Jimmy came back in a stronger voice.

> When I remember my poor old daddy, I see
> a dark and angry man all broken up inside by feelin's
> maybe he just couldn't understand.
> I remember him comin' home at night, I was maybe five or six,
> and he'd walk into that tiny house and he wouldn't
> say a single blessed word, not even howyadoin'.
> He'd be all covered in dirt from the docks where he worked—
> when he wasn't out of work. And because, you know, he was so dirty,
> and because he was too tired to hike upstairs,
> and because he was involved in labour he didn't like at all,
> havin', you know, run out of luck on every
> dream he'd ever put his mind to, he'd drag a chair
> into the parlour and sit in front of our radio,
> a big old wooden thing as tall as an icebox and looked to me

back then like the Ark of the Covenant, all shiny wood
and fancy knobs and full of light and sound.

                                      And my daddy would sit
alone there in the parlour of our house,
and listen to some preacher out of West Helena, Arkansas.
Mama would move behind him, touch his shoulder,
and smooth the hair on his neck. She'd bring him water or a plate of food,
and he would turn and bark like an angry dog
all busted up inside, all pained and hurt and only wantin'
to be left alone in the parlour of our house,
the radio up and the lights turned way down low. But sometimes, you know,
I'd sneak beside him quiet as a mouse
and listen with him to that crazy preacher, the bass of that cabinet
boomin' inside my head, and man oh man,
it felt so good to sit there in our house, my little head
a-restin' there against my daddy's leg,
and I would think: It's just me and my daddy, me and my daddy.

Another pause, longer this time, the music building intensity, slowly asserting itself. Like any good blues, it was hypnotic, working its way into a private space.

I remember one night special. I was five or six.
I was upstairs in my room and I heard my daddy
drag the chair, the radio start to rumble, and Mama's voice,
her sad old voice, singin' just like always,
but this time risin' like a scale and cryin', "Baby please!"
I was scared and hurried down the hall
and fell—thumpin' down those fifteen wooden steps and landin'
on my back, and poor old Mama singin':
"Oh, baby, baby please, babypleasedon'tgo!"

Suddenly there was muscle in the snare. The bass played a quirky riff that ran up to the seven and back down to the root. Sonny played chord spasms on the B-3, lots of Leslie. And Jimmy was in full voice.

> That's when I lifted my head and saw my daddy.
> He'd wrestled that big old radio off the floor and into his arms
> and was huggin' it to his chest and staggerin' around.
> I saw him push past Mama with his shoulder, huggin' the radio
> to his chest, at least a hundred pounds.
> He kicked open the door, and when my mama threw her arms
> around his neck, he stomped down on her foot,
> stomped so hard he broke it, and then set off into the night,
> with Mama rollin' on the floor and cryin',
> "Baby, please, baby please, Babypleasedon'tgo!"
> And I remember crawlin' to my feet
> and walkin' to the spot there where the radio had stood,
> and right there on the wall I found a sign,
> a shadow of dust and grease where Mama hadn't ever cleaned,
> the daily smudge of life in the shape of a radio
> that wasn't there.
>   And Mama put her arm around my shoulder,
> sayin', "Oh darlin', what will we do?"
> That's when I put my hand on the wall inside that cleaner space
> outlined with grease and dust, which seemed to me
> the shape of somethin' holy.
>   And I remember what I said.
> I said: "Momma, lookit there, a door."
> And here's the damnedest thing: It was, you know, it was a door.
> All along it was a goddamned door.

That was all there was to the tape, and Cyrus, blinking with bewilderment, looked over at Sonny who was sprawled onstage asleep. Not knowing what else to do, or what to think, he turned off the Revox and sat there feeling stupid.

A few minutes later the rest of the band wandered in, passing around a forty-ounce bottle of Johnnie Walker. Chuck took off his baseball cap and slapped Sonny with it. "Rise and shine, you old fart. Let's rock and roll."

While Sonny sat there rubbing his face back to life, Two Poops walked over to Cyrus. The minute he saw the tape, he gave a knowing smile. "I see Sonny's trying to convert you. I'd stick to the sheet music, I was you." Then he drifted back to the bottle, following it and the other musicians onto the stage.

Cyrus turned back to the charts again, wondering how long it would take him to make sense of all those chicken tracks. From behind the piano, Sonny said, "What the fuck you need, an invite? We're jamming here, hotshot. Maybe you could come and learn a few things, whataya say?"

When Cyrus joined them onstage, Sonny launched into a slinky little bass riff with his left hand, and Chuck immediately locked into the groove. Two Poops fiddled with his horn a bit, but seemed more interested in smoking a cigarette. After twelve bars, Sonny started in with his right hand. Nothing fancy. Simple logical statements. Each proposition flowing from another. Nothing tricky, really, no fire and lightning. But each step was a step higher, a shade deeper, leading to a place that felt just right.

When it was Cyrus's turn he tried his best to imitate Sonny's laid-back approach and even, you know, closed his eyes and tried to imagine he *was* Sonny, as if such a thing were possible, as if he, Cyrus, had any idea who Sonny was or what he was like, and so, of course, the solo, the solo that came out was, yeah, sure, it was pure Cyrus, manic and shapeless, and the more he played the worse it got until finally after several passes through the chord changes he stopped.

Sonny looked up from the keyboard and said, "Maybe we need to slice off another finger, whataya say?" That brought a chorus of disapproval from the other band members, which Cyrus found more embarrassing than the jibe. If Sonny felt chastened, he didn't show it.

TWO THINGS DOMINATED the backstage area: dinner and a dartboard. And over the past few weeks it was the only place where Cyrus had felt anything close to happiness.

The dartboard was built into a six-foot hard-shell case, the kind that all the other gear travelled in. After the crew had taken out the cords and adapters that were required for the PA, they stood the case on end and the dartboard was at the correct height. On the inside of the lid were chalk, slate, brush, spare darts and flights. All day there had been a game going on. When Adrian wasn't busy onstage, you could find him near the board, playing or keeping score or brewing pots of tea.

Dinner, on this night, came courtesy of the Meckling Baptist Women's League—roast turkey with stuffing and gravy, homemade cranberry sauce and mashed potatoes and Brussels sprouts. For dessert there was apple cobbler with cream. Aside from Jim, who was served in the Airstream, the musicians and crew ate together at the kind of wooden tables you find in most church basements. They were served by grey-haired women in print dresses and serious shoes, women who seemed an awful lot like Ruby and who did not take kindly to the teasing and profanity.

When Cyrus had finished his meal, he took his coffee over by the dartboard. Ronnie patted the seat beside him.

"My young friend," he said, "I hear through the grapevine that you have been hard at work all day. I cannot tell you how pleased I am that you have grasped the nettle, as it were."

Cyrus made no reply. His attention was focused on Eura as she wandered through the loading doors and into the night. The past few weeks she had kept her distance, offering him a smile every morning, a wave every night, and not much else.

"How long has Eura been with you?" he asked.

"D.C.? About a year I should think. Jim is extremely fond of her. Has she told you she was once a circus performer?"

"No," he said, both surprised and not surprised. "We haven't talked much."

"Well just imagine, she was part of this little troupe that visited the United States a few years back. The target for some knife thrower would be my guess."

Cyrus could no longer see Eura, but he continued to look in that direction. "Del Conte sounds Italian," he said. "Is that where she's from?"

"I am not entirely certain which country she calls home, but I do know that Del Conte is not her real name. I gave her that moniker myself. Sonny, of course, in all his redneck charm, thinks she is a Communist spy."

Cyrus got to his feet—the thought of Eura sitting alone out there was too much for him to ignore. "Need some fresh air," he said. Then he headed out back.

The sun was down, the night surprisingly warm and still. A light shone from Jim's trailer. Through the bedroom window, he could see Eura, or rather her shoulders and the back of her head, rocking with a steady rhythm. And he heard Jim's voice, soft and languorous: "Mmm, yes. That's the way. Don't stop, darlin'."

CYRUS MADE HEADWAY THAT NIGHT. At least *he* thought so. He managed to block out most of the distractions and, listening carefully to what everyone else was doing, let the music take him where it would. He gave no thought to expressing himself, or impressing others, but let the current lead him. Whenever he felt unsure of himself, he stopped playing.

Chuck flashed him a thumbs-up after the show, but Sonny gave no reaction at all, which struck Cyrus as unfair—he felt he deserved encouragement. So he stayed in the dressing room long after Jim and the rest of the band had gone back to the hotel. He put new strings on his guitar and polished it with lemon oil. He even helped the crew finish the load-out. As a result, he was still backstage when a thin man in a black suit led a group of grim-faced locals over to Ronnie, who was seated at a small table, writing in his daily planner.

"Mr. Conger," the man said, his hands clasped before him, "we have a bone to pick. There was not a single word about Jesus tonight."

"No," Ronnie said, nodding agreeably, "nothing *directly* about Jesus, you are correct. But I'd say in a roundabout fashion most definitely. So not Jesus, but Jesus-*ish*."

The man looked to his group of followers and then back to Ronnie. "Well, no sir, if you'll pardon my saying so, not exactly. Now I can't tell you right off what in the name of the Lord your man was gabbling about, but I know it had nothing to do with the revival of Christ everlasting. And you told us, sir, that it would be so. Think Billy Graham, you said. Think Rex Humbard. But this performance, if that's what you call it, this Jimmy Waters Revival, is nothing but a fraud."

Ronnie got slowly to his feet and extended his hands, palms up, as though he were holding the evidence there for all to see. "It is one of the trials of an artist, I fear. You present a vision and some will see it, others not. And as you know, even Jesus was not appreciated by all who saw him. The spirit moves in mysterious ways and does not move all equally. Tonight, personally, I felt very much in the presence of something holy. I am saddened to hear that you and your friends were unmoved."

Ronnie gave Cyrus a pointed look, and Cyrus grabbed his guitar case and moved toward the loading door. From there he could see Adrian, Kerry and Tom climbing into the cab of the truck. Then he turned and, in a singsong voice, said, "Mr. Conger, the crew is leaving."

Ronnie grabbed the man's hand, pumped it vigorously and followed Cyrus from the room. Undaunted, the irate locals tried to form a human blockade at the end of the parking lot, but the truck and the Cadillac wheeled past them with little trouble. Ronnie slowed just enough to stick his head out the car window and shout, "May the Lord be with you!"

At the hotel in Woodville, thirty miles west of Meckling, Cyrus once again ignored the invitation to join the others at Adrian and Kerry's. He was still disappointed. But the more he thought about his performance, the more positive he felt. He had been comfortable on stage. He had stayed in the groove. Best of all he hadn't let Jim's performance or Eura's presence distract him. Sonny should have said something.

After a long hot shower, his own soapy hands making him ache with loneliness, he dialled Janice's number. She answered on the first ring, which meant she was in her room.

"Hey there," he said, "all tucked into bed?" His voice had a jovial back-slapping tone, entirely at odds with the way he felt. It was the way his father sounded whenever they went anywhere as a family.

"Cyrus? What's going on? Your sister said you were in Campenola."

"I'm playing, Janice. I got this gig that is so weird I can't even begin to tell you. But it's cool, too, you know. I mean, I'm doing it, just like I said I would."

"Well," she said, half-heartedly, "I'm glad. Really, you deserve it. So, like, this is a permanent thing in Campenola?"

"What? No, I'm somewhere else now. Woodville. I'm on tour. A new place almost every day. It is such a trip."

"Well, you'll have to let us know if you're ever close to Wilbury . . ."

The sound of her voice was making his heart ache. He had expected her to be excited for him, but the conversation wasn't going the way he wanted. "So what about you?" he said. "What's new at school?"

She took a deep breath and said, "Sorry. I can't do this right now." Then she hung up.

He lay on his back and stared at the ceiling. It was bad enough he'd hurt everyone back home. Now he had lied to Janice, the one person on earth he'd always been straight with. Life on the road was not at all what he'd made it out to be. Sure, parts of the gig seemed professional, and the musicians were better than any he'd ever played with, but it was nothing like the life he'd imagined. Where were the easy riders, the barefoot nymphs? Instead he was playing to tubby middle-aged couples and their Bible-thumping teens, for blue-haired ladies with hairnets and shawls and ill-fitting dentures. Most curious of all was their reaction to the show, as if they, too, were wondering what in hell they were doing there. It seemed to Cyrus there wasn't a single person on or off the stage who had a clue what the Jimmy Waters Revival was working so hard to revive.

When Hank's batteries died, he was tormented once again by the din of broken souls, the skittering of rats, the starkness and the darkness and the absence of even simple freedoms. He tossed and turned on his bed. The air tasted of stone and metal and human sweat. In desperation, he stood at his cell door for hours and peered into the future. But try as he might, he found no goat or jeep or wide-brimmed hat. What he saw instead in that dark, empty, echoing space was the barely discernible outline of a man, the way you might see a face take form within a shifting cloud of smoke. There had been other men, other faces, but this time it was his father.

Hank closed his eyes, hoping to dispel the vision, but when he opened them again, the face was there watching him, a hovering presence. So he crept back to his bed and lay perfectly still, struggling to breathe as a scene took shape before him.

He was twelve years old. Ken and Gary and Teddy and Pete, they were all in on it, a club kind of, never anyone's idea but something that seemed to well up whenever they were together. They met at Pete's place after school, smoked a few cigarettes and headed downtown in a gang. At Woolworth's they wandered in one at a time and each swiped a toy derringer. ("Hawk" is the word they used—"let's hawk some guns"—like they were birds of prey.) No one wanted them as toys; no one played guns anymore. It was the stealing that was needed, the thrill. It was the knee-knocking amazement at their own nerve. They carried their little treasures back to Pete's garage and hid them in the pot-bellied stove. And the more guns they collected, the more compelled they were to steal again. It became a necessary challenge.

Then one Friday after supper, Teddy Birch got nailed coming out of the store. Ted was only eleven and a big crybaby, and he squealed on the whole gang and brought the cops right to Pete's garage and the stove and their cache of derringers. A few hours later Officer Danny Scanlon, a marsh boy himself, drove Hank out to the farm. Danny told his story in a few words, then drifted out to his cruiser and back to town.

Hank stood in the living room, afraid to move, until his father grabbed him by the arm and dragged him into the yard, out past the barn, through the hissing leaves of corn and into the chicken coop. There, in the darkness, with moonlight filtering through the cracks in the wood, a smell of feathers and chicken shit floating on the damp night air, he watched his father remove his belt and swing it above his head. The big square buckle glinted, then slashed across his mouth, and the last thing he remembered was the taste of blood and the faint tinkle of a tooth skittering across the wooden planks of the coop. "I'll teach you," his father had said, exactly the way he was saying it now, just outside the cell door, the voice, the face, everywhere in the darkness so Hank couldn't sleep at all.

Next morning after roll call he went out to the exercise yard to look for his man, Golden Reynolds, who was practising his footwork, his jabs and hooks, rocking his neck around like a heavyweight before the bell. Hank approached and immediately felt the breeze of a one-two combo bracketing his head, followed by the suitable soundtrack: "Fsshht, fsshht. You down. You done. You dinner."

"Hey Goldie, lookin' good."

"Fsshht-fsshht-fsshht." Three quick body blows, the dance, the swagger, the head feints. "Can I do for you, Hank my man?"

Hank moved in closer, palms held out chest-high, a target for the other man's fists. "Need batteries, Goldie. Those you sold me are dead already. Three weeks and they're fried."

Goldie backpedalled, throwing straight-arm jabs. "Fsshht. Fsshht. Them would be the breaks there, Hoho. Gots ta feed the beast. And jus' soz you unnerstan', new ones ain't gonna be so easy to arrange."

"Meaning?"

"They gonna cost you some. Maybe twenty."

"Out of your fucking mind. The radio cost me fifty . . ."

"Fsshht, fsshht. Gots ta' have batteries, man."

Hank backed Goldie up until he had him against the wall. They were nose to nose. Guards looked over in their direction, and Goldie stopped bobbing and weaving, his arms quivering at his side like they'd been dislocated. Hank leaned in so his lips were nearly touching the other man's ear. He said, "Don't be squeezing me. I need those batteries."

Goldie bobbed into the open, making with the footwork again, his arms still twitching. "No squeeze," he said. "No sleaze. Jus' the facts, Hoho. You want the freight, you pay the rate. Another guy got this kind of grief'd tell you fuck youself, but not Golden Reynolds. Goldie stick with his clientele, you dig? We working together here to make this a better world is how I see it. Now when you be wanting your Evereadys?"

Hank looked across the yard where everyone was doing his thing— shooting hoops, a bit of catch, some just gabbing to hear themselves talk. He said, "I just give you my last fifty. You know that."

And Goldie moved in close and said, "We got options, Hoho. Golden Reynolds got various payment plans."

In Fenton the band had the day off—no concert, no travel, not even a jam because the gear had gone on to Jamestown, the next gig on their sched- ule, about fifty miles down the road. Cyrus was in the breakfast room of the hotel, flipping through the latest *Rolling Stone* (the cover showed a picture of a nutball by the name of Sun Ra) when Eura sat beside him in the booth.

"This is my idea," she said. "We are tourists today. We will see the sights."

He looked out the window of the coffee shop. A light rain was falling from a bruised-looking sky. He turned back to her and said, "What kind of sights were you thinking of? The place looks pretty dead."

She took a sip of his coffee and shook her head with frustration. "Anywhere must be better than sitting around these rooms all day."

He realized then that she had tried to talk everyone else into this half- baked outing and they had all turned her down. Nodding toward the win- dow, he said, "You don't mind the rain?"

"Nnn," she said, luxuriously, "I love the rain. Do you love the rain?"

"It's all right. If you're dressed for it."

"But it is the opposite I was thinking." Her eyes sparkled with laughter. "It is all right if you are undressed. It is what rain is made for."

They rented a sedan at the front desk. Half an hour later they were sitting in the car with a map spread across their laps. Eura pointed and said, "There. Portland. Is that good? It is on the water, I think."

It was the only place within a hundred miles that Cyrus had been to, an annual pilgrimage with Clarence and Ruby. He said, "Portland is a city. Is that what you want?"

"What I want is to feel alive and not dead, not like I am a prisoner of the Jimmy Waters Revival. So a city would not be so bad, I think. We drive here on this little road and see farms maybe, yes? And pretty farmhouses, and stony fields with cows and sheep. This would not be bad also. And in the city—Portland, is it?—we can find maybe some place to eat that isn't this tasteless food, something with spice, okay? Some place with a tablecloth and candles and wine. We can do this, Cyrus, a simple day with a few pleasures. This is not asking too much." She folded the map decisively and handed it to him. "Portland is good?"

"Portland is fine," he said.

Only Portland wasn't fine, not really. Portland meant a world of bad memories. Clarence and Ruby had taken him there every year for as long as he could remember, and every visit was a misery. It was Hank's home and had been for nine years now.

As they sped out of Fenton, Eura sang snatches of songs he didn't recognize, oohing and aahing at otherwise unremarkable scenery while Cyrus tried to figure out how he would slip away from her long enough to visit his brother. Gradually her excitement broke through his dark thoughts and he started to enjoy the drive. He began to wonder if a visit with Hank would be so bad.

He turned in his seat to look at her. She wore black jeans and a yellow turtleneck sweater that covered up the tattoo, but the thought of it beneath the cotton, its tracery leading who knows where, made his skin tingle. Another thing he noticed, now that he knew her better, was that her face had begun to make more sense to him. It was a sequential thing. One time her mouth dominated her face, another time her skin. At the moment, with her initial euphoria beginning to fade, her sad eyes were front and centre. And it was her eyes that made him speak. It didn't matter that she was driving, he wanted her to look at him, to be happy again.

"Ronnie mentioned the other night that you were in the circus."

She thought a moment and said, "Ronnie talks too much."

"So he was wrong?"

"No," she responded quietly, "not wrong. I was in a circus, but it was not what you think. We had no lion tamer, no dancing bears. Our clowns were not so harmless, our music not something you march to. European circuses are very different from what you know. Sometimes darker, sometimes more gentle."

She smiled at him, or at her memories. "Our performers were very talented," she continued, eyes back on the road. "Jugglers, gymnasts who twist their bodies in the most terrible way it could make your head spin. Always, you know, we would try not to defy death but to trick it, to mesmerize it. So it is very different from the circus that you think of."

Cyrus could tell she was both proud and embarrassed to be talking about this. "A circus would be such a trip," he said. "Why'd you leave?"

She looked at him briefly, then turned back to the road. He was sweet and simple and full of promise, and he reminded her of happier times. Finally, she stroked his arm as though soothing a hurt and said, "This is our day to see the sights and have some fun. Please, let us talk about something else."

EURA PARKED THE CAR in front of Portland's city hall, overlooking the harbour, and watched Cyrus walk down the street away from her. The first time she saw him, getting out of Ronnie's Cadillac, she had noticed his gait, so heavy and determined, like a young soldier who believes he is fighting the good fight. Right then and there she had wanted to grab him and warn him about the world. It is always the young who walk this way, without a clue what they will one day be asked to sacrifice.

When he disappeared around a corner, she got out of the car and wandered about the city with her umbrella, not so much window shopping as drifting through the fog and rain. She was glad Cyrus had suggested they split up for a while. It was a relief, for an afternoon, to forget about Europa Del Conte. These people hurrying by on the street did not know her. She did not have to care about what they thought, nor did she have to spend one moment thinking about them. She could give herself up to the past, to the memory of a husband's blue eyes and long blond hair, a nature keyed to enthusiasms.

He had laughed at her for being so indecisive. "This is something you must do," he said. "America is not an experience you turn down."

"And what about you?" she said. "How will you survive without me?"

"I will survive. I am a survivor. And you will come back to me with a thousand stories of America."

"America. I think it is more you are interested in a new pair of jeans."

"This is not a small consideration."

She grabbed the lapel of his leather jacket and pressed her cheek above his heart. "I will be the one who does not survive."

"You will be strong," he said. "The time will fly."

So she left home, and it was springtime and all things seemed possible. The Little Circus had been booked for a tour of America, twenty cities in three months. Eura, who had once been a dancer with the national ballet, no longer performed. She belonged backstage now, a masseuse, her showtimes non-stop. Without her magic fingers, the circus would grind to a halt.

They flew into New York on May 30, 1968, and from the moment she stepped off the plane, her once-in-a-lifetime trip to America went steadily downhill. You will love the cabbies, people told her, but she found them rude and unkempt, their vehicles a disgrace. You must see the architecture, they said, the Empire State Building and the Waldorf-Astoria, and always she wondered at a people who would choose to live and work in such monstrosities. The food was muck, the beer, even those brands that sounded familiar—Stroh's, Blatz, Budweiser—were abominable. From New York to Washington, Baltimore to Boston, her opinion of America declined. The stories had been all wrong except for one detail: the music. Jazz and bluegrass, folk and rock and roll. This was something Americans did better than anyone else the world over. They could, with an honest simplicity, translate the energy of life into something memorable and then make it dance like crazy. It was her one comfort during those three miserable months in America, the one thing she knew she would carry back to friends and say, "This at least is true."

In the middle of August, the Little Circus travelled to Detroit, the one city of the tour where it seemed the world had ended, or was about to. More than a year after the terrible riots, the downtown was still a charred ruin. She

had never seen anything like it, not even in Europe, the scene of so many griev-
ous conflicts. "I do not like this," she said to Alexander, the tour manager. "I
wish we were not in this place."

In almost every conceivable way, she wasn't. She travelled by shuttle bus
from the hotel to Cobo Hall where they performed each night, and by the
same bus back to the hotel. She did not stroll the city streets. She did not
visit the clubs. She merely drifted through the days, her mind already home,
already comfortably back in the cozy apartment near the university.

Then one night Alexander woke her from a sound sleep. It was three in
the morning, and the moment she opened her door to him he pushed her
back into the room. He quietly closed the door and began to throw her clothing into her suitcase. "Anna," he said in a whisper, "you must listen. Get
dressed and do not waste a moment." He was in the bathroom now, scooping
her belongings into a plastic bag, which he tossed into her suitcase. When
she still hadn't moved, he squeezed her arm until it hurt. "Do as I say," he
hissed. "Movemovemovemovemove."

She stumbled into some clothes, followed him out to a taxi and set off
into the night. Once they were on the expressway, Alexander turned to her
with a look of utter desolation and said, "It's bad. They've brought in the
tanks. It is all over."

FOR SOME PEOPLE, Portland was a university town, the home of their
alma mater. For others it was a historical treasure, the site of a frontier garri-
son. For others still it was of architectural interest. But for Cyrus, Portland
meant only one thing: the maximum security prison where his brother was an
inmate. It meant a tense and tedious drive from Wilbury, with Ruby chattering non-stop and Clarence rigidly silent. The trip home almost always
involved his aunt weeping and his uncle driving well above the speed limit.
On both legs of the journey, Cyrus stared blindly out the window while his
aunt and uncle sucked in all the poison in the car and in their own determined
way tried to neutralize it.

So it was no surprise that, without Eura's presence to rev him up, Cyrus
was having second thoughts about visiting Hank. He wandered in the rain,
stopping at five different variety stores before he found what he was looking

for. Even then he walked past the prison entrance several times. It was difficult enough summoning the courage to face Hank after almost a year, but a
visit to Portland also dredged up memories that Cyrus preferred to keep
buried.

Like the sight of his brother handcuffed in the back of a police cruiser,
the car parked on the drive where the poplars stood like sentries, and Danny
Scanlon on the front porch explaining how they'd caught Hank and Pete
Critchlow in LaSalle with a stolen car and Riley's .22-calibre rifle.

Like the sight of his mother wiping away her tears with the heel of her
hand as she said goodbye to Hank, who was off to serve his eight months at
Burwash, a minimum-security work farm for young offenders.

Like that summer after Burwash, Hank's last at home, with arguments
in the middle of the night, slamming doors, a dust-up between Hank and the
old man—no punches, just a bit of wrestling and grunting and maybe the
sudden realization on both their parts that this battle of wills had gotten
nasty, that it was no longer a father and son working out the kinks in a relationship but a clash between two angry men.

Then one night about nine o'clock, Cyrus was riding his bike home
from a softball game, and saw he Hank and Pete Critchlow zooming the
other way on Pete's motorcycle. Ten minutes later a fire engine passed him
with sirens wailing, headed for the marsh. When he stopped to sniff the air,
he could smell smoke all right. He picked up his pace and, turning onto the
Marsh Road, felt a jolt of panic—the smoke was coming from their place.
He could see the fire engine, a crowd of people; but by the time he got to
the farm, all the excitement was over. The chicken coop had burned to the
ground. All that remained was a blackened stain on the earth. Folks stood
around and shook their heads. The firemen rolled up their hoses. No one
had any doubts about how the fire started.

Hank didn't come home that night. Or the next. Or ever again. Several
months later, just before Christmas, there was a flurry of phone calls. That
night their parents drove into the city, and Cyrus stayed home with Isabel.
It was only next morning when Ruby came to the house that they learned
Hank had killed a gas station attendant in a botched robbery in Hounslow,
and that Riley and Catherine, who had been on their way to the police station,

had died when their truck slammed into a hydro pole.

Hank's trial was quick. No one put up much of a struggle; no one talked about hiring the best lawyers money could buy and fighting this down the line. By then the fight had gone out of those who would care. Hank had been trouble from the start. A poor student, an angry soul, the wrong crowd, a chemical imbalance—any number of reasons were put forward as an explanation, but explanations couldn't undo the damage already done, nor prevent what followed. Cyrus and, for a while, Isabel went to live with the Mitchells. The insurance money came up short, and the bank took the farm. There were some who hoped they had seen the last of Hank Owen.

It was Ruby who suggested they visit each year. She was a religious woman. She believed in forgiveness. She said even a wayward soul like Hank needed love and family. And while it was tough at first to be in the same room with him, the person responsible for so much of their grief, it became easier with time because in Hank's presence it was hard to believe in his guilt—and hardest of all for Hank, it seemed. Throughout the trial he acted more surprised than sorry to be there, never showing the proper remorse or gravity.

Over the years they continued to ask him for explanations, but nothing he said ever made much sense to them. He said he could picture the crime and remember certain details clearly—the smell of gasoline, the song playing on the radio (Jimmy Dean talking his way through "Big Bad John")—but couldn't put himself in the scene. He couldn't remember pulling the trigger or getting back into his car. When asked about his feelings that night or what was going through his head, he shrugged and said he felt nothing then and nothing now, not even guilt. In time, of course, he learned to accept his guilt because the facts pointed in that direction, just as we accept that the earth is round though our senses tell us it is not. If everyone believed he had killed the attendant, it must be true. But accepting guilt wasn't the same as feeling it. What he felt, he said, was an emptiness, a lack, as if something important, something necessary to his happiness, had been plucked from his breast.

The psychologist had no shortage of theories about what had happened. He found numerous patterns in the pain Hank left behind; but none of the talk ever made sense to Cyrus. If there was a progression, he had given up trying to understand it and had, in fact, spent much of the past decade trying to disconnect events. Only recently had he come to accept that Hank wasn't responsible for the death of their parents, that bad luck and bad choices often worked in tandem. As for the crimes his brother *had* committed, they pretty much fell outside the scope of Cyrus's natural sympathies. Hank was his brother; everything else seemed like conjecture.

Once Cyrus had passed all the security checkpoints, he was brought to a glass partition that had a phone on each side of it. A moment later Hank walked in, slouchy but unyielding. The first hint of wrinkles coupled with the touches of grey already showing at the temples of his brush cut made him look much older than his years. There were new scars on his face, the initials "HO" carved into each cheek.

"Hey there, Cyrus, whataya know?"

"Nothing, Hank, just like always."

Hank turned his chair around and straddled it, his arms resting on the chair back. "That's good, kid. Keep it that way. Keep your nose to the grindstone, right?"

Cyrus shrugged, the dopey kid brother, and stared down at his lap. When he looked up again he said, "What's with your face?"

Hank touched his cheek. "This? I was bored. You know how it is. So where's the rest of the crew? They can't face me no more?"

"I came alone," he said, still unable to look him in the eye.

There was something uncharacteristic in his voice just then, a kind of stagey nonchalance. Hank looked at him with his coal-dark eyes, comparing that voice to others he had heard. "You came on your own all the way to Portland. What about school, kid? Why aren't you in school?"

A grin eased into place, a crack in the dam. Then, in a rush, Cyrus came alive. "I quit, Hank. I'm finished with that crap. You remember how I told you I played guitar and all? Well, I got a job with a band. I'm travelling, getting paid real well. It's a blast."

Hank sat up straighter as if to get a better perspective. "A musician," he said. "Isn't that a kick in the head. I always pegged you for a farmer."

"Get lost. I never wanted to be a farmer. Never."

Hank leaned forward again and said, "So how's Izzy? Last time I saw her she looked like hell."

"She's okay, I guess. I don't know, we used to talk a lot, me and her, especially after you left. I always thought she was cool. Now it's like she's too busy or something."

"Hey, somebody's gotta be normal in this family."

"Normal." Cyrus snorted. "She's always got a burr up her ass."

For a moment they felt the uncommon warmth that occurs when a younger sibling makes the older one laugh. Hank lit a cigarette then, the phone clamped between his cheek and shoulder. Cyrus said, "Brought you a carton. They'll give them to you later, I guess."

"Black Cats?"

"Hell to find, too. You might want to think about switching to a more popular brand."

Hank blew a smoke ring. "Thanks kiddo. But I never was that interested in what was popular. And look where that got me. But music, eh? I can see that. Music is pretty cool. Bet you have to beat the babes off with a club. How's that old prick Clarence?"

"He's okay. Kind of worried I guess about the cancer. You shouldn't be so hard on him. He's not so bad."

"Yeah, well, I guess it's me. Guess I won't expect an invitation, I ever get out of this place."

Cyrus perked up. "Is there talk? I mean, about you getting out?"

"There's always talk, kid. Don't mean fuck all, really. Let's face it, nobody's gonna be too thrilled by the prospect. Not sure I am, either. Might have to ask my kid brother to show me the ropes. Been a while."

Cyrus felt completely different visiting Hank on his own. There was no one to act as a buffer or run interference or set the tone. It was just two brothers now, looking at how to move on. And he realized he didn't have the faintest idea of what to say next or where to look.

It must have been obvious. Before long Hank motioned to the closest guard that the visit was over. As he stood to leave, he said, "Appreciate the smokes, pal. Keep your nose clean."

CYRUS MET EURA AS PLANNED at the rental car, then walked with her along the main street. She had spent time looking for a suitable restaurant, something that might remind her of home, and in the end had settled on Reggio's, a little place that served bottled dressing on iceberg lettuce, and lasagna made with hamburger and cottage cheese and no discernible spices. The house wine, though, was a sharp Chianti, which by the second glass had softened her anxieties and, for one night, made her more or less resigned to the food and Portland and the Jimmy Waters Revival.

Cyrus was afraid to mention his visit with Hank, and that fear coloured all his thoughts, stilled his tongue. He watched her stare into the shadows of the restaurant. Whether she was walking down the street or dancing across the stage or, like now, lifting a wineglass to her lips, she seemed weightless. And yet, if someone had asked him, Cyrus would have said she was heavier than anyone he'd ever met. She had a sense of gravity, an aura so complex that she appeared at times to be the only live-action figure in an otherwise cartoonish world.

When the waiter arrived with their food, Eura was drawn from her reverie. She leaned across the table and took Cyrus's hand in hers. "I am not sometimes the best company," she said.

He shrugged in what he hoped was a sophisticated manner and looked down at his pale fingers entwined with hers, which were rough and ruddy. She didn't flinch or make an effort to avoid the little rounded nub that marred his left hand, and he was happy about that. Janice was the only one, aside from family, who had been totally cool about it.

To make up for being so distracted, she began to tell him about her job as a masseuse with the Little Circus, how they had come to America, and about the night she and Alexander sought asylum in the United States. "We left Detroit in a taxi," she said, "and talked this man into driving us to a very ugly place called Muskegon. Alexander knew people there. This is something I will never forget."

"Weird place to go."

"It was not for long. Four nights until we decide what to do. These friends, Katarina and Barbara—what is the word, spinsters?—they too were ugly. Back home, you know, you would see these women everywhere, potato faces, but never like this, with bleached hair, with curlers and makeup and so tight capri pants. At first I would have nothing to do with them. They seemed foolish. But they were only trying to live their new life. It was not so long before I was listening to their stories and laughing at their jokes and accepting their kindness like they were family. And they taught me also the second greatness of America: bourbon, which is something that even Jimmy Waters understands. Other than music, it is the only talent Americans have, I think."

She laughed. "These women, their hair was piled like so—" she held her hands above her head "—and covered with, I don't know how to call them, glittery nets. They drank and smoked too much and owned a bar, KayBee's, beside the docks. It was never busy, only five or six people in the days we were there. But then, you know, from all I could see, this town was made only for ghosts. Most of the stores had closed or burned down. Broken pavement, windows covered with plywood. Outside we saw almost no one, so it was hard to think who would come to this bar. But the sisters said when a freighter came in, the town was very busy and their bar was the hot place. Pickled herring, you could get, goulash and bread. The wall behind the jukebox, a big wall like so—" she waved the length of the restaurant "—was covered with postcards from sailors. Liverpool, Gdansk, Lisbon. These women were loved very much, I think."

She poked at her food awhile, then laughed ruefully. "Four days Alexander stayed drunk, feeding quarters into the jukebox, the same Tony Bennett song over and over till I could kill him. Every day I bought the *Detroit Free Press* and asked Katarina to tell me about home. It is very sad, you know, the way the tanks can roll in and everything suddenly is over as if nothing had before ever existed. These women, though, were not interested anymore. They were Americans, and when they had had enough of us, they drove us to Chicago where we declared our wish to defect."

She touched his cheek, letting her hand fall again to cover his. "But this story makes me tired. Tell me about your family. They are musicians, too?"

"No," he said, "not likely. They're farmers is all. Pretty boring."

His words surprised her. "I believe more that farmers are brave. It is a mystery to me how men and women build their lives on something so risky as weather. Joining a circus or playing music, this is logical compared to such a gamble. And yet look what comes. It is a beautiful thing, I think, to take such risk for so much good. I have nothing but praise for farmers." She ran her thumb along the top of his hand, her gaze dreamy, as though she were remembering all the noble farmers she had ever known.

Not wanting her to drift away from him again, he said, "My uncle has an apple orchard on a ridge north of the marsh, and one of my favourite things was to go out at night and climb into one of the trees. September was the best time, still kind of warm, and I'd lie there in the branches and listen. The canning factory in town ran night and day that time of year, and I could lie there in my tree and hear the tractors and trucks rolling into town from the fields, the air full of pickles or tomato sauce or canned peaches. I always think about that when I hear of people who live beside steel mills or sulphur mines. I guess I should feel kind of lucky."

"You don't?"

"No, I do. But I've been unlucky, too." He let his gaze drift about the room. They were the only diners. Everyone else had moved into the small bar to watch the hockey playoffs. Finally, he turned back to her and said, "I keep thinking about my aunt and uncle. I lived with them after my folks died, and they were real good to me, especially Clarence. He's a great guy, bought my first guitar. But I think about him sometimes and it bugs me."

She smoothed the hair off his forehead. "I am sure he did his best . . ."

"Well, that's just it. I owe him a lot, and you know, he was real sick awhile ago. Had a cancer operation. And I just wonder why he stays there in Wilbury, doing the same thing every day on the same stupid farm he was born on. You know? He and Ruby haven't been anywhere. They just get up and do what they've always done like they don't know any better . . ."

She nodded her head. "I have a friend back home, a writer. He has published three novels, and they are very political and smart. The critics say he is maybe a genius. But it is not easy for him. He has no wife, no children. I have seen him go days without eating. One day I asked how his new book was coming, and he shook his head and said, 'It is shit. The whole thing is shit. Do not even talk to me about it.' So, I changed the subject. Six months later I asked again, and again he said, 'All shit. I am completely useless.' I reminded him of the times I had seen him at his typewriter, laughing, waving his arms. 'Six months you have worked,' I said. 'Twelve-hour days. Surely it is better. There is progress.' And he looked at me and said, 'Progress, sure. It gets better. For a while it is almost good. Almost. And then, boom, it is shit again, and I must rewrite it from the beginning.'" She raised an eyebrow at Cyrus. "Maybe this is the same as your uncle. Maybe he, too, is an artist."

THEY TOOK THEIR TIME returning to Fenton, stopping on dark stretches of country road to look at the stars. When they reached the hotel it was past midnight, the lobby deserted. On the seventh floor she led him down the hall past his own room. His pulse was pounding. He imagined the two of them rolling on her bed and how he would trail kisses down the dizzying path of her tattoo. Instead she stopped at room 704 and knocked softly. Right away they were ushered into the smoke and babble, the press of many bodies.

"Tea?" Adrian asked.

Kerry handed him a joint. "He'll need something stronger after a night on the town with D.C."

Eura slapped Kerry playfully across the back of his head and found a square of floor space where she drew her knees up to her chin and waited for Adrian to serve her.

"Here you go, my dear," he said, handing her one of his special cups, a delicate fluted Belleek that had belonged to his mother and travelled with him now in a special padded case. "Give up your cares and rest awhile."

Ronnie, who was sitting atop the chest of drawers, lifted his tin of milk in greeting. "Let me take a moment, Cyrus, to tell you—and I'm sure I speak for all here—how glad we are that you have come by for a drop of Welsh hospitality. If anyone required proof that you have become one of us, to my mind your appearance here seals it. You are now, for sure and certain, a full-fledged member of the Jimmy Waters Revival."

Cyrus found a spot beside Tony Two Poops, who was washing down vitamin C with mouthfuls of Southern Comfort. When offered the bottle, Cyrus took a swig, then a second. On the other side of him, in a rumpled heap, was Tommy Mac, who opened Cyrus a can of McEwan's ale and, with a nod toward Eura, said, "Tha's a right cunt, tha' one."

Two Poops winked. "Our Tommy boy's had a few too many, I think."

"Aye," Tom growled. "A few too menna, but not enough too menna."

A joint the size of a Cuban cigar drifted by, and Cyrus took a hit and passed it on. Two Poops said, "I guess you'll be wanting to put your name on the list."

Cyrus furrowed his brow. "What do you mean?"

"For Eura. You'll have to get on the list. She giving you the flat rate?"

Cyrus took a sip of McEwan's but found it a hard mouthful to swallow. A quick glance about the room offered no evidence that he was being teased. "The list," he repeated.

"Yeah. My turn tomorrow. Got a disc problem that's killer."

Cyrus leaned against the wall, comprehension slowly dawning. "And you've got an appointment with Eura."

"Wasn't for her I'd never be able to stand up."

"And she charges you a flat rate. For a massage."

"Between you and me, it's worth twice the price."

Cyrus closed his eyes and smiled. He saw the Airstream, the bedroom window, Eura's head and shoulders. He heard Jim groaning with pleasure. She was a masseuse.

When he looked across the room again, she had already slipped away; he had missed his chance to continue their night together. Even so, he was satisfied with the progress made. Questions had been answered, doubts allayed, doors opened.

He finished his beer, then another, and was one of the last to leave the party. That night he dreamed about his father, the same dream he'd been having for years. They're running side by side along the Marsh Road, a beautiful night, the moon shining so brightly it casts shadows on the ground. In real life his father had been an effortless runner, and Cyrus normally struggled to keep up. In the dream, however, they both glide peacefully through the darkness, as if they have wings on their feet. Cyrus is talking calmly, his gaze focused straight ahead. Then, without explanation, his father stops running, and Cyrus sails down the road like a summer wind.

Ruby took Janice to the United Church and suggested they sit in the balcony where the organ sounded most ethereal and the light from the stained glass windows seemed most uplifting. Although she normally sat by herself, she was glad the girl had come. It made her feel needed again.

Janice followed along as best she could, but found it odd to be in a church, and to be there with a woman she hardly knew. They were surrounded by friends and neighbours, yet she felt as if she had dropped into a primitive culture. She couldn't imagine anyone taking these rituals seriously, as bewildering to her as face paint, a bone in the nose, a communal bowl of phlegm. Even so, there was something pleasant about sitting in this church with Ruby. Partly it was the fact that Janice could sense a bit of Cyrus in the old woman—the same blue eyes, the same smell of Camay soap—partly it was the sense that Janice was doing something worthwhile, cheering up a sweet old lady. She was enough of a good girl to understand the beauty in that.

When the service ended, they stood outside and let their eyes adjust to the sunshine. Down the block a couple of leather-necked farmers sat in front of the town hall, eating sunflower seeds. A robin sang in a nearby tree. Ruby said, "It was a boring sermon. And they sang all the wrong songs. I should have taken you somewhere else."

"You play the field?"

"Well, I guess technically I am United. But Reverend Jansen's not my favourite. So I generally go where the spirit moves me. This was a mistake. I don't know what I could have been thinking."

The next week they tried the Baptists, and Janice knew right away it was more to her liking. The energetic hymns, all that vigorous dunking, the white robes afloat in the pool of water—here at least she could see why people might get excited about this Jesus business.

But it wasn't until the third week that Janice saw the light. She and Ruby attended a mass at Saint Michael's. It was a cold blustery day, the wind snatching the hem of her skirt as they climbed the steps to the church. They opened the door and there, just inside by the candles and the fountain, was a statue of the Virgin Mary bending over the body of Christ. Janice stood transfixed, the light coming from behind her, the wind swirling around her, the incense and the organ and the softly tinted light speaking to her in a voice she had never heard. She knew without a doubt that this was it, that she would come back again and again, that she had, in the most unlikely place, found a way forward.

CLARENCE CAME IN FROM THE ORCHARD and hung his hat on the peg above his workbench. Although he normally rested on Sundays, he'd been out collecting leaf samples, which he spread on the bench. Everything was running early this year. The buds had already started to open, showing silver-green mouse ears. He pulled out his magnifying glass and adjusted his gooseneck lamp. After several minutes he'd seen all he needed. Red mites. This week he and Frank would have to use the oil spray.

He opened a cola and flopped on the old sofa. It was a cool, damp morning, but he was perspiring. And he was winded, which happened a lot when the humidity was high. Another result of his operation, he figured.

As he closed his eyes and waited for his breathing to return to normal, he thought about Cyrus—an ache like a phantom limb. The two of them had never talked much, and Clarence wasn't the kind for horseplay and games, but he really missed their Saturdays in the orchard, the two of them establishing a physical rhythm, doing what was required. March was the last time they'd worked side by side, cutting out winter damage and pausing at the end of each row to drink a cup of hot tea from a Thermos.

He had tried to pass on to Cyrus a love of pruning—that you cut something back to make it stronger, that you halted its fruitless yearning to increase its yield—and had tried to apply the same lessons to his own life. He believed in limits. He had always found strength in his losses. But some losses cut deeper than others. He'd be the first to admit he had never gotten over the death of Riley Owen. Those feelings were too complicated for a simple man to unravel, a crazy knot of grief and guilt and jealousy that had maybe left its mark on Cyrus, too, driving him away for good. But where to begin in puzzling it out? The glove? The girl? The grave?

He remembered clearly the day the Donahue sisters showed up at high school. Their father, Jim, a doctor from Waterford, had just moved to town to set up practice. He had an enormous handlebar moustache and round wire-rimmed glasses in the fashion of Teddy Roosevelt, and dressed always in a black suit. As Jim walked his daughters to the front door of Wilbury High that first day, a girl on each arm, he seemed ready to burst with pride. And rightly so. His daughters, Ruby and Catherine, were the most beautiful girls Clarence had ever seen.

Ruby was the first-born, and had she been an only child, she would have captured the heart of every boy in town. But Catherine, three years younger, was not only more beautiful but more spirited than Ruby, who had a serious and retiring nature. In the presence of Catherine Donahue, few could resist the chase. Certainly not Clarence.

He was handsome, strong and intelligent. His father was reeve of the county and one of the most successful farmers in the region. It seemed only natural that the two families, the Mitchells and the Donahues, would become friendly; and naturally enough, Clarence tried everything in his power to make Catherine love him. He fought battles for her, ran touchdowns for her, talked till he was blue in the face, and still he failed to produce a spark. She saw him as a friend and nothing more. Since she treated all the boys that way, Clarence wasn't too concerned. He went off to college with the belief she would one day come to her senses and understand he was the right man for her. But then the war started, and Clarence enlisted in the air force right after graduation, despite the deferment offered farm boys. By the end of 1940, he was stationed in Devon, where he worked in the ground crew of the air base, his knowledge of all things mechanical saving him from combat.

As it turned out, it was young Riley Owen who fired Catherine's imagination, dirt-poor Riley with the lovable spirit of a dreamer but the laughable dream of playing for the Detroit Tigers. Halfway through his first year in Toledo, he came home with a busted knee. He was on crutches until Labour Day and talking about joining the war effort as soon as he was well enough. But then he met Catherine at a church picnic. In the weeks that followed, they were seen around town together or sitting on the Donahues' wide front veranda, ignoring the disapproving looks of her parents. One month later, and a week before he was to report for basic training, they caught everyone by surprise and eloped. Clarence heard the news in letters from his folks: about the marriage, about Riley's return to the farm and his deferment and, eight months later, about the birth of Hank.

Clarence loved them both, but when he returned from overseas, it killed him to see them together. It killed him to see Riley failing to measure up to all that Catherine deserved, farming not by choice but by default, falling deeper and deeper into debt and further and further behind, growing angry and sullen and unlovable. It also killed Clarence to see Catherine suffering, to watch her lose her bloom and her spirit. And this, too: it killed him these past few years to watch Cyrus, how there were moments the two faces, Riley's and Catherine's, would fade in and out of focus like those stupid 3-D pictures of Jesus on the cross. The whole thing, really, from start to finish, it just killed him. When he closed his eyes sometimes, he could feel it like a great big hole inside him where his heart used to be.

When Ruby returned from church, she walked over to the barn where he was still nursing his soda. She looked good, not exactly happy but content, all things considered. When she saw him, though, she sank a little, her mouth losing its upward curl. "Time to move on now," she said. "There's more to life than this."

He knew she was right. He knew that Cy's leaving was inevitable, that this boy and his dreams should not be seen as the symbol of a failed life. But then it wasn't just Cyrus he was thinking about.

HANK KNEW BETTER. Of course he did. You watch your back. You keep your nose clean. You don't make waves. He knew that. He'd said as much to his little brother. And some other time he might have done things differently. But this wasn't another time. The way it is, brother.

He walked away from his metal press where hundreds of licence plates waited to be stamped. He just walked like a free man out of the room and along the corridor to the laundry, walked with such purpose and determination that the guards didn't think to ask what in hell he was doing. In the laundry he stepped up to Golden Reynolds and said, "Enough. No more fucking around. The batteries."

Goldie looked away. "You talking about?"

"I want those batteries, and I want 'em now."

Goldie checked the placement of his friends and stooges around the room. "Hoho," he said, sidling closer, "you lookin' a bit tense. Maybe could use some lovin' is what I think. The Golden touch."

Another time it wouldn't have worked this way, but this time it did. Hank slammed Goldie onto the cement floor and was choking him with his bare hands. A moment later muscular forearms pried them apart. Two, three, then four men held Hank still as Goldie rose slowly from the floor and dusted himself off, all cool and casual. He studied the ceiling a moment, shifted his weight and balance, then moved in and landed a vicious kick between Hank's legs.

"Lesson number one," he said.

FOURTEEN

I sabel got the call about Hank, and she and Ruby set out immediately for Portland. At the prison infirmary, they were told that he had been transferred to the main hospital downtown.

The man on the phone had told Isabel that Hank had been "worked over pretty good," and she'd pictured him the way a prizefighter might look after a rough bout. She certainly hadn't imagined the crumpled mess in the bed at Portland Memorial, or the cage of iron rods and clamps that had been built around him to keep his pelvis and upper body immobile.

He was sleeping soundly, and Isabel and Ruby stood a few moments staring at the wreck before them, the scabs and bruises, the initials carved into his face, the metal truss like some instrument of torture. For the next hour they tracked down nurses and, eventually, the doctor, who told them Hank's spine had been fractured in several places, and that it was still too early to know how much nerve damage there'd been. He would most likely be a paraplegic the rest of his life.

Hank was still asleep when they returned to the room, so Ruby went to get them lunch from the cafeteria. While she was gone, he opened his eyes. "Hey," he croaked, "if it ain't Dingdong Fuzzybell. How ya doin'?"

She moved closer and frowned at him. "You really did it this time."

He laughed at that, one wheezing bark that made his face crumple with pain. When the creases faded, he licked his lips and said, "A bit of rough-housing is all. You know how it is. Boys will be boys."

She hugged herself as though she were afraid she might lose control. "Don't you care about anything?" she said. "Ruby's worried sick."

"Give me a drink there, will ya?"

She manoeuvred the cup through the metal scaffolding and brought the plastic straw to his lips. When he finished drinking, he said, "I care about things, Iz. Like I'm worried you look like a damn scarecrow. Why don't you eat, for God's sake?"

"I do eat. And this isn't about me."

"I'm just saying I care. And that dopey brother of ours. Did you know he came to see me?"

"Cyrus was here?"

"Few days ago. The guy even brought me some Black Cats."

Ruby came in just then and dumped the sandwiches and cartons of milk on the windowsill, fluttering around Hank's bed like a big wrinkled moth. After she settled on a hardback chair beside him, Isabel raised her eyebrows and said, "Cyrus was here."

Ruby looked around. "While I was gone?"

"Last week. He came to visit this jerk."

Hank stared straight ahead, with a slight trace of a smile. "What I wouldn't give to be in his shoes right now," he said, "playing music, seeing the world. He looked real proud of himself. Cracked me up."

News of Cyrus lifted a weight off both Ruby and Isabel, allowing them to fill the air with bright chatter. This made it easier for all of them. Hank could lie there with his eyes closed and let their stories of Wilbury wash over him; they could decorate this grim space with a few reminders of home and avoid having to think too deeply about Hank's life.

They stayed a second day, but it was not as successful. Hank had lost his patience with them. Their presence now clearly a burden, they spent the bulk of their time talking to prison officials and learned that Hank would likely remain in the hospital for another two weeks. After that he would be trans-ferred to the prison infirmary. Eventually he would be moved to another facility where he could get around in a wheelchair.

Next morning the two women drove home. Isabel was so worn out that it was a struggle to keep her mind on the road. She stopped for coffee at every service centre. It was only as they pulled into the driveway at Orchard Knoll that she turned to Ruby and said, "I've been meaning to tell you since we left town the other day, but it never seemed the right time. And I know this isn't the right time, either, but I don't have much choice here. Gerry and I are separating." She looked out the side window, unable to meet Ruby's gaze, and told her about Ginny Maxwell and kicking Gerry out of the house and how maybe they would be putting the farm up for sale.

Ruby took a deep breath and held it before letting it out in a long sibilant whisper. She had heard the rumours. Word travelled fast in a place like Wilbury. She touched Isabel's hand and said, "I'll pray for you, dear."

Isabel pulled quickly away. "I don't want you to pray for me. I just wanted you to know."

"Well, okay. I'll pray anyway."

JANICE WOULD ONE DAY CLAIM that her career as an artist began that first Sunday at St. Mike's, just inside the door with the wind whirling her skirt about, with the smell of candles and incense, and the dark beauty of all that stained glass. But the statement was only partly true. In a way, her career began the day Cyrus disappeared, for it was that feeling of abandonment that led her to befriend Ruby and begin her tour of Wilbury's places of worship. Yet, even that was not the whole story. Before the emotional upheaval of Cy's departure, there were those dreary art classes at Wilbury High, under the lifeless tutelage of Mrs. Velma Fleck, in which Janice produced unremarkable charcoal sketches, oil pastels and pen-and-ink drawings of the dusty objects Velma kept in her cupboard. There were the trips with her mother to the art gallery in Detroit, too, and the coffee-table books she flipped through whenever she was bored. There were the rainy days of arts and crafts at summer camp.

This much *was* true: Janice came home from the Catholic church and immediately took out pen and paper. Her first impulse was to jot down the details of the experience, to explain to herself the emotion she had felt. She sat for the longest while, the nib of her pen poised on the page, as she recalled the way the light, coming from behind her through the open door, cast a shadow on the Christ figure, but left Mary fully lit. Along with the perfume of incense and candles, she had smelled fresh-cut flowers and women's perfume and the unaccountable sadness of mothballs. The entire picture, coupled with Ruby's chatter and the dense murmur of a hundred families jostling in the pews, was what she intended to get down, in point form if need be. But an odd thing happened. On a whim, she moved the pen down the page in a single stroke, a thin graceful arc that hinted at the shape of a head, the curve of neck and arm, a longer stretch of leg. She paused then, surprised by what she'd done; and more curious than committed, she tried to remember the fundamentals Velma had tried to drill into her head. By morning, Janice had covered her bedroom floor with half-finished and completely worthless sketches of The Pièta.

Had this been any other time in her life, she would have put aside her pen and paper the next day and never given them another thought. She had always been easily discouraged when things did not go her way. Her dancing lessons, her tennis and figure-skating lessons—she quit them all after a single season. But this was different, as exciting to her as singing in the band, only more personal, more private. She liked the idea that she could explore her feelings through something as sensuous as a line. And for the first time in her life, her failures inspired her to try again.

Several days later she stopped in to see her high school guidance counsellor, the reptilian Mr. Dietz. Without a word of greeting, she said, "My choices for university. They're all wrong."

"Yes, but Janice, the paperwork was sent off weeks ago."

"I know. It's just hit me that I don't want to go to university."

Dietz grimaced and waved her into a chair. "Last-minute nerves. All very understandable. Have you told your parents how you feel?"

"Well no, of course not. I didn't want them to have a stroke or anything before I checked it out. The thing is, Mr. Dietz, I almost made a terrible mistake, and I've just got to make it right. I want to apply to OCA. I can do that, can't I?"

"The art college." He nodded thoughtfully, touching his upper lip with the tip of his tongue. "Yes, I suppose. But even if you did—"

"I'd need a portfolio, wouldn't I? Jason Browne told me he had to submit fifteen different pieces of work from different media."

"Yes, that's important. They'd be looking for signs of talent. But I have to tell you, Janice, we've been over this ground already. I remember sitting here with your mom and dad, looking at your marks, your aptitude scores. You're one of our best students. Definitely university material. Don't sell yourself short."

She said she understood but needed to consider all options. She took an OCA brochure just in case, a college calendar and application form, and walked out of the school. Then she went straight to the Three Links Hall and pored over the material. The main obstacle, as far as she could tell, was coming up with a few pieces she wouldn't mind showing to someone. In five years with Velma Fleck, she had yet to accomplish that feat, and would more or less struggle with the notion throughout her career. She never called herself an artist. As far as she was concerned, she was simply making progress, taking necessary steps.

AFTER ISABEL RETURNED FROM PORTLAND, she handed Sheldon Demeter her resignation and moved across town to Regal Real Estate, a smaller operation originally set up by Len Griswald but, since his death, run by Nellie, his wife. The two women got along well. Nellie, a widow for almost eight years, knew everything there was to know about living without a man. "I loved Len," she liked to say, "but all things considered, life is better now." Under the present circumstances, with divorce a very real possibility, Isabel found Nellie's attitude refreshing.

One day, not long after her move to Regal, Isabel sat in her car outside her old office, waiting for Sheldon to leave. When he drove off to an open house, she slipped inside to talk to Lawrence Bell.

"Hey there, Larry, how's it going?"

"Can't complain, Iz. You?"

She nodded her head and looked around, as if she hadn't been there in years. "I might have a buyer for that listing of yours on Orange Street."

"Hey, no kidding. The little bungalow?"

"Yeah. Just working out the finances. How low will they go?"

"It's pretty firm, Iz. You know, maybe a couple thou'. We get down to real numbers, maybe as much as five grand, but not much more than that. Young couple?"

"No, a stupid woman who's ditching her sleazebag of a husband."

Larry slowly lifted his gaze until he was looking her straight in the eyes. "You sure, Iz? Everybody makes a mistake one time in their life."

She shook her head. "The only mistake was mine, Larry, and I'm finished making mistakes. You'll have an offer the end of the week."

IN THE YEAR OF OUR LORD 1971, Ruby Mitchell turned fifty-six. She had successfully made it through "the change," as the ladies in her church group referred to it, and in comparison to the horror stories she had heard others tell, the transformation had been gentle—no sweats, no moods, no sleepless nights. If asked how it felt on the other side of fertility, she would have said it reminded her of the sweet silence that settled on the house when the grandfather clock wound down.

Aside from that biological hush, which she had come to regard as a minor blessing, she had no notable physical complaints. Unlike so many women her age, she had her health. And why wouldn't she? She had never smoked, never had more than a few sips of wine in her entire life, ate sensibly and like most farmwives got plenty of exercise. Some of the cattier members of the church group might add that she had never suffered the trauma of childbirth—no rips, no tears, no stretch marks—and that was a leg up she would readily acknowledge. But she had not been spared a mother's grief. Didn't she sorrow for Hank in his prison cell, even more so now that he had lost the use of his legs? Didn't she regret each day the friction that existed between her and Isabel? Didn't she lie awake each night and wonder if Cyrus was safe and well? That they were not her own children made it even more difficult in a way, for she was not simply acting as a mother but also trying to be their one connection to their true mother and, at the same time, to measure her efforts against her own memories of Catherine.

These concerns, not to mention the death of a sister and the illness of a husband, had deepened the care lines of her face and added a complicated texture to her days, an ever-changing mixture of joy, apprehension, guilt, grief, pride and gratitude. And now she had another worry: the change that had come over Clarence since his operation, and even more so since Cyrus walked out of their lives.

Ruby once confessed to Catherine that she had admired Clarence long before she loved him. He was president of the student council at their high school, always so well-dressed, wearing a V-necked sweater over a shirt and tie, his shoes polished, his posture soldier-straight. He organized relief drives for some of the poorer families in town, enlisting Ruby and her sister in the noble cause. He was intelligent and charming, with an even temper and seemingly unlimited patience and energy. Most of all he was kind—and never kinder than he was to Riley Owen, the young boy he had taken under his wing. But now, for the first time in her life, Ruby had discovered a side of Clarence that was less than admirable. At first she thought her husband's self-pity was a question of belief, that he hadn't taken Jesus into his heart. Lately, she had started to wonder if he had ever taken anyone into his heart, even her.

She was the one who started most conversations. She was the one to initiate Sunday drives and weekend getaways and their few sexual encounters. She recalled the way he would shut her out of his bad moods, rolling onto his side in bed and rebuffing her every advance. He would think it a sign of courage, the way he swallowed all thoughts of his illness and didn't make a peep. But Ruby knew that was more a case of endurance. Courage was different. Courage was what you found not in your descent but at the bottom of your fall, the very thing that allowed you to start over, to climb back up toward the light.

After she had tidied the lunch dishes, she wandered into the yard. The air was warm, a beautiful May afternoon, and she walked out to the packing shed to sit with Clarence. He had just returned from the orchard, where Frank and a handful of college students were thinning the crop with bamboo poles. He was at his workbench with a handful of leaves and branches, looking for signs of the next pest. The radio was tuned to a Tiger game. She turned it down and said, "Tell me what's eating you."

He looked up a moment and then back to the magnifying glass. "I guess I've been thinking about those Cortlands we've got in cold storage," he answered. "Should have sold them when the price was up."

"And that's why you haven't spoken to me in almost a month? The Cortlands?" She laughed and touched his hand. "Come on now, you can do better than that. I think it's more like you blame me somehow for Cyrus leaving. Or that maybe you think you're the only one hurt."

"Ruby . . ."

"Don't 'Ruby' me. These are things we should handle together, Clarence. You think I don't need comfort? You didn't even come with us to Portland. If you'd seen what they did to Hank—"

"I didn't want to see Hank."

"Well no, I know that. That much is clear. It's like you don't want much of anything these days." She rubbed his hand with both of hers. In a softer, more sympathetic tone, she said, "Twenty-five years, Clarence. We've been married twenty-five years. And I was thinking, it's the two of us now, just like before. Maybe it's time for a change."

He bowed his head and swallowed heavily. When he turned to look at her, all she saw was fear.

AT THE END OF JUNE, Hank moved into the Willbourne Correctional Institute, which even as an address seemed a step in the right direction. There was a feeling of hope in the idea of correction, of making something right. A penitentiary, by contrast, sounded painful, where lost souls wearily awaited final judgment. It didn't hurt that Willbourne was brand new, with low-slung buildings set against a rural backdrop. There were no stone walls, no barbed wire, no armed guards. Inmates called it the Country Club.

Hank had a ways to go before he'd get to see much of the place. He was still confined to his bed and had weeks of rehab before he'd even get into a wheelchair. But the metal brace had been replaced with something plastic and portable. And he had a new radio that required no batteries. He could listen all he wanted. Away from Portland's dour cellblock, of course, the need for music wasn't as pressing. He could be choosier in what he listened to. Some nights he turned the dial back and forth, scanning the airwaves for hours. He wasn't sure what he was looking for. Maybe nothing. Or at least nothing he could explain.

A week after they slipped across the border into the United States, Cyrus had his first real breakthrough. They were in Arbutus, Ohio, a mid-size steel town close to Cincinnati. The turnout was poor, but the show itself was surprisingly good, at least for Cyrus. He heard the music better that night, started to understand things the others took for granted.

If Jim's music was about anything, it was about changes. In every song, they shifted keys, shifted tempos, shifted from one groove to another, anything to bring the music in line with Jim's stories. And until that night, Cyrus had had no idea how to anticipate when a change might come or where it might go. There were neither verbal nor visual clues. But in Arbutus, he noticed that whenever Sonny played a certain chord in a certain way—Cyrus didn't know what the chord was, but it sounded complicated, what Janice used to call a spider chord because it stretched out in so many directions—he was giving a sign that a bridge to a new place was under construction. Most of the time it signalled a key change, but if that chord was combined with a confusing rhythmic figure, and if Chuck's drumming got scattered and chaotic, then it was pretty certain they were moving to another groove, too.

Because of this small discovery, his playing showed some spark for a change. Even Sonny noticed. As they left the stage that night, he actually patted Cyrus on the shoulder and said, "How about that, the new dog learned an old trick."

Cyrus, wanting to savour the moment, decided to stroll back to the hotel rather than ride in the bus, but he soon regretted his decision. What he really wanted was to be with Eura. Instead he was alone in the darkness, his elation turning by degrees into a dull ache.

Around midnight, he wandered past a small pub down by the river and saw Tommy Mac sitting at the bar. Cyrus slid up beside him and said, "Bad luck, drinking by yourself."

Tom nearly fell off his stool. "Ye fuckin' idjit, ye should have yer bollocks mangled."

"How come you're not with the others?"

Tom took a long pull on his draft beer and slammed the empty glass down on the bar. "Not a fuckin' camel now, am I? A canna be waitin' fer tha' shower a wankers."

The room had a few booths, a handful of tables and a long wooden bar. The place was packed with serious-looking drinkers, men with thick necks and faces that had been rearranged some, women with ponytails and bad teeth.

Cyrus leaned closer to the big Scotsman and said in a half-whisper, "I'm underage, I think. Why don't you see if you can buy me a drink?"

"I dinna think they give two fucks even ef ye came from Jupiter." Tom turned to the bartender and said, "Gie-us another, will ye? And a Bood-weiser for me mate here, Wing Commander Owen, who plays the guitar like a-ringin' a bell."

The two sat there through several drinks. With little prompting, Tom told Cyrus about the old days, booking concerts in Glasgow with Ronnie. In return, Cyrus offered stories of Wilbury. He couldn't get over the fact that this strange and curious creature beside him had followed a circuitous route from Scotland, and that Cyrus had, by a twist of fate, made his own way from Wilbury, and that they had both ended up in this smoky bar on the outskirts of nowhere, swapping tales of days gone by and, in the process, laying the groundwork for tales yet to come, tales that would now include them both. He felt grown-up and real and part of something. He felt that anything might be possible.

Tom excused himself to go to the washroom, and while he was gone, a woman sat with Cyrus at the bar. She said, "I heard your friend say you were a guitar player. I am so-ooo into music." Just like that her hand was on his leg, much too intimate to be merely friendly or an accident. And although he could hardly see her—he couldn't see much of anything through the haze of alcohol—she seemed beautiful and sexy and the embodiment of everything he had dreamed of.

When Tom returned to the bar, he understood the scene immediately. With a simple nod of farewell, he shuffled outside and back to the hotel. Cyrus ordered another round, and another, and got very stupid.

She took him to a frame house on a street of condemned buildings. The place smelled of natural gas and cat litter, and the woman led him up a rickety flight of stairs to a darkened room. They smoked something she called Thai stick, which was a hundred times more potent than the homegrown Janice got from her cousin outside of Toronto. The woman took her clothes off and danced around the room the way young girls sometimes pretend to be ballerinas. And she was laughing and singing, and then down on her knees undoing his pants, pulling him onto the floor where they fucked. There was nothing lovely about it.

He left the apartment around dawn and wandered the empty streets without a clue which way he was headed. Everywhere he looked he saw broken windows and the nervous scrawl of graffiti. In the parking lot of an abandoned factory, he threw up and, for the first time in years, let himself cry, not because he was in pain but because he was scared—of what might have happened, of what did happen, of how he had let a beautiful night become ugly.

Back at the hotel, he had just enough time to shower, pack his bags and climb onto the bus. They had a three-hour drive to Kitsee, Indiana, and for most of that time Cyrus busied himself with his guitar. Anyone else in his condition might have tried to catch a bit of sleep. But few things were as comforting to him as the weight of the Les Paul in his arms. Besides, he was young and resilient and, more than anything, wanted to understand that bridging chord he had discovered.

All his life he had played simple blues tunes, music that a self-taught sixty-year-old slave from the cotton fields could master on a dime-store instrument. Now, uncertain how to proceed, he wandered blindly up and down his fretboard, listening for something familiar. He started with a major chord, a G, added the dominant seven, the F, and knew it was still too pure, far too G-like even if he used the F as the bass note. Step by step he tried adding other notes to the chord—the E, the C, the A—trying different inversions with a variety of bass notes; and although he couldn't find what he was looking for, he began to appreciate that chords were more interesting than he had thought. Solos and riffs had first attracted him to the guitar; chords had seemed dull and faceless. Now he was beginning to see how complicated they really were.

When he caught Sonny watching him from across the aisle, he said, "I'm trying to find that chord you play."

"What chord you talking about, exactly? Been known to play a few."

"You know, that one you use as a bridge when we change keys. I can hear it now, but I don't know what it is or how it works."

Sonny looked at him squarely, and for once there was neither sarcasm nor disdain. "Try the dominant over a six," he said. When Cyrus gave no hint of comprehension, Sonny leaned closer and said, "What key are you in, G? Try a D chord with E as your bass note."

Quietly and carefully, he tried what Sonny had suggested. But without the context, he still wasn't sure. So he vamped for a while on G7, a funky little groove on a single chord, what a lot of Jim's music was like. After about sixteen bars, singing a little melody in his head, he slid up to the D chord and wrapped his thumb around the neck to play the E on the bass string— and there it was, a bridge, a shift to higher ground. By uniting those two elements, the dominant and the six, he had forced the melody into another key. With that one step he had made a return to G virtually impossible. The world had shifted to A.

Cyrus could hardly sit still. It was like finding a tunnel in the backyard or a hidden passageway behind a panel in his bedroom. He knew this would lead him somewhere interesting, maybe even to treasure.

RONNIE CONGER LOVED THE SOUND of spring peepers. They sang to him from the ditches and creeks of this back country road, mile after mile of them joined in a single voice. He loved especially the idea that he had brought this song together by his passage through this rural county, and that this song existed only for him. It was a symbol of his life, the nomad's world he shared with Jim and the rest. Some things exist only in the flow, and if you stop moving long enough to inspect it, to analyze it, the song, their song, would separate into discrete elements.

Not that they had stopped moving much over the three years since he had befriended Jim—hardly long enough to catch his breath, in fact. They had travelled up and down the Eastern seaboard, around the Midwest and central Canada, hoodwinking church groups wherever they went. In every town they used the church halls, ate the wholesome potluck dinners, counted on the promotional network and fundraising skills of each community and delivered, in return, the Jimmy Waters Revival, which was never what those good folks had bargained for and was, as a result, another bridge burned. Ronnie knew it was only a matter of time before every church group in America would be wise to them. Fortunately, he had reason to believe they were on the verge of better things.

Their first recording, "JimJam," had been a modest success. Adrian had recorded the track live at a show in Schenectady, and Ronnie, surreptitiously using the cash held in reserve from the lads' salaries, had had just enough money to press five hundred singles, with no flip side, and mail them out to radio stations across North America. The song got a fair amount of airplay on campus stations late at night. It seemed a good fit with Dr. John the Night Tripper and the Velvet Underground, a nice segue from Captain Beefheart. But those who looked for the disk in their favourite store were out of luck—it wasn't there.

Then, just two weeks ago, Nate Wroxeter came sniffing around, suddenly, no hard feelings. He had heard the record and, after a bit of negotiation, had agreed to set up a few gigs in the underground club scene. Better still, he had offered to front Ronnie enough cash to make a proper record and print up some bios, a few pics.

Ronnie had no illusions. He doubted they would ever hit the big time, but it was never about that in the first place, never about getting rich or wild excess or making history. It was something other, something pure and almost private. What mattered was that the band, after a number of false starts, was starting to jell. No one else believed him yet, but Ronnie was convinced that it was only with the addition of Cyrus that the group made sense, as though they had all been made for each other and, in coming together, created a perfect emotional space that, were you to hold it to your ear, would offer a heavenly sound.

RONNIE'S GOOD NEWS HAD AN IMMEDIATE EFFECT. They still travelled to a different town each day, still played concerts, but Sonny was spending all his free time in the Airstream with Jim, working on a new tune to record and sometimes calling in Chuck or Two Poops. Though Ronnie had lobbied on Cyrus's behalf, it seemed that guitar would not be required this time around, and that was a real blow for Cyrus. There was one consolation, however: over the next few weeks he had a lot of time to wander on his own.

Cyrus did that a lot in Wilbury, especially in the years after his parents died. Aimless jaunts down country roads and farmers' lanes, sometimes going all the way into town and cruising suburban streets that seemed as perfect and dreamy as something on TV; quiet rambles through neighbouring woodlots; or, best of all, wandering about the murkiest, muckiest reaches of the marsh and knowing intuitively that by simply being out in the world and open to suggestion, he would stumble on neat stuff: the snowy owl with the broken wing that he reported to the nature centre; the hobo living in the culvert by Spring Creek; the wheel from a DC-3 that landed in Curly Wilson's soybeans one summer.

Now, with the others busy working on a new record, he fell into the same old routine, strolling through these poky towns, nosing around the shops and parks and promising laneways, chatting with salesmen and waitresses, the average folk on the street. When he got back to the hotel, he'd tell Eura about all the wonderful things he had discovered. It was a successful outing, he felt, if he could make her laugh or raise her eyebrows in wonder.

One day, on a whim, he brought her a jar of pickles from Poland.

"What is this, Cyrus?"

"I don't know, I thought you might like them. I thought they'd remind you of home."

"Home I remember, thank you. Besides, these will remind me of Poland, which also is not necessary."

A few days later he popped into a photo booth at a train station and sat for the standard goofy poses—sticking out his tongue, goggling his eyes, puffing out his cheeks. When he returned to the hotel, he gave the photos to Eura. "Here," he said. "So you can remember me."

"I see you every day. Besides, these will remind me of what is not you, which is, I think, useless."

On a day off in Blayne, Missouri, they went for a picnic in the park. It was a beautiful afternoon in mid-June, eighty degrees with a light breeze, a blue sky dotted here and there with flat-bottomed clouds like ten-gallon hats. They stopped at a grocery store for bread and cheese, a whole salami and a bottle of Spanish red. Then they spread a blanket beside a pond and lazed the day away.

Eura sang to him in a language he didn't understand, ancient-sounding melodies in an ancient-sounding tongue. With his head in her lap, she braided the ends of his long silky hair. When she finished, she swept the bangs off his forehead and said, "I look at you and I am sometimes angry with the Jimmy Waters Revival. You are so young to be living this life with us. You should be eating pie with your aunt and uncle. You should be having a sweetheart and going to dances and driving around in a big American car. You should be falling in love and making foolish plans, and instead you are here with us."

"Who says I'm not falling in love?"

"I say this," she replied, pushing him roughly away. "And if you do not believe me, I will hit you."

He shifted then, so he was lying beside her, his face pressed lightly against her hip. He knew that if he touched her anywhere else their afternoon would be spoiled. He was content to smell the warm cotton of her summer skirt and beneath that the subtle florals of her perfume.

A while later she said, "Tell me about a time when you were happy."

"I'm happy right now."

"No, when everything seemed perfect."

He thought a moment and said, "I remember one time, I'm pretty young, not even in school yet, and I'm on the kitchen floor with a toy truck. My mother is there in the picture, or at least her legs and feet. She's cooking dinner, and I'm driving my truck between her legs, probably making her crazy. And I can hear her singing, which is the best part. My mother loved to sing, and she had a real good voice, too. Her folks were rich, I guess, so she took lessons when she was a kid. You know that kind of fancy vibrato in opera? She could do that. You'd never know it to look at her, though, a bony little thing like a bird."

Eura looked down at him and said, "Your father, he was rich, too?"

Cyrus laughed at that and rolled onto his back, his arm draped over his face. "My dad was about as poor as they come. His folks had a farm on the marsh. When my parents got together, her folks had a fit, I guess. Her dad was a doctor and had big things planned for her. After Mom and Dad got married, her folks never spoke to her again. They moved to San Diego a while after that. I never did meet them."

"She must have loved your father very much."

"Oh yeah. You see pictures of him from back then and he looked like a movie star—real handsome. A baseball player when he was younger. My uncle says he never saw anyone throw a ball better'n my dad. He was scouted by the Tigers and spent some time in the minor leagues. Then one day he got hurt and went back to the farm. Never played again."

"It was better for him, perhaps."

"Farming? I don't think so. He was never much good at anything to do with farming. What I heard, his father wasn't much better. When Dad took over, he had all sorts of big ideas, but nothing ever worked out, and we lost the farm, lost everything."

She turned on her side until she was facing him. Running her hand across his cheek, she said, "That is not such a happy story, Cyrus."

"You tell one then."

"I am tired of my stories."

WITH EVERY PERFORMANCE, Cyrus got better at following the twists and turns of Sonny and the rest of the band, and on the night after his picnic with Eura, he had his best show ever. Everything seemed to work. In one song, he and Jim got into a call-and-response thing, Jim saying, "I know," and Cyrus answering with his Les Paul: *dwee dow.*

"I know."

Dwee dow.

"I know."

Dwee dow.

"I know that my heart is a canyon deep and wild."

Dwee dow dweedy-oh dweedy-dweedy-deedah-dwee.

After the show, Cyrus was so pleased he could hardly sit still. As he walked with Eura toward the bus, he realized he couldn't face the prospect of moping around in his room. What he wanted was to sneak off with her. So he grabbed her by the arm and said, "Let's walk back."

She studied his face a moment and shook her head. "I know what you are thinking, and you should think of something else."

"I want to walk back to the hotel with you."

She pushed his hair off his shoulder and let her hand linger at his neck. "You want more than that. But I will tell you what. You should go on the bus with the others. Let Sonny tell you what a genius you are."

He handed her the Les Paul instead and walked into the night. He followed the main street until it ran out of buildings and headed into farm country, past big brick turn-of-the-century homes, wide fields and little wooden sheds by the road where the wife or maybe the kids would sell produce when it was in season. It was a beautiful night, the stars shining brightly, the air warm and full of familiar smells: freshly turned earth, the sweet stink of cattle and the unmistakable perfume of strawberries.

So many times he had wandered through the dark in just this way, after a fight with Clarence or Izzy, after a night with Janice, or sometimes after nothing at all. It was almost as if, in the darkness and the solitude and the subtly shifting textures of the night, he felt more at ease, more deeply connected to the heart of things.

He got back to the hotel well after midnight. The lights were on in the

Airstream, but there were no sounds of music or talk. Upstairs in the hotel, he listened a moment at the door to Adrian and Kerry's room and, from the quiet, could tell there was nothing happening there, either. But he wasn't tired; he was wired. So he drifted down the hall to Eura's room. He could see a line of light from under her door. He knocked softly.

After a moment she said, "Go away."

"My guitar," he said. "I need it."

"We are leaving early tomorrow. You need to sleep."

"I want my guitar."

A minute later she opened the door and backed into the room as if she was afraid to stand too close. She was wearing a bathrobe, which she clutched tightly around her.

His guitar case sat on the carpet just inside the door, but he walked past it, looking greedily around. "This is the first time you've invited me into your room," he said.

"You invited yourself."

On her bedside table she had spread a white cloth and hundreds of silver pins. Beside the cloth sat several glass vials, each one holding a different coloured liquid. A faint smell of rubbing alcohol lingered in the air.

"What are you doing?" he said, nodding toward the pins.

"I am minding my own business. You should do the same."

He leaned back against the wall and shook his head. "Why won't you let me get close to you?"

"You are close to me."

"Not close enough."

She tightened her grip on her robe. "Close enough for now."

Without another word he grabbed his guitar and walked to his room. Sonny was snoring inside, so Cyrus sat in the hall beside a room-service tray of dishes and began to noodle on the unamplified instrument. In his head he heard a mid-tempo shuffle in G, very B. B. King. He waited a moment, trying to retrieve that mood from his walk along the dark country road, trying to tap into that bottomless well of emotion. Then he played the seven, the F, and gave it a sweet shiver of vibrato. A few licks followed and they were good; but they owed more to B. B. King than his feelings for Eura or the mysteries of the night, so he stopped and tried again. This time he grabbed the A on the first string and bent it up a semitone to the minor third, letting it shimmer for a bar before wandering erratically through the blues scale. Again, uninspired. He tried starting on the fifth, on the major third; he tried it with the flatted third and the fifth plucked together. And each time he ended up with some awkward combination of notes that said nothing at all about the way he felt, and managed to say nothing in a way that was utterly graceless.

He was all too aware of the kind of music a real player like Sonny would produce under the circumstances, or the solo Eric Clapton would squeeze from his instrument if he felt even half as much for Eura. He launched into the guitar intro to one of his favourite songs, "Waitin' on You," by B. B. King.

Ba-doodle-la-doo dal-lee-doop
Ba-doodle-la-doo dal-lee-dah

That was the trouble. He could play nearly every blues solo ever recorded, from Robert Johnson to Johnny Winter. Every lick was memorized, categorized and catalogued, ready for instant recall. But when he tried to come up with a single phrase that summed up how *he* felt about Eura, there was silence, or worse, noise.

He studied the fretboard of the Les Paul. Clearly, there were only so many notes and, therefore, a limited number of combinations. Maybe that was the problem. Maybe everything that *could* be played *had* been played. And with that thought he packed away his guitar again and set it inside the room. Then he went back out to the parking lot. Just the sight of the night sky made him feel better. The Big Dipper and Cassiopeia and the great arc of the Milky Way reminded him that some things were inexpressible. He had nothing to be ashamed of. Perhaps Eura was too big and too distant and too bright to be captured by a few melodies.

Bringing his gaze back down to earth, he noticed Jim out by the Airstream, coaxing the dog to do its duty. Before Cyrus could slip away, Jim turned and said, "It is a magical night out here, my son. The wind sweeps toward us from across the continent, bringin' us a million stories." He tucked the dog under his arm, then closed the distance between them. Putting his other hand on Cyrus's shoulder, he said, "What's wrong? You look as though your heart is in your throat."

When Cyrus shrugged, Jim leaned closer to peer into his eyes. After a moment, he smiled and said, "If I'm not mistaken, this *is* a matter of the heart. You're in love."

Cyrus looked away. "Not love," he said. "More a feeling of—" he dragged a hand through his hair "—I don't know, of feeling like the whole world is trying to pass through me, only it can't."

"What's stoppin' it?"

"I don't know. I was playing my guitar before I came out, and when I closed my eyes I could feel it there as sure as anything, this big, big thing just waiting, but I couldn't find the right notes, you know?"

"I do. And I'll tell you this. I don't want to hear about your guitar right now. This is no time for musical theory. Talk to me about love." And with that he set the dog on the ground and covered Cyrus's eyes with his big fleshy hand. "Do you see her? Tell me now, what's the first thing you think about?"

Cyrus could feel a blush creeping up his neck and cheeks. His skin burned where Jim was touching him. After a bit of squirming, he closed his eyes beneath that massive hand and said, "Her lips, I guess. Her lips are great." And it was Eura's lips he pictured, like the graceful wings of a seagull in flight.

"Mmm-hmm, very nice. Her lips. You kiss her then, maybe pull her bottom lip right into your mouth like it's a section of Christmas tangerine, and your hands, your hands are wild for somethin', aren't they? Sure enough have a mind of their own. You reach out and . . ."

"I touch her hair, her head."

"Yes, indeed, you muss her hair and tilt her face so you can kiss every nook and cranny. She's wild for you, too, isn't she? What's she doin', Cyrus? How's she touch you?"

Cyrus can scarcely breathe. In his mind Eura is rocking against him in that graceful dance of hers. And in a hushed voice, he says, "Her hips."

"Oh my my, she's a devil, rubbin' her sweet thing against you. She wants it bad, and all you gotta do is sing the song, my friend, cozy up and sing the words she wants to hear."

Jim removed his hand and Cyrus said, "What words does she want to hear?"

"I would ask you the very same thing."

Cyrus wheeled around and took several steps toward the hotel. Turning there, he said, "I don't get it. I never know what you're talking about."

"I don't suppose you do. But you were sure enough with me tonight."

"Onstage, you mean."

"Yessir, you were right there with me. It was good what you did, playin' off my words like that. Works both ways, you know."

Cyrus nodded uncertainly, then walked slowly across the parking lot. At the hotel entrance, he stopped once again to look up at the stars. In just a few hours he had gone from fulfillment to longing. He had taken his playing to a higher place and discovered almost immediately how much farther he had to go.

Ronnie knew Wade Resman from the early days, working side by side on that first tour of America with Scot Free. Back then Wade was owner and chief technician of a company called Resman Sound and Light, renting out the appropriate gear for rock-and-roll tours and, for the right price, acting as soundman. Drugs, a bitter divorce and a serious lack of insurance had brought Wade to the brink of bankruptcy. He was now permanently off the road and had invested his last few dollars in ReSound, a low-end recording studio on a desolate stretch of county road between Buffalo and Rochester.

Wade had set up shop in an old general store—white clapboard, wide wooden veranda, with thick black curtains covering the plate glass window at the front. On one side of his property was Vinnie's, a big auto-wrecking yard with a high plank fence topped with razor wire; on the other was a scrubby field covered with billboards, none of which had been updated in five years. It was not a busy road. The only noise Wade ever had to contend with was Vinnie's arc welder, which occasionally set up a high-frequency hum in the studio's amplifiers and mixing board.

It wasn't for sentimental reasons that Ronnie chose ReSound for Jim's next recording. It was the fact that they got four days of unlimited access, the use of all the gear, Wade's not inconsiderable talents as an engineer, and a sixteen-track tape for the cost of one day in a more established studio. So what if the place had a Hell's Angels vibe? So what if everything was held together by duct tape? It was good enough for rock and roll—a statement that, to Ronnie's mind, was less a compromise than a seal of approval.

The night before the sessions began, Ronnie asked Cyrus to drop by his hotel room. "I suppose you have already surmised what I'm about to say, my friend, but frankly, it looks as though this project will have to take wing for now without your fine talents." The boy stared sullenly at the carpet. Ronnie squeezed his shoulder. "What this means, Cyrus, is that the rest of the week is yours. Perhaps there is something you've been meaning to do. Visit the family, see the sights. Eura, too, is at loose ends. I have already offered the use of the Fairlane should she wish to travel somewhere. Possibly you two could work something out in that regard."

Eura called Cyrus shortly after that and asked him to drop by so they could make plans.

"You're inviting me in?"

"To talk, yes."

He noticed immediately how tidy her room was—both beds were made, no clothing anywhere. She'd done something to soften the lighting, too. She wore the same bathrobe he'd seen the other day, her hair still wet from the shower. With a wave of her hand, she indicated he could sit on the bed. She remained standing by the television set.

"What did you have in mind?" he asked.

"Well, Buffalo—this is a fine place to leave us." She took a deep breath and looked across the room to the door, as if having second thoughts. Finally she said, "It is not such a bad idea, I think, that we could maybe go some- where, the two of us. We have had some practice already. . . ."

Her voice trailed off. She pulled her robe more tightly around her. It was his turn to open up. "I think you already know how I feel," he said. "Why don't you just tell me what you're thinking."

"Because I am afraid of that. Maybe you will think I am crazy. Maybe you will not like me anymore."

"Maybe I already think you're crazy. Maybe I *don't* like you."

She stepped forward and laid her palm on the top of his head, as though

that might tell her something about him she did not already know. Before
he could grab her hand and pull her close, she moved away and disappeared
into the bathroom. A moment later she returned, carrying the white cotton
cloth he had seen before, and spread it on the empty bed. From her closet
she removed a small brocade bag, about the size of a purse; from inside it she
took several vials of coloured liquid, a small bottle of rubbing alcohol and a
plastic case filled with silver pins. She sat opposite him and said, "I do not
know where to begin."

He looked at the paraphernalia beside her, then back to her face. "Why
don't you just start talking. Maybe that'll lead you to the beginning."

She smiled that Cyrus could say something so wise. Summoning her
courage, she said, "The first thing I must tell you is that I am married to a
man I will love all my life."

Cyrus lay back on the bed and closed his eyes as she spoke of her
husband, of their apartment near the university where he taught botany, of
their two cats, and their windowsills thick with cyclamen and African violet.
Of the tanks that ended everything.

"He's still there?"

"I can only hope. I miss him more for every day I have been here."

"You could go back."

"No. Not possible."

"And he can't come here?"

"No one has seen him for months. They have taken him where they take
all enemies of the state."

"And that is . . ."

"I don't want to think."

The more she talked, the lonelier he felt. Every word moved her another
step away from him. All his boyish fantasies melted under the heat of her
deep love for her husband. He had thought that he might one day take away
her loneliness and pain, but he would be lost in the enormity of her suffering.

When she had stopped talking, he sat up and said, "You're telling me this
so that we can travel together and I won't act stupid."

"This is a reason," she replied. "Also, for me, so I do not act stupid. And
maybe because I need help, and fate is saying I should trust you."

That she would rely on him more than the others lifted his spirits. "Are you in trouble?"

She rocked her head from side to side, weighing the question. "Not in the way that you think. I need to ask a favour, and I need you to not think badly of me. I need you to be as kind and gentle as I know you are and to please not make judgment." Without another word, she opened her robe just enough to reveal her neck, a bit of breastbone and another portion of the tattoo. The vine rose in a sensuous line from the top of her breasts and circled the base of her throat. From there it spiralled up the left side of her neck and got lost in her hair. It was this last bit he had seen before. He recognized the plant from his years on the farm.

"Nightshade," he said.

"Belladonna, yes. His name for me, his 'beautiful lady.' He knew everything to know about flowers. Same family as potatoes and tomatoes."

She pulled her robe tightly around her again, then slid beside him, hugging his arm. He looked at the pins, the coloured vials, and said, "You did all that?"

In response she turned and pulled up her hair. The tattoo did not in fact circle her neck but stopped roughly under each ear. The final bits of leaf and flower lacked the definition of the rest. "You see," she said, "how I cannot reach. I am making a mess."

He touched one of the berries, a spot on her neck he would have thought impossible for her to reach. He felt an overwhelming desire to kiss each berry and flower and follow that vine wherever it would lead. Instead, he backed away and said, "It must hurt."

"Some parts are worse than others. I am used to the pain by now. But I am so slow. To look in a mirror and do this makes me want to scream."

It was then he understood what she was asking. "You want *me* to stick pins in you?"

She shifted a short distance away, the better to look into his face. "This is what I do. When Sonny and the others are jamming at the hall or shooting their pool or playing cards, I am here. It takes me very long to do even one flower, so I must work at it every day. If we travel, you must see me do this, that is all. And maybe, sometimes, if it is not asking too much, you could help with these places I cannot reach. It is not so hard, Cyrus. I can show you. Just ink on a pin."

He turned to the blank screen of the television, but he already had all the sad news he could handle for one night. Staring at his hands instead, he said, "I guess the big question is why? Why do you do it?"

She rose to her feet as though he had touched a sensitive spot. "Why do you play music? Why do others paint pictures and write novels? It is how we make sense of time."

THE NEXT MORNING, a Saturday, they set off in the Ford. Eura insisted they go to Wilbury. "If we could go to my home, I would take you there," she said. "We can't, so we go to yours."

Cyrus knew it was the right thing to do—let everyone see he was happy, healthy and alive—but he wasn't sure he had the strength just now to answer their questions. Eura was adamant, however, and by midday they were on the outskirts of Wilbury. He pointed out landmarks. He tuned in the local radio station. And little by little he warmed to the idea of showing Eura his roots. He was amazed, too, how different everything seemed. It wasn't that the town had changed, but that he could see it more clearly.

He still had a key to the Three Links Hall, so he headed there first, figuring they could flop for a bit while he made a few calls and figured out a plan. To his surprise, the band's gear was gone, the furniture, too. It had never occurred to him that everyone would pack it in after he left. Eura waited patiently while he worked out the puzzle.

He knew that Isabel worked on Saturdays, so they got back in the car and headed downtown. He pointed out the Vogue Theatre, and the greasy spoon where he and his friends congregated after school or rehearsal. At Demeter Real Estate, he took two steps into the room and stopped: not only was Izzy not at her desk, but her desk was gone. So were her filing cabinets and the framed print of kids skating on a frozen pond.

Larry Bell looked up and said, "Hey, Cyrus, long time no see. How's the gee-tar comin'?"

"Okay, I guess. Where's my sister?"

"Come again?"

"Isabel. Where is she? Where's her stuff?"

Larry scratched his head and laughed awkwardly. "Jesus, Cy, she hasn't worked here in a while. She's at Regal now."

He drove farther down the main street, turned the corner at Woolworth's and parked in front of Regal Real Estate. He was relieved to see Isabel's familiar belongings inside. Nellie Griswald was bent over the drawer of a filing cabinet when he walked in. "Hello, Mrs. Griswald."

"Cyrus? How are you doing? You just missed her. She goes home for lunch these days. How's the music?"

"It's good," he said. "Real good."

Then he ran back out to the car and flopped in the seat. "Just missed her," he said, feeling oddly elated, as though it had all become a game, an elaborate chase. "Drive out this way," he said, pointing to the west. "We'll catch her at the farm."

They passed the water tower, the train station, and the farmers' co-operative. He pointed out the gravel pit on the Fourth Concession, and on the Fifth, the acres of greenhouses that belonged to Mike Delvecchio, the richest man in town. When they turned onto the Seventh, he had another and even bigger shock. Regal Real Estate signs were tacked to fence posts along Izzy and Gerry's farm, announcing it was for sale.

Cyrus told Eura to pull into the driveway. He knocked at the door, but there was no answer. He walked around the house, peering in the windows. The place was empty. Not a stick of furniture. Back in the car he held his head in both hands. "It's like a bad dream," he said.

A moment later Eura touched his arm. "Someone is behind us."

He turned to look out the back window and felt an immediate wave of relief sweep over him.

ISABEL HAD PLANNED to go home for lunch but instead had a burger at A&W. Lorrie Buxton, another agent at Regal, had shown the farm recently and had forgotten to put the key back in the mailbox, so Isabel had offered to do it for her. She wanted to look around and make sure everything was okay, knowing from experience that some agents could be real slobs.

Isabel was pleased to find another car in the driveway. She parked behind it and took a moment to check her look in the mirror and slip into performance mode, all energy and twinkle. When she was ready, she got out of the car and walked slowly toward the house, as if to illustrate that country-side like this demanded a slower pace, an appreciation of earth and sky. She approached on the driver's side, smiling her most benevolent smile. But the minute she noticed Cyrus in the passenger seat, her heart lurched. To go months without seeing him, and then to come upon him suddenly, in a strange car with an older woman—older than Isabel, even—was a shock.

He opened the door and stepped onto the driveway. Isabel said, "If it isn't the prodigal brother."

He looked at the house, the barn, the road. "What's going on, Iz?"

"It's been an interesting few months."

They followed her back to town and the little bungalow she now called home. The short drive allowed her to calm down, remind herself that Cyrus was a man now. She would try not to judge or jump to conclusions.

At the house, Cyrus made the introductions. Isabel said, "Del Conte, is that Italian?" And the woman laughed and said, "For some it is. For me it is a foolishness. A stage name."

"So you're a performer like Cyrus."

Eura touched Cy's arm. "He is an artist. I am a clown."

"Don't believe it, Iz. When she dances, it's like ballet or something."

Isabel put water on for tea and set out a few stale biscuits and a couple of apples, cored and quartered. She called Nellie and said she wouldn't be in till Monday. When everything was ready and they were seated around her kitchen table, she turned to Cyrus and said, "So fill me in. You left in kind of a hurry."

True to form, he kept his explanation brief. He managed to hook up with the Jimmy Waters Revival, he said, the right place at the right time. They had travelled to a new town almost every day, mostly in the States. Great bunch of people. It was hard to explain what kind of show it was.

He looked to Eura for help, and she nodded at Isabel and said, "It is not what you think, this wild music and people you see on TV. Someday he will maybe go off on his own to be young and reckless. The Jimmy Waters Revival will not hold him long. But for now he is safe."

Soon enough it was Isabel's turn to explain about Sheldon Demeter, the farm, the divorce.

Cyrus listened carefully, the skin around his eyes going all crinkly, as if he were hearing about some gruesome medical procedure. "Wow," he said, "that is such a kick in the head. What are you going to do?"

"Do?" She spread her arms out. "You're looking at it, Cyrus. The good life."

Her answer seemed to catch him by surprise. He looked down at the table and back up again. "What about Clarence and Ruby? How are they taking it?" he asked.

"I don't know. Okay, I guess. Ruby's saying her prayers. Which reminds me. We should let them know you're here. You are staying awhile, aren't you?"

He shrugged. "I'm not sure how welcome I'll be out there."

"Stay here," Izzy said automatically. "Eura can have the spare room. You can have the sofa in the den."

"I hate to be a bother, Iz. Maybe a motel or something."

"Your sister," Eura said, "is worried. Can you not see? You should spend some time here with her. Besides, I have seen enough hotel rooms for a while. If she is kind enough to ask, we should be smart enough to accept."

Isabel wasn't sure what the relationship was between these two, but her brother could do worse, she figured, even with the difference in age, even with the foreign accent and the bit of tattoo on her neck.

RUBY INSISTED THEY COME FOR DINNER, and Isabel took everyone in the Buick, first driving out to the marsh so they could give Eura a glimpse of the farm they used to own. With Cyrus fidgeting in the back, Izzy described how the early settlers had built a dike (what was now the Marsh Road) then drained the land and set to farming it. She caught his eye in the rear-view mirror and said, "Wait till you hear the latest. A company in the States sent geologists up here to do some tests. People think there's oil out there."

Cyrus snorted dismissively. "Sounds like another bullshit story Sam Loach dreamed up."

"Well, Sam's involved all right, but it wasn't his idea by a long shot. They signed him up just like they signed Benny Driscoll and most of the other farmers out here."

"They're selling out?"

"Not selling, no. They signed a contract. This company pays a flat fee to drill test holes. If they don't find oil, that's the end of it; the farmers are all up a few hundred dollars and no sweat. If they do, then Sam and Benny sell the oil rights for so much a barrel. You better believe half the folks out here are dreaming in dollar signs these days."

When Cyrus stepped from the car at Orchard Knoll, Blackie was all frantic, poor fella, nuzzling and whining. Ruby kept turning Cyrus around, kissing his cheeks, touching his hair and hands. "I have *prayed* for this day," she said more than once. With Eura, however, both Ruby and Clarence were overly polite, as though they were saving all their warmth for Cyrus.

For dinner, Ruby had cooked his favourites: cornflake chicken, coleslaw and mashed potatoes with mushroom gravy. As the evening progressed, and as they found out more about Eura—a co-worker, that's all, a friend—their uneasiness with her faded away. Clarence, in particular, became most attentive. Cyrus and Isabel exchanged glances more than once as they watched him pour on the charm.

After dinner they sat in the living room with tea and *kuchen*. Blackie lay at Cyrus's feet. Clarence said, "Ever since you've been gone, you know, Ruby has found herself a new little friend. I hardly see her anymore."

Ruby rolled her eyes. "It's nothing of the sort. I've just had a few visits with that nice Janice Young. She's even come to church with me."

Cyrus laughed out loud at the idea of Janice in church. "How is she?"

"Oh," Ruby said, "very well, I think. She's excited about some new idea of hers. Won't tell me what it is exactly." Then she sighed deeply and said, "You'll never know how much you scared the dickens out of her, out of all of us, Cyrus, running off that way."

"I never intended to leave so soon. It just sort of happened."

Clarence snorted and said, "Your aunt here was having conniptions when they found that body out by the pump. I told her you could look after yourself, but she wouldn't listen."

"What was *that* about?" Cyrus asked. "They ever solve the mystery?"

Ruby sat forward on her seat. "No, they did not. And imagine, they're pretty darn sure this poor fellow was a musician. I would have had kittens if I had known that at the time."

"They don't know for certain," Isabel countered. "That's just a suggestion from the autopsy."

"A bass player, wasn't that the idea?" Clarence asked. "Had to do with the calluses on his fingers." He looked at Cyrus. "That sound right?"

"Makes sense. There'd be the regular calluses on his left hand. And most bass players don't use a pick. I know Seth used to get huge blisters on the index and middle finger of his right hand."

"That's right!" Ruby exclaimed. "That's just what they said last week in the *Gazette*." She walked over to the wicker basket that held their newspapers and rifled through them a moment. "Here," she said, pointing to the article, "just like you described it."

What caught Cyrus's eye was the photo of the dead man—just a kid, really—and underneath it, the caption: Do You Know Him? Cyrus handed the paper to Eura and was about to change the subject when he noticed her take a deep breath and quickly fold the paper in half. Her hand trembled slightly when she gave it back to him. And in that moment the subtle clues and suggestions of the past few months came together, and he knew it was this mystery man, not fate, that had brought Ronnie all the way to Wilbury.

AFTER IZZY WENT TO BED, Cyrus waited an hour before he slipped off the sofa and tiptoed to the spare room. He knew Eura was awake. He leaned closer to her in the dark and said, "It was him, wasn't it, the bass player before me."

She rolled over to face the wall. "You should go to sleep."

"I can't. I keep thinking maybe we should call the police."

She sighed deeply and turned back to him. "Do not think too much about this. It is not for you. I will handle Mr. Ronnie Conger."

Then she lifted the edge of the covers for him and he nuzzled closer. When he tried to kiss her, she turned him around so his backside nestled against her and she could press her face between his shoulder blades. When he tried to reach behind to stroke her leg, she grabbed his hand and tucked it against his chest. "Be thankful," she whispered. "It has been a good day."

He was tempted to try again to embrace her, but he thought better of it. He was happy enough to be in her bed and to have her arms around him.

JANICE HAD TAKEN OFF her Sunday skirt and blouse and had just pulled on jeans and a T-shirt when Cyrus rang the doorbell. When she saw who it was, she threw open the door and ran straight into his arms. "You bastard," she said, squeezing him with all her might. "You prick." Then she untangled herself and dragged him toward the den, half-running, half-skipping, all the while keeping up her tirade. "You prick, you bastard." She threw him onto the sofa and straddled him, gazing excitedly into his face.

He touched her cheek and fought back the lump in his throat, completely undone by the sight of her. "You're looking good, Janice."

"Fuck you, Owen. Fuck you. How could you just disappear like that? You're such a prick. And I've got so much to tell you."

He laughed, because her energy was irresistible. And he said, "Well I hear you've been going to church with Ruby. What's *that* all about?"

She rocked her head from side to side. "I've been on such a trip this past while, you wouldn't believe. Me and Ruby, every week at St. Mike's. Can you believe it? I've been reborn." A troubled look flickered across his face, and she hugged him once again. "Not like you're thinking, you big dope. But everything's changed. Come on, I'll show you."

She was on her feet again and dragging him upstairs to her room. The walls were covered with drawings and paintings: pencil, pen and ink, charcoal, acrylic, watercolour, gouache, tempera. There were plaster moulds and sculptures, metal pieces welded together to make goofy-looking statues, mixed-media jumbles made of wood, cloth, bits of coloured plastic and scraps cut out of photographs.

Cyrus held his hands atop his head like a prisoner of war and said, "What is this?"

She stood behind him and wrapped her arms around his waist. "This," she said, "is my future."

"Since when? You hated art, remember?"

"Yeah, well, surprise, what I hated was Velma Fleck's stupid ideas about art. Five years, Cyrus, five years and the only thing she taught us was to draw what you see. If she said it once, she said it a thousand times. 'People, people, people: draw what's there!' And then it hit me that she was all wrong. Art isn't drawing what's there, it's drawing what's *not* there. And when I figured that out, I knew it's what I completely had to do."

She circled him until they were standing cheek to cheek. "Speaking of what's needed," she said. She began to undo his jeans.

He swallowed hard. "Look, hold on." He led her to the bed and sat beside her, taking her hands so he could keep them under control. "I came back with a friend, and we were planning to be here a few days, but something's come up. We're leaving soon." He shrugged. "I couldn't go without at least seeing you . . ."

"Oh. Well. Sure. Now you know I'm fine, right? Now you can just piss off again."

"Janice, don't be mad."

"I'm not mad. Besides, I'll be gone soon anyway. I've applied to the Ontario College of Art. Come September I'll be in Toronto." She took his hand, kissed the palm and said, "What about you, Cyrus? How's the gig?"

He had practised countless times the little spiel he planned to give her, about the adventure, the education, the electricity of life on the road, but his words got tangled in his discomfort. He shrugged and said, "I think I'm in over my head, but I'm learning tons and getting paid and travelling. It's mind-blowing, really. You wouldn't believe these people." Then, unable to resist any longer, he leaned forward and kissed her, pulling her bottom lip into his mouth. "Don't hate me," he said.

She pushed him back and shook her head. "What I hate is not talking to you. No one understands, Cy. They think I'm screwing up my life."

He wasn't exactly sure *he* understood, either, except her sense of frustration. He wrapped his arms around her and rocked her side to side. "I'm on the road all the time, kind of unreachable. But I'll try to stay in touch. And wherever you end up, tell Ruby your address and phone number. I'll do the same, if I ever get settled. That way we can always track each other down."

He kissed her one more time and got to his feet. "An artist," he said, warming to the idea.

She watched him walk to the door and was tempted to run after him. Instead she fell back and closed her eyes, remembering a sunny autumn day in grade nine, the two of them walking along the railroad tracks after school and revealing secrets that made them special. She was doing most of the talking, telling him how much she admired her dad, what a great guy he was. And then she realized what a stupid thing that was to say to someone without a father.

At first Cyrus didn't reply. He picked up a cinder and heaved it at a hydro pole. "My uncle's pretty great, too," he said, unable to meet her gaze. "Clarence bought me a guitar. It's nothing fancy, but it's pretty cool. Electric and everything. I pick it up sometimes and don't even play a note. I just hold it, you know? I just hold it."

He looked up at her, half expecting her to mock him. Instead she smiled, and he smiled back. They each took a step forward. And another. She lifted her chin. He lowered his head. Their first kiss.

CYRUS AND EURA DROVE straight to Buffalo, the American plates on the Ford all the passport they needed to cross the border. They got to the hotel late in the afternoon and walked directly to Ronnie's room.

"Ah, my wandering friends," he said when he opened the door to them. "I had rather expected you would stay away a good deal longer, visit a few scenic locales."

"We did," Cyrus said, pushing into the room. Eura followed him and they sat together on the small brown sofa. "We went to Wilbury."

"But of course, the home ground. Your family is well?"

"Just great. And guess whose picture we saw?"

Without waiting for a response, Eura pulled the *Wilbury Gazette* from her bag and handed it over.

Ronnie studied the picture a long while. Then he sighed and said, "Yes, now I see. You have cut short your vacation because you are looking for an explanation. You want to know how this all came about. You want to look into my eyes for signs of guilt. Ideally you want me to tell you a story that will allow you to sleep with a clear conscience."

"The truth maybe is more what we were thinking," Eura replied.

Ronnie sat on the edge of the coffee table, his head bowed, his hands clasped. "The truth is a slippery thing. Let me tell you what I know." He seemed relieved, as though he had been longing to speak of this matter.

"When I first met Cal," he said to Eura, "he was in much worse shape than even you, my dear, so deeply broken I never would have chosen him had I known. But in his short time with us, he did make great strides. I saw you and the others take him under your wing, and for that I cannot thank you enough. We did more for that boy than anyone had ever done before. He told me so himself, not in so many words, of course—he was not much for sharing vulnerabilities—but in little ways."

He looked out the window then, weariness lining his face. "Twice in our short time together I found him unconscious in his bed, an overdose. It was frightful, I can tell you, to see him lying there like a corpse, that beautiful boy. Both times I dragged him into a tub of ice water. I slapped his face and pinched his arms and legs. And both times, you know, his eyelids flickered, and I was able to pull him onto the floor and towel him dry. Then I walked him up and down the room, plying him with room-service coffee and chocolate bars until finally—and I will remember this all my life—he struggled out of my grasp, backed up a few steps and blew me a kiss, like a Hollywood starlet saying farewell to her fans."

Ronnie got to his feet, jammed his hands into his pockets and began to pace the room. "I curse myself for not being able to save him a third time, but for a few blessed months, we gave him music. Surely you remember his face onstage. I could weep right here just thinking of it. Such pure joy and surprise. No matter that he was hopeless on his instrument, no matter what hell he put me through each day, I was repaid each night by that face. Was it not spectacular, my dear?"

Eura nodded soberly. When she started to speak, he stopped her by holding up his hand. "No one knew where he was from," he continued, "or if Cal was his real name. But one thing I know, he deserved better than to die in some second-rate hotel on the outskirts of Ironville. So I asked a few of the lads to help me lift him gently into my car, and I drove until sunrise and lo and behold I was in a beautiful place, with fresh breezes off the lake, and fruit trees and big black fields. I sat him up against a building so that he could look across to a distant horizon. I placed all his favourite things around him and bid him farewell. How could that be wrong? How could any of that be wrong? Tell me one thing you would have me change."

"Maybe truth is slippery," Eura said, "but so is poetry. What do you think, Ronnie, that it would matter to Cal where the police found his body? But it would matter to you and Jim."

"My dear girl, be reasonable." He held his hands out like a minister urging his congregation to put their trust in the Lord. "Of course it matters to Jim. That is precisely the point I have been trying to make. And it matters to me and you and Cyrus here. It matters to Sonny and Tony and all the people we touch. There is not one of us who came untroubled into the fold. I don't know how or why it has happened this way, but we are, almost in spite of ourselves, a healing machine. So yes, there was another motive. What we have here is something larger than all of us, something that I, for one, do not understand. But I know one thing: our being here, our journey from town to town, makes the world a slightly better place and makes our lives more respectable. Who is willing to tamper with something like that for the sake of formalities?"

SEVENTEEN

The Ontario College of Art turned down Janice's application. She'd been too late with her forms. Better luck next year.

Deciding she would not give up so easily, she travelled by train to Toronto, where she asked for and got an assessment of her portfolio. One week later, she received a letter from one of the instructors she had met, Jonathan Davis. "While the submitted work is unquestionably of some merit," the letter stated, "we do not feel it warrants special status for admission."

Her parents believed that would end it. They had planned for Janice to study law at the University of Toronto, just like her father had, and for the longest while that had seemed to her a logical step. But not anymore. She moved to Toronto in September and found a basement apartment. She worked as a waitress in a string of crummy restaurants: a coffee shop at the train station, a greasy spoon down by the beach, a well-known chop house near the racetrack, walking her feet off for puny tips and maximum hassle. In her spare time she worked on her portfolio and audited courses. She cruised the museums and art supply stores.

Early the next spring she read about a new restaurant, Kolours, that would be opening soon. It sounded hip and fun, and she dropped by while the place was still being renovated and talked the manager, Kostas Louganis, into giving her a job. He looked like Yul Brynner in *The King and I,* right down to the thick gold earring. Even standing amid the construction debris and plaster dust of his would-be restaurant, she could tell he was the most handsome man she had ever met. Just looking at him made her blush. Thinking about it years later, she came to believe that he was the best thing that happened to her that year.

When Kolours opened, it *was* fun. Its white walls were brightened here and there by flashes of floral accents. The wait staff were smart and energetic, the food inventive. At that time in Toronto, those wishing to dine out had few choices—either overpriced steak houses or a handful of French restaurants that had the gall to set up shop in franco-phobe T.O. The city had never seen a place both lighthearted and dedicated to fine food.

Janice didn't have the natural gifts of a great waitress. She was not outrageously pretty or voluptuous, and she had no reliable tricks for improving her memory. She frequently forgot part of an order and had to ask who ordered what. That she garnered more tips than anyone else was a source of genuine mystery to the rest of the staff—but not to Kostas. "People like you," he said.

Because of her tips, she was able to work a four-day shift, and that left her plenty of time to work on her art, write in her journal, read, walk, cook. She was learning so much, she wondered how much value there might be in formal schooling. Besides, being around Kostas was an education in itself. Every Tuesday night, he opened the bar and kitchen after-hours so his friends—musicians, actors, writers—could come for a proper meal. The musicians played, and people sang and danced and talked until, inevitably, Kostas ended up alone in the kitchen, weeping about the beauty of his life.

It was during one such evening of wine and food, music and song, that Janice saw Jonathan Davis a second time. "I remember you," he said, looking a bit glassy-eyed. "Have you applied again?"

"Still thinking."

"Really. A change of heart?"

"You might say that. I'm learning a lot on my own. And I don't really know how much you can teach art anyway."

He smiled. This was funny. "Is that what you think we do, teach art?"

She folded her arms and leaned back against the wall, feeling woozy herself. "Silly me," she said. "Tell me then, what *do* you do?"

He moved closer. His words when they came were hushed, as though he were sharing a great secret. "We create tension," he said. "We are an engine of frustration. On the one hand, we give you the tools and space and time to do whatever you please. But we also take great pains to point out to you— and this should not be underestimated—that virtually any idea that comes into that brain of yours has already been done to death."

"Perhaps you've been teaching too long. You sound bitter."

"Do I? I don't feel bitter. Maybe a little drunk. And lonely. How about we go somewhere and fuck."

"Sorry. I never fuck lonely drunks. So you might as well point that engine of frustration somewhere else."

"Hey, that's funny."

"Well, you're not."

"No, in fact I am funny. And smart. And lots of other good things. I'm just a little drunk right now. Why don't you give me your number and I'll call you when I'm in better shape."

"I don't think so. That student-teacher thing, you know."

"So you are applying."

"Haven't decided yet."

"Well do it. There's no other option if you're serious about art."

"Funny, but you'd never get that impression talking to you."

"Truth in advertising. Art's a pain in the ass. You have to be insane to think you'll ever be successful—a bit of wisdom you'll never read in one of our course outlines. But if you find the prospect exciting—and I confess, I think it's a brilliant way to spend your days—then apply. But don't say I didn't warn you."

Three months later, in September 1972, she started classes. Her parents cheered up, now that she was enrolled at a legitimate school, and agreed to pick up her expenses and tuition. Even so, she continued to waitress three nights a week.

Throughout that first year she worked with the Virgin Mary and Christ in different situations, different materials. Jonathan had been right: the school provided a banquet of opportunities—metal, pottery, neon, wood, fabrics—and ample time and space to investigate them. Wisely, she remained focused on the one theme, exploring its significance across a broad spectrum of possibilities. As a result, at the first-year students' year-end show, her pieces stood out as the work of an artist with vision, though one of still-limited abilities. Kostas, as proud as any father, bought several of her sketches for the walls of his restaurant. "I put big price tag on each," he said slyly. "*Huge* markup. When they sell, profit is yours."

He took *Motorcycle Mama,* a pencil sketch of the Madonna in horn-rimmed glasses, capri pants and a sleeveless top. A brooding Brando figure in leather jacket and jeans slumped between her legs and smoked a cigarette. He bought a series of small pen-and-ink sketches, too: of a boy sitting motionless on a swing with his mother sailing high on the seat next to him; his mother giving him an "underdog"; his mother perched on the bar above him and looking down with a serene grace.

Janice's favourite piece in the show, which no one bought or seemed to understand, was a painting she called *Coming Home.* It showed a grey-haired woman standing in the driveway of a farm, a spooky old house looming in the background and the fields spreading out to the horizon where storm clouds are massed. The woman is supporting a large Latin cross with the transverse beam braced on her arms, and the upright resting on her shoulder—not as Christ would do it, facing away from his burden so he might drag it through the town, but rather embracing it, giving it her love. More than anything Janice had ever done, it seemed to convey a hint of the invisible. She was glad no one bought it. She wanted it for herself.

EIGHTEEN

In the winter of 1973, Isabel and Gerry divorced. She had dated a few times over the past year, but romance was a low priority. Since the farm had sold, she'd been plotting out the best use for her share of the money. She knew she ought to let it sit in treasury bills awhile—she had a job, she could cover her expenses easily enough—but the thought of that money ate at her. She thought she could take her little nest egg and build something substantial with it.

Reg Foster actually had the nerve to phone her with an investment tip, something about a boatload of sugar sitting off the American coast. "Guaranteed 25 percent profit," he said. "In three months." But she squared her shoulders and told him to go fuck himself. It was something she'd been dying to do for ages but hadn't, for Gerry's sake. Her only regret was that she didn't say it to his face.

Invest in what you know, that was the conventional wisdom. If it was true at all, it left her with limited options: real estate and farmland. So when Jeb Wheeler started to make noises about putting his forty-acre parcel up for sale, she drove out to look at it.

Jeb was a widower with no children and had landed in a nursing home after a stroke. He wanted to sell the land fast, thinking he'd need the money to tide him through his final days. But vacant land that hadn't seen a plow in ten years would be tough to move, and she told him so.

He closed one eye and thought awhile. "What's the going price?" he said weakly. "I heard Boychuk got five hundred an acre."

She moved closer so he wouldn't have to use so much effort. "Ron Boychuk had a better location, tilled fields, and even with that he waited three years to get his price. I honestly don't know who'd be interested, Jeb."

"But you'll give 'er a try, won't ya, Izzy girl?"

She came back the next day with a proposal. She'd buy it now for a minimum bid of $250 an acre, a round figure of $10,000. She'd keep the land on the market four years, the first year at $500 an acre, the second year at $400, the third year at $350, and the fourth year at $300. Whatever it sold for, she'd take back her ten grand and give him the remainder, minus fees.

"Could be I'm a dunderhead," he muttered, "but I don't see where you'd wanna be doin' that, Iz, tyin' up your own money attaway."

She took a deep breath and laid her cards on the table. "Seems to me you've got immediate financial needs, Jeb, and I can help. That's a fact. And here's another: the bank'll give me 6 percent on my savings. In other words, if I give you the use of my money for four years, I give up $2,400 in interest—a fair piece of change."

"Sure as shootin'."

"And here's why I'd do that, Jeb. I don't think anyone will want your land anytime soon, but I've got all the time in the world. So if no one buys your land, I give up $2,400 in interest and get your place for $5,000 less than I figure it's worth. You win, I win."

"Course if I die tomorrow, you make out like a bandit."

She smoothed the wrinkles on his dry old hands. "I think you know me well enough to know that's the last thing I want, Jeb."

In the end, he accepted her offer. He died six months later. Now she owned a useless piece of land that would cost her five hundred dollars a year in taxes. Two weeks after Jeb's funeral she was complaining about that very thing to Ross Pettigrew, the golf pro at the local course.

"I'd give my eye teeth for a piece of land like that," he said. "A town this size and we don't have a blasted driving range. It's ridiculous."

Never one to back away from a good idea, Isabel made Ross an offer. She'd provide the land, he'd manage the property and arrange for everything else: the clubs, the markers, the driving pads, maybe a prefab building and a pop machine. In no time they'd each be clearing a minimum of five grand a year—a perfect money machine.

Those were fine times for Isabel. She loved her house, her job, her new-found freedom. Since the divorce she'd flown off for two quick getaways, first to Chicago, then New Orleans. She and Ross had a four-day weekend of golfing in Phoenix planned in the new year. He was too young for her, but what the hell.

The last week of August she drove to Willbourne to visit Hank, just as she'd done about once a month since he'd moved there. Getting his spine rearranged had in many ways straightened Hank right up. Some of the anger had been bled from him, the edge dulled. Two years in a wheelchair had taught him a little patience and self-respect. Ruby called it a miracle. Isabel wondered if it wasn't more a necessity.

She wheeled him into the gardens rather than sit inside. Her first words to him—and it had been that way all summer—were about Benny Driscoll, how rich he was getting, how the land first farmed by their family was sitting on an ocean of oil. If there was one irritant in Izzy's life now, it was this scab that needed to be picked. She drove to the old place some nights to watch the gas flare burn, the marsh painted a lurid orange. There was a new paved road and a concrete bridge over Spring Creek. The Bailey bridge had been too small for the drilling rigs and the oil trucks travelling to and from the wells; and rather than tear down the original structure, they plunked the new one beside it and moved the road over. There were storage tanks, too, and a scattering of pumps that worked night and day. Although no one had seen official figures, it was rumoured that Benny and the farmers surrounding him were each pumping a thousand dollars a day out of the ground. The idea of it made her weak, as if it were her life they were pulling from the earth.

Hank found it all very funny, called Benny and the others the Wilbury Hillbillies. If he had any bitterness, it was about their father. "He would have blown that chance, too, he was such a loser. I bet he wouldn't have signed the agreement in the first place."

They sat together in the sun, eating a couple of peaches she had brought. During the past few visits she'd begun to talk about the future. She had already set in motion a request for an occasional day pass. In a few years he would be eligible for parole, and she had suggested he live with her in Wilbury. Her house had only one floor, and she could get it outfitted with ramps and handrails. The prospect made Hank feel nauseous.

When he finished his peach, she gave him a paper towel to wipe his mouth and said, "What if I can swing an outing? Any preferences?"

He looked across the garden, a grin easing into place. Then he turned to her and said, "I'd love to see the kid play. He's coming, you know. I heard it on the radio. That'd be cool, wouldn't it, seeing the kid play?"

THE JIMMY WATERS REVIVAL was on a roll, and had been since the release of "JimJam #2 (The Door)."

Wade Resman turned out to be a genius, pulling together one of Sonny's incomparable grooves, Jim's rap and a weird-ass background of jungle percussion and layered keyboards. As a final overdub, they got Cyrus to play a solo over the fade-out. Wade had wanted a sound that was full of echo—like Jim's dad fading into the sunset with the radio in his arms—so he laid Cy's amp inside the grand piano and wedged the sustain pedal down so all the strings inside could vibrate in sympathy. A single note from Cyrus set up a hundred overtones.

It stirred something in radio programmers, too. The day the single was released, it started to generate excitement. And with the success of that record, Jim was signed to a major label. They recorded two LPs, both of which cracked the Hot 100. The tours took on a different tone. Nate Wroxeter was on the case these days, and all the papers were in order—the visas, the manifest, the tax forms. Jim bought himself a brand new Winnebago, and a refurbished Greyhound to replace the school bus. They graduated to a better class of hotel, a better sound-and-light system. They were booked into rock clubs and concert halls, with cut flowers and platters of food and buckets of Heineken in the dressing room. And fans. Young men came to study the guitar wizardry, the keyboard magic, the complex rhythms. Some worshipped Eura's every move. But most came for Jim, believing he had something important to say and would one day make it clear to them.

Cyrus, who had always wanted to belong to something large and bewildering, arrived at the gig in Toronto long before the scheduled sound check. He loved to sit in a hall and watch the beautiful chaos of the road crew nimbly manoeuvring through the sprawl of drums and speakers and microphone stands. The crash and boom, the heft and groan, the feedback, the laughter—it was the kind of scene you might find at the heart of a busy port, the pandemonium that speaks of a world in transition.

When it was his turn onstage, he fingered his favourite lick:

Ba-doodle-la-doo dal-lee-doop
Ba-doodle-la-doo dal-lee-dah

And as he played, he concentrated on the pure physical path of his music, how the vibration of the strings above his pickups created an electronic pattern that passed through his guitar cord to his amplifier, where various vacuum tubes and diodes and condensers translated that pulse back into sound, but larger and louder and infinitely variable. From there, a microphone in front of his amp picked up those notes and changed them once again into a flow of electrons, which raced down a series of cables and connectors to the back of the huge mixing console out front, where Adrian worked his magic—boosting this frequency, tamping that—so Cyrus's notes would, in theory, fit perfectly into the acoustic space. Reshaped to this larger purpose, his music moved on to the massive amplifiers beside the mixing console. These, too, boosted the strength of the signal, making it heavy with promise. From there, that pumped-up electronic sculpture travelled, via two thick cords, to the side of the stage and plugged into the tower of speaker bins positioned there, whereupon the notes, Cyrus's notes, came roaring into the open space like the voice of God and echoed off the back wall to greet him.

He wondered sometimes whether his own life would follow a similar path, whether he would trace a helter-skelter pattern across the globe, honed and sculpted by the rigours of the road yet gaining strength and power. He believed that a larger destiny awaited him than that of a faceless sideman in the Jimmy Waters Revival. And while the band's recent success pleased him, it was Jim's scene, his gig, and they were all in tow to make it real.

When Cyrus put down his guitar and moved off stage, Tom lumbered over and said, "Cuppla wankers out front say they know ye." He wiped his nose with the back of his hand and added, "The one, a fair old boiler, says she's yer sis."

It took a moment for the news to sink in. If Cyrus had been expecting anyone to show up, it was Janice. But preparing himself for the sight and sound experience of Isabel did not prepare him for the shock of seeing Hank fidgeting in his wheelchair. Cyrus had written a few postcards—"Greetings from The Buckeye State!" "Georgia's Just Peachy!"—but had never made it to Willbourne. He was shocked the difference a few years had made. His brother seemed to inhabit half the space he used to, so gaunt and grey that Cyrus could scarcely believe he was only thirty-three.

"Hank," he said. "Isabel. Jesus, what a surprise!"

HANK BELIEVED IN THE ROUGH HAND OF JUSTICE and was glad he'd been caught and punished. And though he couldn't remember all the crimes he'd been charged with, he could remember some. His punishment, even if you included his brush with death and subsequent paralysis, was the type of accounting that jibed with his personal moral code: you do wrong, you pay. It was a kind of harsh bookkeeping that was easy enough to calculate within the narrow confines of a prison.

From the moment Isabel came to fetch him for his weekend pass, however, he began to suffer unfamiliar pangs. His paralysis had seemed a minor grievance within the context of his prison term, but when they drove away from Willbourne he was shocked to see normal people going about their normal routines. In some part of his brain he'd forgotten how much latitude a person had in life. Men and women jogged along the river. He saw whole families riding bicycles together. And the traffic—he was certain that when they first locked him up the world hadn't been so chaotic.

Then there was Izzy herself. He was used to the idea of her as an independent woman, a wheeler-dealer, and he'd seen for himself the improvements in her wardrobe, the expensive jewellery. But the car, a royal-blue

Mercedes sedan with cream leather seats—why hadn't she told him about that? The minute she peeled out of the parking space, he felt queasy. He remembered how much he loved driving the old man's pickup, the thrill of fishtailing on a gravel road, the sexual tingle as the pedal touched the floor and the needle ticked over to a hundred. And if driving that pickup had been special, a clunky rustbucket stinking of feed and manure, what kind of kick would a machine like this be, with the freedom to cruise the radiant high-ways of the promised land?

Isabel seemed to be wired on amphetamines. When she wasn't chattering non-stop, she was singing along with the radio. She talked out loud to the other drivers. "Oh, nice. Hey, maybe signal, fella. Come on, Granny, move it or lose it." At first he found it funny, all her blather. But after fifty, sixty miles, he began to tire of it. In Portland, and even at Willbourne, he very seldom had a conversation that lasted more than a couple of minutes. Even the few visits he had each year were brief, because whenever he'd had enough he would shoot the guard a certain look and the ordeal would be over. Now he was stuck in the all-too-cozy confines of a luxury sedan with no way out. Worse, he'd forgotten how every moment out here was a potential decision. Stop for coffee? Want a doughnut? What about the scenic route? Mile after mile, his mood grew darker and heavier, until he wished he'd kept his mouth shut about seeing Cyrus play. He had half a mind to beg Isabel to turn the damn car around and take him back to his cell. But that would have been uncool, and the only thing he had left was his cool, an attitude that said, "You can lock me up, you can break my body, but you will never frighten me." He couldn't very well show his little sister how much her presence unnerved him.

At a truck stop, Isabel got them burgers with fried onions, and a couple of milkshakes. They ate in the car in sudden and blissful silence. He chewed slowly, the food tasting of memories. When he finished, he crumpled his paper wrappers and said, "The last time I had fried onions on a hamburger was the Wilbury Fair."

He closed his eyes and remembered the midway, the crown and anchor games, the saltwater taffy and cotton candy and the irresistible sweetness of fried onions. He saw Jenny Duckworth in her white blouse and black slacks, crossing her eyes at his dumb jokes. They shared a burger and fries, then

wandered over to the horse barns where they patted the quivering rumps
of Clydesdales. Upstairs, above the stalls, they admired displays of prize-
winning pies and crocheted doilies, foolscap sheets covered with the hand-
writing of schoolchildren. And best of all, no matter how he turned the
memory, he found nothing unhappy, nothing dark or disagreeable. Just two
kids having fun.

He turned to Izzy and said, "What happened to Jenny Duckworth?"

"I don't know that anything ever happened to her. She married Bill
Wittle, the guy she'd been dating since grade 12. They bought the house next
door to her parents. She works as a cashier at A&P, just like her mother. Bill's
a trucker for Jenny's dad. It's like a script."

Hank whistled his amazement. "Bill Wittle. I always kept my distance
from that little prick. His whole family was nuts. Poor Jenny." Then he
laughed out loud, one little bark, because it was an image he would never
have conjured on his own—Jenny and Bill.

They drove into Toronto on Highway 401, and Hank sat wide-eyed and
white-knuckled as they rocketed through the tangle of cloverleafs and over-
passes, surrounded by twenty lanes of hurtling metal and menace. They
turned south on the Don Valley Parkway, and ten minutes later turned onto
a congested street in Greektown. Halfway along the block to his right was a
grubby-looking theatre called The Music Hall. The marquee announced that
the Jimmy Waters Revival was playing that night at eight.

"Hey," he said, remembering what the whole day was about. There was
a dreamlike quality to those letters up there, that frame of unlit bulbs. It didn't
seem possible that he could be here and seeing this.

Down the street, he saw a few dismal shops and a scattering of Greek
restaurants, and he ached with longing for the feel of pavement beneath his
feet and the seduction of lights and faces and window displays, all of it,
everything, as alluring as a centrefold. He rolled down the window and
sucked in the aroma of car exhaust and roasting lamb, then turned to Izzy
and said, "You think he'd be here yet? I mean it's only, what, four?"

For the first time since they had left Willbourne, Isabel seemed at a loss.
She chewed her bottom lip and stared at the traffic streaming by. "I don't
know," she said. "I mean, look at all those trucks out front. And that

Winnebago. Looks like someone is here." She got out of the car, set up the wheelchair and helped Hank into it. "Let's see if we can find him. If he's not around, we can go for a stroll."

The front of the theatre was unlocked, and Isabel manoeuvred the wheelchair through one set of doors and was halfway through the second set when one of the members of the road crew walked up to them, a short, squat fellow with stringy hair, a Scottish accent and a face like a brick wall. He softened considerably when Isabel introduced herself.

A CLASH OF ANXIETIES held the three siblings speechless. Only twice in twelve years had they inhabited the same space, and that had been in Portland, with Ruby and Clarence coaching them along and acting as buffers. Here, in the lobby of the Music Hall, they were on their own.

Isabel had never been behind the scenes of anything more exotic than a high school play. Nor had she ever been to a rock concert. Her tastes ran more in the direction of Johnny Mathis or Gordon Lightfoot. To stand in this dingy lobby, amid the clang and clamour of a show coming together, to see these rude-looking people (like the slab-faced Scot who had fetched Cyrus), the dirty T-shirts, the long greasy hair, the hefting and grunting and swearing, and her brother here, sad sweet Cyrus, a person from another world now, with different clothes and different hair and a different way of standing, was more bewildering than anything she had ever encountered. And as she struggled to take it in, all this newness, she felt put-upon and angry. Why, she wondered, did the simple desire to see Hank or Cyrus involve such a struggle on her part? Why couldn't they be farmers, say, or accountants or sales clerks? She could have handled a simple visit to Toronto or Montreal, could have handled spouses and children. But no, Hank lived in a prison, and Cyrus lived nowhere, drifting across the face of the planet like a thunderstorm, all flash and crash and chaos.

Hank, too, was thrown into a darker mood. If Isabel's life filled him with regret at the thought of all he'd missed, all he would never have, to look at Cyrus was agony. His little brother had become everything Hank once dreamed of. He was handsome and confident and living a life of adrenaline and spectacle. He was making a noise, causing a disturbance, and the world was applauding.

Cyrus was in no better shape. He pumped Hank's hand vigorously. He pecked Isabel on the cheek. But even these simple physical actions seemed unreal. And he laughed and said, "Wow. I mean, this is weird. Hank? Jesus, you're out. Izzy?" He looked at his watch. Ninety minutes at least until the full sound check. "I guess we should . . . I mean, this calls for a celebration, doesn't it? Izzy? We should go for a drink. I mean, Jesus, give me a minute here, I'm losing it."

He grabbed his forehead as though it might come flying apart. And when he looked at his brother again—poor Hank, a pale frail shadow of his former self—Cyrus did lose it, his hand sliding over his eyes to hide his tears and then further down to his mouth to hold in any sounds he might make. That's all Isabel needed to get started. They each turned away, as though it was a crime to feel this way.

HANK AND IZZY GOT THE BEST SEATS in the house, behind the mixing console in the middle of the theatre. There they met Adrian and Kerry, the funny-looking Welshmen who worked the sound and lights.

"Right," Kerry said, "another pair of hands never went amiss. Glad to have ya." He gave Isabel control of stage lights numbered one to four. Whenever he called out a number, she was supposed to bring the fader all the way up or all the way down, depending on its position at the time. "You'll get the hang of it," he said with a wink.

Adrian sat Hank to the extreme right of the mixing console, where he would be out of the way—Adrian had to do quite a bit of dancing around during a show—but also where Hank would have access to the fader that controlled Cyrus's volume in the sound system. A strip of white adhesive tape had been placed beside each fader, with a red marker indicating the neutral position. With each fader on its mark, the sound, at least during the sound check that afternoon, was in perfect balance. For solos, you nudged the fader up so the instrument would ride above the mix. If someone got too loud on stage, the fader would be edged lower to bring their sound back into the mix.

Hank's palms were sweating. Isabel was equally nervous. Watching the crowd file in, listening to the hubbub, she couldn't remember the last time she'd felt this kind of childish anticipation.

With a blink, the lights in the hall went out, and Izzy caught her breath. She couldn't see anything but the little red dots of the console, the green glow of the amplifier meters, and then—and this sent a ripple of excitement through the crowd—the bob and weave of flashlights leading the band onstage. People began to cheer and whistle as, one by one, the flashlights made their flickering way off to the side of the stage again. Then, out of the darkness, a voice: "All this way. All this time. And now you're here. And we're here. Like it was meant to be. So put your groove in motion. Put your heart in gear and give it up for the man, little doggies. Put your hands together and give a great big T.O. welcome to *The Jimmy Waters Revival!*"

A blaze of lights, a blast of sound, a change so sudden and fundamental it's as though the increments of daybreak have been fused into one brilliant moment. A thousand fists salute, a thousand voices lift in greeting, some people already on their feet and making their way to the front of the stage.

There is colour and noise and action. A great bear of a man in a black leather suit lumbers up and down the stage, whipping the crowd into a higher frenzy whenever he approaches. The drummer on his riser, a man consumed with fever, thrashes out a rhythm with his arms and legs, body and head. Another man, pouchy and grizzled, crouches like a *bandito* behind his barricade of keyboards. And another, surrounded by toys—conga and clacker, whistles and wood blocks, rattles and shakers, gourds and gongs—leaps up and down to the beat like a diver on a high board. A woman, Cyrus's friend, half-dances and half-glides about the stage in a leotard and skirt too delicate for words.

At first Izzy can't find Cyrus. It's all too confusing. But then she spies him between the drummer and percussionist. He's dressed in white, his hair a golden swirl, his mouth a thin red line. He seems far too serious for a night so bright, as though each note is a matter of grave importance. The drummer twirls his sticks. The singer rants and rages. The percussionist urges the crowd to clap along. But Cyrus is still, contained, rooted to his spot onstage. Izzy loves his little mannerisms: the way he fusses with the knobs of his guitar, the nod of his head before he begins a solo and the way he rubs his nose when he finishes. Every now and then he bends slightly forward, not in any pattern but with a secret rhythm, and she thinks of a flame atop a slender candle, sensitive to every whisper and breeze.

As one song follows another, she begins to settle back in her seat. She brings the lights up or down on command. She begins to understand which sounds belong to Cyrus. It is all too loud, of course. Any other time she would cover her ears. But this is invigourating, like standing outside in a summer storm and not giving a damn if she gets wet.

And what could compare to the final song of the night, a long bluesy number about Erie, Pennsylvania, and family abuse and a big old radio. Near the end, the singer falls to his knees, his hand stretched out like he's touching a wall. Right on cue the stage lights wink out, and a single spot-light focuses on Cyrus as he plays a solo so eerie and echoed and high above their heads, like lightning, like northern lights, that it gives Izzy goose-bumps. Then one by one, two by two, and finally hundreds upon hundreds of hands rise from the crowd, each hand grasping a lighter, each lighter sending up a single quivering flame, a sight so beautiful and tender it takes her breath away.

Hank's experience is different. He has looked forward to this night, and knows the music as well as anyone. But the volume, the press of all these bodies and the significance of what he's doing are too much, the way the soothing murmur of voices can be raised to a level and intensity that becomes a weapon. The bass notes sound like thunder and pummel, the snare drum a thousand slamming doors, the guitar and keyboard needles and pain. With each song he slumps lower in his chair. He closes his eyes and forgets about the knob that controls Cyrus's volume. When the last notes have echoed, when the house lights have come up, he remains perfectly still, drawn into himself until the storm has passed.

AFTER CYRUS HAD SIGNED AUTOGRAPHS and posed for pictures, he found Isabel and Hank near the mixing board. It was clear from the look on Izzy's face that there was no point in trying to tell her how poorly they had played; she wouldn't believe him. Instead he let her splutter and exclaim until her fervour abated. Hank didn't say much at all. Mr. Tough Guy.

Izzy suggested they stop for drinks at the hotel room she had rented. So they hopped into the Mercedes and headed for the Royal York. On the way,

Cyrus heard the latest: Clarence had regained some weight; Ruby was as strong as a horse; Blackie had died; Benny Driscoll had built a mansion north of town; and Janice had spent the summer in Italy with one of her instructors. About herself, Isabel said that life was treating her well—and that much was evident from the Mercedes. When Cyrus asked her if there was a man in her life, she smiled and said, "Several."

At the hotel they ordered beer and munchies, then kicked off their shoes. Being together had stopped feeling like some crazy dream and begun to seem a natural possibility.

Hank lifted his bottle. "Cheers, kid. You're a real star."

Cyrus waved his arm in the air before anyone could drink. "No, forget that," he said. "I didn't even play well. It's you, Hank. It's your day. I mean, it's historic."

Isabel raised her bottle to both toasts, but anyone studying her face would have seen the shadow of restraint, the hint of pain. Neither of them had toasted her. But then they wouldn't, would they? It was always the same, the two boys seeing each other, understanding each other, and giving no thought to her. It was the way of the world. People focused on the extremes and paid no attention to what really mattered—the good and the decent and the selfless.

The more she drank, the gloomier she felt. Cyrus did all the talking, telling them about the things he'd done, the places he'd been, the lessons he was learning about music and life. She was surprised at how self-obsessed he'd become, how insensitive. Every one of his stories seemed to deflate Hank a little more.

Unable to stand it any longer, she brought her beer bottle down with a *thunk,* and said, "Well, Cy, that's enough about us, what about you?"

He flinched at the sarcasm and sat up straighter. "I thought you might find it interesting."

"Baloney. You don't give a hoot what we're interested in."

Cyrus squinted at her. "What's your problem?"

"My problem," she said, enunciating perfectly, "is that you're full of yourself."

Her face just then—the older-sister look, as if he was completely hopeless, completely useless—added a little heat to his next words. "You can't stand to hear how great my life is," he said, "because it makes yours sound like shit. You're jealous."

She looked at Hank, who was fidgeting uncomfortably, and then back to Cyrus. In a cool, measured voice she said, "I don't envy you at all. Right now I pity you because you don't have any idea what you're doing. If you did, you wouldn't act this way."

He nodded his head and got to his feet. "Just so you know, I'll tell you what I'm doing, Iz. I'm walking out that door and going to my hotel. Tomorrow I'll be back on the road making a name for myself, and before you know it, I'll be rich and famous and you'll be a fat middle-aged real estate agent in Wilbury who never did anything. Big deal. And then we'll see who's acting right and who's acting wrong." He clapped his brother on the shoulder and walked out of the room.

When Hank said, "I wish he could take me with him," Isabel threw a handful of ice cubes at his head.

CYRUS TOOK A CAB to the Park Plaza and went straight to Eura's room. His guitar was there; the pins and ink were on the bed. She had waited for him, even though it was late. She poured him a glass of wine, as she did every night, and they sat quietly awhile.

For two years now he'd been her accomplice, helping tattoo the hard-to-reach areas. In return he was allowed to watch her work. He knew better than to expect a show of skin; she went about her business in a modest way, opening her robe just enough so she could concentrate on the chosen area: a flower here, a bit of vine, a red berry. What brought him back each night was the feeling of intimacy. Not only had she shown him her secret and enlisted his help, she had grown increasingly comfortable in his presence. They often sat for hours, Eura bent over some part of her body, Cyrus absently exploring the fretboard, and chatted amiably about the silliest things, like an old married couple after dinner. Twice since Wilbury he had spent the whole night with her, but both times were innocent, with Eura hugging him from behind and holding his hands in hers.

She dipped a finger into her wine, brought it to her lips and said, "It is too late to work now. Tell me about your night with your brother and sister. Were they very impressed?"

He didn't have the courage to mention the argument. He couldn't bear

for her to think poorly of him. Instead he said, "More shocked than anything, I guess." Then, needing to say something truthful, he began to tell her
about Hank—the troubled boy on the marsh, the hardened criminal at
Portland Penitentiary, the broken man of Willbourne. And in saying the
words out loud for the very first time, Cyrus realized what a sad story it was,
how sorry he felt for Hank, for Izzy, for all of them.

He turned out the lights and sat on the floor with his guitar. It was
becoming a minor-chord kind of night, and every song he played sounded
with heartbreak. Every phrase had a face and a history and a sense of loss.
Sometimes a note would shimmer, a single note, and try as he might he could
find nothing that followed, and it would hang there, growing sadder by the
moment, until it fell of its own weight.

Finally Eura said, "This music is too full of tears for so late at night.
How am I supposed to sleep?"

In reply he put aside his Les Paul, kicked off his clothes and crawled
under the blankets, not with his bottom tucked against her but sliding
into her embrace, their lips and bellies and hips aligned. This time she
put up no argument but matched him sadness for sadness. When at last
they were still, he nuzzled her ear and said, "From now on, no more
tears." And she hugged him with all her might and wondered how anyone could be so young.

Next morning when she awoke, Cyrus was on the floor again, tooling
around with his guitar. She smiled uncertainly. "Play a happy song," she said.
And without a second's hesitation, he launched into "Waitin' on You." This
time he even scatted along:

Ba-doodle-la-doo dal-lee-doop
Ba-doodle-la-doo dal-lee-dah
Ba-doodle-la-doo dal-lee-doop
Ba-dweedy-eedy-ooo
Baba-do ba-ba-da . . .
Baba-dwee doody-ooo
Doodle-oodle-ee-doo . . .
Ba-do-dah dweedy-eedy-ooo

Dal-lee-doo
Ba-dwee-dee
Ba-dwee-doo.

Her smile broadened as she propped herself up on one elbow. "What kind of song is this to sing, 'dweedy-eedy oodle-ee-doo'?"

He thought a moment and, after a few false starts, came up with two lines of his own:

Don't know what you do with your lips,
Don't know what you do with your hair.

Eura fell back on her pillow, unaware that something significant had sounded in the room. But Cyrus looked at his guitar, at his fingers and then over to the soft snuggled form of his heart's desire. He wasn't sure what had happened, either, but he knew something somewhere had shifted, as clear and fundamental as a switch from sleep to wakefulness. He took a deep breath and tried again. Ten minutes later he had it.

Don't know what you do with your lips,
Don't know what you do with your hair,
Don't know what you do with your hips,
But baby, I declare
That my heart's on fire.
I'm in love with
The itty-bitty things that you do.
Now if you really want to know—
It's unreal
How I feel
About you.

WHILE CYRUS AND EURA MADE LOVE, Ronnie huddled on the floor of his hotel room and sipped a tin of milk. He had just spoken to Delmore Hinton, an agent in the U.K., who had called to confirm that the band was booked on *Top of the Pops,* with a tour to follow starting in six weeks. Even better, the latest single was number eight on the BBC.

The news didn't surprise him. It was all a matter of faith, he figured, ever-widening circles of belief. Jim's solo had created a believer in Ronnie. Ronnie then broadened the circle to include Sonny and Tony and Chuck and Eura. It came to include Adrian and Kerry and the rest of the crew, young Cyrus and Nate Wroxeter. The record company believed. Now, two albums later, the circle continued to expand with each concert, with every record sold, a growing army of believers out there, the faithful. If anything surprised Ronnie these days, it was how easy it had been to set a world in motion. The hard part would be to step back and, in a Seventh Day frame of mind, savour what he'd done. Because if there was a problem, it was this: he had no vocabulary for bliss, no grammar or syntax, and the words he did have were worth nothing at all. One might as well use numbers and equations to describe a sunset.

So what do you do when a dream comes true? Do you laugh? Do you cry? Do you gibber like a monkey? Or do you sit on a scratchy carpet in your boxer shorts, aching with the loneliness of a young god?

He could pick up the phone and order anything he desired—food, drugs, sex—but where was the sense in that? Instead he got to his feet and turned on his cassette player. He owned only the one tape, which held but one song. He stood there with his head bowed, his eyes closed, and listened, scarcely breathing.

For most of his life, Clarence had dedicated himself to avoiding change, or at least minimizing it, his life a constant battle with blights and bugs, jet stream and market. He and his father and grandfather had created acres of identical fruit by grafting each tree by hand. He knew exactly when to prune and spray and thin, and he never wavered from his duties.

His efforts to maintain the status quo were grounded in an appreciation of risk, of what was at stake when things went awry. He had crop insurance for freak hailstorms and May frosts. He read every bulletin from the Department of Agriculture. Lately he had taken to buying futures contracts on Chicago Mercantile, which cost him a few pennies here and there per bushel but were a sensible hedge against a blind drop in prices. And although he never in his wildest dreams worried about losing the farm (he'd have to be a complete fool to foul up an enterprise as successful as Orchard Knoll), he worried about falling short of the mark. He was the third Mitchell to work this farm, and all his life he'd admired the efforts of his father and grandfather. He'd inherited good land, good trees, as generous a growing season as he would find in Canada. More than anything, he'd inherited a sense of natural responsibility. This was not just a job. He was the caretaker of a precious resource.

The only area of his life where he'd failed at risk management was his friendship with Riley Owen. He had tried to protect his friend, to keep him happy and healthy, especially in those first years after the war. But Riley's confidence was so shaken, his unhappiness on the farm so palpable, that he seemed to lose the will to do the right thing.

Clarence, a teetotaller, followed his friend into the Wilbury Hotel and tried to cheer him up. Riley would nod and listen and make promises. Occasionally he'd perk up and try something new, like the year he planted a field of pumpkins, or the time he was convinced he'd make it big with egg-plants. But he always ended up in worse shape than before, wallowing in his failures. He drank more then, his mood darker and angrier. Sometimes he took it out on Catherine; and Clarence, thinking the alcohol complicated matters, refused to accompany his friend into the hotel anymore. So Riley drank alone, or worse, with men who had even less character than he did.

Clarence, so accustomed to the trade-offs that made life pleasant and predictable, didn't know how to deal with his friend's behaviour. It sickened him to see the boy with the golden arm become a slouched and bitter drunk, a man capable of beating a child with a broom handle, of smacking his beautiful wife for trying to intervene. After a while, Clarence gave up on Riley, crossing to the other side of the street if they happened to be walking toward each other.

That went on for the better part of a year, maybe as much as eighteen months. Then one night in early December, he was coming home late from a town council meeting. It was pissing rain, almost sleet, and he saw Riley stumbling along the road by the golf course, without a hat or coat, his pickup likely in a ditch somewhere—it wouldn't be the first time.

Clarence pulled his truck to the side of the road and opened the passenger door. He knew there'd been more trouble with Hank the past few months. The boy had run off that summer after torching the chicken coop. And the rumour was that Riley was close to losing the farm. So it was pity, more than friendship, that made him stop. It was freezing out there.

Riley slid onto the bench seat without a word, and they drove slowly out to the marsh. Clarence pulled into the parking spot by the house but didn't turn off the engine; all he wanted was to get home to Ruby and a hot cup of tea. But Riley turned and in a lumpy-sounding voice said, "Want that glove back yet?" And before Clarence could respond, Riley started to blubber. It was Catherine this and Hank that and what a great big fool he had been, what a stupid, awful man.

In the first lull, Clarence took a deep breath and said, "I'm not sure I want to hear this, Riley. I don't really know what you want me to do."

Two nights later, both Riley and Catherine were dead.

Thinking about Riley's troubles, Clarence was reminded that some things are immutable, or should be. Do your best. Love your kids. Pay your debts. Care for the sick. Stick by your friends. And until recently, he would have added one final, sacred constant: adore Catherine. But sadly, that bright light had faded, especially in the years since Cyrus had gone. The boy had resembled his mother enough that he'd served as a reminder of her beauty and goodness. There had been times in the past when Clarence had cursed the resemblance, but now, with Cyrus gone, Clarence felt some crucial nerve had been severed.

People in town figured it was the cancer that had caused his long, slow decline. And, no question, his health was largely to blame. He felt sometimes as though life were oozing out of him, drop by drop. He was beginning to cut corners on the farm. The yield wouldn't be as high, but what did it matter? It wasn't as if they needed the money. He'd mentioned to Ruby at breakfast that morning that he was thinking of retirement.

"Oh, brother. That'll be the day."

"Sure," he said. "Get you one of them condos down by the marina. You'd like that. I know you would."

She got up from the table, rinsed her teacup and set it on the rack to dry. Without looking up from the sink, she said, "What would *you* do? I don't know if I could stand it if you were any more miserable than you are now." She shot him a look. "Giving up never made things better."

Since breakfast he'd been sitting on the sofa in the barn. Sitting and thinking—that was all he seemed to do anymore. He struggled to his feet and wandered around the orchard a bit, stopping every five minutes or so for a rest. He crossed the yard and began to circle the house, studying the flower beds as though he'd only just noticed them. As he turned the far corner, he looked in the living room window and saw Ruby crouched beside her table of knick-knacks, her eyes closed, her hands clasping a porcelain figure of Jesus.

The sight of her there, praying like a child, stopped him in his tracks. He was looking into the past at a young girl, long before her parents had moved away or her sister had died or her husband had grown cold and indifferent. He was looking at the present, too, at a woman of fifty-eight years, almost thirty of them married to the same man, a woman who believed in the resurrected Christ, in miracles of love and redemption. But there was the kneeling bride as well, weeping under her veil, weeping in his arms that night in Niagara Falls, and giving him so many years of unquestioning love, honour and respect. This collision of Rubys, her ever-changing face coupled with her perfect constancy, produced an emotion more complicated than he could handle. He turned away from the house and stared across the yard to the barn, wondering what on earth had gotten into him.

FOR TWO SUMMERS IN A ROW, Janice had flown to Florence with Jonathan Davis. They were attracted by the galleries and museums, especially the Uffizi, but the wine and food were important, too. So was the shopping. On their second visit, they drove to Siena to look at the marble quarries. Janice had already worked with soapstone, alabaster and limestone but knew you weren't really a sculptor until you had tried your hand at the Carrara marble Michelangelo had made famous. She wanted to see what a piece might cost.

The quarryman, Antonio, liked them immediately—they seemed so young. He knew by the look of them that their purchase would not be made lightly, and he let them look around a bit, took them for a tour of the operation, before he showed Janice a few facts and figures. He had just shipped to New York a block of pure white statuary marble, eight feet high and two feet square, weighing almost a ton. "You see?" he said. A figure on his clipboard had been circled in red pen, a little more than ten million lira. Even with a growing appreciation of how little the lira was worth, the figure made her head spin. Ten million of anything was a lot.

Antonio did some figuring. "Five thousand dollars, U.S."

That number, so much more comprehensible, was even more depressing. She understood it completely. Carrara was out of her league.

As she was turning to leave, however, Antonio touched her arm and, with a look that was more wince than smile, motioned her into an older section of the warehouse and showed her a misshapen piece that had been sitting there for three years. Altogether the block stood six feet high, but only one of the four sides boasted right angles; the base measured five by seven, the top five by four. And yet the moment she set eyes on it, eyes arguably blurred by the romance of Italy, she saw what she wanted to carve: two wind-blown trees that would lean together and eventually twine. A foundation stone that she and Jonathan might build a life on.

Antonio did some hasty calculations. "This piece—" he tapped the stone with his pen "—*two* tons." Then, with a grand flourish, he drew a circle on his paper and showed her the clipboard. Five million lira. Twenty-five hundred dollars. In response to her incredulous blinking, he waved his arms at the evidence around her. "Three years," he said.

She looked to Jonathan, though she knew she would not pass this up. That night she phoned her father and begged him for the money. The next day she gave Antonio a cheque and made shipping arrangements. When Jonathan asked her what she planned to do with her Carrara, she drew the zipper across her lips.

Her silence saved her a painful explanation later on. From the time the marble was moved into her studio in Toronto, she realized she had chosen the wrong image for what she wanted their relationship to be—not a twining of two spirits, not a unity at all, but rather two separate strengths that connect at regular and important intervals for stability and support and, ideally, a passage to somewhere important.

When she broached the subject with Jonathan, he spoke with a frankness that caught her off guard. "People think too much about love," he said. "What we have here is just another medium for expressing ourselves. I teach, I cook, I play squash, and I live with you. There's nothing fated here. Nothing carved in stone. We choose what we choose. Bottom line is you're one of my works in progress, and I'm one of yours."

After that splash of cold water, she put aside the Carrara and all her romantic notions. Several months later, she studied the pearlescent mass and gradually began to see a life-sized human figure, a stylized Y that arched backward with arms extended to the sky.

TO CYRUS, THE WORD *changes* could mean only one thing: the chords of a song. When Sonny said, "Let's run through the changes," he meant a musical structure, like the one-four-five pattern of your basic blues tune. No other reading came to mind because change was the fabric of their lives—a new town every day, a new hotel, new audience; crossing borders, time zones, latitudes and longitudes; their work itself forever in motion.

But change *was* in the air. On the morning after their concert in Toronto, Ronnie told them about the British tour. "We've taken it to a new level, lads. Watch out now. When we return, the press over here will treat you with a new respect. Nothing like a bit of success across the pond to get their attention. And wait till you experience the audiences over there. Jim can tell you—Glasgow and Birmingham and Liverpool—these people love their music."

Cyrus couldn't believe his luck. Everything seemed to be clicking into place: his playing, his relationship with Eura and now this. His contentment was short-lived, however. The real face of change greeted him next morning. Eura jabbed him in the side with her elbow and said, "I have something to tell you and it cannot wait."

He rolled over to kiss her, but she pushed him away. "This good news Ronnie has given us," she said, "is not so good for me, I think."

He smiled dreamily. He still couldn't believe that they had made love. "As long as we're together, what does it matter?"

She got up on one elbow and looked into his eyes. "I have decided I will quit," she said.

"What are you talking about?"

"I am quitting. I am tired, you know, of the Jimmy Waters Revival. Maybe I can find a job where I do not feel so much like a fool all the time."

"You can't quit, Eura. What about me? What about us?"

She looked away and shrugged, unable to meet his gaze. "Maybe you, too, are needing a change," she said.

"England *is* a change."

"And you should go. Maybe you have seen enough of me already. Maybe this has all been a mistake and we should not make it worse."

"Eura . . ."

"Maybe it is time that you should just forget about me."

When he realized that she was serious, he groaned and pulled the blanket over his face. Though England was calling, he already knew his answer. Finding work would be easy; there was no shortage of bands. He might even start his own. But now that Eura had opened her heart to him, he wasn't about to let her slip away.

Two days later he dropped by Ronnie's room and told him they were leaving. Ronnie was writing in his day planner. Without looking up, he said, "You shouldn't tease your old friend, Cyrus."

"No joke. You'll have to find someone else."

Ronnie sat up straighter and gave Cyrus his full attention. After a moment's thought, he said, "Let me tell you something about Eura, my boy. She is not the sort of woman you share your life with. You are making a terrible mistake. You don't know her half as well as you think you do."

"That's where you're wrong," Cyrus answered. "About her, about me. I've been thinking of quitting from day one. I can't be a sideman forever. I've got bigger dreams than that. This just isn't my scene. It never was."

"Oh, Cyrus. . . ."

That tone—of clucking tongue, of shaking head, of wagging finger—he'd been hearing it for as long as he could remember. Only his genuine fondness for Ronnie kept the anger from creeping into his next words. "The timing sucks, I know. But I've gotta do this. I'm sorry."

"I am sorry, too, my friend. But I'll watch for news of your success."

{ MIND and HEART }

On a raw March morning in 1981, after a long and sleepless night, Cyrus stood shivering on a westbound subway platform in Toronto, contemplating suicide, weighing its possibilities the way a young boy might heft a stone before a plate glass window. Not that he'd gone underground for that purpose. Suicide was the furthest thing from his mind when he set off that morning. Eura was counting on him. Yet the thought had come to him as he stood there: Why not here? Why not now?

The train blew into the station like a storm of grit and stink, and he tightened his grip on his guitar case and kept his eyes fixed straight ahead. When the cars slowed to the perfect speed, his own image began to take shape in the windows of the passing train—a moving picture, one Cyrus replacing the other at exactly the right moment to create a stationary, if somewhat unsteady, portrait of a man in a green army surplus parka and threadbare jeans, with hunched shoulders and unfashionably long hair.

He recalled Ronnie once pointing to their likeness in the water of a canal and saying, "This is our life, my friend, mere reflections on a world in flux. The more we try to slow it down to inspect it, the more it disappears." Like everyone else in the band, Cyrus had learned to tune out Ronnie's chatter. But the image of himself in the train windows, disappearing as the subway slowed to a halt, brought home the meaning of those words.

He slumped heavily into a seat and closed his eyes as the train began to pick up speed again. He'd had a dull headache since rising that morning, and his body hummed with fatigue. For weeks now, Eura had been unable to sleep, and the way she'd been thrashing about and moaning, he seldom managed more than a few hours himself, usually in a chair or on the floor. They were both so bagged, they hadn't played a decent set in a month.

They called themselves Tongue & Groove and were booked as a duo at the Laredo, a country bar in a dreary strip mall on the eastern fringes of the city. Cyrus played guitar and worked bass pedals with his feet. He'd taught Eura a few melodies on a synthesizer, but mostly she sang, badly. When it was his turn to carry the vocal, she played a tambourine and swayed from side to side in tight-fitting clothes.

No one went to the Laredo to listen to music. They went to get drunk. The beer was cheap, the pickled eggs plentiful, and at least once a night, the cops had to break up a fight in the laneway out back. Cyrus couldn't imagine a worse gig, but it was the only kind they played anymore.

Their room upstairs wasn't much better. It was freezing in winter, suffocating in summer; and it reeked of smoke and stale booze and the black mildew that seemed to appear overnight on the plastic shower curtain. He had ordered Eura to stay in the room until he returned from his errand, but he could have saved his breath. With the infection and the swelling and those full-strength painkillers, she was unlikely to go anywhere.

Two days ago he had taken her to a dentist nearby, who told them that a couple of her molars had broken off at the gum line. He could fix it as good as new, he said, but it would cost two thousand dollars—root canal, gold posts, caps, the whole deal. To simply clean it up, get rid of the infection and stop the pain would be six hundred, in two instalments. They said they'd think about it, but they had all of fifty bucks and owed money everywhere.

Cyrus had never dreamed things would work out this way. When the rest of the band went off to England, Cyrus and Eura headed for Chicago. She knew people there, and he liked the idea of being in the home of his favourite blues music. On his first day in the city, he made a pilgrimage to 2120 South Michigan Avenue, home of Chess Records. He got a postcard—

a collage of some of their bigger albums—and sent it to Janice by way of her parents. On the back he wrote: "Gypsy woman told my mother . . ." Eura found them an apartment not far from there, above an Orange Julius. She told him a hundred times that he was a fool to follow her, but she never said it with conviction. They lived on chili dogs that year.

Through a friend of a friend, Eura got them a booking agent, Max Fleishmann. It was Max who came up with their name.

"I see Tongue & Groove," he said out of the blue. "Duos are hot right now. I see a Captain and Tennille thing with a bit more leg, more oomph. You, sweetie, let's face it, we're talking Greta Garbo compared to that mousy bit of fluff, Tennille, chenille, like the girl next door you wouldn't boink if you fell on her. Tongue & Groove, I like it."

He liked Eura is what he meant. He fronted them money for publicity shots, bios, the whole promo pack. He took them shopping for clothes, waxy-looking synthetics that created enough static charge to light Comiskey Park. And because they were pros with a track record and enough of a name that they might wangle some free press now and then, he started them in his top-flight clubs—Holiday Inns mostly, a Sheraton here, a Ramada there—where they stumbled through "Proud Mary" and "Hey Jude" and whole medleys of The Carpenters and Neil Sedaka.

As sad as it was to contemplate now, those were the good times. Soon enough Max realized that Eura was not going to put out for him, and he rolled up the red carpet. "Let's be frank," he told them, "you're not really Holiday Inn material."

The fact was, even Max's days were numbered. By the late seventies disco had done its damage, and clubs that offered live music were an endangered species. Over the course of seven increasingly desperate years, Tongue & Groove bounced from the Max Fleishmann Agency to Talent Plus to Greg Steckle (a.k.a., The Musicman, a one-time protegé of Nate Wroxeter who had done time for fraud and embezzlement). Greg did not come highly recommended, but neither did they.

It was thanks to Greg that they met Lonnie Carswell, the owner of the Laredo. Lonnie took a shine to Cyrus and Eura and offered them the house gig: four sets of hurtin' music from Thursday to Saturday every week for two hundred bucks. He gave them the room upstairs for nothing. "It's not as if anyone else is gonna want it," he told them. "This way, who knows, maybe you'll buy a few drinks, a few meals."

On its own, the seven-year decline of Tongue & Groove brought Cyrus a level of disappointment he'd not been prepared for. When coupled with periodic updates about the Jimmy Waters Revival, however, it was enough to send him into weeks of depression.

As Ronnie had predicted, the band returned from England with a much higher profile. They recorded two more studio albums that each made the *Billboard* charts. They toured Europe and North America almost non-stop, recorded a concert album in London, *JWR Live at the Royal Albert Hall,* and just nine months ago had returned to the United States for what was meant to be a blockbuster summer tour. Then, on the eve of an appearance on *Saturday Night Live,* Jimmy had another meltdown, disappearing into thin air. Some thought it was a publicity stunt, setting everyone up for the tour. But no one had heard from him since, other than a cryptic notice published in *Variety:*

No more tours. No more music. No more nothing.
It's all here. This is the future.
—Jimmy Waters

Cyrus switched trains at Yonge Street and went south to Queen. He then walked east to Church where four pawnshops stood side by side. He walked into the first one, nearly sick to his stomach. A man in a baggy grey sweatsuit sat behind the counter, smoking a cigarette and reading *The Daily Racing Form.* Before Cyrus could work up the nerve to clear his throat, the guy looked at him and said, "Don't want it."

"But it's a Les Paul."

The man feigned weariness and peered over the top of his reading glasses. "You blind? You don't see I got three hanging in the window?"

"Remakes," Cyrus countered. "Those are shit. This is a collector's item, a 1954 Les Paul Standard. Check it out." He hoisted the case onto the glass counter and opened it.

The man looked dully at the golden instrument and said, "I'll give you two hundred bucks."

"But it's worth a thousand at least."

The guy shrugged. "Maybe it is, maybe it isn't. One thing I know about collector's items, about the only thing they collect is dust. Two hundred bucks, take it or leave it."

Twenty minutes later, Cyrus was on the street, the money feeling cold and lifeless in his clenched fist. With the fifty they already had, and the fifty-dollar advance he was sure he could wangle from Lonnie, they had enough for the first instalment at the dentist.

Eura wept when he told her what he'd done. She fell back on the bed and curled into a ball and would not be comforted. "You are so stupid," she said. "You do not even know what is happening to you."

He left the city the next morning in their '69 Chevy Impala. Because the floor of the car had pretty much rusted through, Cyrus had to keep a window open or risk carbon monoxide poisoning. It didn't help that a cold hard rain was falling. Even with the heater on high, he was frozen; and in a matter of minutes, the rugs and his shoes were soaked. That was a minor discomfort, however, compared to the pain he felt when he approached Spring Creek and saw the new stretch of paved road that led to the brand new concrete bridge, so out of place and proportion that it looked like a piece of L.A. freeway fallen from the sky.

When he arrived at Orchard Knoll, Ruby stepped out of the house and partway down a new ramp attached to the side porch, drying her hands on her apron and squinting at the unfamiliar vehicle. It was only when Cyrus was out of the car and moving toward her that she recognized him, not with a shout of joy or excitement but with one hand covering her mouth, the other clenched into a ball and pressed to her belly.

"Do I look that bad?" he asked playfully.

"Oh," she said, almost a sob, "what have you done? Look what you've done to yourself." And because she couldn't bear to look at him, his lank hair, his gaunt ashen face with the dark circles around his eyes, his threadbare clothes, she pulled him into her arms. Then she led him into the kitchen. "Let me make you something. A grilled cheese."

But he held her by the shoulders, guided her into a chair and pressed a soft kiss on her forehead. "Please," he said, "be still. Let me just look at you." He pulled a strand of grey hair back behind her ear and smiled. "It's been so long. How's Clarence?"

She watched his every move, mesmerized by the complicated image, at once so familiar and so strange. "He's feeling better," she said at last. "But then you wouldn't know, would you? Just before Christmas they had to remove part of his colon, Cyrus." She rubbed the table with her thumb and added, "We never know how to find you."

He had never meant to be a bad person, yet that's what he'd become. What else would you call a man who let others worry so much? The last time he'd seen any of them was in 1973 in Toronto when Izzy and Hank had come to see him play, and they had argued. He'd made a few awkward calls on a few of the more notable holidays, the last more than a year ago. He hadn't even called at Christmas.

He took her hand in his. She said, "This time it seemed to hit him harder. With the lung, he bounced back so fast. But this, I don't know."

"But he's okay . . ."

"Well, he had himself a scare. I don't think he's feeling too confident about anything right now. Moves slow, almost like he's afraid to break something. Makes him seem older than he really is."

Ruby looked out the window and down the road. "He likes to get out for a drive these days," she said. "Goes to Clem's every morning for a Seven-Up and a bit of gossip. You may have passed him on your way in." Then she looked at him squarely and said, "You're not doing drugs are you? You look like death warmed over."

"Bit of bad luck is all." He was tempted to mention Eura and the living hell of her teeth, how desperate they were for a few hundred dollars; but it was still too soon for that. Instead he said, "I was hoping you still had my other guitar."

She led him upstairs to his room. The same bedspread. The same clothes in the closet. The same tube of Pick Up sticks on the shelf. The Harmony in its case, beneath the bed where it had always been. Nothing had changed at all, which he found both touching and creepy.

He fiddled with the guitar awhile, the strings so corroded and full of gunk that they felt like bits of wire fencing. The neck was remarkably straight, however. And it was a hollow-body electric, too, which meant he could play it unamplified and it would sound okay. Good for the room at night. Good for his soul, too. He couldn't believe he had ever let this old thing slip from his grasp.

Ruby sat beside him on the bed, her hands folded in her lap. Cyrus looked up and said, "Is it going to upset Clarence, me being here?"

She grabbed his arm with surprising force. "You make one move for the door," she said, "and so help me God I'll brain you with a frying pan."

CYRUS STAYED FOR DINNER—pork chops baked in cream of mushroom soup, with mashed potatoes and peas—and Clarence greeted him with unmistakable joy. And why not? He had believed he'd never see the boy again (unlike Ruby, who had never lost hope). When Cyrus inquired about the cancer, Clarence made light of it, as though it were a minor inconvenience. He preferred to talk about the Tigers. He liked their chances in the upcoming season, he said, and liked the looks of that Kirk Gibson. Cyrus, who hadn't watched a game in years, felt like a traitor and was glad when Ruby changed the subject. She told him what she knew about Janice, how she and her friend Jonathan travelled to Italy every summer.

Cyrus knew a bit about Janice's career. He had read in a magazine how "her primitive figures recontextualized the relationships between our bodies and our emotions." He had cut out her picture and stuck it in his wallet. He had even made it to one of her shows. Although he couldn't begin to understand what she was doing, he was proud of her.

The three of them talked throughout the meal, with none of the tension they might have felt in the past. The most awkward moment came when he asked about Isabel. Ruby took the big serving spoon and carefully trowelled the leftover mashed potatoes into a smooth oval. "I guess you'd probably say she's doing her own thing," she said.

"But what would *you* say?"

When Ruby shrugged, Cyrus looked to his uncle for clarification. Clarence's face darkened, which often happened when he thought about

Isabel, even though he had only the vaguest sense of what bothered him. She struck him anymore as a woman with something to prove. He didn't know what, and he didn't know why, but it gave her an intensity he had always disliked and distrusted in other people. If he were to put it into words, he would say she had become one of those women who make a clatter when they walk, the aggressive clip-clopping of the righteous, as if she was warning everyone to stand clear, that she was on her way. He said, "Your sister has done very well for herself, I'll give her that."

"But what's wrong?"

"Nothing is wrong. She's very successful. Owns, I don't know, four or five farms now, a handful of properties downtown. That girl has more business smarts than a lot of folks give her credit for. She's turned some pretty sweet deals."

Cyrus leaned back in his chair. "You're leaving something out."

"Am I?"

"Yeah, you're telling me these things she's done, only you're using a voice like there's something wrong."

"Well, no, nothing's wrong."

Ruby chimed in. "We're proud of her, Cyrus. That's God's truth. She's doing just fine. And it sounds as though Hank is too. Why don't we call right now?"

Cyrus shook his head. "This is nice the way it is," he said. "Just the three of us. I'll visit her tomorrow." Then he stared into his lap, a sense of shame washing over him. The mere mention of his brother had sounded like a judgment. Cyrus had failed at everything so far, even the most basic requirements of love and duty. It was shocking how little he had thought about any of them.

They went into the living room, and because Ruby's concern was so palpable, he began to tell them about the curious path he had taken, only slightly guilty that he made the travel sound more exotic, the work more meaningful, his life more noble and decisive. The whole point of the story was to allay their fears. In the end, though, a life in the music business was not a tale they could relate to, and he was relieved when they pulled out the photo albums.

He loved the older shots in particular, the ones taken before or shortly after he was born, of Clarence and Ruby standing in front of their '48 Ford pickup or making cider with the windfalls, of everyone posed together on the front steps at a family do. The photos of his parents were almost too much to bear. He set aside two of them—one of his father in dress pants and a sleeveless undershirt, doing chin-ups on a tree branch; and one of Cyrus and his mother on the garden swing. What the photos didn't show was the feel of his father's strong back or the sound of his mother's singing.

He held the two photos in the air and said, "Mind if I take these? I don't have any pictures of them." And that confession, more than the photos themselves, brought a lump to his throat.

Clarence picked up another snapshot, from the last time Cyrus had visited. It was a picture of Eura and Cyrus standing beside the Ford Fairlane. "What about your friend?"

Cyrus looked down at his shoes until he had summoned his courage. "In a way," he said, "that's why I'm here. We've had some trouble."

He had expected the usual reaction, the "Hank reflex" that everyone showed at the first sign of a problem, an emotional distance that might properly be called self-preservation. Instead, they leaned forward, their faces warm with concern. He said, "She needs help. Her teeth, she's being poisoned, I think. And the pain. The dentist we went to, we just don't have the money. That's why I came back for the guitar. I had to pawn my other one. Everything's a real mess."

Ruby and Clarence exchanged glances. Then Ruby said, "You know, Cyrus, I'm upset you would wait so long to ask for help. Don't you know you can always turn to us?"

"I didn't want to," he said.

Clarence shook his head in disbelief. "You Owens are something else. Never had a pot to piss in and still too proud to ask for help. When your folks were having trouble with Hank there, me and Ruby offered to help pay for counselling, you know, a psychiatrist even, but Riley, what a stubborn fool he was. And then after your folks died, we offered Isabel our home and our support, and she turned her nose up. Even after she moved out, we offered to pay for her education, but no sir, she wanted nothing to do with us. And here you are, your friend suffering who knows what, and you're too goddamned stubborn to come ask for help. What in God's name is wrong with you people?"

Cyrus looked across the room at the grandfather clock, at Ruby's table of knick-knacks. "Thing is, me and Izzy actually used to sit in the barn and talk about how nice it would be to live here with you two. But everything changed when Mom and Dad died. I don't know, I guess Izzy was too old, already a person maybe."

"She was just a girl," Ruby countered.

"Yeah, well, I know now how she must have felt. And it's just like you said, Clarence. But when you come from a family of losers, the last thing you want to admit is that you're a loser, too, you know?"

Ruby crossed the room and sat beside him on the sofa. "You're not a loser, honey. Don't ever say that."

NEXT MORNING, Ruby handed him a cheque for a thousand dollars. He looked at it soberly, solemnly, and said, "I don't need this much."

"Then buy yourself something nice."

And suddenly he remembered another day, another cheque, and the consequences that followed. He wondered if every life had recurring themes, identifiable riffs. Did everyone hear their lives changing key, changing tempo, moving inexorably to the bridge?

After a quick breakfast he headed downtown to see Isabel's new office, a modern glass building of irregular shapes and open spaces and improbable potted plants. He spotted her immediately. She was walking briskly, holding a stack of files; but the minute she set eyes on him, a calm came over her, like a studio musician when the take is over, her smile a mixture of happiness and surprise and, more than anything, relief.

She dragged him to her private office and closed the door. The last time she'd seen him he'd been on top of the world, strutting like a peacock; and she had wanted to strangle him. What she saw now, however, gave her no satisfaction. "Look at you," she said. "You're a wreck."

"You, on the other hand, look like a million bucks. Clarence says you're a big wheel."

She moved behind her desk. "Someone in this family had to make something of themselves. Christ, you look like a bum. Don't you ever clean yourself up?"

"I had a shower just this morning, in fact. But look at you, eh? Madame Rockefeller."

She leaned back in her chair, studying him. "I thought that woman of yours would whip you into shape. You two still an item?"

"We're together, yeah. That's why I'm here. Eura needs an operation, and I came to see if I could borrow some money till we get back on our feet." When Isabel opened a desk drawer and pulled out a cigarette, he said, "Still haven't given up the cancer sticks, I see."

"It's the giving up I've given up." She took a deep drag and exhaled the smoke straight at the ceiling. Looking at him again, she said, "I'm sorry to hear about your friend. Of course I'll help. How much do you need?"

"Ruby already gave me a thousand. That's plenty."

She reached into her desk again, pulled out an expensive-looking fountain pen and wrote a cheque for a thousand dollars. "Give Ruby her money back," she said. "It's time we started looking after ourselves."

He tucked her cheque into his shirt pocket and patted it a few times for safekeeping. "So what's the latest from Hank?"

She tossed him her house keys. "Go see for yourself."

He sat up sharply, wondering why Ruby hadn't mentioned this. But then, of course, she had—he had simply misunderstood. He shook his head and said, "I never thought the parole board would give him a break."

"Third time lucky, I guess. I drive him to Hounslow once a week to meet with his case officer, and he lives with me."

"You've got more nerve than I do."

"He's a pussycat, really. When he's ready, he'll get his own place."

CYRUS LET HIMSELF IN through the front door. There was no sign of his brother in the living room, so he tiptoed over to the den, where he could hear the television. Sure enough, Hank was in his wheelchair, within arm's reach of the set and watching the noon news. He was glassy-eyed and unshaven, his hair pulled back in a ponytail. The initials on his cheeks had faded a bit but were still legible. The unmistakable aroma of marijuana hung in the air.

Without turning, Hank said, "You'd never make a good thief, bro."

"Yeah, well, Izzy warned you, that's why." He leaned against the door frame, his arms folded across his chest. "She'd be royally pissed if she knew you were smoking up like this on parole."

"A little recreational weed. Give me a break. How'd you like to be stuck here watching TV all day?"

"You're on parole, dickhead. They'll throw you back in prison. And what about Iz? Haven't you messed up enough for one lifetime?"

"Nice to see you, too, little brother."

Cyrus opened the back door and stood there swinging a tea towel above his head until the air cleared a bit. That was enough to change the mood, too. When he sat down, they started over.

Hank gave Cyrus the up-and-down and, settling back in his wheelchair, said, "I wouldn't be pointing too many fingers if I were you, little brother. All that sex and drugs and rock and roll, you're looking a little worn out."

Hank had always been sensitive to bullshit, so Cyrus didn't bother to embellish the truth. He described as clearly as he could the dismal nature of his life after Jim, the pathetic slide down the musical food chain so that, at bars like the Laredo, he was playing music he hated for people he despised and making next to nothing for the privilege. They had no money in the bank. No apartment. Just the few clothes in their suitcase. A beat-up car that was on its last legs. "If it wasn't for Eura," he said, "I'd have nothing."

Hank looked at him with an air of indifference. "Don't be whining to me, kiddo. You don't know what nothing is till you've been in my shoes."

Cyrus nodded. No matter how bad your situation might be, there was always someone in worse shape, and in his life that someone had always been Hank. "What about you?" he said. "Got any plans?"

"I got things I'm working on."

"Such as . . ."

"Things. You know."

"Things as in a job? A wife? What?"

"Opportunities."

Cyrus rolled his eyes with exasperation, then got up to make them some coffee. Opening cupboard after cupboard with growing bewilderment, he said, "There's nothing here. What do you eat?"

"Iz stops for takeout on the way home. I eat the leftovers the next day."

Cyrus shook his head. "Well there you go. The thing I miss most on the road is real food: Ruby's desserts, the way Mom used to bake chicken, remember? Eura, too. Sometimes she talks about the meals her mother used to make, and it's like torture, so she drags me to these restaurants we can't afford. But man—" he shook his head again "—I'd never live this way if I had a house. What in hell is she up to?"

"Hey, I'm the same. Food, it's just fuel as far as I'm concerned. Gimme a pill I'd be just as happy."

It was one of the great mysteries to Cyrus how three people born of the same flesh could have so little in common. True, there were uncountable disparities between an only child and a third child. And Cyrus had been the only sibling to benefit from the gentle influence of Clarence and Ruby. Still, he was amazed the Owens could share so little.

Cyrus hauled his brother out for some fresh air and a bite to eat. On their way back they were approached by Gordie Spinks astride a great hulking Harley. Gordie had a long red beard and shoulder-length hair topped with a Nazi helmet. Metal studs spelled out "Satan's Wrath" on the back of his leather jacket, which he left open to make room for his belly.

"Hey there, Hoho," he said in a raspy voice, "what's the verdict?"

Hank lazily scanned the street as if he needed to look at something a bit more interesting. "I'm thinking about it," he said.

Gordie tugged on the chinstrap of his helmet and said, "Tell you what. Don't be thinking too long is my advice." Then he roared away.

Cyrus didn't say anything until they were back inside the house and sitting comfortably in the den. He clasped his hands behind his head and, in a voice of weary sarcasm, said, "So, let me get this straight, these 'opportunities' you were talking about, they involve Gordie Spinks? Are you out of your mind? You shouldn't even be talking to someone like that."

"Who else am I gonna talk to? You see the Chamber of Commerce asking me to lunch? You see anybody offering me a job?"

Cyrus went limp with disbelief. "To begin with," he said, "you've got it backward, the way you get everything backward. *You* find the job, the job doesn't find you. And what, you're surprised the Chamber of Commerce isn't interested in you? Why would they be?"

"So I'm stuck with Gordie."

"Only because that's the easy thing to do."

"You don't know Gordie."

"I know him well enough to know you're screwed if you start playing his kind of game."

Hank looked away. "It's not what you think."

Cyrus pulled the wheelchair around so they were sitting knee-to-knee. "Okay, never mind what I think. Why don't you tell me what it is."

"It's too complicated."

"Try me."

Hank looked out the window at cold sky the colour of an eggshell and said, "I needed to clean up a few things when I got out. Gordie helped me, and now I'm paying him back. Piddly-ass shit. You know."

"What, like dealing?"

"No, Jesus, what do you take me for? It's just a couple of favours, then he'll be off my back. Don't sweat it."

Cyrus laughed bitterly. "You've got a real talent there, Hank. Every time you open your mouth I hear famous last words."

"Fuck off."

"No, you fuck off and listen to *my* famous last words. You do anything that hurts Izzy, and I swear I'll never forgive you. And let's face it, without me and Iz and the Mitchells there isn't a single person on this planet who cares whether you live or die."

"Yeah, well," Hank said, "your caring means a helluva lot to me . . ."

Twenty minutes later Isabel came home and found the two of them sitting gloomily at opposite sides of the room, watching *Jeopardy*. "Whoa," she said, "this is a cheery group."

She had a bag of Chinese food, four aluminum dishes with cardboard lids, which she set around the dining room table. There were spareribs and chicken balls with sauces sticky as cough syrup, fried rice, stir-fried vegetables and fortune cookies. She opened a bottle of white wine and poured herself a glass. Then she fetched plates and cutlery from the kitchen and began to help herself.

Cyrus was the first to move. He poured himself some wine and popped a chicken ball into his mouth. While he chewed, he nodded toward the den where Hank was still hunched in front of the television. In a half whisper, he said, "I hope you know what you're doing."

She cleared her throat and then wiped her mouth with a serviette. "Funny, I was thinking the same thing about you. This music business of yours seems to be getting the better of you."

"It's Hank, I mean."

"I know what you mean, Cy. I wasn't born yesterday. I smell the pot in his hair. I've seen the people he meets. I know, I know, I know." She shot a fierce look at the den and then back at her plate. "But what am I going to do, kick him out? His case worker, Jesus, the guy is a case all right. So no help there. What am I going to do?"

"What about Clarence and Ruby? Maybe they could take him for a while. That way somebody'd be with him all the time."

"Cyrus, no, it's not the Mitchells' problem."

"What isn't?" It was Hank now, filling the doorway. "What isn't their problem?"

Isabel didn't hesitate. "You, dummy. All of us. We're not their problem, so we'll leave them out of it."

Cyrus dipped his index finger in the congealed cherry-red sauce and stuck it in his mouth. "They're family," he said. "What if they don't want to be left out of it?"

"They'll just have to get used to it. This is ours, and if we can't take care of it, we don't deserve it."

"Nobody deserves anything," Hank muttered.

When they had finished eating, Cyrus helped with the cleanup. At about nine, he yawned and said it was time to head back to Ruby's. He planned to leave for Toronto early in the morning and felt he should visit with her a bit more. He shook Hank's hand with a meaningful pressure and detected a grudging acknowledgement. He kissed Isabel on both cheeks.

"Don't be such a stranger," she said.

"I'll call. I promise."

"Well, you should think about getting settled somewhere with a phone and a mailbox like real people. How are we supposed to reach you?"

"I'll call. I promise. I'll try harder to stay in touch."

Isabel laughed ruefully. "Your friend, the artist. I saw her last year, I forget now, she was down here for some reason, and I was saying how hard it is to communicate with someone who's never there, never anywhere."

"I'm always *somewhere*."

"Never anywhere that we know of. Your friend just laughed and said we should maybe hire a medium. You know, hold a seance."

"Very funny."

"No, you're right. It's not funny. I've got too many ghosts in my life as it is. I wish I could just call you anytime I feel like it. I wish I could walk over on a Saturday afternoon and we could drink some beer on your porch and have a few laughs. I wish you were around sometimes to give me hell for being a bitch or to remind Hank that he's being a jerk. I'll tell you something, Cyrus, this past while here with Hank, sure, it's been hard, I've hated it sometimes, but I feel like it's something I have to do because it feels right, and this is maybe the first time I've felt right since Mom and Dad died. That makes me think that we need each other more than we let on. Or at least I do."

Cyrus looked at his shoes. "What can I say, Iz? I'll try harder."

"Will you?"

"Well, maybe." Then he walked to the car and sat in the cold a moment, knowing that Izzy was right: he was no more substantial than a figure in a dream.

He started up the Impala, rolled down the window and drove slowly out of town. At Spring Creek he stopped on the new bridge and remembered the night Ronnie came out of the darkness to offer him a bright future. Maybe that was the place to start again. He could track down Ronnie's number and give him a call. Maybe he could take Eura to New York and they could start again. Maybe they could try one more time to put together a kick-ass band. Jim was out of the picture. Maybe Ronnie would be interested. At least he might help them find a new agent. All those things were possible if he called, not so much going back as coming full circle, the way a melody returns for a second verse and gains strength and meaning.

After Jim disappeared, Ronnie focused exclusively on what had to be done. There was a compilation album in the works, *The JimJams*, which required someone to sift through all the master recordings and live tapes in search of a few new tracks. He had to remix a few of the older numbers, write the liner notes, assemble the right photos and credits. It was a labour of love that carried him through the next six months. He ate at the office, he slept at the office. And all the while, there was the hope: he will return.

By Christmas a dark desolation began to settle over him, and by the end of January the emptiness had wormed its way into his heart. Everything he'd worked for—the resurrection of Jim and, one day, the glorious rebirth of The Solo—had gone up in smoke. His faith, if not shattered, was sorely tested. Late at night he stared out his office window at the cabs inching along Avenue of the Americas and knew that Jim was out there somewhere, maybe amid that sea of yellow cars or in the dark river of people that flowed along the sidewalk, in Brooklyn, maybe, or Jersey, or as far away as California or Tokyo, Melbourne or Montreal. Somewhere.

Financially, Ronnie had few worries. RC Music published all of Jim's work. RonCon Productions took 20 percent of all other revenue, including concert receipts and merchandising. The money he'd collected from the band each month as enforced savings had been repaid in full, with an average annual return of 8 percent, but he had used that cash to generate even greater profits (a complicated deal with the record company, where Ronnie paid a large part of the upfront production costs of each record, then sold the finished product for a higher-than-usual cut of sales). If he was frugal, he could afford to do nothing for a long time. But nothing was a bore. Nothing was hard to swallow.

When he wasn't lying on the couch or staring down at the throngs on the street, he was keeping tabs on the only family he had ever cared about. Sonny was playing three nights a week at Bradley's, near Washington Square. Chuck was giving lessons out his apartment in Queens and driving cab in his spare time. Two Poops, in a surprise move, had made a clean break from the music business. He'd met a little honey down in Gainesville, Florida, and two months after Jim disappeared, bought himself a twelve-unit motel and set about making babies. Adrian and Kerry and Tom went back to London, where they had been offered spots with a top-notch sound company. They were already on the road with a band called Marco Polo.

With nothing better to do, Ronnie had caught every performance of the Sonny Redmond Trio. It was at Bradley's one evening that Sonny suggested to him it was time to find another act.

Ronnie, whose long brown hair had been transformed to short platinum spikes, shook his head disconsolately and said, "Another act? My God, allow me to grieve. Allow this poor heart to heal itself. Even if I were to entertain such a notion, what would you suggest? Some addled misfit in platform shoes? Someone who has never heard Lester Young or Earl Scruggs or T-Bone Walker? Is that the sort of thing you would have me do? Now, Sonny Redmond, there is a talent in whom I might invest my considerable energies. But aside from that, my friend, I confess I come up a tad empty."

Still, for several weeks Ronnie took Sonny's advice and drifted gloomily through the clubs of New York, hoping to hear even a few bars of something that might stir his heart. But by the end of the month, he had given up again and was living on a steady diet of marshmallow cookies and weak tea, waking each morning in a Glasgow frame of mind. For the first time in his life, he had neither a plan nor a direction. He didn't even have the strength to see Sonny play anymore.

Then one morning his phone rang and the voice on the line nearly brought him to his knees. "Ronnie," Cyrus said, "how's it going?"

With a deep, calming breath, Ronnie moved to the window and looked down at the senseless patterns of his fellow man, bumping and jostling from cradle to grave, their ceaseless din and tumult at odds with what he had long felt to be his goal in life: to arrange the elements of this world in such a way that they would emit a beautiful sound. He cradled the receiver between head and shoulder and used both hands to open the window and let in the racket and fumes from down below. Then he leaned against the big cast iron radiator and said, "I have wished for many things in my life, some more noble than others, but I can tell you—in fact, I must tell you—that I have longed terribly to hear the sound of your voice again, to look upon your fine boyish features and, most especially, to witness one more time the magic you weave upon your fretboard. My dear fellow, how are you?"

"I'm okay. What about you? I heard about Jim and all."

"Well, my friend, I confess I have been adrift this past while. I cannot even begin to convey to you how bereft I feel, like a man who has prayed with all his heart and soul for a miracle and hears only God's mocking laughter. But that is a discussion we might save for another time. What have you been up to, my lad? Are you here in New York?"

"I'm in Toronto," he said.

"And playing like a demon, I'll wager."

"Well, you know, playing like me, I guess."

"Yes, I well remember the artistry of Cyrus Owen. And you know," he moved across the room and perched on the edge of the desk, "it is funny you should call just now, because I have been thinking about you."

"Really?"

"Let me put it to you directly. I have not been proud of myself this past while. It is commendable—and in our business, perhaps, even necessary—to have dreams and ideals, but one should never become inflexible. I have concentrated too much on what has been lost, when I should have set my sights on finding the next best thing." He let those words land, take root. Finally he said, "You are, my boy. Jim is gone and you are the next best thing. I knew it the first time I saw you."

The words had been drawn from him almost against his will. Worse, it was pure fabrication. He hadn't given the boy a thought in years. And yet, there was an honesty in what he'd said. Even as he spoke, the truth was revealed to him. The boy would be his salvation. Cyrus was the next best thing.

"My question to you," he continued, "is whether you are still playing, and whether or not the two of us could do something together."

"Are you saying what I think you're saying?"

"I am asking, if you are not otherwise engaged, to give me your trust and talent so I might use my resources to make you a star, so that together we can make some scary music. Do you remember, Cyrus? 'Good scary. Scary the way it was meant to be, like it's a lesson or something.'"

Cyrus laughed at that. And Ronnie laughed too. And then they both howled like wolves. As good as a handshake any day.

A MONTH PASSED BEFORE Ronnie made it to Toronto, and during that time Cyrus and Eura got their life back together. With the two thousand dollars he'd brought from Wilbury, Eura had some repairs done to her teeth, he got his Les Paul out of hock, and they rented an apartment. It had been years since they'd had enough for first and last month's rent.

They had taken the first place they looked at, a roomy one-bedroom above an empty storefront in the east end of the city. The apartment had been vacant for some time, but the carpeting still held the imprint of couches, armchairs and end tables and was worn especially thin in the high-traffic areas. The wall of the dining room showed the outline of a crucifix, the wallpaper like new inside the cross. Cyrus touched the wall there, felt the shape of that grease and dust, and remembered Jim's story about the shadow of his father's radio. When he caught Eura's eye, she said, "This is not a door. This is dirt." Even so, he insisted they take the place.

When they got the phone hooked up, Cyrus called Ronnie in New York to tell him the news and ask if it was time to put together a band.

"Gracious, no," Ronnie said. "Let us make no mistakes with this venture. Let us form the vision first and then go forth."

So Tongue & Groove kept up their gig at the Laredo. On their days off, Cyrus worked on a few ideas, while Eura cleaned and painted or searched the junk stores for furniture. If she was excited about the latest turn of events, she didn't show it. She had felt well rid of Ronnie and Jim and all the rest. She loved Cyrus and loved especially that she had him all to herself. Aside from the physical agony of the past few weeks, she had been happy in their life together; and while it would never fill the gaping hole inside her, roughly the size of her homeland, it had allowed her to relax a little, to ease up on the tattoos awhile. Anymore it was Cyrus who pulled out the pins and ink. If not for his interest in it, she might have let it slide altogether.

By Easter, the slush and snow had disappeared in Toronto. Gardens bloomed with crocuses, early tulips and hyacinths. Forsythia bushes had begun to yellow. Lawns were turning green again. One morning as Cyrus was returning from the Italian grocer down the block, where he had bought a pint of imported strawberries and a couple of fresh panini to have with their coffee, a white Mercedes sedan pulled up to the curb. At first Cyrus didn't recognize the man behind the wheel—that spikey blond hair—but when Ronnie opened his mouth, there was no mistaking who it was.

For the next hour they sat around the kitchen table, and Ronnie talked non-stop, extolling the virtues of the neighbourhood, the apartment, the city, and "the absolute tonic" of seeing Cyrus and Eura again. "I only wish," he said, "that I had come sooner. I so love the snow."

Cyrus laughed. "You could get yourself shot, talking that way."

"But it is what I most love about this country. Surely I've told you of my time in Staghorn, Alberta. I made a friend there, a bartender, who once showed me the gear he kept in the boot of his car: blankets, shovels, a box of small white candles. For the weather. It'll kill you, he said. He knew a farmer who had walked out to the road to fetch his mail one day and never made it home again. Wandered in circles until he collapsed. Froze to death fifty yards from the house. Have you not heard that sort of story?"

"Sure. Who hasn't?"

"But what an idea. In England, when they say the country will kill you, they mean it will break your spirit, that you might work for thirty years and have nothing to show for it and end up a broken man. Or they mean the mines will kill you, or the sea, inherently risky jobs. The idea that your country—your 'home and native land,' as you might put it—could simply rouse itself one morning and drive you to your grave, I find that terribly exciting. I love the image of whiteouts sweeping across the landscape like death itself, catching the unwary, the unlucky, and carrying them away. So when we talk about making scary music, my friend, I rather think that is the sort of idea that might inform it. The wolf howl and the wind blow and the icy blast. Music that comes out of the Arctic night."

For the better part of two days Cyrus and Eura listened to Ronnie talk. They met him for breakfast at his hotel; they walked up and down neighbourhood streets; they went out to dinner and drove around in his car, and never once did the words stop flowing. He had a plan.

"We'll call the band 'Jangle,' yes? A subtle reference to our young Django here, but, I hope most clearly, a promise of music that will unsettle and excite."

Ronnie had no interest in the cheap horror of Alice Cooper, or the satanic claptrap of bands like Judas Priest and Ozzy Osborne. Rather he was after something more poetic, more dramatic. "Let us strip the music of its cloak. Take away the sexual pomp and strut, take away the gimmicks and the posing. That Mick Jagger routine is so tiresome. Instead, we will peel away the melody and the rhythm to show the bare beating heart inside." When Cyrus gave no sign of comprehension, Ronnie said, "There's a museum in Paris, the Pompidou. Perhaps you know it."

Cyrus shook his head.

"My dear boy, it is a remarkable building. Imagine: it is built inside out, with its pipes and wires and vents, all its messy inner functions, on the exterior. I see us moving in that direction. Remove pop music's shiny wrapping and show the blood and nerves inside."

Cyrus still didn't understand, but it sounded like something he could embrace. He'd had similar thoughts himself. A return to roots music is how he put it to Eura, songs that come from real life. The prospect of such a thing made the gig at the Laredo seem unbearable, so the next day he phoned and said they were moving on.

For two weeks, Ronnie refused to talk concretely about music. He took them to plays and movies and dance. They went to art galleries and improv clubs. During long candlelit dinners they discussed the state of the world and the nature of love. But what seemed to interest Ronnie more than anything were the few stories he managed to drag from Cyrus.

"You must tell me about yourself," he said. "Show me the blood. Show me the nerves. Tell me—" he looked up at the ceiling "—for instance, tell me about that bridge where we first met."

Cyrus described a young boy dreaming about the future, or lying in the shadows and listening to the creek with his brother; about beautiful April days when pike would cruise up from the lake to spawn, and how Hank would take a pitchfork and spear dozens of them for no other reason than the sheer pleasure of their writhing numbers in a burlap bag.

"The bridge," Ronnie said, "is a potent symbol. And to hear of you there with your brother brings out the emotional truth of it, does it not? I understand suddenly what it means to you, how it is not a bridge for you at all but a great metalworks poem." He leaned closer, their faces almost touching. "And what of the brother? Was it 'Hank' you said?"

Well, Hank was a different story, one that took many tellings, with false starts and second thoughts and self-censored silences. But over the course of a week, it began to dribble out—their bonds, their fractures, their disparate natures. And in time it all came out—the brushes with the law, the trips to the chicken coop, the fire, the poor guy at the gas station.

Eventually Cyrus began to offer information without prompting. He described how proud he'd been of Izzy for having the courage to leave the way she did. He talked about Janice and Ruby and Clarence, and about his own penchant for exploring and getting lost. He talked about everything but his parents, a story that seemed to defy words.

Eura disliked all this talking. She squirmed when Cyrus started to tell their stories: how they had fallen in love, their first trip to Portland, the dreariness of the gigs over the past few years. To her horror, he even told Ronnie about the tattoos, a transgression she would never forgive.

At the end of his third week in Toronto, Ronnie said, "I have things to do back in New York, I'm afraid. Besides, you now have a job to do here." He faced Cyrus and rested a hand on each shoulder. "I charge you with a singular responsibility, my young man. Write me the most heartfelt piece of music about your bridge, the bridge where we first met. And as we have discussed, not the bridge itself but the heart inside the bridge."

Eura raised a more practical matter. "What will we use for money during all of this writing he is supposed to do? He has quit his job."

Right on cue, Ronnie handed her a cheque for a thousand dollars. "I trust that will be sufficient for this past month or so of inconvenience. While I am in New York I will have my assistant send you a draft for $250 a week as a retainer. It is not a king's ransom, but if you are frugal, I'm sure you can make ends meet. When I return I will bring the papers that need to be signed. We are on the verge of great things, my friends. Work well."

He left so quickly that Cyrus didn't have time to explain he had never written a song before, unless you counted that little ditty he wrote for Eura, and that was only putting words to a B. B. King solo.

JIM RESURFACED A FEW WEEKS after Ronnie returned to New York, and every newspaper carried the story on the front page. Cyrus barely recognized his old friend in the photo. His hair had been cut to collar length, and his beard was gone, revealing a strong square chin. He'd lost weight, too, and wore a thin white T-shirt, blue jeans and a pair of work boots. He was standing at the gates of a ranch in New Mexico beside a young man who was holding a shotgun.

The reporter explained how he had driven out with the idea of interviewing the famous musician and had been met with No Trespassing signs. Summoning his courage, the reporter walked past the gate and knocked on the door of a tidy ranch house. Just as quickly, Jim and his young friend marched him right back out to the road, where the photographer snapped their picture. To all questions, Jim replied that he was no longer interested in music or fame, and that he had handed over his earthly possessions, as well as all future royalties, to the Worldwide Church of Jim.

Cyrus phoned Ronnie right away.

"This does not surprise me in the least," Ronnie said. "He has always carried within him the kind of conflict that creates its own spark, its own thunder. It helps to explain his extraordinary success; but his success, I fear, also led to his undoing. It takes a great deal of strength to stand up to something like that. Mark my words, Cyrus. If you do not have your head screwed on, you will lose it."

Cyrus waited a moment, then asked the question that was gnawing at him. "Are you going down there? You saved him once."

"From himself. But this is an entirely different situation. Did you look at the young man with the firearm? None other than Jim's son. And I've seen another photo with Jim's wife in the background, a most formidable woman, believe me. I don't imagine I could do much in a case like that. Now, what about your writing? Any progress?"

Cyrus searched desperately for a suitable reply. "I'm working hard," he said at last.

"No doubt, my friend. And it's going well?"

"I think so. I mean, I'm making progress. I'll call you as soon as I have something finished." Then he hung up before he blurted out the truth, that he was getting nowhere because he didn't know how to proceed. How on earth did you write a song about a bridge?

His lack of progress was not for lack of effort. He rose each morning and played his guitar for hours, stopping only long enough to have lunch with Eura. He played with records, played by himself, laid down chord patterns on his cassette player and tried to come up with catchy melodies, but so far nothing had materialized.

One day, for a change of scenery, he went exploring downtown. He stopped at Long & McQuade and fooled around on a few new guitars, checked out the latest amplifiers. Then he strolled along Spadina, past the El Mocambo, wolfed down some Chinese food at Chungking and bought a pair of black slippers for Eura.

On Queen Street, he walked into a small gallery called the Art Cave. The walls, floor and ceiling were painted matte black; all natural light had been blocked off. Throughout the room there were a few sculptures, and on the wall a handful of oil pastels, each work with a tiny but powerful spotlight trained on it. To his surprise, the largest statue, a stylized human figure nearly seven feet tall, with no arms or legs or head, was the work of Janice Young. According to the small typed card on the wall, the piece was called *Missing Link* and was part of her most successful series, *The Hollow Men*. The price tag was $7,500. A small red dot on the card gave notice that the work had been sold.

Cyrus inspected the statue more closely. The centre of the figure was shot through with a circular piece of Plexiglas about twelve inches in diameter. Inside the Plexiglas, a few items had been suspended: a severed finger with a gold band, a kitschy photograph from the fifties of a couple cutting a wedding cake, a Harmony guitar pick and Wyatt Earp handcuffs.

When he realized what he was looking at, he turned quickly away. After he had regained his composure, he allowed himself to be drawn back to the statue. He circled it and touched it. He leaned close to inspect its every nick and gouge, then backed away to gain perspective.

It was unsettling to see himself on display this way. More troubling still was the implication that Janice viewed *him* as the missing link, that the finger, the photo and the guitar pick were her way of saying there was a hole in her life roughly the size of Cyrus Owen.

Had he read the magazine article carefully, the one from which he had clipped her photo, he might have better understood the nature of her work. "The hollow men," she had explained to the journalist, "are searching for identity. Nameless, faceless, they carry inside them a fractured history, an archaeological jumble out of which they must piece together a personal narrative. To know who they are, they must first puzzle out who they were. But the past is a sentimental fiction. In the end, only art can tell them the whole truth."

Unschooled in the nuances of Janice's work, Cyrus stumbled out of the gallery that day convinced she still carried a torch for him; and when he got home that night, he drank too much before and after dinner. While he was in that woozy frame of mind he did little more than slouch on the sofa with his eyes closed and his guitar in his lap, playing the same chords over and over. All thoughts of the statue had been supplanted by more distant memories of the smell of Janice's skin and hair, her eagerness and confidence and curiosity. And as his hands roamed the fretboard, a memory rose up to him from the depths: that night on the beach when he told her he dreamed of becoming a musician. To her credit, she didn't laugh or make a face. "Go for it," she said. "Don't waste your time dreaming." After that, whenever he figured out a new song, he'd drop by her house and play it for her. And when she started to sing along one night, in that surprisingly husky purr of hers, he felt complete. Later she talked the others into joining the band and found them a place to practise. But of all her many gestures, none compared to that first simple encouragement.

At midnight Eura went to bed, and though he, too, was half asleep, he continued to play till one, two, three in the morning, cycling through the same chords while he let his mind overflow with thoughts of Janice—tossing a football with her father, eating spoonfuls of chocolate syrup straight from the jar. His eyes burned with fatigue, but he couldn't stop, wouldn't let go of this feeling of how it used to be. If he went to bed, she would slip away. If he put down his guitar, the emotional thread would be broken and he might never again feel this close to her.

And, then, with his mind and heart swimming in a sea of remembrance, his hand slipped. Just like that, in the monotonous cycle of chords and fingerpicking, his hand slipped and landed where it had no business landing, a tangle of notes that were clearly a mistake but were not. More like a surprise, like finding the face of love where you least expect it, notes he had known and played but not like this, never like this, never so new.

Aside from that one clutch of mistaken notes in the early hours of the morning, he made no further headway. And the more he attempted to move forward, the more Janice faded from his thoughts. When at last he crawled into bed, the rest of the world was beginning to rise for a new day. He clasped his hands behind his head and watched the sunrise paint the ceiling in pastels, already planning what notes he would try next.

TWO WEEKS LATER, Ronnie asked Cyrus to come to New York to sign the contracts. "It will be good to get away from home and its myriad interruptions," he said, his voice hushed and confidential. "We will be able to talk more freely. About the music. About everything."

Cyrus arrived at LaGuardia the next day with an overnight bag and his Harmony. Ronnie laughed appreciatively. "A sight for sore eyes, my friend. I invite you to the centre of the universe and, look, you bring your work."

Ronnie drove with one hand on the wheel, the other on the radio dial, searching for tunes to discuss. What about this? How do you like that? Couldn't this have been better? Cyrus made few comments. He had always had an uncritical approach to music. To his mind, it all served a purpose.

After twenty minutes or so, Ronnie turned off the radio and looked across the seat at him. "You must tell me what you have been working on."

Cyrus gazed out the side window. "It's kind of hard to describe."

"Oh, I like the sound of that. Uncharted waters. And it's going well?"

"Very slow. To be honest, I haven't written a thing."

"Not a note?"

"Well." He hesitated. "Yeah, I have a couple of notes, but that's it."

Ronnie tapped his fingers excitedly on the steering wheel. "Play me your notes. I'd love to hear what you have."

"In the car?"

Ronnie looked left, then right, and powered up the windows so they were sealed in. "As you can see, we are stuck in traffic on the Queensborough Bridge. What better way to pass the time?"

It seemed so lame, crawling into the back seat to pull out his guitar and play Ronnie the cluster of notes he had literally stumbled on. There were five notes in total, and he played them first as a chord, then as an arpeggio, then in alternating sequence. He played them loud and he played them soft, played them with a syncopated rhythm and then just let the chord ring out and naturally decay.

Ronnie said, "Yes, I believe I know what you mean. It is quite beautiful what you have there, and no question there is a certain *bridginess* to it. But tell me this: where do you see it going?"

"I guess I'm not sure," he replied, mortally afraid Ronnie was about to cancel the whole project. "I mean, I play it over and over, and I close my eyes and know it should go somewhere, but I don't really know where yet." Ronnie looked at him in the rear-view mirror, his eyebrows raised expectantly, and Cyrus stumbled helplessly on. "What I mean, I guess, is that, well it's kind of weird, kind of like that game you play at parties when you're a kid. You know, where they blindfold you and spin you around until you're dizzy, and then you have to do something like pin a tail on a donkey or find your partner or something like that."

"What you feel, in other words, is a kind of confusion."

"Well, yeah. I mean, I play that chord, and even though I'm blindfolded,

I know I'm in a strange room, and that there's stuff around me, most of it useless. But I also know that somewhere in the room is exactly the thing I need. It's like I can hear it vibrate when I play the chord. So I just close my eyes and play the chord and listen for that vibration. And when I think I know which direction to go, I make a move and, bang, I bump into something hard, not what I was expecting, not the right kind of feeling at all. So I try again and head off in another direction and, bang, I hit something else. It's kind of frustrating."

Ronnie's eyes had widened with every phrase Cyrus uttered. "My boy, that is exactly what I have wanted to express but could not. A music of intimations, that bumps against things in the dark." As a final note of punctuation, he honked the horn of the Mercedes, one long brassy blare. Cyrus smiled sheepishly, wondering what he'd just said.

The office of RonCon Productions overlooked Bryant Park. Once inside, Ronnie introduced Cyrus to Brent, a young man with a singsong voice. "I'm Ronnie's ears," Brent explained. He swept his arm in the direction of a desk that was covered with manila envelopes and demo tapes, both cassettes and reel-to-reel. "Another stack arrived just this morning. Pretty soon *I'll* need a pair of ears."

Ronnie led Cyrus into his office and closed the door. It held a large walnut desk, two Morris chairs and a green leather sofa. The walls were covered with gold records and framed concert posters. A moment later, Brent popped in with the contracts.

Before Cyrus left Toronto, Eura had instructed him to sign nothing until he had read every word carefully. She suggested, even, that he not sign anything until a lawyer could look it over. But now that he was sitting in this office, with a friend who was offering to help, with people from all over the world seemingly seeking Ronnie's attention and stamp of approval, Cyrus wasn't going to dither. The Laredo was still fresh in his mind. He signed promptly on the dotted line.

To celebrate they went to dinner at Angelo's on Mulberry, possibly the best meal Cyrus had ever eaten. Afterward they took a cab to Washington Square and walked to Bradley's. The club was packed, the air thick with smoke. Cyrus loved the swanky tone of the place, the long wooden bar, the beautiful Manhattanites, young and old and middle-aged, who had left their various high-rent digs to gather in the name of jazz and the city and whatever advantage they could work from the night. He hadn't noticed the sign out front, and the place was too crowded for him to see the band, but he could hear well enough, the music smoky and playful and rich in sexual innuendo, perfectly in sync with the room. The pianist was especially good, his playing so nutty and off kilter it reminded Cyrus of how it felt to be a kid.

It brought to mind a particular sunny day, in fact. He and Hank were lounging under the bridge, feeling pleasantly bored. With no real plan in mind, Cyrus got to his feet and made his way along the centre of the creek, hopping barefoot from one stone to another, not an easy thing to do because the stones were small and irregular and covered with an emerald slime that felt delicious on the bottoms of his feet. As he made his way along the stream, arms spread like a tightrope walker, he spooked chubs and minnows and frogs. He found evidence of muskrat and raccoon and nearly threw himself into the drink when a large water snake slithered past his foot. When he reached the big drainage pipe at the end of his father's main field, he turned around again to face Hank and—who knows why he would do such a thing?—raced full speed back along the creek, hardly looking at the stones, certainly unable to plan where his feet would land, never thinking for a second that one false step would break an ankle and spell the end of his summer. And when he collapsed on the bank again, gasping for breath, his brother shook his head in disbelief and said, "What the hell was that about? You mental?" And Cyrus laughed.

That's how the piano player at Bradley's struck him, reckless and young and full of life—not the sort of adjectives Cyrus would use to describe Sonny Redmond. "I had no idea," he said, when their friend joined them at the bar. "You sounded so different."

"Different music," Sonny said without inflection.

Cyrus found it hard to believe that Sonny had had this kind of musical ability all along and had chosen not to use it. Cyrus brought everything he knew to every solo, always working at the edge of his capabilities. With Sonny, he realized, there was no knowing how good he really was. It could be he'd never shown anyone his limits.

After the last set, they sat for an hour or so, reminiscing about Adrian's tea parties, Jim's endless rants, those dopey church gigs. When the club manager kicked them out, they waited together on the street while Sonny hailed a cab. Cyrus felt frustrated. All the time they had toured together, Sonny, the best musician he'd ever known, had seemed reluctant to give many pointers. Trying one last time, Cyrus said, "Name one person who really influenced your playing."

Sonny answered right away. "Easy, kid. Before I met Jim, I didn't know how to play at all."

"The solo Ronnie's always talking about?"

"Hell no. His playing was overrated. I mean his words. I had Adrian record every concert so I could chart his raps. Man's a genius."

They shook hands then, and Sonny sped off in the taxi. Ronnie took Cyrus by the arm and walked him slowly back to the office. "I'm afraid you will have to sleep on the couch," he said. "My apartment isn't really set up for visitors. I'll call in the morning. We can breakfast together before your flight."

Cyrus was too wound up to sleep, so he sat with his guitar and watched the sun come up over Manhattan. He kept thinking about Sonny's revelation. It had never occurred to him that you could learn about music by listening to words, especially the words of a crazy man. But he supposed it was true. The old guy sure knew how to talk, and it *was* kind of musical.

He thought about Jim's first line always—"I'd like to tell you a story now, if I may"—and heard the lick immediately:

Ba-dwee
Ba-dweedee
Ba-dweedee-oh
Dweedee-dum.

That's what Sonny had meant when he gave Cyrus that tape to listen to in Meckling. And maybe that's what Jim was getting at in the trailer when he asked Cyrus to forget about his guitar and talk about love—that there was more to playing than notes and chords.

When Cyrus fell asleep on the couch, he had the same old dream. The moonlight. The stillness. His father stopping to let him jog down the Marsh Road on his own. But this time the dream doesn't end there. Cyrus keeps running down to the Lake Road, then farther on to Roxy Beach where the sand is as fine as sugar. He continues to run without breaking stride, stopping just shy of the water where the waves have created a border of weeds and driftwood and empty shells. There is no one around. He can hear his own laboured breathing and the occasional cry of a gull. With his hands on his hips, he turns and looks behind him. Watching him is Ronnie, not Riley. Cyrus doesn't know what else to do. He has run to the very end, it seems, out of land, out of options. Then Ronnie moves beside him, puts his arm on Cyrus's shoulder and says, "Go on."

CYRUS RETURNED TO TORONTO THE NEXT MORNING, his mind abuzz with dreams of the future. There were so many musical ideas he wanted to try, so many thoughts to sort through. But on the bus into the city he realized he had forgotten to buy Eura a present, and that simple oversight filled him with fear. He knew she wouldn't mind—she hated when he made a fuss over her. What bothered him was the total amnesia. He had forgotten about their life together, how she wept sometimes when they made love, how she sang to him as he washed her hair in the bathtub, how she fed him delicacies from around the world—you must try this, you must try that. He had also forgotten the dark attraction of her tattoo and the seediness of the Laredo and the other low-life clubs they had played. He had forgotten about the tangled grief that led back to Wilbury, to Orchard Knoll and Hank and Izzy and his parents' untimely death. For almost two full days he had faced entirely forward. Everywhere he looked, he had seen the outline of a new life waiting for him.

Eura didn't seem that happy to see him. She barely listened to the stories, reacting to news of Ronnie and Sonny as though they meant nothing to her. It was only when they were standing at the sink, washing the dishes after dinner, that she said, "Don't forget, I know Mr. Ronnie Conger with his big brown eyes like a puppy dog."

"What are you saying?"

"I am saying don't think I am a fool."

"I think you're a fool for being jealous."

She glared at him. "You did not even phone."

"It was so late."

"It is never so late. You were not even thinking I was alive."

He put his arms around her and kissed her. "I was. And I was thinking that I love you. You know that."

His words carried an emotional truth that trumped the falsehood he had uttered, allowing him to believe he wasn't lying at all. Eura leaned into him more heavily, adjusting her shape to fit his.

"What I know is something else," she said. "Always I thought that I would be the one to hurt you, you were so young. Now I know the young do not hurt so easily. So I am the one afraid. I am the one who will be hurt."

They made love that night, and Cyrus would remember it as different from most other times. Normally there was a kind of lassitude to Eura in bed, an inertia he could overcome only with a requisite amount of tickling and tomfoolery. Without laughter, and the lighter spirit it brought her, she would often turn away from what he had to offer. But this night she clung to him ferociously and wanted nothing to do with silliness. The look of determination in her eyes, the brute force of her kisses, everything about her proclaimed this was serious business.

After she fell asleep, he tiptoed to the living room and sat with his guitar, trying once again to squeeze some magic from his five found notes. Maybe it was fatigue, maybe it was luck, but as the night wore on, as the city at last grew still, the notes shook off their fixation with the present tense and began to voice a few quiet suggestions about the future. It seemed to him the most exquisite magic to follow that musical line forward, note after note, chord after chord, and feel the past stirring within him.

Next morning, Cyrus called a keyboard player he knew, Pete Marone, and set up an afternoon get-together to fool around on the new changes he'd discovered. Pete wasn't the best musician in the world, and he knew it, but that was his saving grace. He kept his playing simple and clean and never got so cozy with anything that you couldn't talk him out of it. While Pete ran through the pattern, Cyrus improvised—a riff here, a melody there, a couple of breathless solos. After a few minutes, he stopped. At home the chords had seemed so promising, but when it came to playing overtop them, they sounded flat and uninspiring. A drummer and bass player would help, but still . . .

Pete suggested they slow the tempo. He played a few bars to demonstrate, not only slower, but longer on each chord, changing not every bar but every two bars, with a soft, pulsing rhythm. Immediately the progression sounded dreamier, the suspensions more pronounced and yet more delicate.

Cyrus leaned back and closed his eyes, the chords sounding so different and beautiful that he was happy to let them ring out on their own. As he listened, a note became evident, the one note that was missing, so he played it, a single ringing note that carried over two full chord changes and decayed into the third. From there other notes presented themselves: half phrases, recapitulations, then longer and more sinuous melodies that felt to him like a green and growing thing, some kind of organic bloom.

Pete flashed him a thumbs-up. "Very cool. What do you call it?"

And Cyrus laughed and said, "'The Bridge,' I guess. I guess I have to call it 'The Bridge.'"

For the next few weeks they got together every afternoon. Cyrus recorded every rehearsal, and every night he sat down with his guitar and played along with the tapes, letting his mind and his fingers wander until he found something else to interest him. The ideas came rapidly then, from places deep inside, as though some unreachable part of him had thawed. By the end of a month they had a dozen tunes so promising he could scarcely believe he was responsible for them.

Ronnie returned to Toronto in mid-June, and Cyrus made him listen to all twelve tracks, which he did without tapping his foot or nodding his head, his concentration so intense he hardly seemed to breathe. As the tape finished, he opened his eyes and said, "An excellent beginning. I see now why you are excited."

Just like that, Cyrus's good mood evaporated. "Beginning? But I'm blown away. This is so me."

Ronnie nodded. "Don't take my comments the wrong way. I, too, am greatly impressed. I had no idea you had come so far. But you know, I believe

I have more faith in you than you have in yourself. As good as this is, you
have barely scratched the surface."

"But I've never played like this before. It's all brand new."

"I agree. It is authentic music, my friend."

"But . . ."

"But one should never mistake a personal triumph for an artistic one."

"I wouldn't know what to change."

Ronnie got to his feet and began to pace the room. "With what you
have here you could go out tomorrow and play any number of clubs such
as our friend Sonny frequents. You might even get a small record contract.
It is honest and heartfelt music. But I don't want you to play to a hundred
people a night, Cyrus, I want you to play to thirty thousand. I want you to
sell millions of records. And not for the money. I have enough of that to
suit my tastes."

Ronnie stopped at the window and looked at the traffic streaming by.
"We all have a talent of some kind, and mine is a simple one: I can hear the
music in people that is waiting to get out. To be honest, I don't know what I
mean when I say that. But it is what I feel. With Jim, and even more with
you, I can hear what is waiting to be heard. You will be magnificent."

"Sonny's way better than I'll ever be."

"Do you think so? To me there is always something missing from his
playing. He is too much the professional, perhaps, to create truly beautiful
music. But when I saw you that evening on the bridge, I knew that you had
what it takes."

Ronnie turned from the window and folded his arms across his chest.
"Most people," he continued, "are full of dull matter. They are heavy and
inert and terribly boring. A few are born lighter than the rest, and it is easy
to think they are destined to do the greatest good, the best work. But from
my experience, it seldom happens that way. They are not accustomed to the
sacrifices required to accomplish the extraordinary. You belong to a third
group, my boy, those who have suffered great losses, their insides polished
by sorrow. Because Nature abhors a vacuum, each fills up again, some with
bitterness, some with fear, and some—like you, like Jim—with music."

Cyrus didn't know where to look. With a shrug of his shoulders, he said,

"I still don't know what I'd change. I like it all so much." He stared at his knees, worked his jaw.

Ronnie was tempted to compromise, if only to see him smile again, but that would be a disservice to them both. Instead he carried a chair over and sat facing Cyrus. He said, "I have been thinking recently about the origins of music—a fascinating subject, really—and it is my belief that the whole thing goes back to the voice. Think of women talking in a foreign language, a shepherd calling his sheep, or the sounds of lovers, and it is not such a big jump to Maria Callas or Little Richard. Yes?"

"I guess."

Ronnie leaned forward, elbows resting on his knees, and stared at the threadbare carpet. Outside, a car honked maniacally. Across the street a baby wailed. And Ronnie said, "It is too mathematical, what you have done, Cyrus. Talk to me. Make me understand."

EURA HAD BEEN IN HER ROOM ALL NIGHT, working a little with ink and pin. She hated what happened to Cyrus when he talked with Ronnie, the look of nervous excitement that came into his eyes, the look of some- one who, foolishly, had been encouraged to believe too much in himself. At times like that he reminded her of men she didn't like, politicians at the podium or, worse, the men at the Red Lantern with their devouring, possessive look.

She still had nightmares of the Red Lantern and that tiny stage where she moved her hips to the beat—the "fuck music" as the other girls called it—breathing in the sour perfume of cheap champagne and longing, while she looked out on the dull red shadows of the club, the greasy leather booths, the escorts, the drinks, the furtive and predictable choreography of hands and lips, one thing leading to the next with a nearly scientific precision that ended always with the steady parade of silhouettes from booth to private room. It was there at the Red Lantern in downtown Detroit that she first met Ronnie Conger. By then she had already changed her name. She had lost everything else, a new identity seemed a minor concession.

After Muskegon, she and Alexander had stayed in Chicago long enough to be granted asylum. Then they returned to Detroit where Alexander knew a man who knew a man who would help them get established. Right from the start she thought this was a mistake. She hated the ruins everywhere, the unhappiness. But he was so sure. He had already begun to think like an American that anything was possible.

The man was named Jan Kovacs. He had a black bottlebrush moustache and a gold tooth that glinted when he laughed, which was often. He owned Rasputin's, a bar in the suburbs where she was offered work as a waitress. She wore a skimpy costume that made her blush; and when she complained to Alexander about the fat businessmen pawing her and slipping twenty-dollar bills into her cleavage when she bent down with her tray, he asked her to be patient. He would speak to Jan. For now they could use the money. Of his own work he said little, only that he and Kovacs had plans.

One night Alexander didn't come home to their room above Rasputin's. The next day Jan knocked on the door with news that Alexander had been found floating in the Detroit River with a bullet through the back of his head. A gangland execution, the police were saying.

Jan held her while she cried, but said nothing. When her sobs began to abate, he gave her the night off. He would check on her later, he promised. There were things they needed to discuss. Around midnight, he arrived with a bottle of whiskey and some takeout chicken. "I figured you might need something," he said gruffly.

She quietly thanked him and fetched two glasses, conscious of the way he was looking at her, the way he had always looked at her, as though she were a sleek and shiny gun in a velvet case. She brought him his drink then backed away, preferring to stand on the other side of the room. She was not hungry.

"I hate to bring it up at a time like this," he said, waving a drumstick in the air, "but you and Alex owe me a lot of money. And now that he's dead, I'm wondering how you figure to pay."

She froze. "What is this money? If you ask me I am the one owed money. You have not paid me for last week."

"Anna," he said with a kind of rueful chuckle, "Anna, Anna, Anna. Where have you been?" And with that he explained that Alex had borrowed twenty thousand dollars a week ago and promised to pay thirty thousand in one month's time.

She shook her head woozily and put aside her whiskey as if that were to blame. "I do not understand this."

He refilled his glass and stood very close to her, backing her into a corner. "Very simple," he said. "Alexander had plans. He came to me for money, and because I have a big heart, I gave it to him." He shrugged as if this were self-evident. With his left hand he tucked a strand of hair behind her ear. "His big plan was a big mistake," he continued. "I have friends with the police who say it was a drug deal. Something went wrong, someone got double-crossed, and now we have this situation." He traced her jawline with the edge of his glass.

"If you have lost money, it has nothing to do with me," she protested, trying unsuccessfully to move away from him.

Again that chuckle, the shaking head. "Anna, I do not lose money. Ever." Then he pinned her to the wall and kissed her roughly on the mouth, squeezing her breasts and bottom until she managed to claw her way free.

"Get out of here," she said through gritted teeth. "Leave me alone. Can you not see I need some time to think?"

In response, he flopped on her bed. In a dark but playful tone, he said, "Let me tell you a bedtime story."

"Get out of here or I will call the police."

He laughed at that. "Don't act so high and mighty. You're not my type." He slapped the mattress and said, "Sit. I'll tell you a story."

"I am better over here."

"Suit yourself." He focused his gaze on the ceiling, enjoying himself very much. "Poor Alexander. He was going to be a big shot. He had been a fixer all his life with his Little Circus. He made things go right. And this was something he was proud of. He told me so himself. What he didn't understand was that America is not like home. And the real world is not like the circus. He trusted the wrong people, Anna, and now he is dead. A criminal. The police found drugs in his rented car, not to mention a stolen gun. Such a waste."

She slumped against the door and closed her eyes, her fear and sadness rising by equal degrees. Kovacs kept staring at the ceiling, as if the most enjoyable movie were taking place up there. "Now here is the sad part. He left his friend Anna holding the bag. Seems she didn't know about his big score. And that's too bad. You know why?"

Unable to speak, she just shook her head.

"Because the FBI knows that Alexander wasn't alone. Their records tell them he defected to this country with a beautiful woman by the name of Anna Cernik. From what I've heard, the police are a little upset with these two. Imagine, they throw themselves on the mercy of the USA and then get into this kind of trouble. There is nothing Americans hate more than drug dealers."

"I had nothing to do with this."

"I believe you, Anna. I do. But between you and me, I don't think they'll wait for your explanation. The minute they find you, they'll throw your exquisite ass in jail and ask questions later. And then what? No one will give two shits whether you rot in prison. People like you, with no one to fight for them, they get lost in the shuffle. I've seen it happen."

She slid to the floor where she rested her head on her knees. Kovacs stretched luxuriously. "I'm the only friend you've got right now, and you owe me thirty grand. So let me tell you how it's going to be. Rasputin's? You're out of here. This place is too legit for the likes of you. You need a place to hide for a while."

He helped her pack, then drove her downtown to another of his clubs, the Red Lantern, one of the few buildings that remained standing in the whole desolate block. "You can flop here," he said.

She looked at the sign out front, a martini and a naked woman in red neon. The streets were filled with litter and broken glass. The few people on the sidewalk looked like figures from a nightmare.

"Go talk to Marie," he said. "She's expecting you."

"I don't know," she said wearily.

And he grabbed her by the hair and twisted her around to face him. "What I fucking know is that you owe me money. Understand? Now I've got a few ideas how you can work off a bit of that debt, but for now you can start with a bit of dancing. Got it? Shake that money-maker, girl."

So she danced as Ava Muscova from eleven at night until five in the morning, a half-hour on and a half-hour off, seven days a week. During breaks she could rest, or she could mingle and make a little extra cash. Fifty percent went to Kovacs off the top. Even so, she fell further and further behind. "Simple math," he explained. "What you pay me doesn't even cover the interest, doll. Time to think of more lucrative employment."

She knew what he meant, had known all along it would come to that—working the leather booths, the back rooms, the special situations. She knew there would be violence if she didn't agree. She knew her life was worth nothing to him or to anyone.

And then a miracle happened. Ronnie Conger appeared at the Red Lantern, her own personal saviour, and waved her to his table after she had finished dancing. He whispered in her ear about a new life, and with nothing left to lose, she ran out on Kovacs and her debt. Ronnie gave her a new name, Europa Del Conte, and helped her get new papers. It was a leap of faith, of course, but it worked out. Her life became her own again.

So you would think she'd have only good thoughts about Ronnie. But she did not trust him, really. Just as good men are sometimes tempted to do bad things, bad men sometimes do good, she believed. And perhaps more than anything, she disliked Ronnie because he could, with a look, remind her of everything she most dearly wanted to forget. She often wished that Cyrus was not so impressed by Ronnie. She wished they could just go back to the two of them struggling together. She did not like this new world they were entering.

NEXT MORNING, RONNIE LEFT his hotel early and brought them fresh croissants and café au lait for breakfast. He'd found fresh-cut flowers. He placed the *New York Times* on the table with all the significance of the stone tablets of Moses. "I am so happy this morning," he said. "And so excited." He made Cyrus and Eura sit while he served them. While they ate, he suggested it was time to put together a proper band, with keyboard, bass, drums and a vocalist.

Cyrus balked. "I thought we were going to be strictly instrumental."

"Is the voice not an instrument? Do we not want music that sings?"

"But Ronnie . . ."

He held his hand up. "On this point I am firm. These beautiful melodies you are creating will only become more beautiful when you have shaped them for the human voice."

"But we don't have lyrics."

"Nor would we want any. Trust me on this, there must be singing. Your guitar will conquer all in its path, my friend, but the human voice must lead the way."

After breakfast, Ronnie returned to New York, but not before writing a cheque for ten thousand dollars so they could rent a rehearsal space and begin to pay musicians. "The secret to all good writing," he said, "is rewriting. What separates the true artist from the amateur is the burning desire to get it exactly right. I don't want to hear that this is the best you can do, because the best is only the beginning."

Later that night Cyrus and Eura went to a shish kebab place for souvlaki and french fries and a few glasses of beer. Shortly after they returned home, the phone rang. It was Isabel and she was crying. "Come quick," she said. "Please."

I sabel had observed a number of transformations over the past few years: tatty fixer-uppers had become cozy family homes; scrub farmland had blossomed with subdivision and strip mall; the town of Wilbury had lost its reputation as a rural backwater and had become the community of choice for many upper-income retirees from Hounslow; and there was her own remarkable metamorphosis from downtrodden farmwife to real estate mogul. She had four other agents working under her now. She taught a course at St. Clair College, her alma mater. She was a big wheel on the Chamber of Commerce, her opinion sought on most matters of civic importance.

Even so, the recent change in Hank surprised her. All it took, seemingly, was a handful of shirts and ties, a few lightweight suits, a regular haircut and a reason to get up in the morning. Six weeks ago she had offered him a job in her office going to the bank and the post office and the printer, sending faxes, keeping on top of all the piddly details that everyone was too frazzled to deal with. The job was nothing to get excited about, but it had worked a kind of magic. Hank was suddenly focused, making some money of his own, off the streets and out of trouble, and he had truly been a help to them all. Isabel wasn't the only one in town to notice the change in him. People who had previously given him a wide berth were now going out of their way to be sociable. Even his parole officer had been impressed. It seemed a real and true success story, and they all took a bit of the credit.

Near the end of June her bank manager, Bill Bickford, called. "We're holding a cheque here, Iz, from your office. Doesn't have proper authorization." That meant the cheque was drawn on the trust account, where client money was deposited until a deal closed. Any cheque on that account required two signatures, including Izzy's.

"We've been so busy, Bill, I probably just forgot to countersign. I have to go out in a minute. I'll walk over."

"No," he said, "it's nothing like that. Your signature's on the cheque all right. It's just the other one belongs to Hank."

She brought a hand to her breastbone. "I beg your pardon?"

"It's a cheque made out to Gord Spinks."

She looked frantically around the office, realizing that Hank hadn't been in all morning. "Maybe he grabbed the wrong cheque book, Bill. That's been done before."

There was a significant pause, as though he were hoping she would listen to herself. "I suppose that's possible, Iz, but why would he sign your name, too? I'm certain that's been forged. Not anything like your hand."

Isabel slumped in her chair and massaged her forehead. She knew Hank had been friendly with that Spinks character, and she had spoken to him about it. "Thanks for this," she said. "And between you and me? I'd appreciate it if we could keep this little slip-up quiet. I'll speak to him this evening. I'm sure he thought no one would miss a few dollars."

"Well, Iz, the cheque is for fifteen thousand."

Isabel drove straight home but found no sign of Hank there, and no note, so she hopped in her car and began cruising around town. After an hour of that, she went back to the office and asked the other agents if they had seen him. No luck there, either.

She had three appointments that afternoon, the last one ending just before dinnertime. She rushed home without stopping for takeout and found the house just as she'd left it. His suits were in his closet. His jeans were gone, and so was the leather jacket she'd bought him.

After gobbling a handful of cheese and crackers, she climbed back in her car and began to search the town more methodically, asking in restaurants and bars and poolrooms if anyone had seen him. At about ten o'clock, she drove past the fairgrounds and noticed two young boys, one pushing the other in a wheelchair. She pulled over to the curb and stopped them. It was Hank's chair, all right. The boys said they'd found it in front of the grand-stand and, terrified that they were in trouble, gave it up readily and ran off into the night. She stowed the chair in her trunk and drove slowly through the stone gates, into the fairgrounds parking lot. She parked in front of the old grandstand. She hadn't been there since childhood, the time their father took them to see the daredevil show.

She called Hank's name but the only reply was the wind whistling through the empty stands. She walked inside and stood at the railing, gazing out at the muddy oval, which still showed the scars of last week's harness racing. And then she turned and looked up into the bleachers with that great towering slant of roof like something out of history. There, on the centre stairs, halfway up, was a body.

She took the stairs two at a time, then ran down again even faster. At the nearest phone booth she called an ambulance, hoping to God he wasn't already dead. From the hospital she called Ruby and then Cyrus in Toronto. "Come quick," she said. "Please."

Cyrus and Eura arrived at the Wilbury District Hospital long after Ruby and Clarence had gone home to bed. Isabel was pacing the emergency ward, looking pale and owlish. She had been holding up reasonably well. No tears, other than those few on the telephone. But the minute she saw Cyrus, she began to blubber. "He's still unconscious. What they did to him."

Cyrus hadn't seen much brutality in his life. In his darker moments, he had imagined the tableaux of his parents' accident, his brother's crime, but the pictures were short on details and long on emotion. Because of those early tragedies, he shied away from gruesome headlines and Hollywood violence. So the sight of Hank lying so still, his face pulped and purple, his eyes swollen closed, his jaw wired shut, the bandages and tubes and monitors, was enough to make him wobble on his feet. He might have passed out had he not steadied himself a moment by touching his brother's arm.

That simple contact caused Hank to open his eyes. He moved his blood-sticky lips, but no sound emerged from that ruined mouth. Cyrus moved closer and peered meaningfully into the slits of his eyes. And Hank tried again to speak. He swallowed several times, an excruciating ordeal, and in a hoarse, gurgled whisper said, "Stupid."

Cyrus leaned lightly on the mattress, his lips nearly touching his brother's ear. "Who did this?" he asked. "Who did this to you?"

Hank closed his eyes. The lines in his face grew taut. He spluttered deep in his throat and said, "I fucking did."

Later, back in the hallway with Isabel and Eura, Cyrus learned that Hank had also been stabbed several times and had nearly bled to death. If Izzy had found him five minutes later, he never would have pulled through. She told Cyrus about the bogus cheque.

Midmorning, he drove to the Satan's Wrath clubhouse, a two-storey brick building that used to be Hunter's Dairy. Gordie was there by himself, sitting at a metal table and playing solitaire. He had a White Owl clamped between his teeth. He was nursing a can of diet cola.

"Looks like today I'm Mr. Popular," Gordie said. He took the cigar from his mouth and indicated with the soggy end that Cyrus should take a seat. "First I have a little chat with Danny Scanlon, and now this, a visit with Mr. Rock Star. Sorry to hear about your brother, kid."

Cyrus settled in the hardback chair and watched Spinks carefully. "You nearly killed him," he said.

"Me? You got it wrong. We're pals, me and Hoho. I was just thinking I should send him some flowers."

Cyrus could hardly speak he was so full of disgust. "You were squeezing him," he said. "He wrote you a cheque that bounced, and you beat the shit out of him. A fucking cripple, man."

"Whoa, whoa, whoa, Jackson. Let me set you straight. Tell you just what I told Scanlon. I repeat: me and Hoho are pals, okay? Now it just so happens I give him some news awhile back, you know, something I heard through the grapevine, and the dumb fuck gets all excited and tries to give me this money. Go figure, eh?"

"What news?"

"About some guy Hoho knew at Portland, Golden Reynolds. Got himself whacked is what I heard. So I tell Hoho that, and whattaya know he goes all generous and, like I said, tries to lay this dough on me. Not that I was gonna keep it or anything. It was going to charity had my way . . ."

"Cut the bullshit, Spinks. What did Hank ever do to you?"

Gordie blew a cloud of smoke into the air and watched it dissipate. "I don't think you're paying attention," he said. "I personally never laid a finger on your brother. Okay, maybe I'm a little disappointed. He figures to pay a certain debt, shall we say, for services rendered, so to speak. Then, instead of doing what he oughta, he turns the whole thing into a major fuck-up. But that shit at the fairgrounds? That's not my style, kid. Ask your brother. I'm a patient man."

"I'm asking you."

"Okay, so let me clue you in on a couple facts, just between you and me. Some mother in Portland gets his throat slit. Game over. So you maybe can see how that might leave some folks with certain ideas, maybe a bad taste in their mouth. Payback time maybe you'd call it."

Cyrus leaned forward. "You saying Hank had someone killed?"

"That'd be your call there, kid. I wouldn't know all the details, only what I hear. Rumour has it, though, this guy, this Goldie, was the one who worked Hank over in Portland."

Cyrus jumped to his feet, stumbling over the chair. Gordie said, "Be cool, kid. Don't be thinkin' too hard on this. The slate's clean the way I understand it. Nobody owes nuthin'."

"Maybe that's not the way I see it."

He shrugged. "Suit yourself. But maybe think about this: this ain't no game here. This is the real deal with folks who play for keeps. My advice is you just move on. You upset the balance, it'll come back and hurt you. Look at me, I'm the one with the temporary cash flow problem all of a sudden, and you don't see me gettin' all fired up. Some shit you just gotta walk away from."

NOTHING WAS WORKING FOR HANK. His nose was plugged. His eyes were swollen shut. His tongue tasted of nothing but blood. His brain was clouded with chemicals and pain. He couldn't move a muscle even if he wanted to, sealed inside this pummelled vessel, the aching prison of his body.

He remembered (or had he dreamt?) that Cyrus had touched his arm. Aside from that one moment, there'd been nothing to break the monotony— no sunny vision of himself as a park ranger, no wide-brimmed hat or dusty jeep, no natural vistas or cleansing winds, not even the mindless distraction of television—nothing but the same old loop of grainy pictures he'd always had, the looming presence of his father, the acrid smell of chicken shit and feathers, that voice ("I'll teach you") followed by the blows across the face, the shame and the pain and, inevitably, those other dark figures, the grunting voices, the flash of steel and fist, a seemingly endless cycle of lessons learned.

Then Cyrus was there again, and Hank wanted to say something cool, show some attitude, some spunk, if only to make it easier on them both. But his voice didn't work, and he was months away from a high-five. Even a head feint was out of the question. He couldn't curl his lip or shoot the finger. He couldn't grin the wiseass grin. And with a wave of panic, he realized he no longer existed. Everything that made him Hank had been taken away.

Cyrus pulled a chair close so he could whisper into his brother's scabby ear. "You hear me?" he said. "I just saw Spinks. What he told me, honest to God, I feel like giving you a few kicks myself. Tell you the truth, I'm sick to death of even looking at you. I just wanted to say one thing. It's our secret. I'm not going to tell Izzy because, well, I don't know why exactly. I don't want her to hate you, I guess. That'll be *my* job, knowing what a jerk you are. Oh, and one more thing. If you ever screw up again, and I mean ever, I'll kill you with my own hands."

By the middle of July, after auditioning more than a hundred musicians, Cyrus and Pete Marone had found a drummer, a bass player and a rhythm guitarist. Despite Ronnie's insistence, there would be no vocalist, but they were all strong singers should the need arise. They practised every day from noon until five in an empty warehouse by the waterfront. Ronnie had been right about the music. It was far too dense and complicated to work in the context of a band. So now they had gone back to the beginning, but with a kind of blueprint. It was the most fun Cyrus had ever had playing his guitar.

Eura was the dark spot in his life. She tried to be happy for him, but he was already so happy for himself. She knew she should be proud of what he was accomplishing, but he had that amply covered, too. Every day seemed to take him another step away from her; and although his world was growing ever larger, ever brighter, it seemed to have less and less room for her.

In one of his unkinder moments, Cyrus criticized her for wallowing in self-pity. There was some truth in that, and she knew it. But her clearest feeling was bitterness. She had fought long and hard to keep him at a distance, to protect her damaged heart from any more hurt, and in the end she'd allowed him entry to her life only to find that he could never be what she wanted. She needed a love as large as a nation, ten million arms to hold her

and kiss her and fill her emptiness, and he could offer nothing more substantial than melody, the stirring of wind in the trees. This kind of man, she
mused, could only be an artist.

All that summer the band rehearsed, rearranging, rewriting, jamming,
joking around, until they had taken the next step in the musical chain and
become a band not in name, not in legal terms with a trademark and accountants and licensing agreements, but in spirit, their sum so much greater than
its parts. In a matter of a few months they had gone from being perfect
strangers to having the kind of relationship in which each member could say:
I could not play so brilliantly, I could not think this way or know so much or
be so alive without these friends beside me.

At the end of August, Ronnie returned to Toronto to hear what progress
had been made. He spoke briefly to each member of the band (Cyrus had
never seen him so reserved), and then he stood at the back of the room while
they ran through the twelve songs. He didn't say a word between numbers,
which gave the whole scene the feel of an audition. When they finished their
hour-long set, they looked at him and waited.

Slowly, like someone who had been in a trance, he lifted his head to look
straight at Cyrus. "I will remember this moment the rest of my life," he said.

"You liked it?"

"*Like* is not the word I would choose, my friend. I like liver and onions.
I like living in New York. But this is another category altogether. Look." He
held out his hand. "I am trembling."

Cyrus moved forward to squeeze Ronnie's arm. "Were you worried?"

"Unprepared, perhaps. I had no idea you had advanced so far in this
short time. No, my friend, *now* I am worried. You have handed me a thing
so precious I am fearful I might destroy it somehow with my fumbling. What
if I don't have the strength to carry you as far as you need to go?"

"Then we'll get roadies to do it," Cyrus said and laughed again. He felt
wide open. There was nothing so big it couldn't pass through him.

PEOPLE IN GROUPS are a force to be reckoned with—teenagers on a street
corner, soldiers on furlough—but to Ronnie's mind there were few things
quite so formidable as a rock band in full party mode. He loved to watch a

group of musicians strut into a family restaurant or a bar and completely change the mood of the place. He loved to watch the little interactions within a band and knew from experience how tight a group was just by watching them destroy a hotel or sweet-talk a waitress or boggle the mind of some local promoter or DJ. Some would call this behaviour a lack of respect for others, but when Ronnie saw a group get out of line, it spoke to him of brotherhood, all for one and one for all.

With the Jimmy Waters Revival, Ronnie saw precious little of that kind of action. He had enlisted loners into the band—Sonny and Cal, Cyrus and Eura. Their emotional bonds were tenuous, quiet agreements reached during tea parties and jam sessions. But this new project with Cyrus was different. Even without their instruments, the musicians were always jamming, riffing, feeding off one another. They were a group.

To celebrate their achievement, Ronnie took them to dinner at a snooty-looking place called Gaston's. Of the five band members, only Cyrus had seen anything like it, and at first, the heavy silver and fine crystal kept everyone subdued. But that didn't last long. As the wine began to flow, they threw off their inhibitions and lapsed into loud physical comedy. When the maître d' threatened to call the police, Ronnie scooted the lads outside while he settled the bill. Then he suggested they move to a place more suited to their mood—the Pink Pussycat, within rumbling distance of the airport.

A smoke-filled room, lit exclusively with red bulbs, the Pink Pussycat was similar to a thousand other places in a thousand other cities. To some it might have seemed the very image of hell; but to Ronnie it appeared cozy and womblike. Take away the women, the obligatory "champagne" and the deafening music, and you would have a place to meditate. Of course, the purpose of such a place was to meditate on one thing only; and, judging by the immediate reaction of the band, the club seemed to work rather well on that level, too. Within a few moments they were installed in a large semicircular booth, each man with a woman beside him. Bottles were placed on the table. Glasses were filled. Everyone was soon acquainted.

Though Ronnie seldom took part in such sport, he found nothing shameful about it and was surprised others did—those same people who bought music to elevate their souls without ever bothering to make music of their own, who purchased books and works of art for the joy to be savoured but never set themselves the task of creating joy in return. Sex, he believed, was a low form of entertainment, and partners little more than props and staging for a show. He was clear about this in his mind and, whenever possible, encouraged his fellow travellers to think likewise. From what he had seen, groupies were not a reliable option. Too often they misunderstood the basic equation. They wanted a deep connection, while in most cases the lads on tour wanted a brief distraction. With a professional, everyone got what they were after. It was nothing personal.

Before his boys got too enraptured, Ronnie turned to his companion, Ginger, a bosomy young lady with long red hair, and said, "I would appreciate a word with the manager. I was hoping we might be afforded a bit more elbow room, the better to appreciate the view."

A moment later he was standing with a no-neck bruiser by the name of Sal, who counted on his fingers the options available. "You got your basic table service—" he looked over Ronnie's shoulder to Cyrus and the rest—"which your friends seem to be enjoying all right. Or you can go for premier service, which if you want my opinion, ain't such a bargain. If you need a little privacy, you'd wanna pay a couple bucks more and get the exclusive service."

Ronnie raised his eyebrows. "Tell me more."

"Well, you get a real bed for one thing, not a folding cot. You get mood lighting, you get mirrors on the ceiling, the whole deal."

"Yes, indeed, my good man. Now tell me this: do you have—how shall I say this—conference facilities, a banquet room, so to speak?"

Sal's eyes brightened with understanding. "I get your drift there, Jack. We also got a thing called the Rumpus Room. Could be just what you're looking for."

"Yes," he said, "a most excellent idea. I would like, if it's available, to transfer our little party to the Rumpus Room."

"Oh, it's available, but it's gonna cost ya."

"I wouldn't worry too much about that."

"I'll still need the cash up front. Five hundred for the room, plus your incidentals, your drinks, the girls, any extras you might be looking at."

"Yes, yes, my friend, lead us to the Rumpus Room."

Ronnie was playing a big hunch and hoped he wouldn't regret it. But he had a feeling this group of young men was the real thing. His chief concern was Cyrus. On the road with Jim, he had been laid-back, standoffish. Yet so far, on this night of revels, he had been right in the thick of things. Ronnie would have to keep his fingers crossed.

The Rumpus Room was a small apartment devoid of all but a few sticks of furniture. The living area was covered, wall to wall, with mattresses and pillows. The walls were covered with music posters, the windows, too. For mood lighting there was a choice of black light, strobe, or the eerie glow of the appliances from the kitchenette.

Out of the dull red glare of the club itself, the girls looked to Ronnie's eye rather pale and bedraggled, but no one else seemed to notice. It took them no time at all to shed their clothing and tumble together in the middle of the floor. Ronnie pulled the single kitchen chair to the side and sat with Ginger on his lap, observing his boys at play.

"You want to do it sitting?" she purred.

He was scarcely listening to her, his attention focused on the ten glistening bodies on the living room floor like so many sardines in a can. He couldn't be sure who thought of it—he hoped to God it was Cyrus—but someone started barking, which brought a similar cry from all the others, even the women.

Ronnie turned to Ginger. "My dear," he said, "I am afraid I am rather boring company tonight."

She shrugged carelessly. "For you it is better to watch."

"Well, no, not exactly. But, I confess, there are some things I do truly love to see, and this spectacle before us is one of them."

ASIDE FROM RONNIE, who throughout the night had been a model of restraint, the whole crew was physically and emotionally drained when they left the club. Ronnie knew better than to attempt conversation. He hummed quietly to himself as he drove them home, Cyrus last of all. As he pulled the Mercedes to the curb outside the apartment, the sun was beginning to rise.

At each stop along the way, Cyrus had felt his spirits sink lower. He hadn't phoned Eura to tell her he was going out to dinner. When he thought back to the whole dismal unravelling of the evening, he felt sick to his stomach. He had played so well, given it his all and felt the familiar emptiness that followed a high. Then he had simply lost control.

Ronnie got out of the car to open the trunk. As Cyrus lifted out his guitar, Ronnie gripped his shoulder and said, "Do not feel too bad for Eura. This had nothing to do with love. I would even suggest it had not much to do with sex but was an innocent discharge of energy, like a crack of thunder or a flash of lightning across the sky. It may frighten us sometimes with the power it unleashes, but it is meaningless."

"I feel dirty."

"For that I would suggest a long hot shower."

Cyrus tiptoed into the apartment and set his guitar in the living room. He had a scalding shower as Ronnie had suggested. Then he crept to the bedroom door, wondering if he had the nerve to crawl in beside Eura. But the sight of her, hugging his pillow, made him ache with regret. She had spent the night looking at photographs. Some were scattered on the bed; some had fallen to the floor. Those that he could see were from their days with Jimmy Waters—a visit to Mount Rushmore, a tour of the nickel mine in Sudbury; a truck stop in the middle of the night during one of the innumerable breakdowns of the bus.

He knew then that he was losing her, or more accurately, abandoning her. She needed so much, not just love but patience and understanding. She needed a partner who wasn't needy or demanding but rather a healer. For a long time he had been happy to play that role, to tend to her and see her through her many crises. But now there was a spirit moving inside him, and it was big and mysterious. It crackled with electricity. Even if he had wanted to turn away from it, he wasn't sure he had the strength. It was the bright jangled chaos of the future calling.

He fell asleep on the couch, a pillow clamped over his head to keep out the morning light. When he opened his eyes, it was a little after noon, and Eura was kneeling on the floor and watching him, her face a few inches from his. To see her this way, still puffy with sleep and wearing one of his T-shirts, gave him hope that nothing had changed between them. But her first words shattered that illusion.

"You do not love me anymore."

"Eura," he said, his voice clogged and craggy from his night's debauch, "how can you say that?"

"You go out all night with Mr. Ronnie Conger—I do not even want to think of the places he can take you—and you do not give me a telephone call to say you won't be home for dinner, or home for tea, or home to sleep in the same bed . . ."

He reached out to her but she reared back. "I'm sorry," he said. "I should have phoned."

"I am sorry, too," she replied softly, staring down at her bare legs. "I am sorry I was not strong enough to say no to you. Saying no was all I had left. Holding on to the way it was—" she touched her breastbone "—here, keeping it safe forever."

"Eura . . ."

"It was better then, saying no, because even when I was so unhappy, I could know I was at least living in faith. As long as I said no. But you wanted only to hear me say yes."

He sat up now, his head throbbing, his stomach sour. "I don't understand," he said.

"Of course not," she snapped. "If you understood, we would not be having this stupid discussion. If you understood, I would not feel—" She stopped abruptly, hugging herself.

"Feel what?" he said. "Maybe you would not feel what?"

She rubbed tears from her cheek and said, "I gave up everything when I said yes to you. And now I am losing you and will have nothing."

Cyrus felt a stillness come over him, a righteous calm. "Wait," he said. "You think I haven't made sacrifices? You think it didn't kill me to play those Holiday Inns when I could have been touring England and Europe and making records? You don't think I gave up everything to be with you?"

"The Jimmy Waters Revival. This is nothing. You were better off away from those people."

"Oh, yeah, I was living the good life with you, all right, at the Laredo. Don't you understand? Music is the only thing I've ever cared about my whole fucking life."

That sentence hung before them like a crystal, clear and hard and mes-
merizing, its refracted meanings shining every which way. To Eura, it was the
confirmation of everything she had suspected. To Cyrus it was the sudden
transformation of a hundred nameless feelings into a statement of principle.
Then Eura covered her mouth with her fist and walked slowly back to the
bedroom. She closed and locked the door.

At five Ronnie phoned to invite them to dinner. Cyrus accepted half-
heartedly and relayed the information to Eura. After a few moments of
silence, she snuffled indelicately and said, "You go."

He leaned his forehead against the door. In a careful tone, he said, "He'd
like you to come. And I would, too."

RONNIE WAS SENSITIVE to the fact that there might be tensions in the air
and was prepared to assume any persona—master of ceremonies, confidant,
friend, adviser, referee—whatever was required to keep Cyrus functioning at
full power. The boy still had a lot of work to do, and Ronnie's sole focus for
the next while was to keep everything on track. If pushed to it, he would not
hesitate to sacrifice Eura to the greater good.

As it turned out, the mood in the apartment was more encouraging than
expected. He had pictured Cyrus fawning over Eura, punishing himself for
whatever unspeakable acts he had committed or imagined. Instead, there was
a chill in the air, which Ronnie found bracing. Eura drifted about the rooms
with a weak and hollow expression, like someone who had lost all hope;
Cyrus's movements were tight and jerky and full of steam.

They drove downtown with the windows open, Cyrus sitting in the
back. It was a beautiful evening, full of sultry promise. You could see it in the
way people strolled down the street. Gone was the hunched and hurried gait
of Canadian midwinter. In its place was a lazy sashay, all hips and shoulders
and no particular place to go. With a note of false cheer, Ronnie said, "I was
thinking Chinese. Something a bit lighter than the feast we had last night.
Did he tell you about it, Eura? My God, we made pigs of ourselves."

She stared blindly ahead. "I am glad to hear. Lately he forgets to eat. He
will make himself sick if he is not careful. This is something you should
watch, Ronnie. He is not so good at taking care of himself."

Cyrus nudged her shoulder. "Like you're any better."

"I will always survive. I had more than one life before I met you."

"But you weren't always happy."

"Who is always happy? Besides, happiness, I think, is overrated."

They ate at Chungking, and Ronnie kept the conversation as light as possible, which wasn't easy. Cyrus and Eura seemed unwilling to say much to each other. As a result, Ronnie spent most of the meal telling them about Jim's latest antics. He now had his own radio show, which was broadcast from New Mexico. It was becoming a hit, syndicated in every major U.S. city, including New York. There was talk of cable TV.

"I would be happy for him," he said, "if only I didn't feel that every time he opened his mouth, he was tarnishing his legacy. That woman is not helping matters any. The son, too. They are taking advantage of him."

Eura poked at the food on her plate—she did not understand this cuisine, more suitable for cows and pigs—and said, "He has always been crazy. I do not see that this could be different."

Ronnie spoke with the utmost gravity. "There is so much difference I hardly know where to begin," he said. "When I think of what he has given the world, what he still has to give, and to hear him go on this way." He leaned forward confidentially. "It is hard to believe it is the same man making these radio broadcasts. He speaks like the living dead. And the way they parade him around those open-air meetings like some wild-eyed John the Baptist— it's absolutely shameful. Something dreadful has happened to him. I wonder at times if he has been brainwashed."

Cyrus poured himself some green tea and said, "Did anyone *ever* understand what he was talking about?"

"Not fully, of course, but in part. The questing soul, my friend. Whether he applied his talents to the language of music or the music of language, he brought joy to the world. Now he has turned everything upside down. Instead of filling life with magic and miracle, he empties it. At these open-air meetings, which are terribly well-attended, people gather with records and tapes, which they pile into a mound and set ablaze. Did you see the article in *Time* magazine? Jim has been taken up by the Bible thumpers, calling for an end to 'godless rock and roll.'"

"He said that?"

"Not in so many words. His ways have always been hard to decipher. I believe he is talking about a more general proscription. In his own words, 'a time of terrifying silence' that he hopes to usher in."

"Whoa," Cyrus said with a mock shudder. "Heavy."

Ronnie twisted his mouth into a frown. "I am afraid I find this too upsetting to make light of it."

"Then why waste your time with us?" Eura asked, not at all kindly.

"I have called and left messages. They won't even let him speak on the phone. And honestly, what I have observed on TV is not encouraging. Even if I had a few hours alone with him, I doubt I could reach him."

He waved his hands in the air and said he would talk no more about Jimmy Waters. Then he spoke of people he had met in New York, in particular a set designer named Raoul Dupree. The idea, Ronnie explained, was to make Madison Square Garden feel as intimate as a theatre. The hard part would be to create a few icons that were larger than life, both physically and emotionally. To that end, Raoul would need a tape. Ronnie suggested it was time to record a demo, which pleased Cyrus a great deal.

As they left the restaurant, Cyrus suddenly remembered Janice's sculpture. "I have a friend," he said, "an artist. I forget how you just put it, how we need something big and weird. Her statues sure are that."

Ronnie laughed. "Tomorrow promises to be a delightful day. We will find ourselves a cozy little demo studio in the A.M., and in the P.M., we will set off in search of these big weird statues your friend has made, shall we?"

PETE'S BROTHER-IN-LAW had a studio called High Fidelity, on Queen Street West near the psychiatric hospital. It didn't have the best gear or the most welcoming space, but the price was right. From there it was a short drive past Portuguese grocery stores and restaurant supply depots until they came to the Art Cave, where Ronnie immediately cornered the gallery owner. "My good fellow, you had a show not too long ago that featured a piece by Janice Young. I don't suppose you'd have the number of the artist's agent."

The man was short and plump, with beady eyes and a handlebar moustache. "Acts as her own agent," he said.

"Well, then, how might we reach her about a commission?"

The man disappeared into his office and returned with a telephone number and an address. "I wouldn't bother phoning," he said. "She never answers. And even if she did, she'd make some excuse not to see you. If I were you, I'd just drop by the studio. But don't tell her I said so."

Janice rented space in a warehouse on King Street. Ronnie and Cyrus tried several doors before they found one that would open—and stepped directly into her workroom. She was hunched over a marble sculpture that looked to Cyrus like a big, warped slingshot. She wore plastic goggles and a small white mask over her mouth. She was holding a chisel.

In one series of movements she straightened, flipped up the goggles and pulled off her mask. She was dressed in white coveralls, which accentuated the red of her hair. "Can I help you?"

Cyrus still had her picture in his wallet, the one he'd clipped from a magazine; but he wasn't prepared for the sight of her. The last time he'd seen her, her face was rounder and fleshier and not as finely articulated, as though she'd been sculpting it herself and was only half finished. This face, with its more prominent cheekbones and jawline, the hair chopped to a graceless tangle of orange spikes, was one he didn't know, one that had lived and worked without him. Looking at her now, he felt a kind of panic, as if he had returned from a decade of travel to discover he had left a tap running or the stove on or the door unlocked.

Recognition dawned in her face, the flicker of surprise that in an earlier time would have become a headlong rush into his arms. Instead she merely raised an eyebrow and said, "It's you."

"It's me. Been a long time." He hugged her and breathed in her smell, all dusty and warm and slightly sweet, like a gravel road in summer. Her awkwardness in his arms made him feel sad and nervous. Remembering himself, he backed away and said, "This is my friend Ronnie. We were just at the Art Cave."

"And Bernie told you where to find me."

"We promised we wouldn't rat on him."

She made tea, but the presence of her unexpected guests shone an unforgiving light on each step of this familiar process. Her kettle was covered in dust and paint flecks and bits of solder; her cups and teapot were chipped and stained. She was afraid to think what she must look like. She'd been working since eight that morning without a break and could feel the dust coating her face. She could taste her own empty stomach.

More than once she had imagined seeing Cyrus again and how she would present herself—and it was never like a scatterbrain. She hated the act that some artists used to avoid responsibility, claiming they didn't understand taxes, say, or politics, or how to cook or clean or perform any of the daily duties that constituted a normal life. She was suspicious of those who retreated into the world of their creations and let everything else slide. That wasn't being creative but immature. Now she was afraid that she was no better than the rest.

She might have relaxed a little if she had seen herself from Cyrus's point of view. He noticed nothing about the kettle or teapot. In regard to her physical appearance, he was thrilled to have had the opportunity to see her at work, if only for a moment. Granted, that first glimpse of her face had filled him with loss, but the picture of her bending over her marble, goggles on, a fine mist of perspiration on her forehead, made up for that. It was all he needed to know about her past, an image so real and full of implications that it easily filled the gap inside him labelled "Janice."

They stood around her workbench, chatting awkwardly about old names, old faces. He told her that he'd been to one of her shows and had followed her career as best he could. She'd seen him play, she said, years ago. "With that guy who told the weird stories. In San Francisco, of all places. Jonathan and I had flown out for my first show in the United States. It was like a sign, you know? Both there at the same time. Long way from Wilbury."

It hurt to think she had come to hear him play but not to say hello. Worse, he couldn't bear to think about this other man. He wanted her to be happy, and to all appearances she was. But he didn't want to know about anyone called Jonathan. She, too, shied away from more personal questions, and they soon ran out of easy things to say. That's when Ronnie stepped forward. "You are no doubt asking yourself why we would drop by so unexpectedly." He explained to her what they were planning and that they would like to commission a few pieces for the show.

She listened attentively, occasionally shifting her gaze to Cyrus. When Ronnie finished talking, she touched Cyrus's arm. "I can't tell you how thrilled I am that you would ask. You know, I generally don't give much thought to my audience. I don't know who they are or what they like, and I don't want to know. But secretly, I've always wanted *you* to like my work, Cy. I wanted you to think it worthwhile. So it means a lot."

"You'll do it then?" Ronnie said. "You'll design our icons?"

She shook her head. "I'm afraid not. I couldn't. I don't take specific commissions. I just do what I do. If any of my existing pieces are suitable, we might arrange something, but otherwise . . ."

Ronnie became brisk and businesslike. "Thank you, no. Our requirements are very particular. Best of luck to you in your endeavours." He took Cyrus by the arm and ushered him toward the door.

Before they could escape, Janice said, "Thanks, Cyrus. For coming here, I mean. It was good to see you."

He pulled free of Ronnie's grip and turned to face her. There was so much he wanted to say, but every time he found a few suitable words, his feelings rose up and washed them away. She was waiting, looking lovelier than he could ever remember, and he dragged his hand through his hair and said, "It's good to see you, too, Janice. I'm real proud of you." Then he turned and walked away.

That night Ronnie drove back to New York, and Eura made dinner, a rich and fiery goulash, served with heavy rye bread and Pilsner Urquell. It was the first meal she had prepared in weeks, and Cyrus wondered what was wrong. He found out later when she brought him *palacsinta* and coffee. "I have decided," she said, "that I must find my husband."

She had delivered this news, or news very much like it, several times before, and over the years he had learned not to take it too seriously. No one had seen or heard from her husband since 1968 and, like many young men of his education and political affiliation, he was probably dead. Cyrus knew better than to express his opinion on the matter, so he concentrated on his coffee and dessert. She would feel better in a day or two, he figured.

After dinner, Eura kept to the bedroom, and Cyrus slouched on the sofa with his guitar cradled in his lap. He had hoped to work on one of his tunes but couldn't stop thinking about Janice, how great she looked, how much she'd changed. He remembered the way they used to snuggle beneath an afghan and watch TV. She had an opinion on everything and could talk non-stop about any show that was on. She sometimes kept talking even when they made love, teasing, coaxing, instructing until the moment came (and he learned to wait for it) when she would say, "Oh," her voice low and hushed as though she had stumbled on something profound, that single syllable followed by long moments of breathy silence that he always equated with joy.

Work was out of the question now, so Cyrus laid aside his guitar and drank a beer, then another, listening to music by Howlin' Wolf, Paul Butterfield and Taj Mahal. It was well after midnight when he tiptoed to the bedroom. Eura's eyes were closed, but she was only pretending to sleep. He perched on the edge of the mattress and said, "I'm doing this for you, too, you know. I don't understand why you're acting this way, as if wanting to be successful makes me a bad person."

"I am not acting at all. This is the only way I know how to be."

"Well, this is the only way that I know how to be, too. At least I'm trying to be happy. I mean, let it go, Eura. Your husband is dead."

She opened her eyes to look at him and said, "Maybe so, but sometimes he is more alive to me than you are."

The band recorded a three-song demo in the first week of September, and Cyrus immediately sent a copy to Ronnie in New York. The minute it was in the mail, however, he began to have second thoughts. In the studio, the tunes had sounded good; but to hear the stark reality from a couple of stereo speakers in his living room made him cringe. Within two days he had found a thousand things he wanted to change. He was so upset that he phoned Ronnie in the middle of the night.

Ronnie clucked his tongue and said, "It is a demo, Cyrus. A chance to step back and listen to what you have done. The gap between what you intended and what you achieved is the gap between a great artist and a nobody. Move forward, my friend. Move forward."

For the next month the band rehearsed eight hours a day, often stripping the tunes down to the simplest elements then putting them back together. They listened to a lot of music, too, critiquing their favourite recordings, finding out what made them tick. The first week of October, they went back into the studio and recorded the same three tracks, plus a new one Cyrus had written. This time everyone felt better about the result; this time Ronnie phoned to praise the work they had done. It still wasn't perfect, he said, but it was something to be proud of.

A few days after Ronnie's call, Isabel rang up. They had spoken about once a month since the spring, always the same conversation: she was fine; Hank was on the mend and fine; Ruby and Clarence were fine; everything was fine. But the sound of her voice this time told him they wouldn't be having one of those chats. From the initial sigh and the weariness in her tone, he knew there would be a higher truth quotient.

"Hank's birthday's on Saturday," she said. "Four-oh. I was hoping you could make it down. He could use a little cheering up."

"Why? What's wrong?"

"Well, what do you think is wrong?"

He was so surprised by her sarcasm that he stammered. "I thought, I mean, every time I called, you said he was fine."

"How fine could he be? I mean, okay, the tubes are out of his nose and he's off the painkillers, but what's he got? His little sister breathing down his neck, a nurse who treats him like a retard, and TV around the clock. Come and talk to him. He won't listen to me anymore."

He tried to get Eura to go with him, but she'd already seen enough of Wilbury, she said. So he set off on his own and arrived the next day around lunchtime, a glorious afternoon with the trees in full colour and the temperature an unseasonable eighty degrees. He let himself into Izzy's house, but there was no one inside. Out back, through the patio doors, he saw the nurse sitting in the middle of the lawn on a kitchen chair, dangling her bare feet in a child's wading pool. Hank was slumped in his wheelchair on the edge of the driveway. He was listening to a Walkman, the sun beating down on him. He looked like he had a burn.

"What's going on?" Cyrus demanded as he approached the nurse. "I thought you were taking care of him."

"I am his nurse," she said, waddling toward him in her bare feet. "Who are you?"

"His brother. Which means you can buzz off. As a matter of fact, you can take the rest of the week off."

"I will have to talk to Ms. Owen—"

"Get lost, lady, before I throw you headfirst into the pool."

She hastily gathered her belongings and, after a quick trip into the house, piled into a blue Pinto parked out front and drove away. Throughout the confrontation Hank hadn't taken off his headphones or stopped bobbing his head. It wasn't until the woman had gone that Cyrus took a good look at his brother, who had the air of someone in a hospital waiting room, taut and exhausted.

"You look like shit," Cyrus said.

Hank pulled off the headset. "About how I feel, I guess."

When Cyrus tried to wheel his brother back into the house, he realized the chair was mechanical and that Hank could control it with small movements of a joystick. The woman hadn't left Hank baking in the sun; he'd positioned himself there.

The two brothers moved in single file up the ramp on the front porch. Once inside the house, they drifted into the den. When Cyrus asked if he needed anything, Hank looked out the window a moment, tapped his forehead and said, "How about a bullet? Right about here." When Cyrus didn't respond, Hank clucked his tongue and said, "You probably agree with my physiotherapist that this is some kind of opportunity, right?"

Cyrus crossed the room and, on impulse, sat on Hank's lap. He swung his legs over the arms of the wheelchair and hugged his brother's neck. "It's your birthday this weekend, Hank. I came to spend a few days."

"Oh, par-dee. What'd you have in mind, pin the tail on the donkey?"

"I thought we could hang out, that's all."

"Yeah, great, hanging out. That'll be a change."

Cyrus fetched them each a Coke from the refrigerator. Then they settled down to some television. For the better part of two hours, Cyrus kept talking about the shows, the commercials, whatever came into his head. And he wondered if Janice had ever felt this way about him: like Florence Nightingale cheering up the wounded. Maybe chattiness was a normal reaction in the presence of pain.

Isabel came home early, and it was clear that she felt Cyrus's arrival was the equivalent of the cavalry riding to the rescue. "This is nice," she said. "Real nice." She ordered pizza and smiled through the whole meal. After a cursory cleanup, she excused herself and went off for a long hot bath.

The moment she was gone, Hank hung his head and said, "You have no idea how much I hate this."

Cyrus figured he did have some idea. He would have hated it himself. "Seems to me Izzy's doing everything she can," he offered.

"No kidding. Thanks for the info, Brainiac. What do you think I'm talking about? She's got dough, looks, she could do anything she wants, and instead she comes home every night to babysit me. It sucks, man."

"So why don't you make it easier for her, if you feel that way?"

"The only way I feel is I wish Goldie's pals had finished what they started. Fact is, kid, I can't give Izzy what she wants. It's not in me. And what is in me, I wouldn't wish on my worst enemy."

At nine Isabel made tea. She had a quick cup, declared it was her bedtime, then looked over to Hank, who could hardly keep his head up. "What about you?" she said. "You going to try to sleep?"

"What? No. Not yet." He gave his head a shake. "Not ready."

The two brothers sat up awhile longer. They watched the divisional playoffs between the Astros and the Dodgers. It was enough to make Cyrus wish he was watching the game with Clarence, someone who understood the slow majesty of baseball. Hank was always flipping channels, right in the middle of innings. He seemed to have no interest in the sport at all.

Around eleven, Cyrus began to feel the effects of dinner, the long drive and the tension of his brother's presence. He couldn't stop yawning. Hank seemed to be in even worse shape. Every few minutes his head would nod lower and his chin would almost touch his breastbone; then he'd jerk himself up and take a deep breath, as though there might be a shortage of oxygen in the room.

With a big stretch, Cyrus said, "I have to pack it in for the night. Looks like you could stand some sleep yourself."

Suddenly Hank got all speedy, blinking his eyes and nodding like a coke fiend. "I'm okay, kid. But you go ahead and crash."

Cyrus stumbled to his feet, grabbed the remote control from Hank and turned off the TV. "Thing is, bro, I'll be flaking out on the couch here. You're kinda in my room."

"Right. Sure." He motored toward his bedroom. "Sleep tight, kiddo."

Cyrus had no trouble falling asleep; but he woke in the middle of the night with an aching bladder and didn't know where he was at first. When he had it pieced together, he tiptoed down the hall to the bathroom. As he headed back to the sofa, he heard music and noticed Hank's door was ajar. He opened it enough to poke his head inside the room, and what he saw made him flinch. Hank had headphones on and was staring out the window, bathed in the yellow light from the street. His stillness and the colour of his face were that of a dead man. He turned, with the slothlike motion of the massively drugged, and said, "Did I wake you?"

"No, it's fine. I took a leak and heard the music. You okay? You look like shit. Why don't you go to bed?"

Hank removed his headphones, then turned to face him more fully. "I'm cool, kiddo. Just not ready to sleep yet."

Centrefolds covered the wall beside the bed, a pair of binoculars sat on the windowsill, but it was the stereo that dominated the room—tuner, tape player and snazzy-looking turntable, speakers that were large enough to do some damage.

Cyrus moved into the room and sat on the bed. "You in pain? Is that why you can't sleep?"

"I can sleep. I'm just not ready."

"You look like you haven't closed your eyes in weeks. What's up?"

"Forget about it. It's my routine. It works for me."

Cyrus nodded agreeably, then turned to the bedside table. According to the alarm clock, it was three-thirty. He turned back to his brother and said, "Hit the sack, Hank. Big day tomorrow."

"Hanging out, you mean."

"Our very own magical mystery tour. Tomorrow we hit the road."

Cyrus tiptoed back to the den and lay on the sofa, but it took him forever to fall asleep again. He kept thinking how bleak and miserable Hank looked, how his face just then had been the face of their father, or rather the face of their father at his lowest, a version of Riley that Cyrus had all but forgotten. Mostly when he remembered his dad, he thought about the physical exuberance of the man, how he would run full-speed into the lake and send up a fountain spray that would make them all squeal, how he was always the first one off the dock or the first to throw a snowball or climb a ridge, how he was a kid, full of pranks and moods and excess and, like a kid, quick to judge, quick to forgive.

Cyrus knew the other side of the man, of course. He'd made his own trips to the chicken coop (though never as often as Hank), and had seen what his father's silence could do to their mother's beautiful face. But the sadness and doubt had always seemed an aberration, superficial flaws in an otherwise playful man. To see that flaw now mirrored in his brother's face was doubly troubling. It not only reminded him of times he would rather forget but made him shiver with a gloomy thought of his own: that in the disposition of genetic material, Hank had gotten the dark, and Cyrus the light. And when sometime before dawn he heard his brother crying out in the garbled voice of dream-talk, he felt guilty for his many nights of easy sleep.

IT WAS AFTER SEVEN when the sound of Isabel's morning clatter brought Cyrus stumbling into the kitchen. His brother and sister had both eaten breakfast and were sipping coffee. Isabel was dressed for a workout. After one final gulp of coffee, she blew them a kiss. "Be good," she called on her way to the door.

Hank gave him the eyeball and said, "You gonna sit there all day? You got me all excited about our magical mystery tour."

"We're going. Hold your horses." He poured himself a coffee. "I figured we might drive around the marsh first."

"The marsh? I thought we were gonna have some fun. Let's go to Hounslow, for Christ's sake. We could go to the racetrack, have something to eat, see some strippers, maybe even find ourselves some tail. Gordie knows women there could suck the chrome off a trailer hitch."

Cyrus made a sour face. "Just you and me, Hank."

"Oh right, hanging out. I forgot."

They left the house at about eleven with a folding wheelchair in the trunk. At Spring Creek, Cyrus parked the car and rolled Hank's chair over to the Bailey bridge. There was no way he could drag his brother down to the bank, so they just stood in the middle of the bridge and looked around. If he turned toward the lake, the view was pretty much the way he remembered it.

Seagulls wheeled overhead. The air carried the sweet tang of tomatoes from the cannery in town. Cyrus leaned over the rail, pointed to the creek and said, "Remember the summer we spent down there? It was after you came back from Burwash. Just you and me."

"Sorry, kid. Those were pretty crazy times."

"But we had a ball. I thought you were so cool."

"I was cool. Must've been the summer I was banging Ruth Woltz *and* her old lady. No wonder I was with you every day. I was exhausted."

"But you don't remember?"

"I had other things on my mind, I guess."

Cyrus spit over the edge and watched it hit the sluggish flow of the creek. He'd been ready to tell Hank about the other significant moments at the bridge, and how it would be the title of his first album. Now it didn't feel right to talk about it.

They returned to the car and continued out to the old place. Although Isabel had told him what to expect, the change still caught him off guard. No sign of the Owens remained; everything had been knocked down and carted away. With the metal fence and orange flare and paved road, with the pumps and the containers and the signs warning everyone to keep out, it was hard to believe it had once been a farm.

Hank enjoyed Cyrus's discomfort, not because he wanted him to suffer, but because he believed the kid needed this kind of hard lesson. Cyrus, he figured, had a rosy view of the present and the future because he remembered the past as a sunny place—and that was dead wrong as far as Hank was concerned. He should know; he'd been there. The ugliness of their childhood had followed him right into the present, and it seemed pretty certain that it would lead him into the future. The sooner Cyrus clued in to the truth, the better off he'd be. Otherwise it would rise up one day and bite him on the ass.

Hank said, "I wouldn't get too worked up about this, kid. Wasn't such a hot place to begin with."

Cyrus stared gloomily at the pumps as they drew oil from hundreds of feet inside the earth. And the longer he watched, the more he hated the sight of them, the mechanical stupidity of it all, ceaselessly pumping wealth and power. As he drove away, he said, "It's like when you're a kid, one of those stupid things you wish for. What if there was a tap in your house and when you turned it on pop came out. Or what if there was a secret passageway from your closet to an ice cream factory."

Hank laughed, a short, caustic sound. "Pop and ice cream, give me a break. I never wasted my time with piddly-assed wishes like that."

"You know what I mean, the stupid wishes you have when you're, like, five. I used to have this dream when I was a kid, where Mom gave me one of her spoons and I went into her garden to dig around, and every spoonful had money in it, nickels and dimes and quarters. Like that, I mean. Not real wishes you have when you're older."

Hank looked out the side window at the fields of soybeans, trying to remember a time in his life when he'd been that naive. "My dreams were never like that," he said.

"Oh, right, when you were five you were already wishing for Brigitte Bardot and a fancy car."

"Well here's the thing," Hank said, his voice tight with strain, "it was never like that, any of it. Every wish I ever had was fucked. I think back, and I don't remember much about those days. I remember Ma coming back from the hospital with Izzy, sort of. And I can remember holding Izzy, or maybe I just remember a snapshot of me in Ma's photo album. Nothing about ice cream or pop, though. Nothing good . . ."

His voice trailed off just when Cyrus was getting really interested. If he had any hopes about these few days together, it was that they might compare memories of growing up. Maybe talking about stuff would help Hank a bit. As the silence deepened, Cyrus said, "So what *did* you wish for?"

Hank pushed the cigarette lighter in, then pulled it out, pushed it in, then pulled it out. Finally he said, "The first wish I can ever remember, I'd lie in the dark—and this was before we had the bunk beds, so you weren't born yet—and I'd wish the old man was dead. I'd picture him falling out of a plane or a boat and just disappearing."

Cyrus drove in silence for a half mile or so, then said, "I can't believe that's true, Hank."

"Maybe it isn't. Maybe it's just the way I remember it. But what difference does that make?"

For lunch, Cyrus had planned on getting foot-long hotdogs at the town pier. But every favourite childhood spot had provided him with a heartache that day, so he decided to steer clear of the dock and head to Orchard Knoll. If he could count on anyone, it was Ruby.

When he pulled into the driveway, she was outside on a stepladder, washing windows. Hank leaned out of the car and said, "Hey there, good-looking, you wanna come for a spin?"

She climbed down from the ladder and walked toward them, her face full of unqualified happiness. And Cyrus thought what a noble calling it would be to walk through the world making people feel better. He jumped out of the car and gave her a bone-crushing hug, lifting her right off the ground and making her squeal.

After they wrestled Hank out of the front seat and into the wheelchair, they pushed him up the ramp by the side door and into the kitchen. He looked around like he was in a dream. "This place," he said, "you've changed it. The cupboards and everything, they're new."

"Oh, Lord, no," she chuckled. "I've been after Clarence to fix this place for almost twenty years. No, you've just forgotten, that's all. It's been a long, long time."

Cyrus looked from one to the other, unable to believe what he was hearing. "You mean he hasn't been here since . . ."

"I was sixteen," Hank finished. "The summer before Burwash, I guess."

"Izzy doesn't bring you out?"

Ruby gave a gentle shrug of her shoulder and said, "It's not like they haven't been invited. Clarence built the ramp out there to make it easier. But you know that sister of yours. Likes to do things her own way."

She set about making them roast beef sandwiches and a pot of tea. When everything was ready, she joined them at the table. She reached out both hands, palms up, and invited the two brothers to lay a hand in hers. Then she smiled and said, "This is like the answer to a prayer, isn't it?"

Hank and Cyrus coughed nervously and brought their hands back to their laps. Cyrus said, "Where's Clarence? It's not like him to miss lunch."

Ruby swivelled in her chair to consult the clock. "He's off on his afternoon jaunt. Goes downtown for a haircut on Thursdays, has lunch at Kresge's counter and then plays a few games of snooker with Bake Brown."

Of all the surprises of the day, this was the most surprising to Cyrus. "Clarence in a pool hall? You're joking."

"Not at all. Bake even got him onto the golf course this summer."

Both brothers laughed at the image of Clarence in plaid slacks and a peaked cap. This was a man whose life had two parts: work, which took up the bulk of the day; and non-work, which was preparation for the former. When he was tired or it was too dark to work, he'd have his nose stuck in a history book, or something equally dry. Occasionally he'd listen to a ball game on the radio, but that was the extent of his entertainment. He thought television was stupid, and movies a bore. Now he was whacking little white balls around acres of grass.

Ruby waited for the brothers to work through their mirth. She was relieved that Clarence had shaken himself out of his doldrums. "When the doctor first told him to take it easy," she said, "it was just the worst punishment, like he'd been asked to run naked through the streets of Wilbury. You know Clarence. He thought the orchard would go to ruin if he let up even a little. But he got a couple of Frank's boys to help out, and now I think he's finally starting to relax. Still likes to complain how useless he feels, but he doesn't fool me a bit. Getting lazy as a pet coon."

She laughed then, a sound Cyrus had heard countless times in his life. Only now did he realize it was the same as his mother's laugh: three distinct notes, a perfect rising arpeggio of the tonic, major third and fifth, the outline of a chord so sweet and without conflict that it was synonymous with resolution, what all music aspired to.

They chatted pleasantly through lunch and agreed that the discovery of oil had tainted the marsh. You could smell the gas burning off. You could see the flares lighting up the night clouds. Worst of all, Ruby said, was the animosity it had created among the farmers. A matter of a couple hundred yards in some cases meant the difference between those who were oil rich and those who were dirt poor.

As briefly as possible, Cyrus explained what he'd been up to the past while. At the mention of the band and the record he hoped to make, Ruby raised her eyebrows and smiled kindly but had nothing to say. Music didn't seem like a real job to her. When Hank asked what kind of music it was,

Cyrus shrugged and said, "It's kind of weird. You'd have to hear it." As if that were all the clarification needed.

Ruby cleared the dishes and brought them each a bowl of applesauce. When they had finished slurping up the last of it, she said, "What about you, Hank? You've been awfully quiet. You know, ever since your trouble there, I've had to wonder what this world is coming to, that people could do something like that. And they've never found the people who did it?"

"Well," he said vaguely, "I never really got much of a look at 'em."

"It's a crying shame is what it is." She laid a hand on his gnarled fist. "We can thank God that Isabel came along when she did."

Hank shifted awkwardly in his chair and said, "It was real nice how much you came to the hospital, Ruby."

"Well, dear, it's the least I could do."

Cyrus cocked his thumb at Hank. "It's his fortieth this weekend."

"Goodness gracious, don't I know. I was there in your kitchen when your mother's water broke. Riley, of course, had chosen that day to drive into La Salle for some part he was missing. You know how he was. He'd been meaning to fix something for weeks and then, all of a sudden, he needed that part. It was me and Clarence who drove your mother to the hospital. Your dad didn't show up till all the excitement was over."

She looked out the window, her features softening as she retrieved happy memories. "You were such a beautiful baby," she said. "Rosy cheeks, lovely grey eyes like your mother's. She had ideas about you modelling for the catalogue, but Riley nearly had a fit when he heard that."

Cyrus poked Hank in the shoulder. "Aw, idn't he a pretty boy?"

Ruby raised her eyebrows mischievously. "I wouldn't talk there, mister. You were such a doll that everyone thought you were a girl."

Hank hooted at that, and Cyrus leaned toward Ruby, his face glowing with a bright idea. "You gotta come and help us celebrate tomorrow."

"Well," she said, "Izzy has never really extended an invitation."

"I am, Ruby. You gotta be there."

"Oh, honey, I don't know. It might just cause problems."

It was Hank who settled it. He slapped the table and said, "If there's one thing the Owens know about, it's problems, and this ain't one of them. Don't you worry about Iz. We can take care of her. You just be there."

The rest of the afternoon, the brothers drove around town pointing out the highlights to each other: the park where Hank felt up Amy Brousseau, the Landrys' backyard where Cyrus smoked his first joint, Weber Produce where Hank had his first job after quitting school. At Three Links Hall, Cyrus tried to explain the significance of having a place to hang out with Janice and the others, and of the day he bought the Les Paul and discovered his future.

By the time they returned to the house, Isabel was there. She had steaks marinating on the counter and beer in the fridge. She'd bought an expensive bottle of wine. When they walked in the door, she was sitting in the den with her feet up. She'd changed into shorts and a T-shirt and was sipping a tall gin and tonic.

"If it isn't the lords of leisure," she said. "At least you could have washed the damn dishes."

Cyrus pecked the top of her head. "Sorry, Iz. We had a full itinerary. I'll clean up after supper."

"Fair enough. So what kind of mischief did you get up to?"

The brothers exchanged glances and in unison said, "Nothing much."

"That sounds scary. Should I call the cops for details?"

"All very innocent," Cyrus said. "We cruised around town showing each other the hot spots."

"Yeah," Hank quipped. "He showed me his and I showed him mine."

Cyrus fetched beer for Hank and himself and said, "About tomorrow, Iz, did you have any plans?"

"Not exactly. I have an open house until four. I thought we could maybe make a reservation at the Lobster Pot."

"Or," he countered, "I could make supper here. That might be the easiest. Besides, how often do you get to experience my kitchen magic?"

She took a sip of gin and, with an ice cube stuck in her cheek, said, "If it's lethal, only once."

THE PEOPLE OF WILBURY liked to tell strangers that the town was on the same latitude as northern California; but anyone who had spent a few days in the area knew the axis of affinity was closer to the Deep South. The downtown neighbourhoods consisted of huge homes of brick and wood, with wide wraparound porches, the older streets lined with maple and chestnut, sycamore and catalpa. The town hall was a stately brick building with white columns and a spacious portico. Cyrus remembered his parents dragging the whole family there one night after supper. It was the middle of the polio scare, and half the families in town, edgy with fear, were lined up outside to get their kids the oral vaccine.

What most set Wilbury in a southern light was the humidity and the heat and the lush vegetation. It was a place for growing things: the history of the town a history of farmers made wealthy by rich soil, good weather, ample water and a steady flow of hard-working immigrants. Tourism professionals had dubbed the area The Sun Parlour, but Cyrus always felt it should have been called The Sauna. Even so, an October heat wave was an unexpected bonus. And after driving around all day, he was content to sit in the backyard with Hank, drinking beer and splashing his feet in the plastic pool, while Izzy barbecued the steaks and foiled-wrapped packets of potatoes and onions.

Hank seemed to be enjoying himself, too. He breathed deeply the balmy air, smacking his lips in anticipation of dinner. After he finished his second can of beer, he said, "No one asked what I wanted for my birthday."

Isabel turned to him with one hand on her hip, the other swinging a barbecue fork on its leather thong the way a cop might swing his billy club. "Maybe that's because we know what you deserve."

Cyrus thought that was pretty funny. Tapping his forehead like Lieutenant Columbo, he said, "Presents . . . presents. Let me see, those would be the things we give to you but you never give to us, is that it?"

Hank ignored the wisecracks and popped the top on another Schlitz. "A man turns forty," he said, "you'd think his sibs'd spring for something special."

Isabel sashayed over, took a long pull on Hank's beer and said, "Why do I get the feeling I'm being set up?"

"I'm just trying to help you make this the best birthday I ever had."

"Oh, well, that means a lot to me." She poked his belly with the prongs of the fork. "What'll it be, fatso? What's on your wish list?"

He turned from Izzy to Cyrus and said, "You think I'm joking."

"No we don't, do we, Cyrus?"

"Right. Your wish is our command."

Hank nodded seriously. "Okay," he said, "I wanna get laid."

Isabel looked around nervously to see if any neighbours were near. "Jesus, keep it to yourself, will you?"

"I wanna get laid!" he repeated, this time more aggressively.

When Cyrus hooted merrily, she turned on him. "Don't be egging him on, stupid. This is partly your fault."

To which Hank and Cyrus both said, "Uh-oh." When she followed their gaze, she saw the steak and potatoes engulfed in flames.

THE BEAUTY OF A TRIAD was displayed most effectively during dinner. One moment the two brothers teased Izzy mercilessly; the next, Cyrus helped his sister hound Hank's sorry hide. Just as often, Hank and Izzy took turns poking fun at Mr. Bigshot Musician. If there was one thing that bound the three together, it was this sense of fair play.

Luckily the food had been plucked from the inferno without much damage. But then they were all so hungry, it scarcely would have mattered. Hank went at his meal with the grunting gusto that Isabel witnessed every night. When she caught Cyrus staring in fascination at his brother, she sniffed and said, "I've seen better manners in Gerry's pig barns."

Hank put down his T-bone and wiped his mouth with the back of his hand. "You got a problem with the way I eat?"

"Not at all, Hank. It's pure entertainment."

"Good," he muttered. "Wouldn't want you disappointed or nuthin'."

As promised, Cyrus did the dishes. When Izzy came in to help put things away, he said, "What do you think?"

At first she thought he was talking about the job he had done on the dishes. She studied a plate for streaks. Then, in a flash, she understood what he meant. "Oh, Christ, I don't even want to know about it."

"You gotta feel sorry for him. When was the last time he got any?"

"Cyrus," she whispered, "stop right there."

"No, listen, I've been thinking." He grabbed her arm and dragged her into the den where they could talk more freely. "What would it hurt?"

She shook her head. "Have you lost your mind? You going to just waltz a whore into my living room and introduce her to Hank? What about the neighbours? No, never mind that, what about the police? Prostitution is against the law, you know. Besides, I already got him something."

"Not what he wants, though."

"Cyrus, nobody gets what they want. Now drop it."

"Sure, sure, it was just a thought."

They went back outside and sat together on the patio for another hour or so, the fizz pretty much gone from the evening. Izzy had always been an early bird and started to fade about nine-thirty, especially when she'd had something to drink.

Cyrus said, "Look a little bagged there, Iz. Another big day tomorrow. Why don't you call it a night?"

She kissed them each on the head and went inside. Cyrus kicked Hank's chair and startled him from a trance. "Rise and shine, Casanova. The minute she's asleep, we're out of here."

That made Hank perk up. "Where we going?"

"Paradise, daddy-o."

HOUNSLOW WAS A FORTY-MINUTE DRIVE from Wilbury, and they made it to the city before midnight. At the first stoplight, Cyrus turned to Hank and said, "I don't know the first thing about this. What do we do now?"

Hank rolled his eyes, clearly enjoying his greater wisdom in these matters. He mentioned an address and, after a number of wrong turns and detours, they found themselves on a gloomy dead-end street that faced a line of derelict factories. Their destination was a bungalow with asphalt siding and a picture window. The drapes were drawn, no cars out front. The only sign of life was a single string of winking Christmas lights.

Cyrus parked the car at the curb and said, "You sure this is the place? It looks kinda homey."

"This is it. Just say we're friends of Gordie Spinks."

Without a moment's hesitation, Cyrus started the engine. He would have driven away, too, if Hank hadn't yanked the key from the ignition and jammed it in his pocket. "Don't get freaky on me, kid."

"Freaky is you wanting to mess with Spinks again. I say we get out of here and forget the whole thing."

"Well that ain't gonna happen, 'cause I'm gonna get myself laid good and proper, even if I have to drag myself in there on my belly."

Cyrus stared at the dashboard as though he might will the car to start. He said, "You're going to get us killed."

"No," he said, waving his index finger in the air. "I'm going to get us laid. Don't worry about Gordie. Our little problem got sorted out. Besides, he's on my side."

"You say that like it's a *good* thing."

Hank pushed him playfully. "Go on. And quit worrying."

Cyrus left Hank in the car and approached the house. He noticed that the lawn had been freshly mowed. Chrysanthemums bordered the sidewalk. Those simple details helped to stem his rising sense of dread.

Before he could knock, a woman opened the door and said, "What can I do for you, sweetie pie? You look like you're lost."

It was one of those voices some women get, like they've smoked a million cigarettes and had too many belts of harsh whiskey. She had a mahogany tan, a roly-poly figure and looked to be in her fifties, her hair silver grey and cropped close to her head. She had hoop earrings and jangly bracelets. She wore a Bugs Bunny T-shirt and denim cut-offs that showed an awful lot of varicose vein. Her name, he would find out later, was Peg.

He turned to look at the Impala and then back at her. "My brother is out in the car there. He's a friend of Gordie Spinks."

She ran her tongue along the crowns of her teeth, her face full of amusement. "Gordie doesn't have any friends," she said. "Not that I know of. But why don't you come in anyway?"

"Ah, well," he stammered, "I'm really just here for my brother."

"Come in, come in. I hate talking on the porch." She grabbed him by the arm and led him into a small parlour where she indicated he should sit. She crossed the room to a phony fireplace, took a pack of menthol cigarettes from the mantel and lit one up. "So," she said, after she had blown a column of smoke toward the ceiling, "you were saying your brother's a friend of Gordie's. He's come here for some hospitality?"

"That's the idea, yeah. But it'd have to be a special deal . . ."

"Oh, we do special, all right. Special's our middle name."

Cyrus couldn't look at her. She was old enough to be a grandmother. "What I mean is, he's crippled. I might need some help with him."

"Oh, this is sounding like more fun all the time."

"What I'm trying to get at is, it's probably not your regular thing, and he has this idea of spending the night. What'll that cost?"

"Well, punkin', that entirely depends on what your brother wants, but we normally charge a hundred an hour plus extras. I imagine we could give you a special deal, seeing he's a cripple and all. Three-fifty should take care of it. I don't imagine he'll be too demanding. That is, of course, unless you'd like to hear about some of our two-for-one specials."

Cyrus spent the next few hours slumped inside the Chevy. By four o'clock, he'd seen three taxis pull up and each deposit a different woman, who promptly entered the tidy bungalow. At four-thirty, one of them came out and tapped on the window of his car. "I'm Taffy," she said in a nasal twang. "Whyncha come in? Peg's making tea. We don't bite, you know."

He was so physically uncomfortable that he accepted the invitation. "That'd be nice," he said. "Tea would be good."

He followed her into the house, admiring the garden once again, the wrought iron railing of the porch, the brass mailbox and the Muskoka chairs—anything to avoid looking at her. Inside, he could hear the Supremes, and above that, a woman's high giddy laughter and Hank's tuneless tenor.

Taffy led him into a cheery kitchen with a yellow countertop and delicate floral wallpaper. Peg sat at an oak table, working on a crossword puzzle. When she spotted Cyrus, she patted the chair beside her and nodded at Taffy to bring the tea. "This is nicer than sitting outside in your car," she said. "Look, we even got out the good china."

Cyrus admired the cup. Royal Albert. He held it out for Taffy to fill.

"Not often we get visitors," Peg said. "It's mostly takeout these days."

"I kinda noticed that," he said, his eyes focused on his steaming cup.

"And you know, I miss the visitors, the different faces."

"Oh, me too," Taffy said, taking the opportunity to sit in the other chair. "It's like a morgue in here sometimes."

Hank bellowed along with Junior Walker, and Peg smiled. "Doesn't seem to me that brother of yours is slowing down any. Sure you don't want to waste some time yourself?"

"No," he said, grabbing his cup with both hands. "Really, I'm not interested. Tell you the truth, I'm a little uncomfortable."

"No shit, Sherlock. I never would have guessed." To look him in the eyes, she had to lean forward, her chin nearly touching the table. "We're not monsters, you know."

He sat up straighter, still unable to meet her gaze. A place like this felt a whole lot different when he wasn't drunk. At last he said, "I guess I wonder how you can do what you do."

Peg nodded as if to say that was a fair question. In a matter-of-fact tone, she said, "We do what we have to do to get by, same as everyone. The worst thing is I almost never screw for fun anymore, which is a shame. It kind of loses something when money's involved. But it's not so bad. Beats working in a coal mine, you ask me."

"That's not what you hear . . ."

She skated a finger along the rim of her cup. "No question, most working girls got a lousy situation. Pimps, they should all be strung up by their thumbs, as far as I'm concerned. Scum of the earth. But a little business like we got here, just me and the girls, it's all right."

"What about Gordie Spinks? I heard he was in charge here."

She laughed at that, a raspy hack. "Gordie? He's too busy fiddling with that damn chopper of his to run a respectable business like this. Where'd you ever hear a story like that?"

"My brother heard Gordie talking like he owned the place."

The two women exchanged a knowing look. Peg said, "This is my place. I run it, I own it, and I treat my girls like family—the one they deserve, not the shitty ones they were born to. Gordie may have his good points, but between you and me, he's completely useless. And I can afford to say that because I'm his mother."

That news made him flinch. She touched his arm and said, "I know what happened to your brother. The police were here asking questions. Showed me his picture. That boy of mine is a burden, let me tell you, and has been since the day he was born, but he'd never do something like that."

They sat for a long while, sipping tea and listening to Motown—Stevie Wonder, The Four Tops, The Jackson 5, The Temptations. In the end Cyrus actually had to knock on the bedroom door and tell Hank it was time to go. While a part of him wanted to see how long it would take his brother to unwind, he also wanted to get back before Izzy was awake. He wasn't ready for any explanations.

Unfortunately, they got lost on their way out of the city, kept circling the same crazy network of one-way streets. A little before six, Cyrus pulled into a gas station for directions and to drain off some tea. And maybe it wasn't the same station as twenty-two years ago. Maybe it just looked that way to Hank—the same brand of gas, the same arrangement of the pumps, the same stark white light from overhead, the same greasy little office with the pop machine out front and the cans of oil in the window stacked in a pyramid, the same freckle-faced man without a thing on his mind. Maybe it was imagination or being with Cyrus, all the talking they'd done, maybe it was that, the gradual opening up, but Hank squeezed his eyes shut and would not open them. And when that didn't work, he pushed his fists against his eyeballs until he saw fireworks.

When Cyrus got back behind the wheel, he smacked Hank on the shoulder. "You're not getting sleepy, are you?"

"Go," Hank groaned. "Drive."

"What's wrong?"

"Move it, I said. Let's go, let's go, let's go." And when Cyrus still didn't put the Impala in gear, Hank pounded the dashboard and shouted, "Drive the fucking car!"

It wasn't until they were halfway to Wilbury that Hank lifted his head. Cyrus eyed him carefully. "What was that about?"

"I don't know. It was nothing."

"Looked like something to me."

"It was nothing. A little freaked out is all. It happens."

Cyrus realized there was no point in saying any more, so he kept his eyes on the road and stepped on the gas. But Isabel was already awake and sitting at the kitchen table when they entered the house.

"I'm not happy about this," she said, staring at Cyrus.

"We couldn't sleep. We went for a drive."

"Drive, my foot. I know very well what you were up to." She turned to Hank, arms folded across her chest. "I'm trying so hard, you know. I'm trying to make this all work out and it's just not fair." Then she bowed her head, as though she couldn't stand the sight of them.

Cyrus moved forward and touched her shoulder. "Very innocent, Iz. We were driving, honest. We've got ground to cover, me and Hank."

She lifted her head to look at him. "You're a lying shit. You think I was born yesterday?" Then she got to her feet and ran to the bedroom. Half an hour later, she left for work without saying another word.

Hank kept a low profile throughout the day, watching TV, sitting outside for a while with a cup of coffee. Cyrus, who managed a quick snooze, was amazed that his brother could keep going this way. Sooner or later he'd have to sleep.

For dinner, Cyrus decided to make Eura's goulash. Mid-afternoon he went out for groceries and spices, some wine and a few bottles of German beer. Then he phoned Ruby to make sure they were still coming.

He was glad that both his mother and aunt had forced him to do things in the kitchen when he was growing up. He hated it at the time, all that peeling and slicing, but it gave him a real thrill to watch Eura eat his shepherd's pie and stewed chicken. Even his pasta sauce got a passing grade, which was no mean feat. She cared about food, and he had learned to care, too. In fact, their meals, both the preparation and eating of them, were the happiest part of their life together. He had come to regard cooking as not a whole lot different than music. Once you knew a few of the basics, it was largely a matter of what you put in and what you left out. And if you did it right, you could lift everyone's spirit.

By five o'clock Izzy still wasn't home, and Cyrus began to wonder if she would be. He helped Hank clean himself up and get into nice clothes. Then he had a shower, shaved, and dressed in the white collarless shirt and black dress pants Eura had bought for him. He had just finished tidying up and was setting the table in the dining room when Ruby and Clarence arrived, looking thoroughly uncomfortable. They weren't the only ones who were nervous. Cyrus had hoped to have a few minutes alone with Izzy to break the news about their dinner guests. And when his aunt and uncle realized that Isabel wasn't around, they got even more nervous. No one seemed capable of even the lamest small talk. Cyrus wondered what would be worse, if his sister came home or if she didn't.

He got everyone drinks, checked the goulash which, small mercies, smelled delicious. Hank was making an effort to put Clarence and Ruby at ease, and that gesture seemed to be all that was required. Pretty soon the four of them were chatting pleasantly. It was then that the front door slammed, the big vase in the foyer smashed on the marble floor, and Isabel took the name of the Lord in vain.

Cyrus quietly excused himself from the others and attempted to intercept Izzy before she stumbled on the whole scene. The minute he saw her, he covered his mouth. She was drenched with rain, her clothes rumpled and muddy, and she had a huge and obviously heavy cardboard box in her arms, which she was certain to drop any moment.

"Give me that," he said.

"Be careful," she snapped. "It's delicate."

She handed him the box and hobbled to the closet to take off her coat, which was smeared with grass stains and muck. She dropped it on the floor and kicked it into the corner. Cyrus noticed that one of her spike-heeled shoes was now a sensible flat, causing her to move like someone with a peg leg.

"You wouldn't believe," she said. "Some moron is blocking my driveway, in the middle of a monsoon, and I had to park around the corner and carry that damn thing—" She stopped dead when she saw that one corner of the box had been smashed in. "Oh God, don't do this to me." And in an angry spasm, she ripped the shoes off her feet and flung them into the closet with all her might.

The whole picture solidified for Cyrus. She had wrestled the package out of the car—the box had to weigh sixty pounds—and somewhere along the way, her heel snapped off, she fell on her side in the mud and smashed the corner of her delicate gift.

"I'm sure it'll be fine," he murmured.

"No," she replied, "it's broken. Everything's broken. Everything will always be broken." And with that she stormed into the bathroom.

Cyrus laid the box on the floor, ran quickly to the den—"She's a little upset. I'll talk to her."—and then ran back to the bathroom. He opened the door a crack and said, "Are you decent?"

"Go away and let me calm down."

"I need to talk to you."

"It can wait, Cy. I'm a little stressed right now."

He edged into the room with his hand over his eyes, then closed the door behind him. "It can't wait, sis. It's better, I think, if you do all your calming down at once."

"Meaning . . ."

"I invited Ruby and Clarence for dinner. They're in the den."

She took a deep breath, let it out, then pulled his hand from his eyes. She was still fully dressed. "I'll be okay," she said. "Give me ten minutes. Really, I'm glad they're here. It's a nice gesture." As he turned to leave, she touched his shoulder and said, "Carry that box to my room, will you? I want to surprise the bastard."

He did what she asked and noticed that she'd bought Hank a synthesizer only slightly less sophisticated than the one Cyrus's keyboard player used. It had to have cost her two grand at least. If she had asked him for advice he would have told her she was nuts to buy an instrument like that for some-one who didn't know how to play "Chopsticks." But of course she never asked his opinion.

IT COULD BE IT HAD SOMETHING to do with the showbiz nature of her job, standing in front of people all day doing the same song and dance, but Cyrus was amazed Isabel could breeze into the den like she had never had a tantrum, like Clarence and Ruby were frequent guests at her house and she at theirs, like everything was the way it should be and not the way it was. There she was, all fresh and powdered and expensively dressed, her face beaming with pleasure because it was so good to see them. Really. And supper smelled so good. And wasn't the table lovely? And look at Hank and Cy—why, they looked almost like gentlemen.

Ruby and Clarence's act was equally surreal, like they were sitting with the queen, afraid to breathe lest they spoil everything.

After a few minutes of chit-chat, everyone moved to the table, where Cyrus served them goulash in bowls, with little side plates for rye bread and carrot-and-apple salad. And who would have thought such a thing could happen? Not Ruby or Clarence, not Hank or Isabel, not even Cyrus. Before long the combination of food and drink began to loosen tongues and inhibitions. Little by little they became more themselves, not always a good thing, but in this case, maybe.

Cyrus mentioned that he and Hank had driven around town and how disappointing it had been. Oil wells with their industrial stink and blight. Acres of housing where there'd once been open fields. Acres of greenhouse glass, too, as more and more farmers opted for greater control over the elements. A downtown area that was rundown and decrepit because most shoppers flocked to the new mall down by the lake or preferred to drive all the way to Hounslow.

He hadn't meant to criticize Isabel, but to her ears it sounded that way. Many of his complaints were about deals she'd arranged—the mall, for example, and the Jenner subdivision—but she'd heard it all before. She dabbed at her lips and, in a condescending tone, said, "You can't stop progress, brother dear. People want new homes. They want to shop where it's convenient. It's only human nature."

Hank sucked at his teeth and said, "They can bulldoze the whole damn town, you ask me. Nothing but bad memories."

Clarence, who had yet to utter a word at the table, cleared his throat and said, "Funny thing about memories, Hank, is how stubborn they are. Those oilmen already knocked down your house and your dad's barns. They've covered the farm with more metal than a scrapyard so you wouldn't half recognize it. And I don't imagine that's helped your memories one iota. Or has it?"

Hank nodded at the old man's wisdom. "You're right, Clarence." Tapping his forehead with his index finger, he added, "It's up here I need to do some bulldozing."

After dinner Cyrus made coffee and they sat in the den with cake he had bought at the bakery. Soon it was time for gifts.

Ruby and Clarence gave Hank a brown cardigan sweater that was total Perry Como. Hank was a good sport about it. He put it on without comment and did up all the buttons. Cyrus, who had already given Hank his present in Hounslow, had to offer him something at the party, so he handed him the cassette of his demo. "My own stuff," he said with a shrug. "Hope you like it." Then Izzy and Cyrus disappeared and came back carrying the synthesizer, which they laid across the arms of Hank's wheelchair. While he poked stupidly at the buttons, everyone else looked from the keyboard to Isabel, their faces full of questions.

In response she said, "He's up all night listening to music. I thought, you know, if he loves it that much . . ."

"Sure," Clarence said, nodding soberly, "a person has to stay busy."

Isabel looked at everyone and wanted to scream, because no one got it. It wasn't about staying busy. And it wasn't about buying affection or impressing everyone with her generosity. It was about hope—for Hank and, in a way, for all of them. She wouldn't have been able to say much more than that. It was all pretty vague in her mind. But when she closed her eyes in bed sometimes and gave thanks for the way her life had changed, she often thought about the day Sheldon Demeter rubbed her nose in Gerry's infidelity, the day she sat in her car and found her strength. And if she could wish one thing for Hank, it was that he would find *his* strength—the way she had found hers, the way Cyrus, the little prick, had always been strong—and that one day he would reach inside where he felt most empty and find what he most needed.

After everyone had oohed and ahhed over the keyboard, Izzy said, "We'll let you practise a little before we expect a recital." Then she and Cyrus carried the synthesizer into Hank's room.

Before the Mitchells went home, Ruby dug some snapshots out of her purse and passed them around: Hank as a toddler, all chubby cheeks and pink skin with a mop of dark brown curls; as a five-year-old, perched on his father's shoulders and squealing with glee; at ten, scrubbed squeaky clean and modelling his new Sunday suit from the Eaton's catalogue; as a sixteen-year-old rebel with greasy hair, his arm around the buxom Amy Brousseau.

"You were such a beautiful little boy," Ruby said wistfully.

Izzy couldn't get over the picture of the clean-cut fellow in the new suit.

"Look at you," she said, a note of laughter in her voice. "Look at your leg. You're modelling like you're in the catalogue, for crying out loud."

Cyrus brought over the photo of the young dude with his babe. "And look at this one," he crowed. "Talk about Mr. Cool."

Hank wasn't laughing. People could tell him he'd been happy once, they could show him pictures of a bright-eyed boy, but it meant no more to him than the idea that we are all descendants of apes. Maybe it was true, and maybe it was important, but it all happened a long time ago and, anyway, what could you do with information like that? So he nodded stupidly and said, "Look at that. Some getup." But his heart wasn't in it. He breathed a sigh of relief when Ruby and Clarence got up to leave.

He followed them to the door and thanked them for coming. "And for the sweater," he added hastily. "It's nice and warm."

"Well," Ruby said, "you won't need it for a few weeks yet. But this winter it should come in handy." Then she knelt down and kissed his cheek. "I know your sister's awful busy, so any time you need a ride somewhere, you give me a tinkle, will you? I'll be your chauffeur for the day."

Cyrus suddenly pictured Ruby sitting with Peggy Spinks while Hank had an afternoon rendezvous. It was such a surprising yet satisfying image that he nearly laughed out loud.

Izzy stood behind Hank's chair, like an anxious mother with a sick child, one hand resting on his shoulder, the other smoothing his cowlick. "Oh, now," Izzy was saying, "I'm not all that busy. And you've already got enough to worry about with Clarence. We can muddle along."

HANK'S ROUTINE WAS SHOT TO HELL. Normally he'd watch television after Izzy went to bed, flipping through the channels until he was blind with fatigue. But Cyrus's presence meant he had to hang out in his room.

He poked at the synthesizer awhile, but he wasn't in the mood for making that much effort, so he pulled on his headphones and listened to his favourite radio station until he'd heard the same ads two or three times. By then the steam had left his system, and he settled back a bit and worked his way through his cassettes, none of them from the current decade. He didn't rock his head or tap his fingers as he listened, just stared out the window at the writhing dance of the maple across the street.

He'd seen ghosts out there in the shifting shapes of the night, seen his father's face pressed to the window, the gas station attendant sitting in the tree, Golden Reynolds crouched by the windowsill. It made no difference when Hank closed his eyes because the faces were inside his head. Because of that, sleep was nearly impossible. The only thing that worked was the routine; the only sleep he found was at the end of his endurance when darkness fell upon him in a blink. Even there the faces intruded, shaking him awake a few hours later.

After he'd listened to every tape in his collection, he put on the cassette Cyrus had given him. He was curious, but he also remembered the last time he had heard his brother play in Toronto and how miserable it had made him feel.

He leaned forward uneasily, his head full of tape hiss and electronic hum, the amplified whisper of his own breathing. Then, rising out of that background noise, a tremulous sound reminding him of the way poplars quake before a storm. A chord on a keyboard, five notes. And he closes his eyes in a kind of swoon, and sees the driveway of their farm and the poplars that line both sides. Bass and drums creep behind the chord, the kind of rhythm that makes him want to walk, not marching music really but walking music, a rolling gait that moves him step by step down that driveway. He sees the red-brick path that leads to the house. And with the chord quivering and the bass and drums loping along, the guitar begins to sing its melody, leading him up that path, past his mother's spice garden and into the mud room. It's all there, everything the way it's supposed to be. He takes off his rubber boots and his jacket and walks into the old kitchen where his mother sits at the table, feeding dry bread and vegetables and quartered apples into a meat grinder because it's Thanksgiving and she's making stuffing for the turkey, the bread-and-vegetable mixture spilling out of the grinder like a rainbow. And she opens her arms and says, "Come here, honey. Give Mommy a hug." He runs into her velvet embrace, and the smell of onion and carrot and celery mixes with the poultry seasoning and her lilac dusting powder and makes him go shivery and goosebumpy all over. . . .

Hank played the song again. And again. And each time he saw more of her: the way she curled her hair around her index finger when she was thinking; her laughter when he tickled her; the sound of her singing around the house, always singing, in a voice that made people think of Doris Day.

As he sat in the darkness of his room, lit only by the street light and the eerie glow of his stereo, he realized that throughout his entire life he had bumped against the same pains, the same horrors—the man with the belt, the man with the freckled face, the man with the radio, the man with the friends and favours—but never a trace of her, coming to believe that he would never see her face again, that she had slipped irretrievably into the blackness. And how ironic that a man without a future, a man whose every waking moment had been indelibly stamped by the past, would find it so hard to remember. He could speak her name but feel nothing, see nothing but a few bland images. Now suddenly there she was. She was in his brother's music, a living, breathing presence again.

Ronnie had not only made the most money from the Jimmy Waters Revival, he had gained the most respect. Perhaps he wasn't in the same league as Colonel Tom Parker or Brian Epstein, but look what he had to work with. Jimmy Waters was an impossible act to sell compared to Elvis and the Beatles. That Ronnie had succeeded at all was regarded as a matter of brilliance.

As a result, when he went shopping his new band around, people were eager to accommodate him, wanting to get in on the ground floor of the next big thing. "Jangle," they said, "yes, we are very interested." With a minimum of effort he arranged a showcase in Hollywood at the Troubadour. Every A&R director of every major label would be there.

Throughout the autumn, Ronnie's staff worked on a promo package while he hired a road crew. (No luck talking Adrian or Kerry or Tommy Mac back into the fold.) Raoul Dupree had settled on a design he called "quotidian chaos," the very look of a sound check in mid-stride, with cases and cables and equipment scattered everywhere, and the road crew's muscular shuffle an integral part of the show. When the band was established and able to fill large venues, there would be a suspension bridge that would rise above the clutter and, at certain key moments in the show, extend into the audience so that Cyrus could wander among his fans.

From November to just before Christmas, Nate Wroxeter booked a series of club dates so the band could work out the kinks, test their set for weak spots and awkward transitions, and give Cyrus, a lifelong sideman, a chance to rev up his stage presence. The crowds were largely enthusiastic, and each gig made the whole project seem larger and more inevitable. By the end of the stress test, Ronnie knew he had a roadworthy machine. The band members were strong, confident, and required little or no maintenance, their edges and angles fitting together like cogs of a wheel. The crew worked equally well. And because there were natural leaders in both groups, Ronnie's job would be a cinch.

Finally, on January 24, 1982, the band walked onstage at the Troubadour. Cyrus said, "I'd like to tell you a story now, if I may." And they launched into the dreamy intro of "The Bridge." Cyrus managed to move around the stage and look comfortable doing so, but he was mostly unconscious of who he was and what he was doing. He was blinded by the lights, deaf to any sound other than the band, numb to any feeling other than the music of his life passing through him like a flood.

THE VISIBLE PART OF THE EAR, the seashell, collects sound waves from the world and funnels them down the waxy canal to the eardrum, which converts those waves—crest, trough and amplitude—into mechanical vibrations. The eardrum also separates the outer ear from the middle ear, which is an ingenious little gizmo not unlike the tubes of an amplifier. With the help of three small connected bones—the malleus, the incus and the stapes—the middle ear amplifies the vibrations from the eardrum and passes them on to a much smaller opening called the oval window, which looks on to the inner ear. It's there, in a snail-like contraption called the cochlea, that the business of hearing gets interesting. The cochlea is filled with fluid and thousands of special nerve endings called hair cells. When the mechanical vibrations on the oval window disturb the fluid, the hair cells dance like seaweed on the ocean floor, and that movement sends an electric impulse through the auditory nerve to the brain, which is where it all comes together. Our ears don't hear words or melody or silence. They are a fancy bit of science designed to receive energy, modify it, break it down and pass it on.

What Ronnie heard at the Troubadour, the translation of wave to vibration to electric impulse, sounded remarkably like love. So much so that at the end of the first song, he was struck with utter clarity that he loved this boy like a son. This bridge they had built together, this cascade of notes, this arrangement of light and shade, colour and shape, was nothing more than a bridge between the two of them.

With Jim it had been different. Ronnie had wanted to hear that glorious solo again, a longing on par with the search for philosophical truth or mathematical purity. It was the music that led him to the man. But with Cyrus, it was the other way around. Ronnie found the boy, a child alone in the darkness, before he found the music; and together they had fumbled toward this riot of notes that now filled the room. No question, Ronnie wanted Jangle to be successful, but for the boy's sake, not his own. That realization had caught him off guard. His own desires had taken a back seat. He only wanted Cyrus to be happy, the very thing a father might say.

When the last note sounded and the band left the stage, Ronnie got to his feet and began to mingle. He shared words with Clive Davis, Mo Ostin, David Geffen and a dozen other hitmakers, and it was clear that they had listened but not heard. Their eyes gave no sign of understanding. They said the right words—"Ron, fantastic, call me, we'll talk."—but their eyes were full of distance and pity. At one time or another they had all been in his shoes, hearing the magic no one else could hear, seeing the future no one would believe. They backed quickly away lest he taint them with the evil eye.

Ronnie was a good sport. He held no grudges. He made no judgments. It wasn't about money or the big deal. As far as he was concerned, it wasn't even about music. It was about the boy. And when he had had a good stiff drink and prepared his face and tone and words, he headed backstage to tell the band how it really was, not how it was perceived. They believed him, too, because they could see the emotion shining in his eyes.

The party began soon after. The big names had stolen away, leaving behind the lesser lights and media freeloaders, people too naive to notice or too cynical to care that there was nothing to celebrate. Cyrus and the rest of the band fell into the first category. They dug into the drinks and nibbles with the ferocity of conquering heroes. They laughed and waved their arms madly. They were big and loud and full of themselves. The change, to Ronnie's eye, was bittersweet; and although he was happy enough to allow the illusion to remain, he wondered how long it would last.

His own evening had been spoiled. Aside from the band's performance, nothing had gone as it should. But he would keep that grief to himself and let Cyrus enjoy his moment. To see him there among those people, savouring his own power, made Ronnie smile. It was like the boy had been transformed into pure energy.

IF HOLLYWOOD TAUGHT CYRUS anything it was that bliss has many faces but only one name. He could make the case, with a good deal of certainty, that their gig at the Troubadour was the very pinnacle of his life to date, and that all other high points and low points were merely stations of the cross on the way to that pivotal moment. He stood in the spotlight and the music poured out of him, as though all he had ever felt, all he had ever known or remembered, came flooding out in those few brief songs. To his right, to his left, behind him even, were his fellow band members. To call them friends would minimize their importance. Call them brothers, soulmates who had joined the common cause, who had suffered together, laughed together, broken bread and debauched together, in the trenches, on the bus, who had opened themselves to each other and created a joyful noise.

And what on the scale of excitement could compare to playing for a roomful of Hollywood big shots, to feel with every note he played, every gliss, every bend, every hammer-on, that he had moved out of the realm of make-believe and into that higher reality where dreams come true, where the pretty high school girl becomes a model or movie star, where the poor young ghetto kid makes the NBA, where the geek with his electric guitar stands in front of Clive Davis and David Geffen and they listen and applaud and take him seriously.

When the show was over, when he and the rest had stepped backstage, the feeling remained, the sizzle and spark lit up the room and passed from one to the other as they recounted who played what and how brilliant it was. Then Ronnie came in and testified, and his eyes were wild, his voice high with excitement, and yes, he said, the sound had been glorious out front, and yes, he had heard the fire and the passion and it was stunning, all of it, all of it perfectly stunning.

And in this way bliss begets bliss. As the adrenalin seeped away, as the flash of artistic triumph began to fade, Cyrus wandered into the club, where food and drink had been arranged, mountains of shrimp, platters of smoked salmon and cold cuts and exotic fruits and dips. He'd never had a better-tasting beer than the one just then, a necessary reward. And in the presence of all that food, he discovered his raw emptiness. He gorged on delicacies until Ronnie introduced him to so-and-so of the *L.A. Times* and what's-her-face from *Billboard*, to this person here and that one there, each and every one of them gushing with praise. And wasn't that a beautiful woman, and wasn't she smiling in his direction, with the second beer tasting better than the first, and the food tasting better, too, and the woman looking better each time she turned his way, with her white silk blouse and cleavage, her tight jeans, and the way she smiled in a way that made him smile. And all the while people were pumping his hand and plying him with drinks and food until there, on an admittedly lower level, in a darker and more primitive part of his brain, he runs smack into a particularly sticky patch of bliss, thick and rich and sweet as honey.

And as these things happen, they all head back to the hotel suite where drinks are plentiful, and people offer drugs, and the woman (he'll never remember her name) attaches herself to his side and pumps him up whenever the post-adrenalin fatigue threatens to wear him down, pumps him up with the simplest things, a whispered word, a touch of hand, a certain leaning look that offers the promise of anything he might dream, hanging on his every word, his every move, until the night reaches a certain kind of equilibrium, or perhaps more accurately a certain imbalance, and he takes her hand and leads her to his room where they coil like snakes on the bed— the hissing kisses and hard slithering bodies of fundamental bliss.

What eats at him as she dresses to leave, and especially the next morning on the flight home to Toronto and Eura, is that he's noticed a definite pattern going back as far as his thoughtless behaviour in Fenton and the Pink Pussycat: the arc of his bliss moves in one direction, only ever backward, from the sacred to the profane, from the glittering present to the murky primordial past.

FOR RONNIE, THE PARTY ENDED AT SIX in the morning when the band began tossing wineglasses from the balcony into the big fountain in front of the hotel. With a sharp, almost military tone of voice, Ronnie snapped the lads back into focus and sent them off to bed. Alone at last, he called Brent in New York and got him to set up an appointment with RonCon's accountant and bank manager. He then dialed Nigel Cranston at his flat in Chelsea.

Nigel, a guitarist in the early days of British rock and roll, was now one of the premier producers in the world, Britain's king of alternative rock. But few people in the business knew that he owed his later success to Ronnie, who had taken him one evening to a club in London to hear a group of angry young men called The Brothers Heisenberg. The Brothers had approached Ronnie to be their manager, but with Jimmy at the top of the charts and on his second tour of Europe, Ronnie didn't have the time or enthusiasm for the project. So he foisted The Brothers on to his friend Nigel, who not only signed them to his production company but produced their first record, *Everything Is Everything,* a pretentious bit of art rock that sat on the *Billboard* Hot 100 for three solid years.

When the transatlantic connection was established, Ronnie said, "Nigel, it's Conger."

"You old ponce. How are you?"

"Couldn't be better. Out here in Hollywood just now showcasing a new act. All very exciting, I can tell you. But, how shall I say this, I'm afraid I need a favour."

"I was beginning to think you would never ask."

"I need your exemplary talent, Nigel, and your imprimatur and whatever positive spin I can muster."

"The showcase didn't go down all that well, I take it."

"Well enough that I could secure a contract, I suppose. These people down here are all money men. They only know the deal, not the music. That's why I want you. This project means the world to me. And as I sit here in the cold light of dawn, after listening to an outpouring of music like you can scarcely imagine, I can't bring myself to let these bloodless bastards have it. They don't deserve it, they won't appreciate it, and in the end, won't know what to do with it."

"Sounds like you've got yourself another Jim."

"In a way, Nigel, in a way. A remarkable young guitarist named Cyrus Owen. And what I was wondering, old fellow, is if you still have the same set-up north of London."

"Hidey-Hole."

"Yes, exactly. You see, the more I think on it, the more I'm convinced that the route I took with Jim is the one I should follow again. Which means I will make an end around Hollywood and, if you are amenable, bring my boy over to make a record with you at the helm as soon as we can. Is that anywhere within the realm of the possible?"

"Not only possible," Nigel replied, "it's guaranteed. When do we start?"

They made plans to begin in May, and Ronnie hung up the receiver feeling light-headed. He had only meant to sound Nigel out, not make a firm commitment. He still hadn't figured out how he would finance a project like this. Even with the discounts Nigel was sure to offer, a first-class recording would easily cost him the equivalent of a quarter of a million dollars.

He decided to mention none of this to Cyrus and the others. He would speak to his accountant and banker first. He'd been burning through his savings at an astonishing rate, but he had an idea up his sleeve. It was time, perhaps, for another release from the Jimmy Waters vault of live recordings. If Ronnie played his cards right, he might rob Peter to pay Paul.

A LAWYER, AN ACCOUNTANT AND A BANKER all sit in an office in New York one wintry afternoon, waiting for their client to arrive. When he walks in from his transcontinental flight looking pale and rumpled, he says, "I'll get right to the point and tell you what I need."

And the lawyer, roughly the same age as his client (though appearing much younger, thanks to a loving wife, regular sleep and healthy diet), looks up and says, "I think I'd better tell *you* what you need." He then proceeds to describe the court injunction that has just arrived and the pending lawsuit

brought against RonCon Productions and Future Records by the Worldwide
Church of Jim (hereinafter referred to as "The Church"), claiming damages
and all past, present and future royalties deriving from the sale and airplay of
LP, tape cassettes and any future sound reproduction devices hitherto
unknown, on the unlawful and unlicensed musical compilation known as
"The JimJams" (hereinafter referred to as "The Album").

And the client, this bleached-blond Scot (hereinafter referred to as
"Ronnie"), looks left then right and laughs, a single bark of disbelief. "This
must be some kind of a joke," he says.

No joke, the lawyer continues. The Church claims that the rights to The
Album lie outside the existing agreement, and further, that The Album has
been injurious to the reputation and effectiveness of The Church and its chief
spokesman, one James Waters (hereinafter referred to as "Jim"), resulting in
both emotional and financial hardship. As of noon tomorrow, Future
Records must remove all copies of The Album from stores, retrieve all copies
from radio stations and, failing that, inform such stations that they will be in
contempt of court if they play The Album, in whole or in part, until the suit
has been brought before the court and judgment rendered. Further to that,
The Church is seeking damages of $10 million, above and beyond the royal-
ties already collected and disbursed.

Ronnie slumps into the nearest chair. "Can they do that?"

"They have a case, but not a strong one. I would suggest they're unlikely
to win. But it could take years to sort out."

The accountant's turn. "I have those figures you asked for, but in light
of what I've just heard, I have to tell you they're no longer worth much. A
considerable part of this figure has the current earnings stream factored in, a
large part of which, as you know, is driven by The 'JimJams.'"

"Meaning . . ."

"That prior to this court injunction, RonCon had approximately one
hundred thousand dollars in investable assets through a combination of
short-term deposits and regular cash flow. Until this legal matter is settled,
I would suggest a ballpark figure of sixty thousand might be achievable
without seriously curtailing current operations."

"Sixty."

"Give or take."

Ronnie turns to the banker then. "Looks like it's your lucky day."

The banker, another fine-looking young man, smiles thinly and says, "According to the proposal Brent brought me this morning, you are looking at a project of a quarter million dollars that you had planned to fund 60 percent, while the bank would extend a line of credit up to 40 percent of the amount. If I read you correctly, you now propose to fund a little more than 20 percent and are asking my bank to carry the remainder."

"That is pretty much the size of it, my estimable friend. I am offering you twice the business I had originally anticipated."

Again the banker smiles, and his smile is even thinner. "I believe, Mr. Conger, that that is more risk than my bank is willing to assume."

Ronnie looks down at his small freckled hands. "How many times have I borrowed money from your bank? A hundred? A thousand?"

"That's not the issue here."

"No? Then perhaps you could explain just what the issue is. I've worked with your bank since you were still in diapers and there has never yet been an *issue*."

The banker opens the folder in front of him, scans his papers a few moments and then closes the folder. He looks squarely at Ronnie and says, "All your previous loans, even the one in 1976 for two hundred thousand dollars—" he consults the folder onc more time "—as I say, all of your loans have been secured, dollar for dollar, by accounts receivable, royalties owing but not yet collected." He coughs softly into his hand and says, "To be perfectly honest, Mr. Conger, given the current situation and the possibility of a curtailment in revenue stream, not to mention a dramatic increase in expected legal costs, I would find it hard to extend any further credit and—let me be frank—may have to go to bat for you to prevent my supervisor from calling in your current loans with us."

EURA HAD ALWAYS CONSIDERED CYRUS her crystal ball. She had only to look into his eyes to catch a glimpse of her future. She had seen, for instance, long before it might be possible, how he would one day climb into her bed, just as she could now see the end of their time together, approaching as surely as summer rain across open fields.

She was afraid to think what sort of twisted mess Cyrus might see in her eyes. Guilt, certainly, that she had bent him to her purposes, reshaping him little by little to the template of her former love. Perhaps her crimes were not so big: teaching him to cook and enjoy certain foods; instructing him in the evening stroll and the long breakfast and the lazy afternoon of kisses and Bach; turning his attention to a broader notion of culture and society, to favourite poets and philosophers and masters of cinema. You could easily make the case that she did nothing worse than show a young man where to find meaning in the world. But she would never make that case herself because she knew the truth. Her relationship with Cyrus was essentially pornographic, she felt, a bitter clash of dream and reality that could excite but never fulfill her desires.

When he returned from Hollywood, they argued. She knew that certain types of women found him appealing and that he might easily lose his head. And although she knew she could never make room for him at the centre of *her* life, she panicked at the thought she would not be the centre of his. If she did not exist there, she would not exist anywhere. She had no home, no family, no network of friends. She was lost in this petty North American culture. Without a foothold at the centre of Cyrus's world, she would drift away.

So she sneered at his stories of excitement, found ulterior motives in everything these Hollywood people said and did. "They are polite like this to everyone," she countered when he told her how enthusiastic the audience had been. "They came out, I suppose, as a favour to Ronnie," she said when he expressed his amazement at the turnout. "Free drinks are free drinks."

Within a few minutes of his arrival she had ruined everything. He walked out of the apartment and spent the next few hours wandering the snow-covered streets, only returning to sleep on the couch. But here was the irony: she had been shopping the day before to buy ingredients for his favourite dish. All that morning as she waited for him to arrive she had been daydreaming about his kisses, his soft skin and boyish hungers. And why? Because she genuinely liked him. She had wanted to help him celebrate a special accomplishment in his life. Yet the moment he walked through the door, he brought with him all the radiance of the California sun and made the rest of their life together seem so dark and drab that she felt immediately afraid, as though she had already fallen into the past.

After Hollywood they never did get back on track. They slept in the same bed but didn't touch. They ate together and chatted listlessly, but nothing important was ever said. They were happiest when distracted by movies or the drift of scenery on late-night strolls. When Ronnie called to say, "Nigel Cranston, studio time north of London, twelve weeks to start," Eura quietly caved in, weeping softly for days on end.

AFTER HIS MEETING with the accountant, the banker and the lawyer, Ronnie called Sonia Herscovitz, the agent who had sold him his apartment at the Canyons on the upper west side of Manhattan. He told her he wanted to lease his place, furnished if possible. She mentioned three grand a month. And just like that he had boosted his revenue. The banker, slightly relieved, fashioned a loan for sixty thousand. That meant, with another sixty already in hand, that Ronnie could pay Nigel half the cost of the record up front, with the rest due whenever.

Mid-April, Ronnie called Cyrus and invited him to England to get acquainted with Hidey-Hole. They met at JFK a few days later and, after an hour layover, set off together for London. Ronnie bought them each a one-ounce bottle of Scotch, then lifted his plastic cup in a toast. "To our grand adventure." When Cyrus lifted his glass half-heartedly, Ronnie said, "You're not nervous, are you? Because I can tell you, Nigel Cranston is the salt of the earth."

For the next hour or so, Cyrus tried to explain his troubles with Eura, how they hadn't stopped bickering in the time he'd been home, and how in the days leading up to his departure, the tension brought an icy stillness to the apartment. For forty-eight hours they hadn't said a word to each other. She wouldn't even look at him when he said goodbye.

Ronnie sipped his drink and pondered what to do. Finally he said, "Women have always seemed to me a rather complicated puzzle, and that woman of yours more complicated than most. It may be a tired analogy to say they are like a flower, but I refer not to their beauty or their perfume, not even to their procreative function. Rather, I speak of their intricate connections to the world. They have deep roots in the soil, where they draw in the rain, and who can say how many nutrients. They absorb the sunlight. They take in carbon dioxide and return life-giving oxygen. Women are not like us, Cyrus. They draw strength from relationships you and I do not even know exist. By comparison, we enjoy a simple and often destructive freedom. We are like bees, buzzing blindly about the garden, drawn by the colour and smell to take what we want, with no understanding of the intricate arrangements that underpin our entire existence. But women know these things. They bring worlds together in a fashion we cannot even imagine. I believe we must make allowances for them."

Cyrus stared out the window at the limitless blue, so focused on his own grievances he scarcely paid attention to what was being said. When Ronnie at last stopped talking, Cyrus turned to him, drained his Scotch in a gulp, and said, "The hell with it."

Ronnie had booked rooms at the Gore Hotel, which was around the corner from Kensington Palace. The Gore was the kind of place that appealed to Ronnie but held no charm for Cyrus: lumpy beds, a little breakfast room with white lace curtains and centuries-old woodwork, and a cozy bar that would have seemed crowded with ten people in it. To Cyrus it was the kind of place where grey-haired grannies would feel at home, which, with a rather different inflection, was much what Ronnie might have said.

They had dinner at a Persian restaurant around the corner, and next morning Ronnie drove Cyrus northwest of the city to Hidey-Hole, ten acres of land that housed a Cistercian monastery that Nigel had purchased and turned into a state-of-the-art recording studio.

They met Nigel near the front gates where he had been taking his morning walk. To Cyrus he seemed more farmer than hotshot producer and, despite the Irish setter by his side, not a gentleman farmer, either, but someone with dirt under his nails and manure on his heels, someone who even in a tuxedo would look a bit rough around the edges. He was not one of the beautiful people.

Before Ronnie could begin introductions, Nigel approached the passenger side and opened the net bag he had clasped to his jacket. "Here's lunch," he said excitedly.

Cyrus peered into the bag and immediately recoiled. It appeared to be a bag of brains, or something equally grisly, all honeycombed and delicate and the colour of manure.

"Morchella esculenta," Nigel prompted, as though Cyrus had merely forgotten the name of the grotesque objects. "Found these lovelies fruiting under the apple trees along the road farther on." He unhooked the bag from his jacket and handed it to Cyrus. "Go ahead and get settled. Patrick will show you to your rooms. Oh, and tell him to take these to the kitchen so that Sophie can do her magic. Red and I need to stretch our legs a bit more." Then man and dog headed across the meadow.

Ronnie and Cyrus did as instructed and were soon settled in rooms that were larger and more luxurious than the Gore, which pleased Cyrus greatly. After all, he'd be spending months at Hidey-Hole.

An hour later the phone rang. Patrick said, "Sorry to disturb you, Mr. Owen, but Nigel asked me to tell you lunch will be ready in thirty minutes. Drinks are being served in the lounge, if you'd care to join the others."

He went down immediately to find Ronnie sitting in a leather armchair, admiring the view out the big bay window—a patchwork of fields and hedges and stone walls, a church spire in the distance. Nigel had changed from his walking gear and was dressed in a rugby shirt and track pants. He stood behind a long oak bar. "I'm drawing your man here a pint of Guinness. Can I offer you one as well, or do you fancy something else?"

"A Guinness, sure. Never had one."

"Ah, well then, you're in for a treat, aren't you?"

A few minutes later, Nigel came out from behind the bar with three pints of the famous black brew on a tray. As is so often the case with that heralded Irish concoction, Cyrus's first sip was a revelation, that anything could be bitter and sweet and cool and thick and smooth as silk all in one brilliant gulp. "Wow," he said.

Ronnie laughed and raised his glass in a toast. "Yes, here's to wow. To a perfect pint, a champion of the electric guitar, the world's finest producer and, above all, to a glorious new undertaking."

For the next half hour, Nigel related the history of Hidey-Hole. Then he led them into the dining room where lunch, as promised, featured the mushrooms he had found in the orchard. Sophie, frail-looking and elfin and almost frighteningly pale, not only prepared the meal but served it, and told them in a whispered voice that she had sautéd the morels with yellow peppers, shallots and prosciutto, and moistened it all with a white-wine and nutmeg sauce. The mixture was served on triangles of toast, accompanied by a salad of mixed greens. To wash it down, Nigel offered them "a pesky little Montepulciano."

Cyrus tried to enjoy the meal and the conversation, but his thoughts were elsewhere. After a dessert of raspberry sorbet, Ronnie wiped his lips and said, "My friend and I did not come all this way to sample your hospitality. Rather, I wanted you to meet young Cyrus here, and for him to get acquainted with you, so that we can all feel—as I do already, I confess—that we are on the verge of something extraordinary."

Ronnie then spoke of his vision of Jangle, and the overall philosophy behind "The Bridge," music that had been turned inside out. As he often did, he went on at great length, and Nigel listened more or less patiently until Ronnie mentioned the suspension bridge that was planned for the stage. At that point Nigel's eyes widened. He threw down his napkin and said, "I have something to show you."

He led them to a big workshop attached to the main house. There on a wooden bench sat a twenty-foot I-beam. Welded to each end were crosspieces about five feet in length. Stretched taut between the two end pieces were eight cables of varying dimensions, arranged in order of size. The largest would have been suitable for a wrecking ball.

"I've been wondering when I might use this," he said. And with that he whacked the thickest cable with a rubber mallet, setting up a deep, soul-shaking rumble as though the earth itself were humming.

Cyrus couldn't restrain himself. He ran his hands along the entire length of the thing. "This is so cool," he said. "Can I try?"

Nigel handed him the mallet. "Pentatonic scale in C."

Cyrus, after some deliberation, hit the C and the G, and while the notes resonated, he laid his hand on the crosspiece. The vibrations, like an electric shock, ran up his arm to the shoulder. "What is it?" he asked.

"I don't know exactly. I made it myself from the frame of an old farm wagon. Maybe it's a bridge."

Cyrus fooled with the contraption for the better part of an hour while Ronnie and Nigel chatted about the early days. Cyrus soon discovered that the less he played on it, the better. The strings were so long and thick, and the sound waves they set up so rich and sustained, that single notes or simple chords worked best—but they were more than enough. He could have soloed over that geological drone forever.

For the rest of the afternoon, Nigel gave them a tour of the grounds and outbuildings, saving the studio for last. Although Cyrus had recorded two albums with Jim, he had never been in a place of such reverent stillness. To stand there even a moment was to feel sound willed into being. Again, he ached for the feel of his guitar, the monumental roar of his amplifier.

As they headed back to the main house, Ronnie took Cyrus's arm and waited a moment for Nigel to move beyond range of their voices. "I can see your flush of excitement," he said. "You are impressed?"

"I can't wait."

Ronnie let his gaze drift across the field. "Yet at lunch you seemed positively downcast. Is it your difficulties at home?"

When Cyrus shrugged, Ronnie nudged him into a stroll, knowing that walking could sometimes set free a troubled tongue. Sure enough, Cyrus began to speak once again about his complicated relationship with Eura.

"When I came back from L.A., I thought she'd be happy, and in a way she was—happy for *me*. But she was even more unhappy for us."

As delicately as he could, Ronnie said, "Have you considered that perhaps she is being selfish?"

"It's not like that. You don't know. I'm the one who's selfish. I'm the one who has to have a career."

Ronnie squeezed the boy's shoulder. "I'll tell you what I am going to do. I will catch the first plane to Toronto and have a talk with Eura. Then I will bring her back with me. She feels left out, poor thing. I should have thought of it sooner."

When Cyrus gave a hopeful look, Ronnie said, "There is joy enough for all in what we are doing, my friend."

A few hours later Ronnie left for London, promising to return in a few days. Nigel poured Cyrus another pint and led him back to the bay window. He said, "I've listened to your demo this past week."

"Oh, man," Cyrus groaned, "there's so much I'd change."

"That's good to know," Nigel continued. "So would I." He looked squarely at him and said, "I don't know if you want to get into this sort of thing now, but we're going to have to work on your sound . . ."

The colour drained immediately from Cyrus's face, and Nigel realized he had overestimated the young man's level of confidence. "Look, mate, what I mean is, you've got a great tone. Really. Trouble is, you use it for everything. Variety, you know. It's the spice of life."

Cyrus opened his mouth but no words came out. Nigel continued. "I've got dozens of guitars here and I don't know how many amplifiers. What we don't have, we can get in an hour from London. Not a problem. But you have to start listening to sounds, try out different gear. Just now, with my toy out there, you copped right away how to play it. Guitars are the same. They all have different personalities."

Cyrus felt as woozy as if he'd been whacked in the head with a stick. "I guess," he said, "I guess I always thought my job was to play, and it was your job to make things sound good."

Nigel laughed good-naturedly. "I wish it was that simple—the flick of a button. But I've got limits, mate. I'm just the outsider. I stand back and encourage you to do your best, and hope we get some magic down on tape. But I can't make it sound better than it really is, or not much better at any rate. I can only work with what you give me."

RONNIE'S PLAN was to somehow talk sense into Eura; but he had no idea what to say other than to encourage her involvement. If she came to Hidey-Hole and saw what a splendid place it was, saw the radiance that flowed from Cyrus's face when he stepped into that studio, she might try harder to hide her own pain. Not that she had ever shown much sense. Ronnie never understood why she stayed in North America when she clearly had no love of the people or culture, when it was perfectly evident how much she missed her home and family. It seemed to him a kind of neurosis to cling to something that drove you crazy. He wondered at times if it was a form of penance, or maybe even a way of remaining faithful—to what or to whom, he had no idea.

From the airport, he drove straight to the apartment. He had Cyrus's key but knocked first. When Eura didn't come to the door, he called from a phone booth around the corner. She picked up immediately.

"Oh," she said, "it is only you."

"You didn't answer the door. I wondered if you were all right."

"There is no one I want to see. The phone, I thought, was maybe him."

"I came to talk to you about that. Can I come up?"

"I don't want to talk much to you about Cyrus."

"I guess I thought we would talk about you."

"That, too, is not so good to talk about, I think."

"You're hurting him. If things don't change soon, you might actually ruin his life. Is that what you want?"

She hung up the phone. When he arrived at the apartment door, she led him upstairs and sat on the sofa, hugging herself as though she were chilled through. Ronnie sat in an armchair on the other side of the room. He could barely look at her. She had always been careful about her appearance, but now she was smeared and dishevelled. She had food stains on her robe. Every visible part of her skin showed some evidence of tattoo.

Eura spoke first. "Maybe you will be the one to ruin his life and I am an innocent bystander." When he didn't respond, she sniffed bitterly and added, "You think I am a poison and should leave him alone."

"Well, Eura, I never—"

"Maybe you think I twist his mind and keep him from making beautiful music. Maybe you would like it better if I would go away."

"Eura, really, I don't know how you could think that. I don't honestly have the faintest idea what it is you want from him or what you give to him. That's none of my business. I only want to help."

"Maybe you think the best way to help is to get me out of his life. Maybe you came here to help me do something I cannot do on my own."

That's when Ronnie realized she was pleading with him, not criticizing. "What are you saying?"

She covered her face with both hands, as though she'd seen a terrible crime. After a moment, she said, "In my country, you know, they say that if you win, you are champion for a year; if you lose, you lose forever. Such is regret."

He moved beside her on the sofa. He took her hands and gave them a gentle shake. "Here's what I think," he said. "I think we should pack you a bag and then fly over to see Cyrus. The two of you can stay in England for the next while. A vacation before the sessions begin."

She removed her hands from his and tied her robe more tightly. "It is strange how we come to the end of things. I am finished wanting. There is no room for it in my life anymore. The same way I can see I am nearly at the end of regret. You know how it is, Ronnie, what a stupid cow I am. So many things I wish were different. And now, biggest of all, is this business with Cyrus, because I knew. I knew . . ."

Ronnie watched carefully, waiting to see if she would continue. After a few more seconds, he said, "What comes after regret then? What next?"

"You tell me. This is why you are here."

He sat forward, clasping his hands together. "I've already told you I think you should fly over to Cyrus." She smiled at him, like he was an impossibly naive child. He said, "If you won't come to England, what do you propose?"

"I propose nothing. I pray."

"That . . ."

"That love will find a way."

Ronnie scoffed. "That he'll give it up and come running to you?"

"I would never dream such a thing."

"Well, and don't think you're the only one who loves him, either."

"I am not so stupid as you think. I have eyes and ears."

"You *are* stupid if you think your love will lead you out of this mess."

"My love, no. But your love, maybe . . ."

"My love?"

"Your love could find the way." She looked at him with a level gaze, waiting for him to think this through. Then she added, "You are not a stranger to this kind of thing, Ronnie, slicing the truth until it is so thin it will fit your purpose. What you did with Cal, you can do again, telling lies for a good cause."

"For Cyrus, you mean."

"For all of us. Someone has to be strong."

NIGEL THOROUGHLY DISSECTED the deficiencies in Cyrus's playing, then excused himself to run a few errands. Cyrus was so hurt by their exchange, so fearful now of the next few weeks and months, that he could rouse himself to nothing more productive than lying on his bed and hugging his pillow. He remained that way until the light in the room began to fade. That's when Patrick called and said, "Dinner will be served in one hour, cocktails at your leisure. Nigel is already in the lounge and said he would appreciate your company if you feel up to it."

Cyrus wanted to lie on the bed and wallow in self-pity, but he knew Nigel had been at least partly right. When he walked into the lounge, he did his best to meet the other man's gaze. Nigel poured them each a pint and said, "I know I've messed with your head a bit, but it's better this way. You'll see. Now we move on. Now we figure out how to make one kick-ass record."

He touched his glass to Cyrus's and took a long swallow. Then, coming out from behind the bar, he led Cyrus into the hall, up a flight of stairs and into a large oak-lined room full of pinball machines and a tournament-size snooker table. Another set of doors led to a soundproof room approximately twenty feet square, a recent addition to the rambling structure of the house. Various amplifiers lined the walls: a Twin Reverb, a Princeton, an Ampeg, a Marshall stack, a Vox, a Mesa Boogie, even an old Traynor. There were flight cases full of effects and pedals and cords, as well as a bank of tape machines. What really caught Cyrus's attention were the guitars, about twenty-five of them on stands, and one guitar in particular—a National Steel, shiny as the chrome on a new car. He had seen pictures of them, heard them on records, but never played one.

"Can I touch it?" he asked.

Nigel shook his head and took Cyrus by the elbow, guiding him to the door again. "I only wanted to show you the room. After dinner you can muck about till your heart's content. Anytime you're at Hidey-Hole, really, you're to treat this room as your own."

At dinner Nigel played the genial host, keeping Cyrus entertained with stories about what it was like to chum around with the Yardbirds and the Kinks.

"Most of us back then felt that if the Beatles could make it," he said, "damn well anyone could. I mean, they were mediocre players. And those songs, okay, some of them were pretty and sentimental, and some had some bounce, but let's face it, they didn't really know how to rock, did they? Now the Who, there was a brilliant band. I'm still trying to figure out what Pete Townshend was doing on 'Can't Explain.'"

"And the Animals?" Cyrus asked. "Did you know Eric Burdon?"

Nigel nodded matter-of-factly. "I was mates with Chas Chandler. It was Chas, in fact, who got me into producing in the first place after he started working with that wanker Cat Stevens. But the Animals, you know," he wrinkled his nose, "aside from Eric's singing, there wasn't much to them. Not like the Who or the Yardbirds. People say Hendrix changed the way we think about electric guitar, and that's true. The guy was our Charlie Parker. But they forget the early Jeff Beck and Pete Townshend. That's still some of the most twisted rock and roll you'll ever hear."

"I love the stuff Eric Clapton did with John Mayall."

"You and everyone else. You couldn't be in London in those days without seeing 'Clapton is God' spray-painted somewhere. The kiss of death, that."

They talked through dinner and two bottles of wine, until Nigel excused himself and stumbled off to bed. Cyrus should have gone to sleep—he was too drunk to do much else—but the thought of that National waiting for him was hard to resist. As he headed in that direction, Sophie, still in chef's whites, asked if he wanted anything.

"Well," he said, tickled by her wispy manner, her lilting accent, "I'd love another coffee if there is any."

"I'll make a fresh pot. Were you headed to your room?"

He pointed to the guitar room. "But, look," he said, "I'll be fine without. Don't go to any trouble . . ."

"No trouble. I'll bring it to you up there."

As she turned to leave, he said, "Just black, Sophie. And thanks for dinner. You're a great cook."

"Oh, well, ta. It was nothing special."

"I cook, too, you know."

She laughed at that, covering her mouth with her hand. At his quizzical look, she began to fidget like a small bird. She said, "It's just I've never heard of a musician ever cooking before. It's how I got to do this in the first place, innit, knocking about with musicians who couldn't stir up a tin of beans."

Her voice faded to nothing, and he watched her squirm, this pale, frail creature who looked as though she rarely sampled the food she prepared. Though she had sharp features, and a body that had all the warmth and attraction of a plucked fowl, he felt drawn to her. "Well, I guess I'll see you in a bit," he said.

Upstairs, the National felt cool and unlikely in his arms. Before he had a chance to get familiar with it, however, Sophie arrived with a small carafe and a porcelain cup. She placed them in front of him, then sat on the floor. "Play something," she said.

Now it was his turn to fidget. Nigel had been right. Every guitar had its secrets and limitations, and he'd discovered neither about the National. He was also drunk. So he opted for the one tune he could play in his sleep. After fingerpicking a few bars, he began to sing along, too:

Don't know what you do with your lips,
Don't know what you do with your hair,
Don't know what you do with your hips,
But baby I declare
That my heart's on fire.
I'm in love with
The itty-bitty things that you do.
Now if you really want to know—
It's unreal
How I feel
About you.

She got to her feet and smiled. "Cheers. See you later."

When she was gone, he idly fingered the intro to "The Bridge," remembering his struggle to write that first piece of music, how for the longest time he'd had a single chord, and how it eventually led to another chord and another until an entire song was born. In the same way, he wondered if his life with Eura had led him to an appreciation of this odd new person. Wasn't it all a kind of progress, coming to understand various complications, various structures that at first seem alien but in time become moving and then familiar? And wasn't the key that original brightness? You play a certain chord, often by accident, and like magic you hear something new, a clear and surprising possibility you don't quite understand but know you will, know you must.

With that thought he put aside the guitar and walked to the kitchen, where Sophie was sitting at a large oak table with her head cradled in the palm of her hand. She had changed into a black T-shirt and baggy cotton pants. "You look tired," he said.

"I forget to eat." She rubbed her face, then looked over to the big walk-in refrigerator. "Scrambled eggs, maybe. Something light."

Before she could move, he put his hands on her bony shoulders and said, "Stay put. I make fantastic scrambled eggs."

He walked into the cooler and returned with three eggs, a wedge of cheddar and a pitcher of milk. The serious look on his face made her want to laugh. She actually had to bite her lip as he mixed the eggs and milk and then cut cubes of cheddar into it. He fired up the stove, dropped a scoop of butter into the skillet and, when it had begun to brown, poured the eggy mixture into the pan. A few minutes later he presented her with the finished product. *"Madame,"* he said with a bow, *"bon appétit."*

She sampled the eggs, then took a second taste and a third. Holding her fork aloft like an exclamation point, she said, "Next time use cream. It gives them a velvety texture. And your pan was too hot. You overcooked the eggs. You want something more like soft custard." In response to his startled expression, she touched his arm and said, "They're good, though. Really. And anyway, sometimes cooking's not about food, or I've always thought. Is music that way? Are there times when playing your guitar isn't about music but something else?"

Cyrus hardly knew where to begin. He only had to think of the Harmony, and hugging that beautiful thing in the darkness of his bedroom, to know it was more than a musical instrument. But even if he could find the words to describe those feelings, they were too personal to share with someone he'd just met. Instead he moved beside her and took her hand in his. "Let's go for a walk," he said. "I feel I could walk all night."

She finished the eggs and told him he could take her home. Then she led him out the back door and along a gravel path, the air so thick with fog that he was soon chilled through, even though he was wearing a sweater.

"Let's go back and get you a jacket," he said. "It's freezing out here."

"Not at all," she replied, opening her arms to the sky. "It's lovely. You North Americans with your central heating are a wee bit soft around the edges. We're built of sturdier material over here."

Cyrus nearly laughed out loud at the idea that she was sturdily built. When he tried to put his arm around her, she jabbed him in the side with her elbow and skipped away. "Don't be trying your fancy moves," she said, "or I'll serve you your bollocks for breakfast."

"I didn't mean anything. I thought you might want to get warm."

"I'd just as soon stay cool around the likes of you. A girl could get herself a broken heart if she's not careful."

"I'm taking you home, that's all." This time when he put his arm around her, she let it stay, and they walked on through the fog, neither of them saying a word.

The path led past the recording studio and down a hill to a wooden gate that opened to a paved road bordered on each side by a thick hedge. A hundred yards down the road they found another gate in the hedge and passed through it to enter another, smaller field. Off to one side stood an oak tree and, chained to its massive trunk, what looked to be a large metal mushroom. When he looked at her with disbelief, she smiled and said, "My caravan." Then she placed her hand against his breastbone and pushed him back toward the hedge. "I really did like the eggs, and I'm glad you walked me home, and some other time I'd love to sit and talk, but if I don't go to sleep right now, alone, I'll be a nutter tomorrow."

Cyrus dawdled back to the house and didn't crawl into bed until three. He woke a number of times that night, wondering where he was. Long before anyone else was up, he tiptoed out to the lounge and, with the first inkling of sunrise touching the sky, dialed the apartment in Toronto, hoping to talk to Eura. But the machine was on, and the tinny sound of his own recorded voice made him ache with loneliness and concern. It wasn't like Eura to stay out so late, well past midnight, Toronto time.

A few hours later, he and Nigel had breakfast, then carried their coffee to the guitar room where they each took up an instrument, Cyrus the Les Paul and Nigel an old sunburst Telecaster.

"Let me show you the sort of thing I want you to work on," Nigel said. Then he launched into the chord pattern of "The Bridge," in particular the clipped arpeggios Cyrus had played beneath the synthesizer solo. "This is a nice little figure you've come up with, but listen how great it sounds on the Telly. Did you ever hear anything that sounded more like twanging metal? Now you try it on your Les Paul."

Cyrus shook his head. "I don't need to. You're exactly right."

They switched guitars. Cyrus tried the part just as Nigel had played it, and knew in his bones it was much better. More than that, the sound of the guitar suggested different ways of extending the line.

Nigel played a few licks over the arpeggios, then held the Les Paul out from him admiringly. "No question," he said, "these are amazing axes. Always sound like dirt to me. Mud and muck and swamp ooze."

For the next few hours they fooled around on a variety of guitars. After a quick lunch, they were right back at it. Nigel had a big workbook in his lap, and together they listened to the demo and picked it apart, phrase by phrase, instrument by instrument.

At five o'clock Nigel excused himself. He had to go to London for the evening and wouldn't be back until the next day. "Sophie will make whatever you like for dinner," he said. "Or I'll tell you what: Patrick and Sophie can take you down the road to the Two Poofs. A few pints and a round of darts might do you a world."

Cyrus tried phoning home, but again there was no answer. He was starting to worry. More than that, he needed to hear her voice and be reminded of the complicated melody of their life together.

When he stepped outside, Patrick was waiting behind the wheel of a vintage Jaguar. "Sophie will meet us there," he said with his head out the window. "Went home to change." Then they sped off in a cloud of dust, the car seeming to fill the narrow winding road. Two minutes later they arrived at a tidy little place with a thatched roof, leaded windowpanes and a bright-coloured sign out front that featured a pair of rotund friars.

Patrick took him by the arm and led him into the back room, where there was a jukebox and a couple of dartboards. Cyrus had never been in a proper pub before. He'd never played darts or had steak-and-kidney pie. Nor had he ever seen people having this sort of fun: these big beefy fellows drilling into the treble twenty while young folk nodded to the rock and roll or, like Sophie, danced non-stop beside the jukebox. Others laughed and talked and seemed like happy drunks, not at all like his father or any of the people he'd seen stumbling out of the Wilbury Hotel or the Laredo. Back home, the idea of going to a bar seemed so uncool. It had never occurred to him that a night of drinks could be uplifting, that a roomful of people bound by smoke and alcohol, music and games and simple chat could seem like one of the secrets of life.

After his third pint, he worked up the nerve to sway alongside Sophie, who danced with her eyes closed and was dazzling in her high-top runners, tweedy trousers and sleeveless undershirt. He couldn't pretend they were dancing together, because he was sure she hadn't noticed him. But then, without breaking her rhythm or looking at him, she pressed her body to his and draped her arms around his neck. "Don't drink too much," she whispered. "You'll spoil it."

He tried to look at her face, but her head was tucked under his chin. "Spoil what?" he asked innocently.

"It. The magic. It's magic, innit?"

And it was. So was the walk home, the two of them swaying along a dark winding road so narrow in spots that, with arms outstretched, it seemed he could almost touch the hedges on both sides. She pulled him into her pasture. She spread a blanket on the ground, the mist swirling out of the north, and they leaned together, saying nothing, moving hardly at all. When the sun began to burn off the haze, she removed her clothes and doused herself with rainwater from a barrel before scooting into the trailer for her chef's whites. She hunched before an open fire and made herbal tea to have with day-old scones. Then they were back through the hedge and along the road to Hidey-Hole, where he tumbled into bed and a deep dreamless sleep.

When he opened his eyes, Ronnie was sitting beside him. The violence of two worlds colliding made Cyrus wince in pain. "I called the apartment," he muttered.

Ronnie touched the boy's arm. "She's gone, Cyrus. Vanished."

Cyrus knew and didn't know. He understood completely and didn't have a clue. Covering his eyes with the palm of his hand, he said, "She wouldn't go. She has no one but me. She has nowhere but there."

Then Ronnie pulled a sheet of yellow lined paper from his pocket. "I found this on the kitchen table," he said.

It was the kind of paper they kept beside the phone for messages. It held very few words, written in her perfect hand.

Dear Cyrus,

I am a thief to sneak away, but it is not possible otherwise because I am weak and need to be loved. Do not hate me.

Eura

Cyrus read the message three, four times, and never stopped shaking his head. Ronnie took the paper and placed it on the bedside table. He said, "I bumped up our schedule. The rest of the band arrives tomorrow."

Cyrus sat upright and swung around so his feet were on the floor. "I have to go to Toronto," he said mechanically. "I have to find her."

"She's gone," Ronnie repeated. "You should let her go."

J anice worked for years on her Carrara sculpture (a month here, a month there), watching with satisfaction as the likeness of a human figure gradually rose out of the stone, and not just any figure but, surprisingly, that of her father, bending backward with arms thrust toward the sky. Unfortunately, the more she worked on the statue, and the more time she spent thinking about her father's joyful approach to life, his commitment to a better world, the more she began to notice, by contrast, the many shades of Jonathan that were not to her liking. Eventually another and darker truth rose before her, and on their return from yet another trip to Italy, she told him she no longer loved him. There was no one else, she said. She just felt their relationship wasn't going anywhere.

"I wasn't aware it had to go anywhere," he said, his tone distant and superior. And she nodded her head as though that was exactly what she had expected him to say. They discussed the matter for a day or two but not with any heat. He didn't argue or rage or make rash predictions. That final day, she watched him quietly pack his suitcase and walk out the door.

For the next while she concentrated solely on the Carrara. She slept at the studio, ate at the studio. When she had finished all the hard slogging— the screech of masonry blades and the painstaking effort with mallets and steel—she started on her favourite part, turning the general contour into a particular kind of beauty with the aid of claw and tooth chisels and a variety of rifflers. She had also settled on a final design. Instead of the one central cavity that characterized her *Hollow Men* series, she had drilled three or four smaller holes no larger than a silver dollar. Each hole would be fitted with a pair of magnifying lenses. Peer through one of the openings and you'd see a bigger and wider world. The surface of the marble would also have letters and symbols, even a few words etched into it—what she had come to think of as "lexical skin."

The shape of her life was far less encouraging, but at least she was busy enough with work that she had few opportunities to miss Jonathan. Then she suffered an even greater blow: a few weeks before Christmas, her father died suddenly of a heart attack. She returned to Wilbury for the funeral and stayed with her mother until the new year, sliding into a deeper sadness with each passing day until finally, her darkness threatening to overwhelm her, she flew out to the west coast and rented a house on Salt Spring Island. She spent the rest of the winter alone there, walking the tide line and searching the debris for some clue to the future. By April she still wasn't ready to get back to a normal routine so she returned to Wilbury with the idea that she and her mother might become better friends. But her mother didn't need Janice's company or particularly welcome it. When Janice complained about the cool reception, her mother squared her shoulders and said, "I'm making a new life. I suggest you do the same. You only get one kick at the can."

On Salt Spring, Janice had wondered whether to leave the Carrara unfinished, like her father's life, and even contemplated having the thing destroyed. But as the sharp edges of her pain slowly softened, she realized that without her father on the planet, she needed the next best thing. So she arranged with Harold Winters, who owned a shipping company in town, to bring her sculpture to Wilbury for the summer. He rented her a bit of warehouse space out by the farmers' co-operative, where she worked most nights. Most days she drifted about in a fog of remembrance.

She visited her father's law office and chatted with his former partners, reminiscing about the summer she filed mortgage documents for them. Another day she sat on the steps outside the Three Links Hall and sang her

way through the old set list, or what she could remember of it. She drove to
the dock and the arena; she spent quiet afternoons at the library. But her
favourite place of all was Lakeview Cemetery, where her father was buried.
She'd sit on the small concrete bench near his grave and listen to the birds
singing in the pines. She didn't always think of him when she was there;
sometimes it was the peace and quiet she was after.

Eventually, as her fog lifted and her pain began to fade, she realized that
her work was the only happiness that remained in her life, the only strength.
Because of that, and because it was in Wilbury that her interest in art first
came to light, she decided to return the favour. She would offer classes in
sculpture and line drawing, hoping to undo some of the damage Velma Fleck
had wrought on the artistic temperament of the community and, in
return, lead herself back into life. She met with Roger Larry, the director
of the Wilbury Recreation Centre, and convinced him to set aside an
area of the complex for classes.

It was mainly retirees who showed up the first night, people she remembered from her churchgoing years before and who already had a moderate
amount of skill. For their first exercise Janice set up a still life of fruit and a
wine bottle. "The bottle and fruit are your subject," she said, "but you are not
allowed to draw them. You can only draw the space around the flowers and
fruit. You can draw the wall in the background, the table beneath them, the
other objects in the room. You must render your subject by revelation."

The exercise was odd enough that she assumed there'd be fewer people
for the next class. In fact, the room was almost full. This time, she asked them
to do paired sketches. "First draw a flower," she said. "It must be realistic, with
petals and leaves and stem. But the mood must reflect your mother, or some
aspect of her—the way she used to stand, the way she looked when she
scolded you. The other drawing will be the reverse. Sketch your mother in
every detail but in such a way that it evokes a flower."

At the end of the second class, after the last of the students had gone
home, Ruby Mitchell showed up. Janice immediately ran to embrace her.
"I've been meaning to drop by," she said. "I've so wanted to see you. Are you
interested in the course?"

"Well, no. Art isn't really my cup of tea, dear. It's more my nephew. Do you remember Hank? He had a spot of trouble a while ago, and according to the doctor hasn't really healed the way he ought to. Tell you the truth, I think he's feeling pretty down, and I was wondering if you thought this sort of thing might help him."

"That's hard to say, Ruby. Does he enjoy art?"

She shook her head dubiously. "I don't imagine he enjoys much of anything anymore. It's more I was wondering if maybe this would do him good—as therapy, I mean. Could I bring him to your next class?"

"Well, sure. You come, too. How's Clarence holding up?"

Ruby looked away, her mouth a grim line. She started to say something and then stopped abruptly, her eyes closed, her index finger pressed to her nose the way people do when they're about to sneeze. After a long moment, she swallowed several times and said, "He says he feels fine, but I think it's back again. I can tell he's in pain. He can hardly stand up straight. He's going through Aspirin like they're candy."

Janice touched her arm. "Has he been to the doctor?"

"He talks about it but never makes an appointment. I don't know if he's just being stubborn or afraid of what they'll find."

"I'm sorry to hear that, Ruby. Is there something I can do?"

"For Hank, maybe. Maybe you could do something for him."

TWO NIGHTS LATER Ruby brought Hank to the class twenty minutes early. She made the most general introduction, then hurried to the car.

Hank had a few simple categories into which he slotted the women he met—sluts, bitches and goody two-shoes—and the woman in front of him, his brother's friend, was clearly option number three. She was pretty, he thought, in an all-American way, wholesome and well fed. Her teeth were straight and white, her eyes clear, her skin and hair squeaky clean. And while she was a little too solid to ever be considered a Miss Universe, he had always preferred women whose flesh exceeded his grasp. What qualified her as a goody two-shoes was her happiness and confidence—a bad combination for a woman to have. The world was a cruel and dangerous place, and Hank didn't think women had any call to be that confident or at ease.

She kept holding his hand and staring into his eyes like there was something there she wanted to understand. When he realized she was wait-ing for him to respond to her greeting, he said, "So you're the artist."

"And you're Cy's brother."

He smiled appreciatively. "That's—what's the word—diplomatic. Some folks'd just out and out call me the murderer."

"Is that what you'd prefer?" she asked, an eyebrow raised mischievously. "Or I suppose I could just call you Hank. That seems simple enough. You can call me Janice."

He looked her up and down without pretending otherwise. Then he said, "I'll tell you straight out, Janice, I know fuck all about art and pretty much couldn't care less. But Ruby thinks it might be the cure for what ails me, and tell you the truth, I've always had a soft spot for the old girl. So between you and me, I'd be just as happy to sit off to the side somewheres while you and your friends do your thing."

"Suit yourself," she said. Then she walked over to the table where she continued to prepare blocks of clay for the class. Every time she looked up he was staring at her. That in itself was not so troubling. Back in her waitressing days, she got used to men watching her with mournful eyes. Even now, when she had a show, a few men would follow her every move, and she was neither flattered nor offended. She took it for what it was, an involuntary reaction from those who were not thinking clearly, if at all. What did trouble her, worming its way under her skin, was the feeling that Hank himself was a work of art, that his hard grey eyes and sensuous mouth, the scars on his face, his slouching posture and the mechanical efficiency of his chair were some-how iconic, as though the figure before her were merely a physical and symbolic manifestation of all the invisible elements of his life. In a way, we were all like that, she knew, wearing our broken hearts on our sleeves, our losses like so many pockmarks—but she had never seen it so clearly.

When the others arrived, she handed everyone a block of clay, even Hank, and gave one sentence of instruction: "Mould a figure that represents the most important thing your father said to you." Then she left the room, returning every few minutes to see how they were progressing and to offer words of encouragement. When anyone asked a question about technique, she answered them; but for the most part, she let them find their own way.

Near the end of the class, she noticed that Hank had left the room. At the table where he had sat, she found his piece of clay, which bore the perfect imprint of a man's fist.

She scanned the class again, then stepped outside, where she found him in the parking lot, smoking a cigarette and staring at the moon and stars. "Your sculpture," she said, "it's very powerful."

He flicked his cigarette butt into the air. Without looking at her, he said, "Maybe 'cause it's not art, it's true."

Those words filled her with hope. She touched the cold metal of his chair. "Art has to be true, Hank. Always. Or else it's not art."

He turned to look at her. "Does your art tell the truth?"

"Well," she said, "yes, I think so. At least I hope it does."

"I'd like to see it, then. See what you think is true."

ON THE NIGHT OF HANK'S first art lesson, Isabel went to dinner with Ross and had too much to drink. Afterwards, she stopped at her office to pick up a few papers that she needed for a meeting in Keppel the next day. While she was there, she took a moment to file away some of the documents that had been cluttering her desk for weeks.

Above the filing cabinet was a map of the deeded property of Wilbury. She'd coloured her own properties bright red, each little square another step away from the past and into her own brave future. Taken together, those red spaces should have been the very image of her independence, the very shape of her dreams. And yet as often as she had studied the map, it had never once given her the sense of satisfaction she craved. Aside from her home on Orange Street and this lovely office, the properties were hers in name only. True, they offered a kind of financial security not to be downplayed, but they didn't speak to her in a single voice, didn't whisper the words she needed to hear.

She sat on the corner of her desk and picked up the framed photograph she kept there. It showed Izzy and her parents and brothers posing in front of the house on a summer day. In the background were the barn and the fields and, beyond that, the old chicken coop. Riley and Catherine had their arms around each other. Hank was flexing his muscles like Charles Atlas.

Cyrus, a mere infant, was nestled in Izzy's arms, trying to grab one of her pigtails. Everyone was smiling, Izzy most of all.

HANK INSISTED ON FINDING his own way home from the rec centre, and Ruby wasn't ready to go back to Orchard Knoll just yet (she had imagined these outings as a chance to unwind a bit), so she drove out to the dock and bought herself a cup of butterscotch ripple from the concession stand. She sat at a picnic table and watched sailboats skate along the horizon. But after a few minutes she started to feel self-conscious, as though she were only pretending to relax. Clucking her tongue at her own foolishness, she got in the car and headed to the farm.

Five minutes later she was back at the house. As she hung her jacket in the front closet, she saw Clarence limp out of the bathroom, wincing with each step. He was struggling to catch his breath and was so unsteady that he had to lean against the wall. She hurried to his side and helped him into his favourite chair in the living room. She knelt beside him, and he placed a trembling hand on hers and said, "Better get me to the hospital."

IT WASN'T LOST ON RUBY that churches these days were empty while hospitals were overcrowded. Those who live by the flesh, die by the flesh, she figured. For that reason she generally kept her distance from doctors and hospitals. She didn't believe in annual checkups or running for help at the first sign of a cold or ache. She trusted in the Lord and common sense.

Fortunately, with Clarence's first two bouts of cancer she'd been able to get him home quickly and on the mend. But this time was different. Right away the doctors had him plugged into monitors and had tubes running down his throat and into his arm and even hooked up to his you-know-what. She wished she could take him back to the farm and nurse him in private. That's what he needed, what he would have demanded if he were even half himself. Always such a proud man, so proper, he never went anywhere without looking his best, wouldn't even go to Farm Supply without cleaning his fingernails. It was agony for her to watch him lying in that hospital bed with his disease right out in the open for all to see.

That night she didn't leave his side to make so much as a single phone call.

But someone spread the word, and first thing in the morning Isabel arrived, looking stern and businesslike. Ruby figured she was about to get a scolding.

"It's like pulling teeth to get answers around here," Isabel said with some heat. "I had to chase doctors and nurses for half an hour before I got someone to tell me what's going on." Then she stopped talking and hugged her aunt. "Poor Ruby," she murmured.

Isabel had never hugged her aunt, and on some level they both registered that fact. She didn't regret the show of affection. On the contrary, it seemed to be part of a general trend in her life. With Hank's return to Wilbury, she was rediscovering her natural sympathies, her need to ache for others, to comfort them beyond the level of friendship. Now, in that grim medicinal space, she felt a sudden and irresistible urge to take care of her aunt and uncle, the closest thing she had to aging parents.

She turned to Clarence then and cupped her hand over her mouth, the message in front of her unmistakably clear. Each of us contained the same terrible truth, and in her uncle, it was rising quietly to the surface.

Jim isn't exactly thrilled with the way things have worked out. He's been in New Mexico for a year now and it hasn't been the sanctuary he anticipated.

At first he'd found reasons to be hopeful. His wife, Elysse, by her own account, had remained faithful, and father and son appeared to have interests in common. Daniel worked at the local radio station as their all-night DJ and resident jingle writer. He played the piano in his spare time and expressed an admiration for Fats Waller. Even so, Jim's return to the family fold was, in most respects, too late. Elysse and Daniel had no room in their lives for such a complicated shape. They had other plans he was unaware of, and wanted nothing more from him than his name and his shine.

He tried hard to make up for lost time. Every night he went to the radio station with his son. They talked about music but also about family. Daniel had the idea that they should get it all down on tape, father-and-son dialogues. At first Jim was reluctant to do so (he had come to hate microphones and tape machines and mixing consoles), but he agreed for the sake of his son. Each night for weeks he sat in the voice-over booth, with Daniel in the control room, and talked into an ancient Sennheiser until he was hoarse, talked about everything really, about Erie and New York and life on the road, and a million other things, too, from the price of gas to the probability of life on other planets.

Eventually Daniel lost interest in what Jim had to say. When he wasn't introducing a song or voicing a commercial break, he was splicing tape in a world of his own. Eventually Jim got the feeling his presence was no longer welcome and that, on some level, he'd given his son everything he required.

It was much the same with Elysse. When she opened the door to him that first day, it was like her prayers had been answered. She hugged him and kissed his cheek, ushered him excitedly into the house. She fixed him his favourite meal. She touched his face and hair and, that very first night, even held him in her arms and let him snuggle with her. But soon the bed was off-limits, and anything more than a good-morning peck on the cheek was out of the question. Food started to come from a can. He was relegated to a cot in the drafty bedroom off the back of the house. When he complained, she told him, "This is all the family you deserve." And those words hurt him terribly because they seemed so true. He deserved little. He had made a mess of everything and knew he was just like his daddy, a dreamer with a madness for leaving.

He had hoped the reunion might turn out differently. He had first come to this place in the desert seeking primary satisfactions—family, love, silence, stillness—but they were not to be. Within weeks of his disappearance, reporters showed up asking questions. They said people wanted to know why he'd abandoned them. And because he was a good man at heart, because he felt responsible, he tried his best to describe what he did not understand. He told them he'd given everything he had, that he no longer possessed words or music. The only thing left was the silence. Yet such was their hunger that they wanted even this, they wanted his silence to be theirs.

He shouldn't have been surprised. He had always been their tool. When his feelings were raw and hurtful, he gave them The Solo; and sure enough, there were those who created worlds with it, carved paths out of the wilderness. When his ideas were feverish and muddled, he gave them The Door; and lo and behold, empires rose and fell. Now he is an empty shell, with nothing more to give; and his own son, his own wife, wield that emptiness to conjure Heaven. It has been months since he has spoken a word to anyone. The father-son dialogues are a distant memory, and yet his voice goes out each week across the nation. More surprising still, people respond. His son and wife have taken him to see the bonfires, the towering black columns of smoke, crowds of people gathering with vinyl and tape and even book, building mounds of hand-held radios and turntables, speakers and components. He is afraid to ask what these people believe.

And so he has risen in the middle of the night. He has packed his bag, his provisions and tent. Turning his back on the house and trailer, he weaves his way west by the light of the moon. The only sound is that of his own scuffling feet, his own laboured breathing. He feels no wind. He senses no water. He follows no tracks or signs, guided by the unseen, the unfelt, the insubstantial, along a ridge and then down a wide, rocky arroyo as it slopes toward the west. A few miles farther on, the gully widens and forms a desolate plain dotted with coarse grass and weed. There is a profound stillness here, away from the hum and thrum of the family compound, an almost frightening hush. He stops to rest and thinks that this might be what he has been searching for, the kind of emptiness from which all things are possible. He sets up camp. He sits in his tent and sips his water, nibbles his food. The silence around him rivals his own.

When the sun is up the next morning, he peers out at the heat, watching as the desert sends its many inhabitants to pay their respects—lizards and scorpions, small dusty birds and, around sunset, a female coyote. He tosses her bits of cheese and salami and crusts of bread but only succeeds in driving her away. Later he is visited by a small owl. Above him he senses, but does not see, bats fluttering. As he grows accustomed to the surroundings, he notices, too, that the silence is not nearly so complete as he had imagined. No human sounds, of course, no household sounds, no sounds of modern life, but as he settles into this new place, he hears something very old and very much like music, the soft lament of sand and wind and empty spaces.

The next day unfolds in much the same way, a similar progression of creatures from day to night. The female coyote shows up again but keeps her distance, skulking off when it is clear he means to stay put. As darkness falls, the night grows cool, and the desert score swells with importance. The wind sounds different here, with scant greenery to soften its tone. The sky seems to hum with static. The soil is alive with the ticks and clicks of insects and reptiles. And what binds it all together, gives it sense, is the silent flow of time. The rise and fall of the sun and moon, the passing of clouds across the sky—these are the gods of this secret world, their key and signature.

He wakes occasionally to listen to the night, to breathe deeply the desert wind. Long before dawn, he crawls out of his tent to lie directly on the ground. There is a hint of dew, or maybe just the longing for it. The air is cool and clean. He feels intimately connected to this desert world of drab-looking creatures and coarse vegetation, to the heat of the day and the cool of the night. And as he lies there, he feels something stir inside him. He touches his stomach. He brings his hand to his chest. He holds his head in both hands. Finally he closes his eyes and sees it shimmering before him, a picture, or rather a series of moving pictures like a grainy Super 8, moving forward from start to finish, beginning at the beginning with a shot of the house in Erie—junky tarpaper shack, screen door bangin' something awful in the wind. And as the jerky handheld camera moves in on a close-up of the front door, the credits roll, and then the title, *The Ages of Jim*.

The camera catches it all: The Fall, the tumble down the stairs into chaos and not knowing, his father there in shadows and high contrast, pushing into the darkness with a radio in his arms, knocking his poor wife to the floor. Jim rises without a whimper and touches the mark on the wall, The Door.

Cut to a tidy little house in Little Rock where he lives with his Aunt Corina Phillips, sweet Corina, who teaches him about the piano and then some, while his mother works her fingers to the bone down at Anderson's Dry Goods. A year is all, a year of lessons and illness and books before his father sends word he's got his life back together and wants them to come home. Has himself a job as the manager of a motel down in Port Swaggart. The Waters Inn, he says. An omen, he says. Which means they have an apartment over-looking Lake Erie. Jim's mother isn't happy with the arrangement, all those strangers around, no front porch, no back garden. But to Jim it's pretty darn good, living there by the lake. He helps out in the office. He has his own rowboat, and most days of the summer he goes out early and catches his fill of perch and silver bass. The sun shines every day.

Fade to black. Cue the music, party sounds. Lights rise on his fourteenth birthday, a simple celebration with just the three of them. His father's present is a big old Seabreeze he'd taken from a lady who couldn't pay her bill, and a stack of 78s—Sarah Vaughan and Mahalia Jackson, those voices, those rhythms, as silky and seductive as Aunt Corina's swelling bosom. They dance together, the three of them. They laugh. It feels brand new but nothing has changed. His father is still the same man. A couple of years after he gives Jim the Seabreeze, he leaves on a breeze of his own. The camera watches him walk away. They never see him again.

Reaction shots, mother and son talking, arguing, crying, packing suitcases. His mother catches a bus back to Little Rock and her sister. Jim hitches a ride to New York with the idea he will join the navy and see the world. He's just a kid with a few ideas and no prospects, but he believes things will work out. They always do.

Scenes of the city. The Statue of Liberty. The Empire State Building. The crowds on Fifth Avenue. Scenes of a working life. Lifting crates. Filling shelves. Pushing brooms. And look, a shot of the Glebemount Hotel, where he lived on cigarettes and bruised fruit. And there's a close-up of Elysse, who worked at Gimbel's and thought Jim was the bee's knees. A whirlwind romance, dizzy and breathless. Weeks of dance and chat. Sex in unlikely places. One night they're out on the town and run into Gil Gannon, a buddy of Jim's from way back. Gil says he's putting together a band and needs a piano player. The camera rises to treetop level as the three walk arm-in-arm down the street. In the distance, tugboats work the East River.

Publicity photos, hundreds of them, of Gil Gannon and the Cannons. The suits. The greasy hair. The white socks. The look of pure joy that spills from those glossy black-and-whites.

The good times: the travel, the appearances, the red carpet everywhere, what it's like to be in a band and making records the whole world loves to sing, and not a blessed thing in your head but making music and seeing the world and doing whatever you please. And the bad times, too: the way some get stupid and throw it away, abusing themselves, abusing others.

Scene in Chicago, lobby of the Drake Hotel.

Jim: I feel real grateful is what it is. For everythin'. And The Solo I guess is a kind of reward. There are a thousand musicians who can bust my chops. So why me?

Reporter (nodding): A reward . . .

Jim: I'll tell you what I think. I think the Solo was lookin' for me, the way lightnin' looks for somethin' to strike. And I was there. It passed through me like a current, and that's all I know about it.

Flashback to that poky little recording studio just off Woodward Avenue in Detroit. There's Morton DePew, Gil's producer—sour breath from sucking on a pipe all day, but a classy guy. Then Gil bursts into the control room, pumping his arm like a piston. "A fucking hit. A fucking hit. A fucking hit."

Jim doesn't say it, but he figures the song is not one of Gil's best. It's all there on paper, kind of cute and catchy but missing something, he thinks. Can't all be gems. So he settles down at his keyboard and slips on his headphones, all set to overdub his solo, not really thinking or excited, just letting it happen. At the end of the second chorus, he sits up straighter, takes a deep breath and exhales. And that's it. Like breathing. He just exhales and the music comes out in a perfect shape, the thing that was missing. The missing link. And all he did was exhale and his fingers did the rest. It passed through him. The Solo passed through him like a charge.

The reaction shots, the confusion. Gil gets on the intercom and says, "What the fuck you been smoking, you play a solo like that?" So Jim records a few more tracks for the hell of it, but nothing else feels as good. And each time they go back to the original it sounds a bit better. Still pretty weird, but better. They decide to sleep on it. Next morning it's like a veil has lifted. Everyone nods yeahyeahyeah. Took some getting used to, they all agreed.

But the fans, they're crazy about the record the minute it's released. Number one in its first week. Stays there most of the summer. Tune into any station that year and you hear it, and you hear DJs talking up The Solo. There's Chick Camino at WNBC in New York playing "Don't Look Back" forty-eight hours straight. Camera pans the kids lined up around the corner for the *Ed Sullivan Show*.

People call Jim a genius. He's voted the best keyboard player in America that year when even he doesn't know what he's done. Not that he's going to argue. He's having a ball. Womenfolk, in particular, are terribly kind, and none kinder than the lovely Elysse, from Taos, New Mexico, who works at the fragrance counter at Gimbel's and loves him, who stays with him longer than he ever expected she would, and who bears him a son, a little angel they call Daniel.

The family snapshots: Jim in scrubs, Jim with cigar, Jim leaving the hospital with bundle of joy in his arms. Changing the diapers. Feeding the Pablum. Playing the lullaby. But there's a growing concern on his face. The words are coming, those five painful words that tear worlds apart: The show must go on.

No surprise, the years become a line of days—buses, planes, trains, cars, spotlights, flashbulbs, autographs, screaming fans. And then a funny thing happens, but not so funny when you think about it. Every day is another town, every night another concert, and even though Gil has a pretty long string of hits by then, you can't help but feel the audience has come to hear one song, and in fact one part of one song: The Solo. Jim isn't about to disappoint. He's a professional; he's grateful. But after a while he gets a little antsy about the whole thing, the way you might if someone holds you down too long. He starts messing around in rehearsals and sound checks, looking for a way he can change that solo, liven it up. But nothing he tries is ever as good, and that makes him more determined. Yet here's the thing: The Solo is too perfect to change, like gospel or something. Soon he's fiddling with his other solos, trying to nudge *them* closer to perfection. In the end, it's like he isn't expressing himself anymore, he's expressing The Solo. Like a millstone, a dead weight, it's starting to make him nutty, until that day on *American Bandstand* something snaps, talking there with Dick Clark and trying to keep it together, when something snaps and he pushes through the curtains and disappears into thin air. Elysse and the kid, tired of waiting, had already gone to New Mexico without him, so he heads for the only true home he's ever known: Port Swaggart.

Talk about your before and after. Look at the difference a few years makes. The happy family, Little Rock behind them, are back together again. They're standing in front of the Waters Inn. A new beginning. And then look, the broken man, the runaway, lying on a mucky mattress in a broken world. And he's so messed up it's easy enough to think it's all his fault, as if in tearing down his career he has torn down everything.

Scenes of a frantic sleeper. Ronnie Conger shows up out of the blue. Two weeks later they're in New York, and Jim's already looking more himself, more together. And it strikes him that maybe Ronnie is *his* solo, the exact shape that had been missing from his life.

So he doesn't complain too much when Ronnie brings those people around, those musicians. He's not interested in the piano anymore, but he's trying to be polite for Ronnie's sake. And then one night, lying on his bed, he hears music, lovely stuff that sounds to his ear like the kind of thing his daddy used to listen to on the radio, that preacher down in West Helena, Arkansas. And he walks over to the door, you know, to check it out, and sure enough a fellow is sitting at the piano and rolling out a lazy gospel groove, and it pulls him in as sure as a magnet pulls steel, right into the middle of the room, except it's the living room in Erie that he sees, with his father's radio and his hardback chair and his plate of food, and all these things, you know, the wallpaper and his mother hugging herself in the kitchen, all these pictures and memories and feelings gather in his throat like a pressure and he just starts talking.

It takes them all a few goes at it to really figure out how the damn thing is supposed to work, but once they tune in, it isn't long before they have themselves something special. Jim is happy then. The sparkle is back in his eyes. And he thanks the Lord for Sonny Redmond and Ronnie Conger and all the generous souls who help him move backwards and forwards through time. Then one night after a rehearsal, the day before they are to appear on *Saturday Night Live,* he looks up at the stars and feels empty. He has nothing left to say, and that nothing of how he feels is maybe all his fault, he thinks, because of how selfish he's been. All his life. More than anything, he wants to be like Ronnie, the missing piece, the perfect shape in someone's life. And that means one thing: he has to find Elysse and their son.

Even though that, too, is a kind of selfishness, another kind of self-fulfillment, it seems logical in a way. In music he had uncovered his feelings; in his feelings he had found his stories; in his stories he had found his understanding; and from understanding he had hoped to reach out to his family with whom, he believed, he would find happiness . . .

Jim opens his eyes and sits up. The sun is painting the desert landscape in battlefield colours. A warm soft wind polishes the sand. He can see it now from start to finish, clear as day. The ranch, the family—these are not options. Whatever comes next will not be found here; whatever he needs is somewhere beyond the horizon. He will know what to do when the time comes.

Somewhere behind him the coyote sends up a single arching note, a sound as old as the hills but so full of life and meaning and purpose that it makes him shiver. By comparison, all the music he's made, all the stories he's told, are a pale imitation. Without turning, he can sense the animal watching. Jim knows he's been an inconvenience, a disruption in the natural order, but he also knows he can do better. The spirit is moving again. It will lead him, he's sure, to a greener place. He feels the flow and knows it's some kind of revival.

Cyrus took Ronnie's advice and remained at Hidey-Hole, where he let work take hold and transport him. The arrival of the other band members helped, and for the first week they rehearsed in the studio every day. When Nigel decided they were ready to get down to serious business, Ronnie knew it was time to leave. He couldn't stand to watch the recording process, he said. "Would I ask Houdini to show me his tricks?" Instead he drove down to London, where he would work out of the Gore Hotel.

Cyrus had done more recording than anyone else in the group, but he had never been in a studio that compared to Hidey-Hole, the bells and whistles of its technology like something from a spaceship. Nor had he or the others experienced anything as rigorous as Nigel's process. They spent a full day fiddling with the drum sound, loosening the skins until there was no snap, then covering the heads with wads of paper towel and gaffer tape to remove frequency spikes. They followed much the same process with the other instruments, adjusting volumes, altering tones, with no thought of how the musicians might respond. When Pete complained at one point that they might not play as well under these circumstances, Nigel said, "It's not about playing, mate. You go on the road to play. Making records is work."

If Nigel's search for sound was exhaustive, his demand for performance was exhausting. He recorded up to twenty takes of each track and just as many overdubs. After each take he said, "Perfect. Let's do another," so that they began to hate the songs before the sessions were half finished. The worst, they realized, would be the final mix. At that point they would all be held hostage to Nigel's quest for perfection.

They recorded eight hours a day, seven days a week for six weeks, time enough for two hundred cups of rancid coffee, three thousand games of pinball, the same ten songs playing over and over, sometimes on the big punishing speakers, sometimes on the little two-inchers that simulated a car stereo. They argued a lot, especially when the grooves didn't groove, when the songs didn't sing, but they laughed, too, and danced and got righteously stoned. Sometimes, in the wee hours of the morning, if they had been to the pub for drinks, Cyrus would creep into the echoless space of the studio for a moment of privacy. He'd lie on the floor beside his amplifier and listen to the whispery silence, or puzzle over a phrase or bit of groove, or, in the mystical magic of predawn, get all philosophical and deep.

At times like that he often had mixed feelings about what they were achieving. The music sounded real but unlike anything he had expected, as different as he could imagine from those early tapes he'd made with Pete or those first demos. And while he was proud of many parts of the record—the long guitar solo over that droning I-beam, for instance—he hardly recognized it as his own. After months of writing and rewriting, always focused on the bridge and creek, the farm and marsh, his family and Janice, he had imagined one long anguished cry of an album, music that spoke of blood and tears and broken hearts. Instead he heard something hard and shiny and mechanical; he heard cities groaning, numbers crunching, the bright complicated structures of science.

After six weeks, Nigel told them to go home. "Don't play," he said. "Don't listen to anything. Get lost. A month maybe. Then we'll see what we have and start the final mix."

Cyrus was tempted to stay in England, but with the recording on hold, his days were increasingly dominated by the great aching wound that was Eura. In the studio, he had put her out of his mind, which in many ways was music's central grace: the ability to drain the world of everything but rhythm and melody. Now she filled his empty head and heart like a spring. She filled his ears and his mouth and his eyes. She filled his empty arms and crowded his bed. Now that his work was finished, there would be no forgetting. He would have to go home and pick up the pieces.

FIVE DAYS LATER he landed in Toronto, and it seemed as though he'd been gone an eternity. Familiar objects had taken on the quality of icons: the door to their apartment with its lacy curtain, grey with age; the long narrow flight of stairs to the second floor; the checkerboard tile of the hall landing where he liked to sit and play his guitar for the echo.

The apartment itself was much as Ronnie had described it, a scene of hurried departure. Dresser drawers had been left open and empty, though not perfectly empty, always some article left behind in the rush: a pyjama bottom, a single woolen sock darned and redarned at heel and toe, a single earring. A suitcase on the bed held a few small items—a scarf, a belt, two pairs of scuffed shoes, a purse—and he realized that he not only felt abandoned but robbed, as though in casting aside his love and their life together she had also decided to burgle the apartment. She hadn't, of course; she took just what belonged to her. But he couldn't help feeling he had a claim on her clothes, her face creams and toothpaste, the way she smelled and the way she sounded and the way she filled his life with emotions that were not always pleasant but were something.

Ronnie had emptied and wiped down the fridge. He'd thrown out all perishables and taken out the garbage. Everything else was just as she'd left it. And the closer Cyrus looked, the sadder he became. It was true, she took nothing of his. Worse, she took nothing of theirs, as though she wanted no reminder of their time together. The photo albums sat untouched on the shelves in the living room. The records and cassettes were just where they were supposed to be. Nothing had been removed from the bookshelf or even the mantel, where she liked to display the mementos they'd picked up in their travels together. Most hurtful, she'd taken from her wallet the photo-booth snaps he'd given her way back when, of a young boy making silly faces. That she would stop in her flight to toss them on the coffee table seemed an act of cruelty. Beside the pictures were the keys to the Impala.

He listened to the answering machine in hopes of hearing her voice, a few words of regret, a promise of return. What he heard instead were his own calls from England, the pathetic and disconsolate sound of a phone hanging up, over and over again. Aside from that, there was the wheedling voice of the landlord, wondering when he could expect the rent. The last message on the tape was from Isabel, sounding hushed and serious.

"Better get home," she said. "It's Clarence, and it doesn't look good."

He phoned her right away and got no answer. He phoned Ruby. Again no one home. He phoned Izzy's office, then remembered it was a Sunday. That's when he decided to head for Wilbury. Why bother to unpack? It wasn't as if the apartment felt like home anymore. He grabbed the car keys and his suitcase and walked around back to the Chevy, which was more decrepit than he had remembered, a patchwork of rust and graffiti, all four tires slashed. Undaunted, he hiked down the street to a rental outlet and was soon behind the wheel of a brand new compact.

He forced himself to enjoy the drive. He paid attention as the sun set. He noticed the fog that rose out of the surrounding fields and began to creep across the highway. It was beautiful, in a bleak sort of way. And partly because of the fog, partly because of the cold and empty apartment he'd left behind, he found himself looking forward more keenly than he would have expected. He couldn't help wondering what would loom out of that grey cloud.

He arrived in town at nine o'clock and went directly to the hospital. Clarence's room was full of people—Ruby, Hank, Janice, Izzy, Reverend Jansen—and he noticed immediately the complicated way in which they were all connected: how Ruby sat beside her husband, clasping his large hand in both of hers; how the minister waited quietly for the opportunity to share his strength; how Janice stood beside Isabel's bony shoulder while Hank, with a look of gritty determination, held on to Clarence's foot, as though he could physically keep him from the other world.

As Cyrus entered the room, they turned—not at once, but by degrees, depending on their level of distraction, until all five were shaking his hand and touching his shoulder and whispering how wonderful it was he'd made it. Then they parted to give him access to his dying uncle; and facing the unmediated horror of Clarence's illness, he began to feel the full weight of his own life. He took Ruby's seat and held his uncle's hand. "Clarence," he said, though there was absolutely no indication his words might be heard, "it's me, Cyrus."

He was relieved they had given him some space, some private time, and there was so much he could have mentioned, the gratitude, the admiration, the sadness and guilt. But in the end those sentiments were too difficult to express. Instead he gently squeezed the old man's hand and said, "Everything's going to be fine." After a few more minutes of silent communion, he let Ruby return to her rightful position. An hour later his uncle struggled briefly, then stopped breathing forever.

After that the family was pushed to the periphery while the doctors made the death official. In the jittery vacuum created by the family's loss, Isabel took control. "Ruby has to sign papers, then I'll take her to Worrell's to make arrangements." She looked at her watch. "I doubt we'll be out of there before eleven. No way is she going to the farm tonight. She can stay at my house. What I need is someone to go to Orchard Knoll to get a few things." When Janice volunteered, Isabel nodded efficiently and said, "Maybe you could take Hank with you and when you're done there, go back to my house and change the sheets in his room. He can sleep on the couch a few days till we make other plans."

When Isabel looked at Cyrus, he moved forward and helped her lead Ruby down the hall and into the last empty years of her life.

BY DAYLIGHT, Orchard Knoll was the kind of tidy setting you might find gracing a colourful calendar or children's book—the bright red barns, the stately brick home, healthy trees in orderly rows that stretched across the land as far as the eye could see. But that night, with the orchard covered in a shifting blanket of fog, and with Clarence's death fresh in her mind, Janice found it a far more meaningful place. Troubling, to be sure, but in the way that art can trouble. This is the Orchard Knoll a great painter would have captured, she realized, the farm that wasn't visible to the untrained eye, that only showed its true face to those who were quiet enough and patient enough to wait for revelation, or in times of upheaval such as this, when people and

objects unwittingly revealed their secret natures. As she sat in the driveway with Hank and stared at the silent farmhouse, she felt bright and
breathless, her senses on high alert, as though she were in the midst of a
deeply creative act.

She was thankful when Hank handed her the keys to the house and
suggested she go in alone rather than wrestle with his chair. How often were
you given the opportunity, an hour after someone's death, to stand perfectly
still in their home and listen and watch and soak it all in without a single
living soul to disturb the infinite currents that swirled through every room
and tickled the hair on your arms and neck?

For a long while she stood motionless just inside the door, with the lights
off. Instead of the profound silence she had expected, she heard the pert
rhythm of a dripping tap, the soft purr of the refrigerator, the steady back-
beat of the grandfather clock. Outside, she could hear Hank working his way
along the dial of her car radio. Behind that, there was the hoot of a barn owl
and, far away, the faint roar of the lake, still agitated from yesterday's storm.
These sounds, meaningless in themselves, seemed to gather weight and
significance in the empty house. A complicated music, but as evocative of
this time and place as anything she could imagine.

Finally she flipped on a light and put together a few necessities for Ruby.
When she returned to the car, Hank was leaning out the window, his head
resting on his arms. After she stowed the suitcase in the back seat, she
nudged him with her hand and asked point-blank what was on his mind.

"Me? Nothing much. In prison, you think a lot about open space and
weather and shit like that. I guess I'm trying to appreciate it while I can."

She fingered the keys in the ignition. "Were you close to Clarence?"

"Not really. Guess I never gave him a chance. Guess I've never been that
close to anyone, though I was always partial to Ruby. Makes me laugh just to
look at her sometimes. Never could get over how she was the opposite of my
mother—the two sisters, you know—and at the same time how they were
exactly the same. Never could figure that out."

At Izzy's bungalow, Hank showed Janice where the clean sheets were
kept and led her to his room, where she stripped his bed and made it again
with the fresh linen. He was uncomfortable about the whole thing, especially

the wall of pin-ups behind her. When she finished, he said, "Don't suppose you'd like to take those down."

She looked behind her as if she hadn't noticed the centrefolds at all. "You sure? Maybe Ruby'll get a kick out of them."

Hank had never been able to take teasing from anyone who wasn't family, so he turned away from her and rolled himself into the kitchen. When she joined him again, she said, "I put them in your dresser. They'll be safe there." She looked at the clock, the counter, the cupboards, and down the hall to the front door. "Unless you can think of anything else," she said, "I'll be on my way."

"You think I'm a jerk."

She tried her hands in her pockets but that didn't feel so good, so she tucked them into her armpits. "If you knew me better," she said, "you'd know I'm not like that—judgmental, I mean. So, no, I don't think you're a jerk. I don't really know what you are. An artist maybe."

He laughed weakly, almost against his will. When she looked at her watch, he said, "I hate the idea of waiting on my own for them to show up. You feel like going somewhere?"

"Well," she said, not exactly wild about the prospect. Something had been stirred in her back at Orchard Knoll, and she wanted to go to her studio space out by the farmers' co-operative.

But there was a part of Hank that liked nothing better than backing people into a corner, and he sensed rightly that he had Janice in such a position. He moved his chair closer and said, "What about this truth I've heard about? I showed you mine, maybe you could show me yours."

As they drove across town, they realized they hadn't eaten since morning, so they stopped at Stewart's Drive-in for burgers, onion rings and mugs of root beer. Hank, who often had difficulty remembering his time in Wilbury, was flooded with memories of Stewart's. The laughs with his pals, the hot and heavy action with Jenny Duckworth and Donna Pulaski and a string of other faces that had lost their names. Or better still that spring night, about two in the morning, all the other cars gone, the parking lot full of shadows and shadflies and empty wrappers, and Milly Green slowly working up the nerve to take his thing in her hand, everything as slick as Christmas, when who comes roaring into the lot but Dickie Bernardi, Milly's ex-boyfriend, only Hank didn't know that. And Dickie, because he's huge and on the football team, thinks he's invincible, and sure enough when he sees Milly in the front seat of the Owen pickup truck he goes apeshit and tries to pull her into his car. That's when Hank put a few things straight. He kicked in Dickie's front teeth and left him coughing blood on the asphalt. After that, Hank was king of the hill, the coolest cat. Certain girls lit up like candles whenever he came near; everyone else stayed out of his way. Like a dream come true.

Janice was the type who wouldn't have given him a second look back then. His charms were lost on women like her. They didn't get it, didn't understand who he really was. And where some guys had other characters they could use in a pinch—they could be shy or smart or sporty or sexy, depending on the circumstance—he just had the one character, which hadn't done him much good recently.

"Came here all the time," he said, when he finished his burger.

Janice nodded. "Cyrus and I stopped after every gig. You can't imagine the stuff we used to talk about."

And it hit Hank that he couldn't imagine his brother at all. Most of what he remembered about Wilbury came before Cy was ten years old, hardly even a person. Feeling a small space open inside him, an emptiness that needed to be filled, he turned to Janice and said, "Tell me about him. Anything you like."

She sipped her root beer, then said, "He sure thought the world of you." But that was such an old-lady comment, and so clearly did not hit the mark, that she tried again. "In the band we had this thing called The Hank Standard. Whenever we made a decision, Cyrus would say, 'Okay, maybe, but would Hank think it was cool?'"

He laughed. "The Hank Standard. I like that."

"One time," she continued, "I even saw him defend your honour. Bryce McKutcheon was making wisecracks about you being in prison, and Cyrus went right after him."

Hank gave the low whistle of astonishment. "I've seen that McKutcheon. He's built like a Mack truck. Cyrus decked him?"

"Well, no, he actually got himself beaten pretty bad. Cy's only fight that

I know of. 'Stickin' up for his bro' is how he put it."

Hank wasn't all that tickled by that last story. Maybe she intended it that way, to show him what a negative influence he'd been. As if he needed any more of that kind of information. Janice, too, felt increasingly uneasy. Not that Hank seemed like such a bad guy, but the more she got to know him, the worse she felt about herself. Of all the people who had moved through her life, Cyrus had always had a special place, her first love. And yet she realized how selfish she'd been back then. She'd given almost no thought to what it must have been like to grow up in such a sad and painful family. She took what he gave her and gave what she had, without looking beyond or looking deeper.

When they finished eating, they drove out to Winters Shipping & Receiving and parked around back so Hank could manoeuvre his chair up the paved ramp of the loading dock. He felt right at home. This was the kind of place he had worked when he first quit school. The heft and groan, the sweat and ache. Given his present physical predicament, he'd give anything to do that kind of work again, to feel the power of his limbs, the pumping of his heart. Janice led him along a dark hallway and into an even darker storage room. From the sound of their echoes, it was a huge space, like a gymnasium. "Wait here," she said, "while I get the lights."

The darkness enveloped her in two seconds, and as he listened to her retreating footsteps, he realized that, for a night that had started out so poorly, it was turning out pretty well. Clarence's death had been good in a way, all of them in that room watching him go. And although it was tough to see Ruby upset, Hank was glad he'd been there. The experience had brought him a few steps closer to a place he was meant to be, and the clearest indication of that was the relative peace and calm he felt just now sitting in the dark. Nothing at all like those anxious nights in prison, the shadowy faces leering at him out of the empty space.

It was Cy's tape that had started it, he figured, and the picture of their mother, Catherine, floating into his mind as though she were swimming up to him from the murky bottom of a lake. He'd played the tape constantly the past several months, and each time another little piece of his life seemed to rise up to greet him: the smell of Wildroot Cream Oil, the taste of Beemans chewing gum or NuGrape soda, the sound of his mother singing "Tennessee Waltz" or "Stardust." Often those little snatches of memory were enough to trigger larger recollections, like the time he and his friends went swimming in the rock quarry on Rinders Island or the time he tickled Izzy until she peed her pants, each memory becoming a signpost for others, leading him, it seemed, down a very different path that summer, from Cy's tape to the drives around town with Ruby to the art classes with Janice, all the way to that emotional gathering around Clarence's final breath.

It wasn't always a sunny thought he stumbled on, of course. The more he remembered his childhood, the more he remembered exactly why he hated his father, remembered how much they fought that last summer, one night after supper even wrestling in the dirt by the barn, neither one of them landing blows, but understanding all too clearly that it was over between them and the only thing left was to hurt each other. It wasn't always a one-way street, either. With all the trouble he'd caused in his life, it'd be easy to blame himself for everything, but that wouldn't be right. They both had problems, both did wrong; yet Hank was the only one still paying. Not that he'd ever been smart about it. He should have run and not looked back. But he kept licking the same wounds, circling over the same territory. Burning down the coop, that was plain stupid. And all those dark months in Hounslow, getting into more trouble and more pain and more trouble. It was stupid. He'd always been stupid. He was just so stupid.

He peered into the darkness for a glimpse of Janice. He listened closely for her footsteps. And then, all at once, a blaze of overhead work lights. He blinked once, twice, and there before him, dead centre in a huge empty room, was a pure-white figure falling backwards, a man falling backwards with his arms flying up in complete surprise, a dopey-looking guy surrounded by lights, just some poor fuck doing his job, doing what he was told, when bang he gets hit full blast by the unexpected, the unexpected bending him over backwards so his face is staring straight up at the sky, and his arms fly up in total fucking surprise, and bang, the surprise, the unexpected, bang, it's right there blooming on his chest like flowers, the poor bastard, and on his arm, and one just above his belt buckle. And all he said, all the guy had said, was "Can I help you, mister?" That was all he said, standing there in his white

overalls and white T-shirt like he wanted to be extra visible that late at
night, "Can I help you, mister?" And even now he can remember how that
one stupid line made his blood boil, as if he'd ever wanted or needed anyone's
help. Can I help you. What the fuck was that? What did the guy expect? It
was about never wanting help. It was about I can do this myself. It was fuck
you and you and all of you because I don't need your help, which, really, was
the kind of thing that could catch a guy by surprise, send him back on his
heels and bending over backwards. Because the guy was not too bright. Some
local farm boy who didn't have a whole lot of smarts in his favour, and yet he
had this perfectly normal job, pumping gas, maybe fixing an engine now and
again or changing a fan belt, certainly not hurting anyone and probably making
his folks proud, when bang, something unexpected catches him right there
near the collarbone, and there above the belt buckle, and in one wicked whip-
crack his body bends backwards, his arms fly up and he goes stumbling into
the gas pump and falls to the ground, a bit of snaky thrashing, his nice white
overalls totally fucked now. Then he's lying there still, and Hank is breathing
so hard it's like he's run a hundred miles, only he just got out of the car, a
snazzy little red Corvair, noisy as fuck, and like a bad dream where you forget
important things, he suddenly remembers how he got the car, how he stole
it from the parking lot at the racetrack, and he stops for gas, right, the thing
needs gas, and the stupid-looking guy comes towards him in his nice white
outfit, so fucking proud of those overalls you want to tear them to shreds, and
the guy is such a loser, with buckteeth and zits and a face you just had to hate,
saying, "Can I help you, mister?" and without thinking (how do you think
about something like that? You don't. You just do it) he reached under his
shirt where he had a little .22-calibre pistol in his waistband, the kind of
thing you'd take out to the dump to shoot rats, and he pulled it out and
without saying anything, without thinking anything, he just squeezed the
trigger, and the guy flew backwards like he'd been hit by Sonny Liston, his
face looking up at the stars and his arms with a life of their own, and the guy
went down, heavy, he went down heavy and his chest was gurgling, his whole
body doing this snaky bit of thrashing until suddenly he's still, and Hank
looks at the gun in his hand, and he looks at that stupid fuck falling backwards and he feels an emptiness like he has never known before, like there is

no air left in the world. And he looks up and there she is, Cyrus's friend Janice, and there is that guy frozen forever in mid-fall, his arms flying up, his back bent nearly in two, blown away by surprise, except Janice is looking at Hank as though he's the one who's been shot, and Hank holds his hand out to show her the gun, the cold metal in his fist, and all he can say is "I did it. I did it," over and over until even that is beyond him and he begins to sob, a whitewater flow so powerful and turbulent he can't fight it, he can only let it take him.

CYRUS AND ISABEL SAT SIDE-BY-SIDE at the dining room table, both leaning heavily on their arms, too tired to speak. They had given Ruby a sedative and tucked her into Hank's bed. Then they set about sedating themselves. When the wine was gone, they started on the Canadian Club. They took turns looking at the clock, took turns pouring the next round, took turns peering out the front door for signs of Hank and Janice. Neither spoke to the other about the concerns they might have.

When they heard the front door open around two in the morning, they moved soundlessly to the front hall. Whatever angry words Isabel had been teeing up, she quickly put away the moment she saw Hank. It looked as though he'd been weeping for hours, his eyes bloodshot and swollen. She was touched by the notion that her hard-edged brother, who had seldom shown a speck of consideration for others, was grieving this way for his uncle. She knew he had a fondness for Ruby. Even so, she was surprised to see him so upset.

Cyrus was more interested in the way Janice looked. As strong and confident as anyone he knew, she now seemed completely shell-shocked, as though she'd been shaken to her core by something. He only hoped Hank hadn't done something stupid.

Janice spoke first. "I'm sorry," she said. "My fault. We finished here early, and Hank didn't want to wait by himself. I showed him what I've been working on. The time got away from us."

Without a word or gesture, Hank put his chair in gear and motored toward his bedroom. Halfway there he remembered Ruby, turned his chair around, and rolled himself into the den where he flopped on the sofa, his back to the room. In response to Cyrus's raised eyebrows, Janice shook her head and backed sheepishly to the door.

"Thanks," Isabel said. "We couldn't have managed without you."

Cyrus offered to walk Janice to her car. "I was just leaving myself," he explained. "This hotel's full."

"I can put cushions on the floor!" Izzy protested.

He held his hand up like a traffic cop. "It's all right, Iz. Any other time I'd take you up on the offer, but the last time my head hit a pillow was about forty-eight hours ago in England. If I don't get some serious sleep, I'm going to collapse. Tomorrow, okay?"

On the sidewalk in front of the house, Janice offered to let him stay at her mother's. "She's in Florida," she said. "She won't mind."

He stopped to look at her squarely. "And you don't mind?"

"No, why would I?"

"I don't know. It's been a long time, Janice. I'm not sure I even know who you are anymore."

"Well, if you'd rather not . . ."

He grabbed her wrist as she was about to move farther away. "I don't want to make things awkward for you, that's all. I only just heard from Iz, you know, about you and Jonathan."

She pulled her hand away and took a step closer. In a softer, almost apologetic tone, she said, "The only thing that's making me feel awkward is this stupid conversation. Would you like the spare room or not?"

"Yes. And a ride, too, if you don't mind. I'm a little drunk."

That simple decision lifted a weight off both of them. Cyrus led her to the rental car, where he grabbed a battered suitcase from the back seat. Her vehicle, a vintage Volvo station wagon, was so full of wood, cement, plaster, metal, plastic buckets and several gauges of wire and mesh that it was hard to find a spot for his suitcase. Anyone looking inside would think the car belonged to a construction worker.

Once they were driving, he looked at her and said, "So what's with Hank? I've never seen him that way."

Janice had always been good about secrets. Private knowledge might inform her art, but only in the most roundabout way. She could proudly declare she had never broken a confidence, never snitched. So even if she had understood Hank, she would have been reluctant to reveal anything to Cyrus. As it was, she had no idea why his brother was so upset. He had told her about that terrible night at the gas station; but that was old news, surely. He'd been convicted of those crimes. He'd had years behind bars to come to terms with his guilt. Why the sudden breakdown? Why did he feel the need to confess to her, repeatedly—unless that was the curious way he related to women. In any case, there was nothing she could or would reveal about the matter, so she shrugged her shoulders and said he'd been upset. When Cy persisted, she looked at him and, in a flippant tone, said, "I don't know, he's *your* brother."

The Young house was exactly the way he remembered it: same wallpaper, same smell of fresh flowers and furniture polish. The guest bedroom, where he dropped his bag, had the same chenille bedspread, the same Andrew Wyeth print above the dresser, the same bookcase with the same books and framed snapshots. To Cyrus, that had always seemed the definition of old age—people who were unwilling or unable to face change and who arranged their world as a fortress against it. But now, as he sat and listened to Janice moving about the room next to him, he felt the appeal of such a fortress. He remembered like it was yesterday how much fun the two of them had had together, making love on this very bed, whipping up a batch of brownies and watching the soaps after school, hanging out at the Three Links Hall and being able to say anything and have her understand. He had half a mind to knock on her door right now and talk until dawn about where they'd been and what they'd seen and what it meant to be who they were. But he was already so tired and drunk, and the pillow was so inviting, that he fell back fully dressed, wrapped himself in the bedspread and let the darkness carry him away.

NEXT MORNING CYRUS OPENED HIS EYES to find Janice sitting beside him, her hand resting gently on his cheek. "Your sister just phoned, looking for you," she said. "She wants you to call."

He closed his eyes again while he reconfigured the who, what, where and why. For a fraction of a second, he had thought he was back home in

Toronto, and that Eura had settled on the bed beside him. When he opened his eyes again, Janice was watching him closely. He took her hand in his and said, "It's weird, the two of us being in this room again."

"Is it?" She let her gaze settle on a distant corner of the ceiling. "I think we've always been in this room. And we've always been at the Three Links Hall and at school and drinking root beer at Stewart's. Just like, in a way, I'll always be a student in Toronto. My father will always die. I'll always be there when Clarence takes his last breath. You know what I mean? It's all here." She touched a hand to her belly. "If you could look inside, you'd see it: a jumble of stuff like you'd find in an attic."

Cyrus didn't have a clue what she was talking about, but he knew one thing: he was still the silent partner, the straight man, and she was the one with all the words.

"I'll make coffee," she said. "If you hurry, maybe we can talk a bit before you get pulled too much into the day."

He showered quickly and phoned his sister, who said Ruby was doing fine, all things considered. It was Hank who worried her. "He's still asleep," she said. "And it's not like I'm tiptoeing around. I wonder if I should wake him just to see if he's okay." Cyrus understood the concern. They had talked earlier about how unnerving it was to live with someone who slept only a couple of hours at a stretch. Before he could comment, she said, "I've been working out some details for the funeral, and it struck me you might not have a suit with you."

"Good guess. I don't own one."

"Cyrus, even Hank has a suit."

"Yeah, well, what would I do with something like that?"

"Oh, you know, go to funerals, a wedding or two, maybe a graduation, all the normal milestones you've somehow avoided."

"Don't act like I've missed out on the good things in life."

"Maybe you have and maybe you haven't. That's not the point. You're going to a funeral tomorrow and you don't have a suit."

"So maybe I won't go. I find that shit kind of gruesome."

Izzy exhaled loudly, and then said nothing, as though she were counting to ten. Then, in a tone that was calm and matter-of-fact, she said, "Can I tell you something? If you don't join us, I may never speak to you again. You understand?"

"But Iz, that religious crap is so hokey."

"Maybe you should try telling Ruby that. Anyway, I don't have time for your teenage bullshit. I've already called Samuel's and told them to expect you. If you're there by noon, they can have the alterations ready by closing tonight. And don't worry about the expense, it's on me. This is important, Cy, whether you know it or not." Then she hung up.

In the music business, it was normal for thirty-year-old men to act like teenagers, and when Cyrus was in his world, doing what he was meant to do, it all felt good and right and natural. It was only when he came back to Wilbury that he felt odd in any way. Izzy never gave him any slack, of course, never considered how hard it was for him to be out of his element. But then she'd never been much of a teenager herself, one moment a young girl, and the next married to Gerry Muehlenburg. She was bitter, he figured. Even so, her words had gotten to him. After all, Ruby's offer to buy him a suit twelve years ago had led him to the Les Paul and Ronnie Conger, to Jim and Sonny and Eura, to the road up and the road down, and now, with his record half-finished, a road pointed toward the stars. Who could say what surprises this new offer might bring?

Downstairs, the sight of Janice puttering in the kitchen further complicated his mood. For a fleeting moment he saw what it might have been like had he taken Ruby's cheque and bought that suit, if he'd finished his year of school, say, then gone on to university and married Janice the way everyone would have predicted. Here she was, a healthy mind, a healthy body, the closest friend he'd ever known. They could have had kids and gone on vacations and done great things. And it would have worked out, he had no doubt about that. They had always been great together. And while you could make a case that he'd never been more alive than when he'd been with Eura, he could also say that he'd never been happier than with Janice.

He sat quietly at the table and let her bring coffee, let her fiddle with the toaster and bread, the butter and jam. When she sat facing him, he asked what she'd been up to the past while; and she told him about her art classes at the recreation centre, how liberating she had found the move from

Toronto. She was thinking of relocating permanently, she said. For his part of the history lesson, he restricted himself to professional matters—putting his band together, recording in England with a famous producer.

"That is so great," she said.

And Cyrus should have been happy, should have been full to bursting with pride and a sense of accomplishment. But he wasn't.

FOR MORE THAN TWENTY-FIVE YEARS Samuel's Fine Apparel had been clothing the Wilbury elite—the doctors and lawyers and dentists, the wheelers and dealers like Isabel Owen. You could get Burberry there. You could get Aquascutum and Lacoste.

Cyrus had never set foot in the store (he'd always bought his school clothes at Feldman's Men's and Boys' Wear down the street) and was glad Janice had offered to tag along. Her parents had bought most of their clothing from Ben Samuel. She shopped there too, occasionally, for kilts and cashmere and fine cottons. So Cyrus let her do all the talking and, except for the odd shrug from him now and then, make all the decisions—about the colour, the fabric, the length, the cut. Even so, he didn't breathe normally until they were back on the street again.

"I guess I owe you lunch for that," he said. Taking her by the elbow, he led her along the main street to their old hangout Marlowe's, where they sat in the window booth and had the Teen Special, which unfortunately was a disappointment. The burger was mealy, the fries weren't real, and the shakes were thin and tasteless. Of course, Junior Marlowe wasn't manning the grill these days. He'd been dead for several years.

After lunch they drove aimlessly around town, ending up at Memorial Park where they lazed in the sun and took turns pushing each other on the swing. As the day wore on, they spoke more freely, moving gradually from safe and sanitized topics until they were floating freely in the ebb and flow of who they were and what they thought. By the end of the afternoon Cyrus was able to breathe another sigh of relief. She was still his pal. She still laughed at his jokes.

At six o'clock they returned to Samuel's for a final fitting. Even Cyrus had to admit he looked good. When he moved toward the change rooms to get back into his jeans and T-shirt, Janice grabbed him by the arm. "Leave the suit on. We'll go back to the house for five minutes so I can change. We should go to the funeral parlour." In response to his pained expression, she buttoned up his jacket and said, "Come on, pop star. I'll show you how it's done."

Isabel was so happy to see them walk through the door together, and to see Cyrus looking so handsome and respectable, that she rushed across the room to greet them. "My goodness," she said, "don't you look swell."

"Don't push it," he warned. "I'm here against my will."

"That's fine. Against your will looks good on you." Then she led them over to Ruby, where they spoke a few phrases of condolence.

It was downhill from there. The very idea of modelling his grief for everyone in town seemed ghoulish to him. He couldn't get the hang of it. And Janice, not officially part of the family, had made herself scarce, loitering in the wings and smiling encouragement whenever Cyrus looked especially bleak. When Frank Pentangeles walked into the room, however, the whole mood changed.

In most ways that mattered, you could say that Frank and Clarence were good friends, though they seldom moved in the same circles. There had been mutual respect and affection and a long history of shared labour. And fun. Frank loved to tease and fool around. But there was no joking now, no levity. He dragged himself toward Ruby like he was the heaviest man on earth. Then he knelt beside her and wept, occasionally wiping away the tears with the heel of his hand but mostly just letting them flow. The rest of them exchanged uneasy glances, and Cyrus wondered what would happen if Frank couldn't stop. Worse, this open display of grief had already brought tears or the threat of tears to everyone else in the room—what if they all lost control? What if this contagion of tears spread down the street and along the block, from neighbourhood to neighbourhood, until the town lay down in sorrow?

Cyrus should have known better. Frank was many things, sometimes too loud, too sentimental, too emotional for his own good, but he was not a man to lose control. This was a matter of openness. And when he had finished pouring out his grief, he rose, squared his shoulders and walked directly to the open casket where he placed his hand over his friend's heart, made the sign of the cross, then turned and walked away.

Once everyone had regained composure, Izzy quietly suggested to Hank that he, Cyrus and Janice go and have a drink. "Ruby and I will stay awhile longer," she whispered. "Then we'll join you for a nightcap." When he resisted, she gave Cyrus a look that said she needed his help. Hank had slept most of the day, but even now, trussed up in his suit, he seemed dopey and depressed. It was hard to believe that Clarence's death had laid him so low.

With a nod of acknowledgement to Isabel, Cyrus got behind the wheelchair and started pushing his brother toward the exit. "Come on, bro. Looking at you in that monkey suit is getting me spooked. Let's get hammered."

But no one was in the mood for a drink, and Hank least of all. He glowered darkly at Cyrus and Janice and was unable to rouse himself to even a few words of chit-chat. A few minutes later, he rolled himself into the den, flopped on the sofa and fell asleep in his suit. Cyrus took that as their cue to leave.

At Janice's they were able to breathe more easily, speak more freely about the evening. Janice agreed the spectacle of Frank's sorrow had been deeply affecting, but in some ways, the stilted platitudes of everyone else spoke to her most clearly. It was as if they'd been so shaken by Clarence's death that they completely lost the ability to express themselves and had to lean on stock phrases and sentiments like so many prosthetics.

The biggest surprise of the day, she thought to herself, had been Cyrus's uneasiness that afternoon in Samuel's. He had let a small-town shopkeeper and the simple act of buying a suit unnerve him. And while it was true that he lacked the language for such a transaction, she still found it laughable, as though he were a stranger to civilization.

He'd matured in other ways, of course. Back in high school, he'd grow pink and flustered whenever female classmates acknowledged his presence. But that afternoon he'd made wisecracks with the waitress at Marlowe's, chatted amiably with a young mother at Memorial Park and watched with unmistakable appreciation as women passed by on the street. The idea that the scope of his personal growth over the past decade extended no further than sex, drugs and rock and roll made her bristle with sarcasm, and she was wondering how to broach the subject, when he reached over, placed his hand on her knee and squeezed it affectionately. "You're even more beautiful than I remember, Janice."

"Ah," she said, her index finger held up as a warning.

"Maybe we should go upstairs and, you know, snuggle a bit."

"Yes, well, we've been there before, remember? A long time ago."

He leaned closer. "But look at us. We both need comfort."

With Jonathan out of her life, Cyrus was the only person she might conceivably love right now. She never doubted that for a moment. She had loved him almost as long as she'd known him, even when she and Jonathan were together. That didn't mean she was without reservations. For one thing, Clarence's death had reawakened her own sense of loss over her father's passing, and unlike people in the movies, she had never found grief that romantic. No amount of touching would heal these wounds. Only time.

She took his hand off her knee and dropped it in his lap. In response to his inquisitive look, she shook her head.

"Is that 'No, not right now,' or 'No, buzz off'?"

"Not now," she said.

AFTER BREAKFAST, Janice took Cyrus out to the warehouse to see her monument. All morning he'd been working hard to show her there were no hard feelings. He was loose and goofy and as talkative as she had ever known him. The effort on his part made her feel better about everything.

When she showed him the sculpture, he circled it repeatedly, running his hand along its contours, at one point even embracing it. "Wow," he kept saying, "this is cool." He looked through the lenses. He backed away from it and moved closer again. "What do you call it?"

"*2B Young.*"

"Byron Bradley Young," he said. "That's neat. A happy tombstone." And unable to restrain himself, he hugged her with all his might.

After an early lunch, they headed to the United Church. Cyrus wanted to sit at the back with Janice, but she dragged him up front so he could sit next to Ruby. Isabel was on the other side of her, and Hank was fidgeting in his chair at the end of the aisle. The service was so dreary that at one point Ruby leaned over and, in a voice that wasn't as whispered as it ought to have been, said to Cyrus, "The Mennonites do it better. Those people know how to sing." Not long after that, the men from Worrell's Funeral Home wheeled the casket down the centre aisle and out to the hearse. The family followed in a limousine, and behind that was a long line of other cars, including Janice's Volvo.

Cyrus had sketchy memories of his parents' funeral. He remembered the feel of Clarence's big warm hand surrounding his that day, and how his uncle never let go of him throughout the service, as if he thought Cyrus would try to follow his parents if given half a chance. He remembered, too, how Izzy had winced each time Ruby tried to hug her, how sharp and flinty she'd been in her grief.

At Lakeview, the men from Worrell's set the casket on a sling-like contraption above the grave. Cyrus felt kind of wobbly on his feet, and he searched the crowd for Janice's face. He could have used her stabilizing presence just then. People were crying softly, dabbing quickly at their eyes. Reverend Jansen said a few more words. Then the casket was lowered into the ground.

Cyrus watched the long, slow descent of that polished box, caught the hollow sound as it came to rest in its concrete enclosure. He might have tumbled into the gaping hole, if Izzy hadn't grabbed his elbow and said, "Steady." And that one word, more than the service, more than the limo ride, more even than the final moment of Clarence's life, brought a lump into his throat. It was what Clarence had said, he remembered now. They had stood just like this, a ten-year-old boy and a sorrowful middle-aged man, as Riley and Catherine were laid to rest. His parents had driven off with no special farewell, no meaningful looks. They just walked out the door like it was any other day and not their last, leaving Cyrus to stumble blindly through days of bewilderment and pain, coming in the end to teeter at their graveside until his uncle drew him closer, his arm around his shoulder, and in a calm reasonable voice said, "Steady." That was all he said. Steady. A man as good as his word.

Now Izzy had said the very same thing, served the very same purpose, and he felt so grateful that he turned and kissed her pale powdered cheek. That caught her completely off-guard, and they both would have tumbled into the open grave if she hadn't been standing so squarely.

Janice rushed forward to help Izzy edge him into the shade of a large sycamore. The rest of those in attendance took that to mean the service was over. Some drifted slowly to their cars; others offered Ruby one last handshake or smile of condolence.

When Isabel was satisfied that Cyrus would be fine, she looked around to see how her aunt was bearing up and noted that Ruby was her usual tower of strength, from the looks of it offering more comfort than she was receiving. When Isabel saw Hank, however, or rather the person talking to Hank, she had the biggest shock of the day. There, kneeling on the grass and waving his arm, was Gerry. Believing this to be a crisis that needed her attention, she marched directly over to the two men.

"I was sorry to hear about Clarence," Gerry said, hoisting himself to his feet. "I always admired him."

Over the past decade, she had kept tabs on Gerry—it was hard not to in a town like Wilbury—and she'd been a little annoyed that he seemed to do just fine without her. He and Ginny Maxwell had stayed together, not at all what Isabel would have predicted. She had thought Gerry would bounce down a long line of tramps and end up a sad and solitary man who couldn't look after himself. Luckily for Ginny, he had gotten out of pigs altogether and had started a small greenhouse operation—seedless cucumbers, with one house producing geraniums and marigolds for local gardeners. Ginny had quit her job at the Gaslight Room and worked beside Gerry in the greenhouses or out in their little booth on the highway. To her credit, she had always had an artistic flair. Most people in town now owned one or two terracotta pots that she had hand-painted.

"Well," Gerry said, as though he was working up to an unpleasant task, "I guess I better talk to Ruby."

As he turned to leave, Isabel touched his arm and said, "Clarence admired you, too, Gerry. He liked the way you ran the farm."

Those words stopped him in his tracks. He knew they were untrue. He could remember clearly the way Clarence had treated him, always so critical, and remembered, too, the more painful part: how dearly he'd wanted the man to approve of him. So he closed his eyes and searched Isabel's statement for hurtful edges. But for all her faults, she'd never been cruel. She had simply been blind about this fact, the way she'd been blind about others. Gerry said,

"It was good to see you again, Hank. And you take care, Iz." Then he did what was right and walked over to Ruby, who'd always been kind.

AT FOUR, THE FAMILY WENT BACK to the house, and Izzy poured them each a stiff drink. She hauled out platters of food and put on soft, inoffensive music. She had decided it was time to get plastered. But first they needed a toast.

For as long as she could remember, even when her parents were still alive, it was Clarence who said something to commemorate an occasion. But he was gone now, and her brothers had never shown a talent for choosing the right words, so Izzy assumed that this task, too, would fall on her shoulders. It was Ruby, though, who held her glass high and said, "This is one sight your uncle didn't get to see enough of, the three of you together like this. He didn't show it sometimes, but he loved you all very much. And I can tell you, this would mean a lot to him."

That was all it took to begin the ritual of remembering the dead. Isabel talked about those lazy summer nights of Tiger baseball and Coca-Cola and the rich perfume of the apples in the packing shed. Cyrus offered a hymn of thanksgiving that culminated in the purchase of an electric guitar. Even Hank, whose relationship with Clarence had been strained, was able to share a memory of his uncle coming to help Riley one day, the three of them up in the loft of the barn and discovering a wasp nest, or rather, being discovered by the wasps and chased yelping and cursing all the way to the house. What he remembered best, he said, wasn't the sting or their comic skedaddle but the way they sat on the screened porch afterwards and dabbed themselves with calamine lotion, and how Clarence kept talking about the looks on their faces, the sight of them hightailing it across the yard, until he had them all laughing till their throats were sore.

Long before the stories ran out, Ruby excused herself. She was tired, she said, and would see them in the morning. Then she kissed them each on the forehead and went off to Hank's room. It was barely past six o'clock and the sun was still high in the sky.

Izzy poured herself another drink, then looked at each of her brothers in turn. "You know," she said, "for once, I think the Owens actually did the right thing."

Cyrus finished his drink and helped Izzy clean up. As he walked back to Janice's house that night, with the setting sun deepening the green of the lawns and trees, with each house, even the poorest, emanating a wholesome glow, he considered what Izzy had said. Was there for every moment in life a perfect word, a perfect action, something that not only fulfilled that instant's potential but transformed it into something larger and more uplifting than anyone had imagined?

Janice opened the front door as he walked up the flagstone path, then led him into the kitchen where she fixed them each a whiskey. She knew he needed silence right now not chatter, and as difficult as it was, she waited for him to speak if he needed to, or to sit quietly if preferred. They remained that way for several minutes, holding hands over the tabletop, neither of them touching their drink. Finally he said, "When you work on your art, how do you know when it's exactly right?"

This was not what she had expected. She took a sip of her Scotch and said, "I don't know. I guess I don't think in those terms. I mean, exactly right for whom? When my work pleases me I stop, which is a kind of rightness. But right in some objective sense? Who could know something like that? I don't. I don't care. It's enough that it pleases me. Why?"

He shook his head. "What about your life? Do you ever get the sense that what you do is exactly right?"

"Not often," she said. "Most of the time I feel like I mess up royally."

"Me too. Always." He looked around the kitchen, a spare scientific place, not at all like Ruby's kitchen, or the kitchen he had shared with Eura in Toronto. He could easily imagine Mrs. Young in this room, putting together picture-perfect meals from *Better Homes and Gardens*.

Leaning forward, he said, "When I play, you know, not always but often enough, I do exactly the right thing. I'm onstage in front of a crowd, the band has set up this beautiful groove, a perfect shape that's missing one part, something I'm not even aware of until just the moment it's needed, and you know, nine times out of ten I have the part they need and I put it right where it's supposed to be. It's weird."

"But working the way I do, Cy, I have only myself to worry about and myself to blame. You're lucky. I remember my piano lessons and singing in the band, and it was never like that, what you're talking about. It sounds like you've found something quite magical."

"Religious is what I'm thinking," he said. "It feels like maybe it's something I believe in."

NEXT MORNING, the Owens took Ruby to Orchard Knoll. She wanted to go through Clarence's things and divvy them up accordingly. Some of it she would junk, some was too precious for her to part with and the rest could be claimed by anyone who felt the need. But in practice, the decision-making was not so easy. Ruby hated to see any of it thrown out. Surely Cyrus needed a set of ratchet wrenches? Couldn't Hank use a set of onyx cufflinks? And what about those back issues of *Canadian Orchardist*? In the end, the Owens were primarily interested in photographs, though Hank pounced on Clarence's Zippo, built like a tank, and kept flipping it open and closed until they had to ask him to put it away.

Poring over the snapshots, they puzzled out the path of the baseball glove that Isabel had safeguarded since Riley's death. All along she'd assumed it was her father's glove. But she realized now, by comparing a series of photos, that the glove had passed from Clarence's hands to Riley's. Ruby filled them in on the whole story.

"Your uncle was always of two minds about that darn glove," she said. She pointed to a picture of Riley when he was about twelve years old, the glove tucked under his chin as he wound up to throw a pitch. "Those were pretty lean times for your Grandpa Owen. There was no way he could buy Riley the things he needed, so Clarence took him under his wing. He liked to say that he'd only ever been certain about two things in his life: that he loved Riley like a brother, and that Riley had more talent in his baby finger than all the rest of the folks he knew put together."

Isabel leaned forward and touched Ruby's arm. "He must have been pretty certain about you, too, to stay married almost forty years."

Ruby laughed at that and rubbed her nose, as though the notion tickled her in some way. "The way I remember it," she said, "it wasn't like that at all. It wasn't until after the war that we started dating, you know, after Clarence came home from Devon. I had already started to wonder if I was going to end up an old maid. Everyone was getting married. For heaven's sake, even my little sister had a husband and two children. But Clarence wasn't one to rush into things. It took him forever to propose. So really, I think it was maybe more the opposite, dear. I think you could say our marriage worked out the way it did because he *wasn't* certain, and maybe, in my own way, I wasn't either. One thing for sure, we had to work at it every single day."

Ruby picked up the photograph of Riley posing on the grass of Briggs Stadium with Hank Greenberg and Charlie Gehringer. "Hindsight's a terrible burden sometimes," she said. "Clarence always blamed himself, I think, for the way things worked out for your father."

The three siblings studied that glossy black-and-white photo and wondered if it could possibly be that simple, that their lives might have been brighter and sunnier if only Clarence had kept his glove to himself.

Izzy lifted the picture from the table and asked to keep it. She already had the glove; it seemed to her that the two things belonged together. When Ruby agreed, Isabel scanned the photo again, knowing that her memories of Tiger baseball and Coca-Cola would never be the same.

Ronnie had come to accept the fact that he would never hear The Solo again. Even so, he didn't begrudge his hours of toil and tribulation for the Jimmy Waters Revival. The mystery had deepened in other ways, leading him to the music of Cyrus Owen and his bridge. So it wasn't regret he felt when people mentioned Jim's name. It was the heartache you might feel if a father or son or prophet became a traitor to the cause. How else to describe the hurt created by the Worldwide Church of Jim?

Brent and the rest of the staff at RonCon Productions had resigned en masse because they hadn't been paid for months. Worse, the court injunction and suit for past royalties had seriously undermined the funding for Cyrus's album. Ronnie needed the equivalent of a cool hundred thousand dollars to finish the project. While he could probably forego payment a bit longer, he was loath to draw on Nigel's friendship any more than he had already. They had received a significant discount, and even when charging full price, a place like Hidey-Hole was a money-losing proposition.

Ronnie's solution had been to send Cyrus and the band back home while he went to London to investigate alternative finances. With few options remaining, he made a trip to see Tommy Mac's old mate Alec

Walker, who ran some girls and drugs but also a bit of loan-and-groan out of a flat in Shepherd's Bush.

Alec looked much the way Ronnie remembered. He had a round freckled face with doe-like brown eyes and moist red lips that put an exceptionally good front on teeth left brown and rotting from a steady diet of Irn-Bru, McEwan's Ale and the odd wrapper of fish and chips. His wardrobe had been updated, however. Instead of hand-me-downs from his father and his brothers, he sported black leather pants, white bucks, a Hawaiian shirt and vintage porkpie hat. To look at him, you would think he was a complicated man.

He was slouched in a swivel chair, his shoes propped on the desk. He didn't seem surprised to see his old acquaintance. He clasped his hands behind his head and smiled broadly, as if he'd been expecting him for some time. "The one and only Ronnie Conger."

"Mr. Walker, how's business?"

"Can't complain. And you, you bugger, you look like the Bank of bleedin' England. What can I do for you?"

Alec had the unnerving habit of gazing distractedly about the room whenever he spoke. The moment he came to the end of his words, he slowly turned to confront the person with a cool inscrutable expression. Ronnie met that gaze and held it. "Tommy Mac gave me your whereabouts," he said. "I've a business proposition." He mentioned the sum required.

Alec stared at the ceiling where cobwebs dangled in unfelt currents of air. His eyes gave nothing away, but a faint smile quirked the corners of his mouth. Steepling his hands beneath his chin, he said, "It isn't every day a man like you comes crawling to a man like me."

"I'm hardly crawling. I'm offering you a bit of business."

"Of course you are. Doing me a favour. Spreading the good fortune."

"Call it what you will."

Alec sniffed. "Money like that takes a while to arrange."

"I've got time. You can reach me at the Gore."

Two days later, Alec called and said thirty thousand pounds was the most he could offer, regular terms, take it or leave it.

Ronnie agreed. Then he tidied up a few outstanding debts in London (most notably at the hotel) and paid off some of his American Express bill. He called Nigel and told him what he could offer as a second instalment. The rest would be forthcoming, he said. Could they resume work?

Nigel had suggested more than once that they settle accounts later, after a deal had been struck with a label. He knew his friend wasn't the kind to stiff him. But Ronnie was funny that way, always had been, more comfortable borrowing from a stranger than a friend. Nigel figured it had something to do with being a Scot.

FOR THE FIRST FEW WEEKS BACK IN TORONTO, Cyrus couldn't sit still. He had never in his life cleaned a floor or a toilet or an oven, and over the course of three days he cleaned them all. He bought a new armchair and futon. He painted the kitchen cupboards canary yellow because he thought it would make the place look brighter.

One night on a hunch, he went out to the Laredo, hoping to find Eura there. But Lonnie hadn't seen her since the last performance of Tongue & Groove. Cyrus asked people in the neighbourhood about her, but the only person who remembered Eura was Peter Liu, who owned the Two Star Variety at the corner. Peter remembered the nice lady for sure. And a man with grey hair. They drove off in a fancy car. The man was not from Canada, Peter was sure of that.

Cyrus figured it was one of Eura's relatives, some uncle maybe, or a brother-in-law who had come to bring her home to an official widowhood where she could tend her vines with the proper sort of concentration. Almost any other arrangement of words would have left him with more hope. This was what he had long feared, that Eura would one day come to her senses and do what was right, triggering in Cyrus that particularly noxious heartache that was equal parts guilt and grief.

One night in desperation, he called Janice and asked her to come to Toronto. "You could stay here with me," he said. "We could have some fun." But she was too busy. She had her classes and her sculpture to finish. Maybe at the end of the summer, she said.

In mid-August, Ronnie rang up in high spirits. "Time to come back, my lad. You and Nigel have a record to finish."

"What about the others?"

"Yes, well, I thought perhaps just the two of you."

Cyrus, who remembered all too well how it felt to be shunted to the periphery of a project, said, "That's not fair, Ronnie. We're a band. They deserve to be there."

After several seconds of transatlantic hiss, Ronnie cleared his throat and said, "You're right, my boy. Don't know what I could have been thinking. All for one and one for all."

Two weeks later, they returned to Hidey-Hole. Nigel had worked up a rough mix that was more polished than Cyrus had anticipated, and for the first time since he'd begun work on the album, he was able to forget the million little problems and puzzles the music presented and hear it the way someone else might hear it—the solidity of the bass and drums, the surprising shape and movement of the keyboards, and through it all the lines of his guitar, blooming here and there into bright unforgettable colour. The more he listened, the more unbelievable it seemed. He wasn't this good. None of them were. How had they done this?

To celebrate their achievement, they took speakers, an amplifier and a hastily dubbed cassette of the album, and made their way down the road to commandeer the Two Poofs. All the regulars were there and were more than happy to put aside their darts and conversation to join in the festivities, as long as Ronnie was picking up the tab. Nor did they let the difficult rhythms, quirky solos and moody atmospherics deter them from having a rocking time. Everyone tried to bounce along with the music. Some played air guitar. Others hooted like cowpokes on the range.

That night Cyrus's bliss took on another guise. He felt lighter than air, driven higher by the rising currents of his own sense of accomplishment and the deep gratitude he felt for all those who had helped lead him to this very spot, most of all Ronnie, who believed in music like it was something holy. With each new round of drinks, Cyrus clinked glasses with his old friend, and each time, his voice increasingly muddled, he said, "We did it, man. We fucking did it."

Ronnie was silenced by this show of affection, and several times had to struggle to hold back tears. After last call, when everyone was moving back under the stars and heading home, he clapped a hand on Cyrus's shoulder and, in a breathless voice, said, "You have always, you know, been like a son to me." Then he planted a soft kiss on his temple.

Cyrus was unable to respond properly to such a heartfelt expression. After six pints of ale he could scarcely make out his friend's face. Instead he gave Ronnie a witless grin, then staggered into the middle of the road where he tilted his head back and lifted his arms skyward.

Sophie came out of the pub shortly after that. Cyrus had danced with her most of the night and had watched with equal fascination when she laughed and danced with others, because she was moving to his music, his rhythms. Now all he wanted was to lie with her on the ground outside her trailer. He asked ten different ways if he could spend the night with her, but she knew better. She had seen it all before. She knew there was nothing sadder than people who had come to an end of celebrating. This was no business of hers.

BY NIGEL'S RECKONING, the final mix would consume the better part of a month. It was after the sessions were finished, he said, that the real work took place. Ronnie absented himself at the first opportunity and travelled down to London where he had arrangements to make—a wise choice, considering his aversion to the studio experience.

Day after day Nigel examined the sounds on each track, polishing the tonal characteristics, splicing together performances from twenty different takes, adjusting the levels so that certain instruments would dominate at one time then give way to others. He fiddled with the spatial positioning, some sounds centred while others could be heard dancing left or right on the periphery. Anyone unfamiliar with the rituals of the studio might think Nigel insane, twisting his multicoloured dials a click to the left, a click to the right, over and over and over again, his movements quick as reflex. He spent a whole day feeding a snare drum track through a variety of filters and effects, making minute adjustments in levels and frequencies and tone like a man in the grip of a mysterious compulsion. Whenever he asked the band's opinion on some technical refinement, they seldom heard any difference. By the end of the first week they were giddy with boredom.

Cyrus was glad now that Sophie had had the good sense to keep him at a distance. He might have spoiled the easygoing nature of their friendship with emotional chaos. And without her having to say a word, he knew how disappointed she'd been that he had thought of her even briefly as something he might fuck. As if that were her only value, a dumping ground for his excess emotion.

They went for long walks. They sat in the pub or on the grass outside the studio and talked for hours. He told her about the recent funeral and what an important character Clarence had been in his life. From there it was an easy transition to talk about Hank and Izzy and Ruby, and his long history with Janice. In return, she gave him the merest sketch of her childhood, of growing up in a council flat in the east end of London, of her early escape from that dismal grey world and her determination to live a joyful life. They often held hands when they walked. They danced cheek to cheek at the pub. His favourite thing of all was to lie face down in the grass and let her walk barefoot along his spine like it was a tightrope.

When Ronnie returned to Hidey-Hole at the end of the second week, he had a scrape on his cheek, which he'd gotten in a fall, he said. He seemed distracted and edgy, and when he heard how little progress had been made, the energy drained out of him. For a few days he forced himself to sit in the studio and hustle things along, growing increasingly impatient with Nigel's glacial pace. Then, as the tension in the control room reached the breaking point, the two had a shouting match that ended with Nigel ordering his friend back to London immediately. Ronnie nodded soberly and agreed that Nigel knew best. He insisted, however, on taking Cyrus with him.

They left the next morning with a few cassettes of the rough mix. Ronnie's idea was to get them into the right hands, stir up a little excitement in the industry. In particular he wanted Bobby Mason to hear the tape. Bobby, who had managed Scot Free way back when, was now a top fellow at the BBC. He could almost single-handedly make or break a record in England, the very kind of help that Ronnie needed.

It was Bobby's day off, so they dropped by his flat in Chelsea about mid-afternoon. "Just in time for breakfast," he said at the door. "Salmon and eggs, Conger. Too good for the likes of you, ya bugger."

Ronnie said, "My friend Cyrus I was telling you about."

Bobby offered a thin smile then turned and headed for the kitchen. He wore a pair of plaid boxers and nothing else. He was a slim, almost bony man with a deep tan, which seemed to Cyrus entirely out of place in England. A gold chain hung from his neck and tangled in a bounty of grey chest hair. He was drinking a Bloody Mary. A young woman who looked to be half his age was prancing between the bathroom and the bedroom with a towel wrapped around her, her flip-flops making a clatter on the parquet floor. As Bobby added smoked salmon to the whipped eggs, he said, "You eat yet?"

"Yes," Ronnie lied. "Just did in fact." Casting a look around the apartment, he said, "Still up to the old tricks, I see."

"Same person, aren't I? See you brought a tape."

"My young friend's masterpiece. I want you to be the first to hear it."

He took the tape from Ronnie and looked at it suspiciously before tossing it into a wicker basket half-filled with unripe fruit. Then he turned on the burner beneath a big skillet and cooked the eggs. As he stirred the mixture, he said, "You have to wonder sometimes, men our age farting around with pop music." He spooned the eggs onto a sky-blue plate and carried it and a second Bloody Mary to a small balcony crowded with white cast iron patio furniture. After his first bite, he twisted his lips with disgust and pushed the food away. He knocked back half of his drink and, fixing his gaze directly on Cyrus, said, "So, what's it like?"

At first Cyrus thought Bobby was asking how it felt to be on the cusp of great things, instead of a jaded over-the-hill executive. Fortunately Ronnie came to the rescue and gave the entire spiel about Jangle, his voice taut with excitement, his eyes feverish.

While Ronnie talked, Bobby studied Cyrus's face. In the first lull, he got up from the table to retrieve the cassette. When he sat down again, he held it between thumb and forefinger, the way you might hold a weapon you were hoping to dust for fingerprints. He leaned closer to Cyrus and said, "I get twenty of these dropped on my desk every day. Pathetic, really. What have you got on this thing, four songs?"

Cyrus cleared his throat nervously. "The whole album."

"And why not? It's your masterpiece. You poured your heart into it. But you know what? No one cares." He knocked the cassette against Cyrus's hand. "We're not dealing with art, here, we're dealing with product. Soap flakes. The only thing that matters is the package. It's what record companies do, you know, design packages. Boggles the mind how much they spend to convince punters that soap flakes are sexy and exciting. And you? You have to fit inside the box, don't you? That's what it's all about. Are you boring enough to be labelled cool. For your sake, I hope so. Because cool is important, even to me. Let's face it, without cool, I don't get laid. I'm an old man."

Back in the car, Ronnie stared vacantly out the side window, not saying a word. He squeezed Cyrus's arm and smiled weakly. "I wouldn't worry too much," he said. "The man loves music. It runs through his veins. He grouses that way because he hates to be taken for granted."

For the rest of that afternoon and all of the next, Ronnie and Cyrus raced around London meeting with influential figures in the British music scene: the pop music critic for the *Times,* A&R directors of several record companies, a handful of writers from various music industry publications. Aside from Bobby, everyone expressed great curiosity about Jangle and seemed genuinely pleased to meet Cyrus.

After their second day on the town, they returned to the Gore feeling drained but cautiously optimistic. Ronnie had been a dynamo since they'd left Hidey-Hole, never stopping for a moment, and that energy, that sense of mission, had spilled over to Cyrus. He was proud of the way he'd handled himself. He'd often heard others complain about the dreariness of promotion, but he couldn't think of a better way to spend a few hours than to talk about his music.

As they waited at the front desk for their keys, Ronnie remembered he had left something on the front seat of his rental car and ran out to fetch it. A moment later the sound of commotion drew Cyrus's attention to the front door, where he saw Ronnie struggling with a man. Cyrus was halfway to the street when the stranger, wearing a Tottenham Hotspurs football jersey, reared back and punched Ronnie in the face, sending him to the ground in a heap.

What came next, though, was even worse. Ronnie struggled to a half-sitting position, propped on one elbow. Blood was coursing down his face. The man in the Tottenham jersey kicked him under the chin and sent his head crashing to the pavement. Then he picked Ronnie off the street and tried to push him into the back of a grey panel van.

Without thinking, without a single attempt at rational argument or civil interrogation, Cyrus, who'd been in only one fight in all his life and who had never successfully landed a punch, ran to the curb and grabbed the man's arm, trying desperately to pry Ronnie free. "Stop," Cyrus said through gritted teeth, baring down on those hard grubby fingers with all his might. "Leave my friend alone."

Like that terrible dream of childhood when the monster turns away from its initial victim and sets its cold malevolent eyes on you, the man let go of Ronnie's limp figure, which was now half in and half out of the van, and with no effort at all, like he was scratching himself or brushing a lock of hair out of his eyes, calmly grabbed Cyrus's left hand and, in one surprisingly graceful motion, twisted it back with such force that he dislocated the bones of the wrist.

A blinding white pain, and the next thing Cyrus knew he was lying on the sidewalk. He had just enough strength to lift his head and see Ronnie disappear into the back of the van. Cyrus said something then, some bleat of incomprehension as the brute closed the rear doors and walked past him toward the passenger seat. It might have ended there—it would have ended there if Cyrus had done what was smart—but he lunged at the man, or tried to, managing only to sprawl on his side. The thug turned slowly and laughed. Then, as a kind of afterthought, he lifted his scuffed black boot as high as he could and stomped on Cyrus's throbbing left palm.

When he opened his eyes again he was lying on a stretcher. Scenes came back to him, not in a flood but intermittently, like lights flicking on across a vast dark city. Ronnie falling to the ground. That big black boot. Turning to the door to see Ronnie struggling with the man. The twist of wrist with the bone nearly breaking through the flesh, the magnesium flare of pain and his weightless descent to the pavement. The sound of commotion and the turn toward the door, his stumble down the steps and into the fray. Tottenham Hotspurs, sour smoky breath. A policeman kneeling beside him, a kind and concerned expression on his face, a gentle voice. That big black boot poised above him. "Stupid git." The crushing, obliterating pain. A jostling drive through narrow city streets. "Good as new in no time, sir." The look. The look in Ronnie's eyes as he was stuffed into the van. The look of pure understanding and acceptance. No words exchanged but eyes locking on and not letting go until his head disappeared inside the van, no longer struggling. And at the hospital a nurse with a sweet round face. Doreen on her name tag. Doreen touching his shoulder and telling him to close his eyes and try to take deep breaths, they would have him feeling better in a jiff. But every time he closed his eyes he saw the boot and the wrist, and his dear old friend shoved unceremoniously into the back of a van.

When he opened his eyes a second time he was in a hospital bed, his left arm encased in plaster, from elbow to fingertips. The policeman was there. Doreen, too. She brought him a glass of water and placed the straw between his lips. She dabbed at his chin where a few drops had dribbled.

The policeman moved closer and opened his notepad. "Eyewitnesses described a struggle. The driver of the van, a man in a jersey, your friend and yourself."

"Where's Ronnie?"

The policeman cleared his throat and said, "We know where *you* are. We hoped you might help with the rest."

Cyrus closed his eyes and immediately he saw it all again, from the first sound of commotion to that sickening crunch of heel on bone. Finally he opened his eyes and said, "He took Ronnie. A man I've never seen before." Then he told the policeman everything he remembered.

Doreen gave him a sedative and told him to sleep. Later that day, Nigel brought the rest of the band around to visit. They were heading for Heathrow directly from the hospital and would await further developments in Toronto. But Cyrus had nothing to say to them and cared little what sentiments they had to offer. After twenty minutes or so of awkward small talk, they left for the airport, and Cyrus gave himself up to another sedative. When he opened his eyes again it was morning, and a doctor was looking at him.

"You'll be discharged today," he said. "We've done what we can for now, but there was extensive damage to the knuckles. You will require reconstructive surgery to regain even rudimentary mobility in the joints."

Cyrus lay there without expression, unable to move or speak. Doreen came into the room a few minutes later to confirm her own suspicions. She held his right hand and touched his fingernails, which were long and carefully shaped, a necessity for the kind of fingerpicking he did. She then inspected the left hand where it jutted from the plaster cast, the nails almost painfully short, the proud callused flesh on the fingertips. The hands of a musician, she knew, just like her son. And the sadness of her face was all the permission Cyrus needed to pour his bitterness into his pillow.

THE SEARCH FOR RONNIE CONGER LASTED THREE DAYS, and each day the newspapers roused themselves to increasingly feverish speculation. The most popular fiction involved the drug trade, a theory accepted by many because Ronnie had been a noted figure in the music business. Those who knew him best denied such allegations and said they'd never known him to partake of illegal substances. Even so, there wasn't a paper in all of Britain that could resist running a picture of Ronnie's father, the Reverend Archibald Conger, along with all the sordid whisperings. The family, each story stated, had no comment.

The only solid lead the police had was the licence plate number of the van, which an eyewitness had jotted on his arm. Unfortunately, the vehicle had been reported stolen the day before, so no one could reliably suggest its whereabouts. In the end it was a security guard at a public garage in Putney who found Ronnie lying in a fetal curl and barely clinging to life in the back of the van, the victim of a vicious beating. A five-pound note was taped to his forehead.

From the beginning the reports from the hospital were not encouraging. Ronnie's brain had suffered extensive damage; it was able to keep the heart beating, the lungs pumping, but not much else. A few reporters made the trip to East Kilbride. They published photos of the family home and the hall where Ronnie promoted his first show. When they approached Ronnie's parents, however, they were met with stony silence. It was only on the first Sunday, as Archie and his ailing wife struggled up the steps of the East Kilbride Baptist Church, that anyone got a rise out of the old man.

One reporter shouted, "Will you be saying a prayer for your son?"

And Archie wheeled around and said, "My son and I do not worship the same god." Then he pushed through the great wooden doors, into the cooler sanctuary within.

Charles Doernhoffer, a reporter for the *New York Times,* eventually put two and two together and wrote about a music mogul in financial ruin, who had begged and borrowed to bring his latest protegé to prominence. In New York, bankruptcy proceedings had already begun, the story noted. Former employees of RonCon Productions were suing for back wages. Only Nigel had taken the high road and told Doernhoffer: "The heartbreaking part is that this latest project of Ronnie's will probably be held up in the courts for quite some time. The banks have confiscated the master tapes. Everyone wants their pound of flesh, it seems. For my part, I have forgiven whatever money is owed. All I want is for my friend to get better soon." Doernhoffer ended the article by saying, "Ironically, Conger's quest for the future of music balanced on the unknown, and unlikely, shoulders of a young Canadian guitarist, may have cut short any possibility of a future of his own."

Cyrus was so wounded by the disparaging tone of that last sentence that Nigel suggested they invite the press to Hidey-Hole to listen to the rough mix of the record so they could hear what Ronnie had been so excited about. "Right now you've got their attention," he said. "Use them. The more they write about you, the closer you'll be to a deal. And a deal would solve one of Ronnie's major problems. Everybody wins."

Several days later a horde of reporters descended on the studio. Nigel had spruced the place up. Patrick, outfitted in a tuxedo, walked around with flutes of champagne while Sophie, in chef's whites, offered a sampling of hors d'oeuvres she'd prepared. Cyrus realized that he was not uppermost in Nigel's mind, and that the effort and expense were for the benefit of Ronnie and his woeful financial situation. But Sophie, he knew, had worked especially hard on his behalf.

Before the listening, Cyrus forced himself to walk up to total strangers and introduce himself. Those he'd met before, he greeted warmly. It was not difficult to express his own excitement about the record and how glad he was that they had come. When asked for particulars about the project, he was able to ape Ronnie's comments. Inevitably, though, they wanted to talk about the injured hand or poor Ronnie lying in his hospital bed.

Mid-afternoon, everyone filed into the studio. A set of headphones waited on each chair. The reporters took their places, while Nigel and Cyrus remained in the control room behind the mixing console. When Nigel started the tape, Cyrus excused himself and went outside to sit with Patrick and Sophie. She touched his arm and said, "It'll be all right, you'll see."

"They won't even hear it," he complained. "It's not music to them. It's a story, and I'm the villain."

"You can't be," she replied lightly. "You're an artist. A creator."

Cyrus was moved by her confidence. But it didn't brighten his mood. He had looked in the eyes of those star makers, scanned their faces, and knew they thought poorly of him. They would weigh his music against Ronnie's tragedy and be appalled.

NIGEL COULDN'T COUNT THE NUMBER OF TIMES he'd previewed music for industry insiders—including this same sorry handful of reporters—and he'd thought he'd seen every reaction, from absolute boredom and irritation to ecstatic jumping and jiving. But he'd never seen this kind of serious reflection. In an odd way, with the eerie half-light of the studio seeming just then like an isolation booth, with the headphones, the grey, solemn faces, he felt as though he were watching a group of war criminals on trial. Except they were the judges. They sat unmoving on their twelve chairs. No one tapped a foot or a finger. Some sat with heads bowed and hands clasped. Others slumped in their chairs and stared bleakly at the baffles on the ceiling.

Nigel himself wasn't sure what to make of the record, even after the hundred or so times he'd listened to it. The production was top-notch, of course; he'd done everything he could to help Ronnie in that regard. And the music probably deserved some attention if only because it confounded so many expectations. But somehow it didn't feel right to him. The grooves were good, the chords interesting, the melodies strong. But it was missing a cock, he felt. There was no sense of the hunger that was central to all music. A young rocker's appetite for sex, even Bach's joyous desire for Jesu—it was all uplift and longing, and this record had none of it.

"You are right," Ronnie had said when Nigel brought up his complaints, "this is not about sex, it is about love. It is not about desire, but fulfillment. It is not entertainment, it is art."

Nigel wasn't surprised to hear Ronnie say this. He'd always thought of him as some latter-day Saint Jude, the patron saint of lost causes. He'd made a star of Jimmy Waters, so it had seemed conceivable that he could do it again with Cyrus. But now all bets were off. By the look of things, it would be a miracle if Cyrus played the guitar again. And the doctors doubted Ronnie would ever regain consciousness. It was asking too much, even of a saint, to work miracles from a coma.

In the weeks after Clarence's funeral, as Ruby ambled stupidly up and down the aisles at the A&P and tried to think single portions, no leftovers, or sat knitting on the porch after a solitary dinner, she recalled the conversation she'd had many years earlier with Janice, who was still in high school at the time. "How can it be that there is one thing," Janice had asked, "one thread, and you pull on it and the whole fabric comes apart? How could we not know our lives depend on something like that? Shouldn't they teach us that at school?" Ruby had suggested that that was more properly a subject for religion, but now her answer seemed altogether too patronizing, and she wondered if maybe religion was flawed in that way, producing the kind of certainty that limits the natural range of sympathies.

Of course there'd been no shortage of sympathy flowing her way. Isabel invited her for dinner once a week. Hank kept her company on afternoon drives. The women in her church group were always talking about a bus tour somewhere. Even Janice called now and then to see if she wanted to tag along to Hounslow or wherever she was off to. Ruby had no complaints on that score. Everyone had been very kind. If she had any beef, it was that she had not had enough time to sit quietly by herself and make sense of her new situation. Janice had been right. There were times in a life when everything comes undone, or threatens to. And while a well-placed stitch could hold it all together, sometimes it was better to let it unwind and start over.

Ruby was lucky. Clarence had provided a financial foundation on which she could build any life she chose. This had come as a shock. She had her own savings account where she stashed a few dollars now and then. And she knew about the cash flow of the farm account; it was her job to write the cheques and itemize their expenses. But the extent of Clarence's investment portfolio surprised her. She'd heard him talk about the stock market with other men, heard him say he owned a few shares of such-and-such, a bit of what-have-you. But when John Dixon, their lawyer, explained how well off she was, she'd been completely floored. Whether she leased the orchards or let them fall into ruin, she'd still have all the money she would ever need. Clarence's blue-chip stocks and government bonds would see to that.

Her first reaction was anger. All those years of scrimping. The trips they hadn't taken. The choice cuts of meat she'd foregone because they were too dear. All the treats she'd denied Cyrus because she believed they couldn't afford them. But her anger lasted only a short while. Happiness, she knew, was a talent. Some people had it and others didn't. And all the money in the world couldn't buy it for you if you didn't have the gift. She and Clarence had been two of the lucky ones, or so she'd always felt. Maybe that's why they'd been able to save so much in the first place. They weren't the kind to chase after a bigger home, a fancier car, imported food and drink. They'd been satisfied with what they had.

Not that it had always been clear sailing. The first years of their marriage had had a few rocky spots, arguments over nothing, stupid jealousies and tantrums. There were times when Ruby was sure she was losing him. But she never did. And as the years went on it seemed less likely that she ever could have. Clarence once said they were like an apple tree that hadn't been pruned properly, where two branches had rubbed together over the years until they not only lost their original shape but moulded themselves into a single living piece of wood. If so, that now meant that a large part of her would no longer burst into green, no longer bear fruit. For as long as she lived she would feel, deep inside, a part of her that was no longer alive.

At the end of her first month of living alone, she invited Isabel and

Hank to dinner. She made chicken and potato salad—enough for an army—
and they ate at the picnic table in the yard. After dessert, they set off down
the lane that led to the back of the orchard. With Ruby on one side of Hank's
chair, and Izzy on the other, they passed between Spartan and Pippin,
McIntosh and Empire, the trees heavy with fruit. Ruby told them she'd been
thinking about the farm and the rest of her life, and feeling confused.

"The girls think I should move to town," she said, as though she were
confessing a sin. "And I never was a country girl at heart, but to lose
Clarence, and then lose my house and all of this . . ." She smoothed Hank's
hair. "It might be too much in one go."

They stopped at the top of the ridge. From there they could look down
the long slope to the marsh. Isabel said, "Maybe your friends are right. It's
hard to see how you'll manage out here on your own. What are you doing
about this year's crop?"

Ruby looked around and sighed. "Wade Dobbins from D&B Orchard
offered to help with the harvest."

"Well," Izzy said, "you only have to say the word. I'd be more than happy
to find you a place in town. Whatever you want to do."

"Well that's pretty much the problem right there. I'm not used to wanting
things. I mean, married to Clarence, I never wanted for anything. Certainly not
for myself. Wouldn't really know how."

Isabel didn't believe Ruby could be all that selfless. If it was true, it
marked a clear difference between them. Izzy had always gone right after the
things she wanted, maybe because she'd learned at an early age how easily it
could all be taken away.

"Speaking of wanting things," Isabel said, pointing down the hill toward
their old place, the link fence, the storage tanks, the wells that were no longer
pumping. (It turned out there had been only a fraction of the oil down there
that everyone had figured on.) "I made an offer this afternoon."

"An offer," Hank said with disbelief. "On what?"

"I'm buying the land back from Benny Driscoll. I wasn't going to tell
anyone yet. I wanted to surprise you."

Hank leaned over the side of his chair and spit onto the gravel. "You
surprised us all right. What do you want with a hellhole like that?"

"I don't know," she said. And she laughed then, her shoulders hunched up and her eyes sparkling with a little girl's mischief.

WILBURY WAS ABUZZ WITH OWEN NEWS. The story of Cyrus's misfortune, especially his heroic attempt to save his manager, got front-page coverage in the *Gazette*. Almost as exciting was the word around town that Isabel was buying back the family farm. Considering her reputation for shrewd real estate transactions, a few local businessmen were trying desperately to figure out what on earth she was up to. The mayor, Milt Iverson, wondered if he'd somehow missed a subtle change in zoning.

For the first time in her life, Izzy thought she might have taken on more than she could handle. She had to keep her business on track, her employees humming, Hank out of trouble and more or less happy, her students at St. Clair College motivated, her business connections well-oiled. Add to that the emotional upheaval of buying back their land, and she was spread pretty thin. Even so she spent the better part of two days trying to track down Cyrus. She got through to the hospital just after he was discharged. She zeroed in on the Gore but only after he had checked out. She had the name Nigel Cranston, at a place called Hidey-Hole, but so far she'd had no luck. She would let the Canadian embassy do the rest.

She had also made it her business to look out for Ruby's welfare. She set up an appointment with Clarence's accountant, Wilfrid Thiessen, to go over Ruby's financial affairs. Ruby heard once again how wisely Clarence had invested, and how he had provided an ample income for her.

"About the farm . . ." Wilfrid said.

But before he could get any further, Ruby held up her hand. "I've already made up my mind about that. I want the kids to have it," she said. "Clarence and I talked about it many times. It's what he wanted, too."

Izzy shook her head sadly. "We couldn't afford that, Ruby. Soon as you change ownership, you trigger a capital gain. We'd have to sell the farm just to pay the taxes."

Wilfrid held up his hand. "Ordinarily, yes. But, as I was about to say, Clarence was a very prudent farmer. Aside from Ruby, you three were his only family; so every year, even before your folks died, he deeded each of you a small portion of the farm, all perfectly legal. Though he took a slight tax hit every April, it was easier to pay it in increments, he figured, than in one great whack. So, Ruby here couldn't sell Orchard Knoll even if she wanted. It doesn't belong to her. It belongs to you and Cyrus and Hank in equal shares. Right up there on the barn, isn't it? The Mitchell family."

Isabel was not a sentimental woman, but that last statement made her catch her breath. She could not even look at Ruby.

That night after dinner, she got a call from Cyrus that was maddeningly short on particulars. In response to her legitimate questions about what had happened and how he was doing, he said, "I'm okay, I guess. I called to ask if you could lend me some money."

"Come home and we'll talk about it."

"Look," he said, "you know what I've been through. My friend's in a coma. I need a few operations myself. I thought you could help me out."

"Come home, Cy. The people there can look after your friend. Your project can wait. Come home and get better. That's what home is for." And before he could say anything else, she launched into a brief description of all that had happened, shading everything in golden tones to make it seem more appealing. She saved until last the story of the Mitchells' generosity, and how he was now part-owner of Orchard Knoll.

When she finished talking, he said, "About that money . . ."

"Think about what I said, Cyrus. Then we'll talk."

He did think about it and called an hour later with what he figured was an ideal solution. "Sell my part of the farm for me, Iz. Better yet, you're a wheeler-dealer, buy my share. I'll give you a discount."

"I couldn't."

"What's it to you? I'll never be a farmer. Buy my share. That way it stays in the family and I get some of the cash I need. It's the only thing that makes sense."

"Sense." She spit the word out like it was covered in mould. "You have never in your life made sense. What do you know about it? No, I will not sell your piece of the property. No, I will not buy it from you. Please don't ask me again or I'll hang up. I'll send you money, but only enough for a plane ticket home. After you have your operations, and after we talk, if you still need some money, and if it makes even the tiniest bit of sense to me, I'll see what I can do. Though I'm warning you, I'm a bit strapped for cash myself. You're not the only one with things on the go."

After a long pause, he cleared his throat and said, "Don't talk to me that way. I'm not some stupid kid you can boss around. Better still, Iz, don't talk to me again, period. I'm tired of your fucking sermons. Got it? Forget this call happened. I don't want your money." Then he hung up.

SOON AFTER THE SPECIAL PREVIEW of Cyrus's album, the first published reports began to surface. A few were kind, even mildly encouraging, but for the most part, those who had come to Hidey-Hole had nothing good to say. *Buzz* gave the worst review, suggesting that Ronnie's misfortune was not without a bright side. "At least," the article stated, "when Conger went down for the count, he had the grace to take this pretentious pick*meister* with him. With any luck, we'll hear no more jingles from Jangle."

Nigel was very considerate, offering the comforts of Hidey-Hole as long as needed; and for the next few days, Cyrus stayed in his room in a kind of blank nausea. Sophie finally dragged him out for a walk and made him eat. They stopped at the Two Poofs and shared a ploughman's lunch. Sitting outside on the patio, beneath a sun umbrella, she touched his fingertips where they jutted from the plaster cast. "This is you right here," she said. "Your friend Ronnie—that's you, too."

Every day for a week Nigel and Cyrus drove into London to visit their friend. Eventually Doreen took them aside and said, "The family's been told, but you two have acted more like family than anyone, so I thought you should know. It would be a mistake to think he'll ever get better." The two men digested that bit of information and nodded soberly. They had already accepted that as the likely outcome. It didn't mean they couldn't do what was right and visit from time to time.

Doreen bowed her head, almost shamefully, and added, "There is nothing more we can do for him here. Beds are scarce. He'll soon be transferred to long-term care." When they didn't react, she added, "His family is unwilling to fund the extra cost of private care. Without some other direction, he will most likely end up at Scrivens Park." The last two words were delivered with an inflection of disapproval. They told her they understood, and set off to inspect the nursing home where their friend would most likely live out the remainder of his days.

What they found was not a proper park at all but the old parade ground of the Scrivens Army Barracks, weedy, pitted asphalt and coarse unkempt grass where local drug dealers plied their trade. The main barrack, looking very much as though it had been through a war, had been transformed into a nursing home. One glimpse was enough to convince both Nigel and Cyrus that it was no place for a man as fine as Ronnie Conger; and as they made their way inside, they were shocked that anyone would have to live his final days with so little dignity.

They approached a tiny, round-faced woman who was carrying a clipboard and looking officious. She was at the end of a long shift, her little nurse's hat no longer sitting straight on her tight grey curls. Her name tag identified her as Erna. Nigel swept his arm about to indicate the general state of things and, unable to hide his revulsion, said, "What *is* all this?"

Erna followed his gesture with her tired eyes, and in a slight Jamaican accent not entirely drained of its music, she said, "This is Scrivens, sir. Are you here to see someone?" She scanned her clipboard as though searching through a list of sanctioned visitors.

Cyrus jumped in. "A friend of ours is coming here. We wanted to check it out. You know, to see if he'd like it."

"Honey," she said, a chuckle in her voice, "people who come here haven't got much talent left for liking. Look around. Not one of them is ever going to notice this isn't Buckingham Palace."

"It should be condemned," Nigel blurted out. "It's a disgrace."

Erna held her clipboard across her bosom and sighed. "You'll get no argument from me. But what are you going to do? These people have nowhere else to go. And the government has nowhere else to put them. So we do the best we can with what we have."

Nigel and Cyrus spent the rest of the day investigating a few of the more affordable private nursing homes on the list Doreen had provided, but there wasn't a single one that seemed the right place for Ronnie, and they returned to Hidey-Hole in the dark, feeling tired and fed up. All day, The Who's most chilling lyric had rattled around in Cyrus's head. And though he usually felt that being alive was the greatest of all good fortune, he had now begun to appreciate that a person might want to die before he got old.

Nigel invited Cyrus to join him for a nightcap. Standing together at the bar, the moonlight their only illumination, he poured them each a large glass of brandy and downed his drink in one gulp. When he had finished with the facial contortions, he slapped his glass on the bar with enough force that it might well have shattered.

"I could do this myself," Nigel said, his words hissing like steam, "very quietly. Just pick up the tab because we're mates. I can afford it. But fuck that. And fuck them. It's time to make a ruckus."

He had decided to organize a benefit concert. He wanted to shine a critical light on Ronnie's family and their false pieties, but even more on the shameful state into which social services had fallen. As Nigel laid out the details of his plan, he peered into the darkness outside the window, as though he could divine the future out there. He could get Noel Plaice to promote and organize the concert, he said. Noel owed Nigel favours. They could use the grounds at Knebworth possibly. If not, there was always Wimbledon. He listed all the big-name bands he could count on. There would be stories in the papers about Ronnie's brilliant career and subsequent misery, abandoned by his family and his country.

Cyrus nodded encouragement but didn't share the same enthusiasm for the project. As he went to bed that night, two sore points kept him from getting much rest. If anyone had earned the right to appear onstage for Ronnie's benefit, it was Jangle. Yet that was impossible. Cyrus had several operations ahead of him and months of therapy before he could even begin to hold a guitar again. That fed directly into his second disappointment. He was a young musician struck down in his prime and with few, if any, prospects of ever playing again; yet no one had spoken of a benefit in *his* honour, if only to rescue his album from the limbo of the courts.

Cyrus knew he could voice none of these complaints without appearing selfish. Ronnie needed his help. Everything else had to wait.

WHEN HER DEAL CLOSED, Isabel drove to the old place and set her plans in motion. A team of workmen tore down the chain-link fence. Though the pumps and storage tanks had already been carted away, there were large sections of sheet metal, splintered wooden palettes, hoses and tubing and wire to be collected from the property and carted off to the dump. The ground was stained black with oil, which Benny Driscoll had foolishly tried to burn off. The place still had the scorched taste of disaster.

Once the land was cleared of debris, she had Joe Filmon remove the contaminated soil. He made a hole five feet deep and fifty yards square. When people drove by and saw the backhoe and dump trucks, they wondered if Izzy was planning to put up a skyscraper. In the back of her mind she was thinking greenhouses like the ones Gerry had built.

The first time Hank came out with her to see it, he just shook his head critically. He had no sentimental attachment to the land, and he didn't suppose she had either. He figured she'd lost her mind, pouring good money into a place like that. But once the property had been freed of all debris, and especially after Joe began to dig, Hank began to think more positively, began to think that maybe one of his own dreams, however truncated, might come true.

"Tell Joe to go deeper," he told her. When she explained they had already removed the contamination, he said, "Doesn't matter. Go ten. Go twenty if you can. Can't be too safe." When she complained about the expense, he said he would chip in. When she reminded him he didn't have any money, he told her he would ask Ruby. When she asked him why he was so interested, he said he had an idea.

For two more days she had Joe pull out soil and cart it away. At ten feet they struck water. By the next morning the hole was a five-acre pond, which Hank dubbed Lake Isabel. She wasn't amused.

The next night after dinner they drove out and parked at the side of the road, the sun still low in the sky. A humid breeze blew in off the lake. They didn't bother to get out of the car.

"Now we plant trees," he said. "Poplars at first. They grow like weeds. A few willow. We plant grass, too, and get Joe to lay a gravel path all the way around the pond." When Isabel still didn't get it, he said, "A campground, Iz. Two years from now we could have people in trailers out here. With lots thirty feet wide, you could have twenty around this pond alone. We stock it with fish, build a little rec room somewhere . . ."

She turned in her seat and gave him her most scornful look. "Who in their right mind is going to want to stay out here?"

"Me, for one. I could be the manager, you know. I get myself a little mobile home, maybe a little shed where I can fix things. A little sit-down mower to keep the place tidy. I could hire some local kid to help me in the summer. I got it all figured out, Iz. I need something to do. I need to get out of your hair. I can do this. I know I can."

When she didn't respond, he cleared his throat and told her about his dream from his prison days, the park ranger, the jeep, the wide-brimmed hat. "It's not the Grand Canyon," he said, "but it'll do. Whataya say?"

She stared out the window of the car for the longest while. There was already a pair of seagulls floating around the pond. And she said, "You have to promise to wear the hat."

After two days of planning, Nigel and Cyrus returned to London to visit Ronnie. His condition was the same. His expression was the same. His hair, the angle of his chin, the position of his hands folded across his stomach—they were all the same. Lying there, seemingly dead to the myriad stimuli of the world, a great tangle of tubes and wires and patches connecting him to the technical marvel of modern medicine, Ronnie looked to Cyrus like the kind of arcane gizmo you might find in the recording studio, as if he had found a way to transform himself into music's perfect receptor.

While Nigel sat beside Ronnie's bed and spoke softly about what he was planning, Cyrus got the latest report from Doreen. Pneumonia was the danger now, she said. Then she took his broken hand in hers and reminded him he had his own medical problems to take care of. He nodded, though he had no intention of following her advice. That would mean going back to Toronto, and he wasn't ready to do that just yet.

Cyrus returned to Ronnie's bedside and listened to Nigel chat about the football scores. When they were preparing to leave, Doreen came in and said there was a man on the phone. "He wants to speak to someone in the Conger family. I thought you two might be close enough."

Cyrus followed her down the hall to the nurse's station. A familiar voice on the other end of the phone said, "I have only just heard. I have only just heard and my heart aches at the news, and yet, and yet I want so much to give you my deepest condolences in this time of sadness. He was like a saviour to me, your Ronald. He saved me and anointed me and brought me out of the wilderness and gave me a voice. I tell you truthfully that I would take his place if I could."

Cyrus waited until the first pause in that mellifluous flow of words, and then said, "Jim, it's me. It's Cyrus Owen."

"Oh, Lord," he said. "This is luck. When I first read the news, I knew I had to reach you somehow and tell you how sorry I am for your misfortune, one musician to another. Tell me, now, what is the prognosis? When do they think you will play again?"

Cyrus explained what the specialists had told him, but to hear it in his own words, without the doctor's authority, made the outlook seem hopeless.

Jim clucked his tongue sadly. "Get yourself home, young man. Do not dilly-dally with somethin' like this. The stakes are too high."

"I intend to," he replied, "but not just yet. We're organizing a benefit concert for Ronnie. I have to stick around for that."

After a moment's pause, Jim cleared his throat and said, "I know I am not the star I once was, not that I ever was such a big attraction, but I would be most honoured if you would consider me as a possible performer. And, if not onstage, then in some other capacity. I have realized this past while that I owe Ronnie more than I could ever repay. I would be most grateful, you know, if I could help out."

Cyrus took Jim's phone number, in a place called Waldorf, Nebraska, and said he would phone in a day or two. But considering the role Jim's music had played in Ronnie's life, Cyrus more or less promised him a spot onstage.

Nigel was thrilled. "A reunion of the Revival," he said excitedly. "Imagine if we could convince Gil Gannon. It'd be fucking brilliant."

Cyrus called Jim the next day. A woman answered on the second ring. "Billie's House of Music, Billie speaking."

"Sorry. I was looking for Jimmy Waters."

"He's with a customer right now. Can he call you back?"

"Well, I guess. I'm calling from England—"

"Lord love a duck!" she exclaimed. Then, half-covering the mouthpiece, she shouted, "Jim, git your fanny over here. It's that fella from England." Back in her phone voice, she said, "He's coming. And next time don't be so mealy-mouthed. I imagine this is costing you an arm and a leg."

Cyrus heard what sounded like a bit of sexual roughhouse, full of slap and tickle and girlish giggles. Then Jim said, "Young man, I am in high spirits today. This is good news, I hope."

When Cyrus said they wanted him to reunite the Revival, Jim actually whooped with delight. "The very thing I wanted to hear. I have already taken the liberty of callin' Sonny and the others, and they are ready to roll. I would prefer to have you with us, naturally, but considerin' your circumstances I have asked Derek De Groome to fill in, as he did so well when you and Eura left us those many years ago. But if you could talk that lovely lady of yours into joinin' us onstage, I'd be most honoured."

Cyrus cleared his throat and said, "I haven't spoken to Eura in a while. We split up. I don't even know where she lives."

"Ah, what a pity. I did think you two would last. But then I never have been very wise in matters of the heart."

In order to bring the conversation back to a safer footing, Cyrus said, "You work in a music store?"

"Hard to call it workin', my friend. I am havin' the time of my life."

NIGEL WAS BACK IN THE STUDIO, producing an album for Newton's Apple, a band that had seemingly perfected the art of stadium rock. (Every record contained six or seven ponderous tunes of drug-induced splendour and implied significance that always—and this was the secret—sounded best in the vast echoing confines of a football stadium or hockey arena.) At the end of each day of recording, the band returned to the pleasures of London, and Nigel turned to the arrangements for the benefit. He seldom had more than a word of greeting for Cyrus. Sophie and Patrick had switched their focus to the studio's new clients. Sometimes Cyrus felt he had become invisible; at other times he thought he had become something even worse, something only partly visible and wholly upsetting.

In the days after he had spoken to Jim and made the arrangements for him and the others to fly over, Cyrus did little more than stroll about the grounds of Hidey-Hole. As the promotion for the concert increased, however, reporters asked him to explain what Ronnie was really like, to describe the dreadful attack. The interviews invariably left him feeling sorry for himself. He almost always ended those days with a few solitary rounds at the Two Poofs.

After one particularly depressing interview and the ensuing pints of bitter, he called Janice. More than anything, he wanted to hear her voice, one of the happiest sounds he had ever known. But this time he heard worry. She had read the news stories and had spoken with Izzy. She wanted to know how he was doing; she wanted details. And no matter how he tried to shift topics, she came back to her central concern until, finally, he told her everything.

"I'm supposed to have a few operations," he said. "But it doesn't look good. I don't know what I'm going to do."

"Are you asking for advice?"

"No," he said, "not really. I just wanted to hear your voice, I guess. How are things there?"

She told him that Isabel had bought back the old farm and was turning it into a trailer park, with Hank as superintendent. "Just last week," she said, "he bought a mobile home. He's already living out there. Drives around in a little golf cart. I'm invited for dinner tomorrow night."

Every time he phoned Wilbury, it seemed the fabric of the world had become unravelled and knitted together again in some new pattern. "I assume Izzy's paying for all this," Cyrus said.

"I'm not the one you should ask. It's none of my business. But I think Ruby helped him get started. She's been very generous lately."

"I guess you heard about Orchard Knoll. Bet you never thought I'd be a farmer."

"You'll also be a landlord soon. Ruby's living in town now. Izzy found her a condo down by the marina." Cyrus wasn't surprised that Ruby wanted to live closer to her friends, but the news hit him hard. The combination of Ruby and Orchard Knoll had always been his salvation. When he didn't respond, Janice continued. "I told you, didn't I, that I was thinking of moving to Wilbury more permanently? I mean, I'll always keep my studio in the city, but being back here, even at my mother's place, has been good for me. My work is going well, I feel good about my classes, I've enjoyed being with Ruby and your brother and sister, and, well, they rented me the farm, Orchard Knoll, I mean. Two weeks from now I'll be living out there with all those apples. Donny Pentangeles, Frank's son, is going to help me move around some of the equipment in the barn so I can work out there. You don't mind, do you?"

What he minded was that he wasn't in Wilbury with her. The people he cared about—Janice, Hank, Izzy, Jim—hadn't forgotten him, but they had created new lives without him. In a voice drained of energy, he said, "That's fine, Janice. I'm glad you're staying out there. Maybe I'll come see you someday."

"You'd better, and soon. Right after you see about that hand."

They said their goodbyes, then Cyrus went to his room and tried to sleep, wondering what he'd done so wrong that his life had turned out this way.

THE BENEFIT WAS MORE SUCCESSFUL than anyone had bargained for. Sixty thousand people arrived on the chilly grounds of Knebworth to witness the spectacle. The BBC filmed it for a special. Nigel recorded every second of it for a live album. There were T-shirts and posters on sale, information booths, petitions to be signed. They made the front page of both the *Guardian* and the *Times*.

The backstage area was a paparazzo's dream: David Bowie and Elton John in animated conversation in the food tent; Peters Frampton, Townshend and Gabriel mugging for the television cameras. And that sense of communion carried over to the show itself, which became a monster jam session with several drummers, banks of guitarists and no end of singers and percussionists and keyboard players.

The highlight, of course, was the surprise reunion of the Jimmy Waters Revival. Even jaded press hounds leapt to their feet as Jim bounded onstage to a loping blues groove. He closed his eyes, threw his head back, threw his arms wide and let the crowd's energy flow through him. When at last a stillness fell over that vast sea of people, when the only sound was the soft pulse of the bass and drums, a few muted chord spasms from

Sonny's B-3, Jimmy stepped up to the microphone and said:

> I'd like to tell you a story now, if I may, about the birds,
> the birds we see each day—the meadowlark,
> the robins, wrens and chickadees—and how they've all descended
> from those massive howlin' greedy beasts
> the allosaur and stegosaur and *Tyrannosaurus rex.*
> And I was wonderin', you know, about these birds,
> and thinkin', if it's true—and really, this is many millions,
> this is many million years—but,
> if such things could ever be, and through some kind of magic
> a dinosaur transforms into a bird,
> a bluebird in a tree, what on earth could *we* become?
> What could I become for you; and
> all you lovely children, what could you become for me?

The crowd roared in approval, fists punching the air. At the same time, the rest of the musicians began to file onto the back of the stage, twenty, thirty, forty people rocking side to side with the groove, while Jimmy said:

> This is somethin' we must understand.
> If some squiggly protozoa from the deep primordial
> slime can develop new behaviour,
> a backbone and a brainpan and the jivey wires inside,
> the blood and lungs and pumpin' heart of you
> and you and you, all sittin' in this regal place and lis'nin
> to the man—well if, you know, it can
> make that crazy leap all the way to me and you,
> it makes this whole thing kind of special, don't it,
> almost like a famous solo spinnin' out its line,
> and every note's another step in time.

> Maybe that's the way it is, another kind of music,
> and we don't know enough to play the part.

We feel there's somethin' missin' but we just can't find the notes
in our heads, or even in our hearts.
But oh my blessed children, lissen here, lissen here.
Don't you feel the shape of somethin' holy?
It's in the air around you—don't you feel it drawin' near?
Just close your eyes and lissen to it only.
It's there in the music of two billion hearts a-beatin',
the jangle of those jivey wires inside.
So let it out, let it flow, let the world rejoice
to the fundamental thunder of
our single lifted voice. Fill the empty space
with songs of love and laughter, and
let yourself embrace at last the sweeter life hereafter.

The audience applauded wildly as he strode away, an ovation that built to a resounding climax of hands and voices and stomping feet. When he returned for his encore, he was wiping his face with a white towel, the entire stage cloaked in darkness save for the spotlight trained on his movements. He waited patiently for the cheering to subside. Then, he said, "I'd like to introduce you to a friend of mine. Mr. Gil Gannon."

The audience roared again, though many remembered the name only dimly. As Gil moved to his microphone, Jim slid quietly to the back of the stage and took his position behind Sonny's B-3. He adjusted the microphone to accommodate his extra height, and when he was comfortable, when everyone had given him a look of readiness, he leaned forward to the mike and said, "This goes out to Ronnie. We're all lookin' forward, friend." Then he counted in Gil Gannon's biggest hit.

Gil had gained weight over the years and lost the agility and grace he once had. His voice had dropped an octave. His hair was a comical poof, his face swollen and glistening. He moved about the stage with the heavy deliberate step of an old-time boxer. His suit had the cut and shine of Las Vegas, and not the big-time casinos but the dingy off-the-Strip places that featured washed-up singers and foul-mouthed comics. And yet none of that mattered. He sang as well as he ever had, believing every word.

Keep on ridin' with the herd,
Runnin' with the pack,
Flappin' with the birds,
But honey—don't look back.

Jim had been playing some in Waldorf, just enough to show people how the keyboards sounded. Occasionally Billie talked him into a song or two—she loved to hear him do Fats Waller. So he was not without chops. But the solo in "Don't Look Back" required real technique, an edge he'd lost over his years of refusing to play. So, from the moment Cyrus told him about the concert, Jim had practised that solo, playing it over and over again until he could repeat it perfectly, like a prayer. And when the time came, when the band moved through the second chorus and the setup for the instrumental break, when Gil and the other musicians and all the people in the audience turned to him expectantly, Jim was ready to give them The Solo, that raging, Dionysian howl of the free spirit.

But at the very moment he should have begun, when he should have started his signature two-octave gliss up to the minor third, he paused, not a long time, maybe a beat or two, and then quietly began to weave a simpler, sadder, more thoughtful melody, one that summed up more accurately the feelings of the moment, the lives lived, the opportunities lost, the circumstances that had brought them all together. He hadn't planned it this way. He had wanted to play The Solo one more time for Ronnie's sake. But in the end it wasn't possible. He didn't have the spirit within him to breathe life into the youthful phrasing of long ago. It meant nothing to him anymore; he could scarcely remember who it was that had once played those notes. You can't step twice into the same stream. Instead he played the melody that hovered somewhere between his heart and mind. It was a more dissonant line this time, heavy with suspensions, the nines and fours, the non-chordal tones; but it was not difficult. It required more feeling than pizzazz. And when he played his final note on that final chord of the passage, he closed his eyes and kept them closed until the song ended. He hoped that Ronnie, that everyone, would forgive him.

THE PARTY BACKSTAGE WOUND DOWN after about an hour. The good deed had been done, and everyone had someplace to go. Back to a tour or a recording. Back to lovers and families and friends. The goodbyes were emotional, tinged with a feeling of satisfaction.

Cyrus, too, had somewhere to go. He had an apartment in Toronto and the prospect of surgery. Not surprisingly, he found it hard to work up much enthusiasm. He didn't mingle or make merry. As soon as he could, he caught a ride back to Hidey-Hole.

After a sleepless night, he asked Sophie for one final fry-up. He had nearly finished eating when Nigel walked into the room with a guitar case. "I was going to have Patrick drive you to Heathrow," he said, "but then I thought we could visit Ronnie before your flight. I've dubbed a cassette of the concert. We could play it for him. Oh, and here. I want you to have this." He set the guitar case beside him. "The National."

Cyrus stared at the blackness of his coffee. "I can't play, remember?"

"You'll think of something. For now a simple thank-you would do."

They left Hidey-Hole early in the morning and were at the hospital by ten, carrying a portable cassette recorder, two cassettes and two sets of headphones. The authorities had backed off on their plans to hustle Ronnie into a long-term care facility. He could stay until other plans had been made. When Doreen saw their gear, she wasn't pleased. "No rock and roll parties in here, I'll have you know."

"None," Nigel promised. "Just wanted our friend here to listen to the concert we put on for his benefit. Thought it might cheer him up."

She looked warily at the two of them. "I was at your concert, and it was too loud. We can't be having it loud like that in here."

Again they promised to behave, then hurried to their friend's room. Nigel put one pair of headphones over Ronnie's ears and offered the second pair to Cyrus, who had absolutely no interest in hearing the concert again. It had been painful enough the first time. He had no desire to be at the hospital, either. He'd made his peace with Ronnie. Now that he'd decided to go back to Toronto, he wanted to get on with it.

After a few numbers, Cyrus took off the headphones and walked down the hall. When he found Doreen, he gave her his address and phone number. "Let me know how he's doing, will you? I have to go home." He waved his busted hand. "If it wasn't for this, I'd stick around."

She kissed his cheek. "He's a lucky man to have friends like you."

As he walked back along the ward, he tried to think of his own life in those terms. Who'd look out for him when he couldn't look out for himself? Who'd sit by his bedside when he went in for his operations? Time and again, the answer to the question was the one person he couldn't bring himself to speak to just now: Isabel.

He sat beside Nigel and tried unsuccessfully to solve the crossword puzzle. Nigel got them coffee from the canteen, and they chatted casually about the previous night, exchanging catty remarks about various performers, wondering why it was that every artist, sooner or later, became a caricature. Cyrus suggested it had something to do with getting old.

"Look at Gannon," he said. "He's stuck in a time warp. Like parents. When they're young, they keep up with the trends, and then at some point they just stop caring or something. A switch gets flipped and that's it. For the rest of their lives it's the same hair, same weird clothes. A guy like Gannon— it's like he's making fun of himself."

Nigel disagreed. "Gil still cares what people think. He wants to be cool in the worst way. But he knows it will never happen, and it drives him batty. Even if he has a comeback, he won't be cool, he'll be nostalgic. But I respect a performer like Gil. He still has his fans. They want to hear him sing the hits the way they remember them. They want him to look the same, act the same, and he obliges. That's what our friend Jimmy Waters never understood, the fans. For Jim, and I think to some degree even Ronnie, music was more quest than communication."

Nigel put on the second pair of headphones. "Almost finished," he said, too loudly. "Jim's introducing Gil."

Cyrus had four hours yet until his flight. He went through a mental checklist to make sure he hadn't forgotten anything. When he looked up again, he screamed—Ronnie was staring at him. Nigel, who had been listening with his eyes closed, jerked to attention and saw what had upset Cyrus.

For the longest while neither one of them seemed able to move. Then Cyrus jumped to his feet and ran to get help, but when he returned with Doreen, Ronnie's eyes were closed again. Nigel was trembling. As calm and reassuring as a primary school teacher, Doreen retrieved the phones from Ronnie's head and handed them to Nigel. "It happens," she said. "It's nothing to get excited about. Just nerves firing."

Some time later Nigel drove Cyrus to Heathrow where they gave each other a hug. Almost as an afterthought, Nigel said, "If the bank ever gives up those master tapes, I'll finish the mix, no charge."

Cyrus nodded his appreciation, though he secretly feared his record would be stuck in limbo forever. Then he marched purposefully into the airport and checked his bags. His gear would follow in a few days.

Jim was sitting in the departure lounge, waiting for a flight to Chicago. "My dear boy," he crowed when he set eyes on him, "my every wish is comin' true. I was sorry we didn't get to chew the fat last night."

Cyrus embraced him. "I thought you'd stick around London awhile."

"No," he said, a ripple sounding in his voice, as though he were enjoying some private joke. "This is no longer my world. I have to get back to my Billie. Got myself a good little thing goin' there, I can tell you."

Cyrus shook his head. "You were great last night. Everyone thought so. This could be the start of a big comeback—the Revival's revival."

"The truth is, my friend, I have been there already. And I believe I have found, at last, my true callin'."

"That silence thing of yours?"

He raised an eyebrow. "Then I would hardly be workin' in a music store, would I?" When Cyrus didn't respond, Jim folded his hands together, leaned forward and said, "I have known salvation, Cyrus, that is the thing. That is the one thing I have tried to get across to people, but they would not hear me, neither my music nor my words nor my silence, deafened perhaps by my own clang and clamour. Now I am trying a simpler approach. I work in Billie's store and try to connect people to the instruments they deserve, the instruments that will deliver them. And if they require, I help them get started. I lead them step by step. I am their teacher." He nodded then at Cyrus's busted hand. "Perhaps it is somethin' you, too, might try."

"You mean, those who can't, teach."

"Not at all, my friend. Those who have known salvation are obliged to show others the path."

Cyrus shrugged, unconvinced. "You could reach more people onstage or with a new record."

"And for every Cyrus Owen who listens to the record and hears his own future, how many others are silenced? For now I'll make a little less noise, shed a little less light. See if I can help people find their own music."

A few moments later, a voice overhead announced that the flight to Chicago would soon board. Jim stood then and shook Cyrus's hand. He said, "Know any horn players?"

"A few."

"I've been thinkin' about this fella I knew way back when, Mance Morgan. Told me once that most players, you know, they take a deep breath before they start a solo, like they're gettin' ready to dive into deep water. But the good ones know better, he said. They know it's only after they run out of breath that they start playin' soulful notes . . ."

Jim's voice faded away. He gazed slowly around the waiting room, as though he hoped to remember it forever. Then he hugged Cyrus and walked slowly toward his flight.

HIS FIRST MONTH BACK IN TORONTO, Cyrus was too busy to feel sorry for himself. With checkups, consultations, interminable hours spent waiting for specialists to show, two separate operations and countless sessions with a physiotherapist, recovering was a full-time job and not one he was especially good at. He couldn't wait to move on.

Just before Christmas, Doreen called to say that Ronnie had died. "The day you left," she confided, "he began to fade."

He briefly debated whether to attend Ronnie's funeral, but the fact was, he had no money. He'd already signed up for welfare and was thinking seriously about pawning some of his equipment until he could get back on his feet. He wouldn't be playing anytime soon. He had one more operation scheduled, and quite possibly a few more in the new year.

The night of the funeral, Cyrus went out and spent his last few dollars in a bar getting "legless" as Tommy Mac used to say. And for the first time in his life, he understood how his father must have felt.

RUBY'S NEW APARTMENT still didn't feel like home. She was afraid to use the gleaming kitchen, and the floor-to-ceiling view of the marina always caught her by surprise. There were times she drifted through the spotless rooms and wondered who she was, where she had come from. Perhaps if she'd been younger, she would have found encouragement in her surroundings, the novelty and sheen suggesting that anything might be possible. Instead she looked around her sometimes and thought that nothing seemed real. That was why she'd been going to church more often, not just Sundays but also once or twice during the week, just to sit on her own and while away some time.

One day as she sat quietly in the balcony of the United Church, the choirmaster came in and began to play a piece of music on the organ ("Jesu, Joy of Man's Desiring," she would later discover). At first she listened the way she listened to all music, that is, with only some distant part of her mind. Music was something she didn't understand, so she rocked her head from side to side. The song's gentle pulse was reminiscent of their grandfather clock, a steady, measured *tick, tock, tick, tock,* that was pleasant and did not interfere with her enjoyment of being in the church, feeling so clean and starched and proper and, in some indefinite way, closer to Clarence. She was glad that there were things in her life that could remain as they had before, that she could continue to feel the comfort of this place.

Little by little, though, the melody of the hymn began to impress itself on her, not so much the tuneful nature of it, because that was much too fast and complicated for her to make sense of, but just the way it moved, *one-two-three one-two-three,* circling round and round like dancers, *one-two-three one-two-three,* just the way, in fact, that Clarence had whirled her around the dance floor on the night of their wedding, *one-two-three one-two-three one-two-three one-two-three,* spinning her faster and faster until she was breathless. And that was it exactly, the two of them dancing, her dress billowing out as they circled the room, the guests that night giving them all the space they required to unfurl their joy. And the more she listened to that three-note rhythm, the more it echoed the sounds of her life, like Clarence counting eleven-quart baskets, a tower of apples that rose shoulder high, like the sound of her shears as she pruned in her garden. It was the sound of her peeling apples and of the farm machinery and the *clickety-clickety* of the train they took out east. It was all there, really, the busyness, the regular routines and cycles of life, the ups and downs, the endless chores and decisions and running around but always in an established pattern that was lovely, that seemed to grow deeper and lovelier with each passing year as though each note of this song represented each day of their lives, sweet and steady and not unexpected, from note to note and step to step, falling in patterns and clear repetitions and connections that fade only to come back again, as though it, this simple life, their simple lives, were the finest art, the work of a genius, and all these little clicking figures and phrases were supported by something larger and more mysterious that reached out to her from across a great divide. She sat and listened now, really listened to this music flowing over her, flowing through her; and as it came to the final four bars, the final ten notes as the music slowed— *one-two-three one-two-three one-two-three . . . one*—she heard words, too, words bubbling out of the music or out of her mind or someplace between, each one aligned perfectly with the rhythm of that quiet resolution, as though it was a song she had written herself, as though the music had pulled out of her the one central theme of her life: "Loved only Clarence. He loved only me." And whether the words were strictly true mattered little to her at the moment. They were true enough, a truth that had been observable in the way they lived each day, in the way God's majesty had been evident to her in every moment of her life.

{ NERVES and BLOOD }

It was Peter Liu at the Two Star who told Cyrus about a possible job opening. Peter's uncle worked at Dominion Optical, a factory that supplied frames to opticians across the province. "Good place," Peter said, shaking his head agreeably. His tone, however, suggested it was not the sort of job he would take. He was a businessman, an entrepreneur. He hadn't come to Canada to become someone's slave.

Cyrus, who had nothing inside him that approximated an immigrant's drive to succeed, and whose self-esteem was sinking daily, took the address from Peter, put on the suit Izzy had bought him and went looking for an interview.

The factory stood four storeys high and took up half a city block. It was built as a warehouse for a large distillery, and the rumour was that in 1930, business associates of Lucky Luciano came to this very spot and bought two thousand empty barrels. Now the building housed an army of minimum-wage labourers, women mostly, from China, the Philippines, Jamaica, Trinidad, Senegal and Somalia. There were a few Canadian-born workers, disenfranchised in some way, through lack of education or natural smarts, through deformity or accident or some penchant for making the wrong choices.

The manager at Dominion Optical, Dean Lawrence, knew from

experience the ebb and flow of his human capital, knew that the amount of misery raining down on his workers was much higher than the national average and that among these people, who were as close to the edge as you could get without falling right over, there would be in any given week two or three who would not return, who would succumb to the forces of inertia, bad luck or karma, or simply the recurring nightmare they had been trying so desperately to escape. He knew this. He'd been on the job long enough to know that even when he was fully staffed it was wise to keep his door open. He would always need workers.

There was a policy at Dominion, handed down by the Schlegel family, who had owned and run the business since its inception in 1938 (when they brought their own immigrant energy and expertise to Canada). The policy was this: Give people a break. Make room for the downtrodden and dispossessed. Run a company cafeteria, with wholesome food sold at cost. Make a decent affordable product, so even the working poor could afford to look good. Those who insisted on the designer labels paid through the nose. Their stupidity, and the shameless markup, helped grease the wheels of the enterprise.

Dean wasn't surprised to see Cyrus Owen walk into his office that April morning and ask for work. The expensive suit, the long hair—appearances meant nothing to Dean or the Schlegel family. It was stories that had built Dominion, and this young man had one. You could see it in his eyes, the way he kept rubbing his misshapen left hand, the way his shoulders slumped forward in defeat when he forgot himself.

They talked for fifteen minutes, enough time for Dean to sense that Cyrus was a good person and, having no education, a failed career and a crippled hand, was suitably qualified to become a Schlegel employee. He was hired on the spot (as it turned out, there was an opening), and the next day Cyrus took his place at a wooden bench, beside a man named Chu.

Chu, with few words, showed Cyrus the basic elements of their job. When an order came in for a certain size frame with a certain length of arm, an order picker walked into the warehouse, selected the required pieces from the shelves and delivered them on a plastic tray to Chu or Cyrus, who then assembled the frames, using the tiniest screwdrivers Cyrus had ever seen.

After the arms had been attached, the tray was set aside and either Gladys or Connie would retrieve it for shipping. In terms of a crappy job, he had expected much worse.

Cyrus, who had never been one to sit and think about things and was even more reluctant to do so now, spent a large part of the day listening to others talk. He heard Sammi's daily report about the previous night's action on the dance floor. At least once a day he heard Gladys reciting her recipe for hamburger soup. Most of the time he listened to empty chatter about the lottery. Every week the employees chipped in money, and as the big day approached, their talk became more animated and full of expectations, falling miserably on the morning after. When Chu wasn't talking about the lottery, he was listing the prizes people had won on the previous night's *Wheel of Fortune.*

What made the first few months bearable for Cyrus was the sight of Tina in the cafeteria each day, her face a simpler and more youthful version of Eura's, her brown hair like a massive haystack, her thin, thrift-store fashions struggling to contain her voluptuous contours. She didn't speak much English and could not have been more than seventeen years old. She was also pregnant, which became increasingly evident with each passing week.

He didn't know where she was from, and he had no idea what she wanted from life, but he found himself caught up in her joys and sorrows. At lunchtime she would pull baby clothes from a bag and show them to the other women, who would cluck and fuss. She showed them photographs, too—maybe of home or her man or her parents and siblings. The other women took good care of Tina. Most knew from experience what she was headed for, and they pampered her and protected her and even, when she wasn't aware of it, said silent prayers for her, she was so young. But in those rare moments when Tina was alone, Cyrus observed another and less encouraging side. She would sit distractedly and rub her belly, her face filled with worry.

After his final operation and convalescence, after weeks of physiotherapy, Cyrus was forced to accept that he would never return to music in any professional capacity. He could hold a guitar and, with some pain and difficulty, play a few chords or a simple melody; but the hand simply did not respond in the required fashion. The doctor told him not to expect much more.

Several weeks later, Cyrus sold most of his equipment, but held on to the Harmony for sentimental reasons, and the National because he loved the look of it in his apartment. He made enough money at Dominion Optical to pay his rent and buy a week's worth of food. The extra cash from his instruments was for entertainment. His favourite spot, Zeke's Open Kitchen, had cheap beer and no clientele. It didn't remind him of Eura or home. If anyone spoke to him, it was about the weather or sports.

Once a week he phoned Janice, or she phoned him, and they chatted casually about the events of the day. For the first time in his life, he had become aware of the world outside music, filling in the dreary hours to and from work by reading the newspaper. He avoided the arts section and anything that reported on the music scene, but was oddly entertained by the political stories, especially those about Pierre Trudeau. (It was amazing that a leader who seemed more interested in ideas than in his constituents could remain so popular.) Primarily, Cyrus was drawn to the scientific articles—a discovery in the heavens, or the latest medical breakthrough. He was reminded that science was the only subject he had ever really liked in school. And with his penchant for wandering and discovering things, he wondered occasionally if he had taken a wrong turn, if he would have been better off doing research or something.

One night at the beginning of July, Janice phoned to say she was coming to Toronto. "A new show of my work," she said. "I wondered if I could crash at your place a few days."

Cyrus had gathered from comments over the past while that Janice could easily afford the price of a hotel room. So staying at his place, he knew, was for personal, not economic, reasons. "Don't expect me to clean just for you," he said.

"I'm talking spic and span, buster. You'll be getting the sniff test, the white-glove test, even the dreaded crisper inspection."

In the end she was hardly in the apartment at all. At the opening, they waved to each other a few times, but Janice was so busy working the crowd that Cyrus spent the night on his own, trying (and failing) to think of something clever to say about her work. It was all too weird for him, this new direction of hers, like bits of junk stuck together. They left the studio late that night and, in the taxi home, she fell asleep against his shoulder. He decided to save the wine and nibbles he'd bought; neither one of them was in the mood. He fixed her a bed on the sofa.

Next morning they had time for a brief, laughter-filled breakfast. She told him about the latest happenings in Wilbury, filling in the details about Izzy's purchase of the old place, and how Hank was living out there and turning it into a trailer park. The picture she painted of the two of them, Izzy completely frazzled and Hank wheeling around in a golf cart, was something that would warm him through many dreary hours at the factory. So would the feeling of sitting with her and discovering they could still be comfortable. It was the hallmark of a true friendship, he felt, that they could be apart for months and pick up right where they had left off.

While Cyrus was at work, Janice met with the art critic from the *Globe and Mail*, taped a short segment for the CBC, and gave a lecture at the Ontario College of Art. It was almost ten o'clock that night when she returned to the apartment, looking completely worn out. He smoothed the hair off her forehead and said, "Have you eaten?"

"A muffin, I think. I mean I bought one, but I can't honestly remember eating it."

He settled her into a kitchen chair, opened a bottle of red wine, brought out a small tub of dried black olives he'd bought at the Italian grocer down the block and then got out a large bowl, a bag of flour, some olive oil and yeast.

"You baking me a cake?"

"A pizza. I'm actually getting pretty good at this."

As she watched him knead the dough, she thought about the power of continuity. His actual movements were unexceptional. He was making pizza dough. Somewhere down this very block, and on thousands of other blocks around the world, you would find other men and women engaged in the same activity. But this was Cyrus. These were the same hands that had peeled potatoes in her mother's kitchen. These hands had played music of passion, cupped her breasts and combed her hair and wiped sleep from her eyes. She had watched him pick apples with those hands. She had watched him do his homework, holding his pen between his thumb and forefinger, like a child who was learning to write. Asleep, he would curl his hand into a fist and cover his mouth. In conversation, especially when he got excited, he would pound his knees like a drum. And whenever he was concentrating, he would flick his thumbnail between his two front teeth, *click-click, click-click, click-click*. It was magic, this continuity, this nearly endless series of hands, all of them Cy's, all of them different but complementary. More than that, it was art. This was how she worked, extending a line so that it might link the most unlikely moments and textures and images in the most necessary ways.

While the dough was rising, Cyrus prepared the toppings: a thin wash of tomato sauce, three mushrooms chopped finely, a palmful of diced green pepper, grated mozzarella and a few slices of prosciutto. After the pizza was in the oven, he lifted his glass, touched it to hers and said, "How'd it go today, dear?"

Her hand lingered on the nape of her neck where a knot of pain had been building most of the day. "It's funny," she said. "You spend so much time getting your career to the point where people will talk to you about your work. And when it happens, it's so dreary that you only want to be left alone. But you must know all about that."

"Not really. I was still working on the first part."

She studied his face a moment. "How are you doing, anyway?"

He wiggled his fingers, as if to test their flexibility. "I sold most of my gear. What company is going to release a record from a guitarist who can't play? Looks like my temporary factory job is a career now."

She remembered a time in her life when her whole world came unravelled. Ruby had thought a little religion might do wonders. Instead Janice had found something of her own to believe in. She sipped her wine and said, "Maybe it's time to look at other options."

"Really? What options? You think stacking shelves might be better?" He turned away then, disgusted with himself. He had vowed he wouldn't be pitiful. With a forced laugh, he said, "I'm reading again. Maybe someday I'll go back to school."

She smiled but not happily. He could tell the damage had been done. Her sunny features had darkened. She was disappointed or saddened or worried—it scarcely mattered what. He'd just ruined their first real chance to talk.

After they finished the pizza, she begged to hear a bit of his album and, good friend that she was, made a convincing show of enthusiasm. But his mood was such that compliments hurt as much as criticism. As he had on the previous night, he made her a bed on the sofa and left her in peace.

Half an hour later she crept into his room and sat on top of him. "You are such a moron," she said. Then she kissed him with so much force that she pressed his head deep into the pillow, as though she were trying to squeeze all the stupidity out of his system. Little chance of that, though. He'd always been stupid. Aside from music, he knew little at all. But he knew this: he loved the feel of her in his arms; her presence there beside him was the expression of something grand. He lay awake all night listening to her breathe. Next morning after breakfast, when she drove back to Wilbury, she took all the brightness with her. When he looked closer at the space she'd left behind, it seemed to glisten.

EVA WAS TINA'S BEST FRIEND AT WORK, and it was from Eva that Cyrus got the scoop: the father of Tina's child was in trouble with Immigration. One day it looked like he would be granted status as a landed immigrant; the next, deported. Dean Lawrence was involved. He'd spoken to his member of Parliament. If anyone could fix it, she said, Dean could.

Cyrus couldn't begin to imagine the uncertainties of immigrant life, always fearful you might displease the authorities and lose your cherished foothold in the land of peace and prosperity. Though on some level the loss of his parents had left Cyrus emotionally homeless, he had never felt that way. With Clarence and Ruby, with Isabel, he had always known he was safe and secure and, most of all, loved.

He told Tina's story to Chu and asked if he had ever experienced that kind of pain. Chu cleared his throat, an impressive array of rumblings and scrapings, and said, "Canada is the best country."

Cyrus then asked Chu where in China he'd come from.

"Austria," he said. "Before Canada I live six months with my brother. In Vienna."

"But before that, in China, where did you live?"

"India. My parents move to India." He then described how, in the middle of the revolution, his mother and father boarded a junk and made their way to Calcutta, where they established a leather tanning business. When Cyrus asked for more details, a troubled look appeared on Chu's face. "Next month I go back," he said. "To Calcutta."

"Are they sick?"

"Two years ago my mother die and now—" he twisted his mouth, searching for the right words "—we finish blessing." He then described the ritual of prayers, how only the poor and desperate were buried too soon.

It was a struggle for Cyrus not to make a face. Those few days of Clarence's funeral had nearly done him in. He couldn't imagine two years of ritual. Little by little, the import of Chu's words began to sink in. He was planning to use all of his vacation time. He had three children and a wife, who, like him, made minimum wage. Cyrus could well imagine how expensive it would be to fly to Calcutta.

That night back at his apartment, Cyrus's feelings of disbelief turned to anger. Chu was wasting so much heroism and good fortune. His parents had set off from a troubled country and sought a new and better life. They worked hard and prospered, raised two sons who in turn sought a better life, first in Austria, then in Canada. It was the stuff of legends, of the building of empires and nations. But to what end? For Chu to land this dead-end job and devote his every waking moment to lotteries and the shallow seduction of game shows? Was that what the dreaming and effort had been for? And then to fritter away his hard-earned dollars on what, to Cyrus, amounted to little more than a primitive sacrifice. Why not throw himself into a volcano and be done with it?

Nothing in his own life had that kind of power over him; he was free of dreams and obligations. All he had was a vague longing, an empty space inside him that might take any shape, that might make any demands if he let it. At one time it had echoed with the music of his life, but now it was silent.

When he told Chu's story to Janice, she was more sympathetic. "You shouldn't be so quick to judge," she said. "It sounds to me like your friend is the one who's heroic. The grand gesture of his parents is obvious. But what Chu is doing is even harder in a way."

"Watching TV and buying lottery tickets?"

"His children. He suffers this life so they can have a better one." When he didn't respond, she said, "You're one to talk. Not exactly setting the world on fire there, are you?"

He was so angered by that shot that he slammed the receiver down. But he called her back a few minutes later. "You're not being fair."

"Well, you're not being kind."

"Yeah, well, fuck you, too."

IN THE FIRST FEW MONTHS after Cyrus started working at Dominion Optical, the guys in Jangle would phone to see what was up and invite him out for a drink. But he never wanted to go anywhere or see anyone, so in time they began to call less and less and finally stopped altogether, which was what he had wanted in the first place. But when Chu went off to Calcutta, Cyrus realized that, as pathetic as it might be, sitting beside Chu eight hours a day, exchanging a few sentences of mindless chit-chat, comprised his entire social life. He had no friends, no hobbies, nothing aside from tipping back a few glasses of beer at Zeke's. When Janice phoned to invite him to Orchard Knoll for the weekend, he jumped at the chance.

The Impala had been carted off for scrap, so Cyrus took the bus to Hounslow and was met at the station by Janice. As he tossed his suitcase into the back of the Volvo, she said, "You'll be happy to know your room is just the way you left it."

"Oh," he said, disappointed that they'd be sleeping separately. "I thought we might pick up where we left off in Toronto."

"Well geez, Einstein, no kidding. I was making a joke. Ha ha. I packed all your junk into the basement the day I moved in. It gave me the creeps, that room."

They drove out to Lake Isabel before heading to Orchard Knoll. His last time through, the old place had still been an industrial wasteland with oil wells and storage tanks and wire fences. Now he saw a vast stretch of mud and weed, with a murky-looking pond in the centre. Two trailers sat beside the pond, one twice the size of the other.

"Looks like Hank's got some company around that mudhole."

"Yes," she said, "Po Mosely." She uttered the words carefully, without inflection. There had already been enough talk around town about Po and

Hank. She didn't want to colour Cy's view of things. It was none of her business.

He turned to her and said, "I suppose you think this is funny."

"I didn't say a word."

"Yeah, I know you didn't. I can hear you not saying a word. Your not saying a word is coming in loud and clear. Why didn't you tell me?"

"Because I knew you'd get weird about it."

She pulled into Orchard Knoll and parked beside the garage. As they stepped out of the car, he said, "You think I'm being weird about it?"

"You're acting like Izzy, which is weird enough for me."

He held his hands out, as though he were balancing two pies. "What did I say?"

"You didn't have to say anything. I could see it in your face."

"What, that I'm surprised?"

"That."

"And maybe a little pissed off that no one told me?"

"That, too. You're also afraid that Hank's going to screw up again."

"And you think that's weird?"

She raised her eyebrows playfully. "You and Izzy. I'm beginning to think Hank's the only sane one in the bunch."

IF ANYTHING MADE HIM FEEL WEIRD it was his aunt and uncle's house, especially with all the changes Janice had made—bold colours, stylish furniture. And making love in Ruby and Clarence's old room was weirdest of all. It was almost too much for him. Had it not been for Janice's customary ardour, he would have lost his concentration.

Next morning he got up at sunrise and wandered through the orchard. There'd been no spring pruning, no thinning, no spraying, no effort to keep the grass and weeds down. Frank was too old to take on that much, and his boys had found work in an auto plant. Who else was there? You couldn't have just anyone mucking around out there. They could do more damage than good. He picked a Winesap and inspected it. The whole crop, both early and late varieties, was a write-off. What hadn't been spoiled by pests and rot would be too small to sell. Worse, the load on some of the trees was so great they might split. A couple more years of this and there'd be nothing much to salvage.

When he got back to the house, Janice was still in bed. He crawled in beside her warmth and kissed her neck. "I think you should stop fooling around with this artsy-fartsy crap of yours and take care of those trees out there. It's breaking my heart to see how wild it's become."

"You own them. Why don't *you* do something about it?"

"It's Izzy who should have taken care of it," he complained. "Hire someone or sharecrop it or something. This is just wrong."

His mood improved over breakfast, partly because of the funny stories Janice told about Wilbury and partly because of the way she moved about the kitchen. She looked beautiful to him, like something green and full of life, a field of corn, perhaps, and he was a summer breeze.

After he helped her clean up the kitchen, they returned to the bedroom and made love again. Unlike the previous night or their last evening in Toronto when they had been frantic and greedy, there was something methodical in Cyrus's approach that morning, as if by clearly labelling and cataloguing her discrete elements—the mole beneath her chin, the arch of foot, the dimpled knee, the swell of buttocks, the deep ridge of her spine, the physical poetry of her shoulder blades—he might later, in the loneliness that was sure to greet him down the line, remember and possibly even relive the splendour of this time together. If he could hold himself outside the beckoning chaos, he might make better sense of what was happening between them, maybe unlock the secrets of this naked duet. But foot and knee, breast and lips, flesh and sweat and breath had their own sort of cadence and value, a physical melody with dynamics that ranged from the susurrus of whispered kisses to the loopiest of crescendos, up and down, round and round, themes repeated, restated, inverted and harmonized until he lost all sense of time and register and meaning and was drawn down inside this thing they were creating, this energy, this wave, this flow.

HANK TOOK A MOMENT EVERY DAY to marvel at his project. It wasn't a dream come true, not even close, but it was something. As laughable as it might be (and he knew some people were laughing), he still felt lucky.

The hardest part of the whole scheme had been talking Izzy into it. Once he'd done that, it was easy to convince her they needed a well and a big holding tank for waste. With money from Ruby he bought a trailer, then a banged-up golf cart from Ross Pettigrew.

The riskiest part of the venture was Po, who'd been turfed out of his spot at the home. There'd been cutbacks to social services, and the authorities figured he could fend for himself as long as he came in regularly for his medication. He was certainly no harm to anyone. He deserved his freedom was the thinking; he needed his self-respect. But freedom brings certain risks, the prime one being the freedom to mess up, and that was something Po frequently managed to do. Invariably, a day or two after he cashed his welfare cheque, some young thug managed to take the money from him. And more often than not, he was so involved in keeping the sidewalks free of paper that he neglected to get his medication. Increasingly he was spending nights at the shelter in the church basement. Ruby's complaints about the matter, how Po was disrupting various social functions, gave Hank his idea.

With Janice's help he drew up a proposal and presented it to the local council. If the town could come up with a trailer for Po, Hank would rent him a spot at Lake Isabel where disturbances were unlikely to be a problem. He would also keep an eye on him and monitor his medication. The councillors discussed the matter, spoke with social services and gave the go-ahead. The Rotarians bought Po a trailer, which Hank described as "no bigger than a breadbox and about as crummy."

He had concerns about sharing his space, of course, but they were soon allayed. Proper and regular doses of medication kept Po as quiet as a mouse, and during daylight hours he had his litter work along the Marsh Road to keep him busy. Little by little, Hank began to appreciate having him around. Sometimes they cruised together around the pond or sat at the picnic bench, not talking so much as inhabiting the same location. Before long, he even had Po fetching things from town and helping out with a few chores. He was certainly strong and, as long as the requests were simple enough, could manage them without too much difficulty. The week before, they had driven over to the beach, where Hank got him to load the cart with wide flat stones. After a few trips, they had enough to make a little patio by the pond. That's where Hank was sitting when Cyrus and Janice drove up.

"Look what the cat dragged in," he called out.

Cyrus turned in a circle to take in the full lunacy of his brother's new home. "And look at you, you bastard, like Ben Cartwright on the Ponderosa."

Hank laughed at that and waved them forward. Janice kissed him on the cheek and, pointing to the stonework, said, "This is new."

He laughed again, knowing it looked kind of crappy but proud of it all the same. "Me and Po made it," he said. "And Cy, check this out." He rummaged under the seat of his golf cart and came up with a paper bag full of bread crusts. He tossed a few pieces onto the surface of the pond. One by one they were sucked under by a black mouth. "Catfish," he explained. "Bill Krause give 'em to me. Ain't it cool?"

It was only then that Hank remembered Cy's troubles, and he turned and looked him over carefully. "How *you* doin', kid?"

Cyrus wiggled the fingers of his left hand. "I'm glad to have the cast off, but I'm still not good for much."

"Hell, at least you can scratch your ass with both hands now."

Cyrus and Janice climbed onto the back of the cart, and Hank drove them to his trailer. There, he levered himself into his wheelchair and led them up the ramp to his living room. "It's not much," he said, "but then I don't need much, right? Winter might be a bitch, I guess. Haven't really figured that one out yet."

The room itself was large and more or less empty. He had his stereo set up on a card table. There was a black-and-white TV and a threadbare recliner, a wobbly wooden chair, a pile of TV tables folded up and leaning against the wall and, propped in a corner, a battered-looking acoustic guitar with a hula dancer painted on the front, an instrument so warped that the strings looked to be six inches from the neck. No sign of the synthesizer.

Cyrus knew what role he was meant to play here—his brother needed encouragement. Under the circumstances, that would require a few lies, or at the very least some exaggeration; but he and Hank had always been straight with each other. These conflicting thoughts made him hesitate, and his silence only made matters worse. Janice wanted him to be helpful. That was probably one of the reasons she had invited him to come down.

He walked to the window to admire the view—acres of mud still bearing the mark of Joe Filmon's backhoe. Without turning around, he said, "I hear you got Po Mosely for a neighbour. What's that like?"

Hank rolled his chair forward into his galley kitchen. He poured water into a kettle and put it on the stove. He grabbed a big jar of Nescafé and plunked it on the counter. Then he turned around and said, "Po's Po, I guess. No different than ever." He looked at Janice, then Cyrus. "I guess I'm the one who's different. Coffee?"

Janice got out a tray, a carton of milk and a sugar bowl. She carried it all into the living room and set it on a TV table. Sounding like the affable sidekick on a talk show, she said, "Po helps you out quite a bit, doesn't he?"

"Yeah, Po's all right. Likes it when I call him my partner."

Cyrus waited a few seconds before he drifted over to the TV table. He tested his coffee, added some sugar, and then sipped again. "I didn't mean anything," he said. "It's good you're doing stuff. Really. What else have you got planned?"

Hank rolled over to the recliner and pulled some papers from the side pocket. "Here," he said, holding them out to Cyrus. "See for yourself."

There were two pencil sketches. The first was a view of the pond surrounded by mature trees, lush parkland and well-tended paths. There were tidy-looking trailers, and people sitting in lawn chairs and chatting with their neighbours. The sun was shining. There were big puffy clouds, a happy couple in a canoe. A flying saucer hovered near the horizon. The second drawing was on grid paper, a site plan showing exactly where trees and paths would go in relation to the pond and parking lot.

The professional nature of the drawings, and the fact that Hank had made them, surprised Cyrus. The classes with Janice had obviously sharpened his brother's perception and trained his hand. More than that, Cyrus was shaken by the thought that Hank, who had spent his life reacting to the past, now had a plan for the future.

When he finally looked up, he said, "This is great, Hank."

"You don't think it's stupid?"

He looked at the pages again. "No, it's a great idea. Really."

While they finished their coffee, Hank talked non-stop about the handful of successes and the many disasters of the past few months. Even his complaints carried a note of satisfaction, however, the way new parents lovingly recount the sacrifices they've made for their children.

When it was time to leave, Cyrus gave his brother a hug. Pointing to the guitar, he said, "You play that ugly thing?"

"I hack away at it, but not much comes out."

After that, Janice and Cyrus drove around town awhile. He didn't pay much attention to the scenery. He kept thinking about Hank and his plans, and how surprising the whole thing was. For lunch, they parked at the dock and got a couple of foot-long hot dogs. Janice said, "He needed that, you know, your approval. He's not always so upbeat."

"He seems to count on you a lot, too." He looked at her and said, "You're not falling in love with him, are you?"

She calmly held his gaze, an indication that she, too, had pondered the question. Placing her hand on his arm, she said, "I'm fond of him. He's unlike anyone I've ever known before. But . . ." She let her hand wander up his arm to his shoulder, his face, his hair, her touch so gentle and reassuring that the rest of her words were unnecessary.

Cyrus didn't have the strength to see any more of Wilbury, especially Isabel, so they stayed in for dinner, drank too much wine and made love until they were exhausted. Next morning, while they were still lounging in bed, Hank phoned. "I forgot to tell you about the party. Think you can come down again next month? It's Izzy's turn to hit forty, you know."

Cyrus chewed the side of his thumb and stared into the darkness of the open closet. "She's pissed off at me," he said. "I'd just ruin everything."

Hank scoffed at that. "Izzy never stays mad at anyone. I know this from experience, believe me."

After a bit of hemming and hawing, Cyrus promised he'd attend the party. He'd already been wondering how to arrange another visit with Janice. Before he hung up the phone, he said, "I'm really happy for you, Hank. This whole new plan of yours seems great."

"Well," he said, "I've been a loser all my life, kid, just like the old man. I guess I figured it was time I tried something else."

CYRUS STRUGGLED through his first week back in Toronto. With Chu still away, he had twice as much work to do. He came home most nights with a sore hand. It was boring, too, to sit all day without Chu beside him, a feeling made even worse by the fact that Tina was absent all that week. Not well, Eva said.

When Tina came back to work a few days later, her eyes were swollen, her shoulders slumped, her eyes downcast. All day long the women hovered around her, clucking and fussing and comforting. Eva told him later that the government had deported the father of the child, news that seemed to cast a pall over the entire department, as if they realized suddenly how much their lives, too, were subject to change. Cyrus suggested they take up a collection, and Eva thought it was a good idea.

It was only when Chu returned to work a week later that the mood began to lift. He brought everyone presents and gave Cyrus a small copper box with a hinged lid. The box was just large enough that it might hold two dominoes, one atop the other, and Cyrus worked the lid a few times and said, "Hey, this is cool. I could keep all my money in here."

The joke went right over Chu's head. With a look of great seriousness, he took the box from Cyrus and set it on the workbench. Then he placed Cy's tiny screwdrivers in the box and closed the lid. "See?" he said. When Cyrus laughed, Chu smiled with relief.

Next day Chu talked more than usual and more poetically than Cyrus thought possible, about his vacation, about his brother who worked now in the tannery, about his parents and their lives. It was clear how much he missed that world, the nights in particular, when he and his brother and father strolled through the city arguing about politics. The food, too, he said. And the heat. And the newspapers he'd grown up with. Cyrus could feel the ache of that longing in his bones, knew from his days on the road how the fanciest hotel in the most exciting city in the world could pale beside the simple idea of home.

The sense of being rootless and alone followed him throughout the day, and that night in his apartment, almost out of habit, he picked up the National. After a few simple chords, however, his knuckles ached terribly, and he knew it was no use. So he sat in the darkness awhile, holding the guitar in his lap, thinking that Janice was right about Chu. Even though he might talk longingly of home, he would stay in Toronto, at Dominion Optical. He was a bridge for his children to cross into the promised land. Without that, none of it made sense. When Cyrus thought of his own situation, he was ashamed he had embraced defeat so completely.

The day before Izzy's birthday, he closed his savings account—nine hundred dollars in cash. After lunch he asked to speak with Dean Lawrence. He took a seat in the single wooden chair in front of his boss's wide desk and said, "I know I've only been here a few months, but I kind of need a few days off." Dean nodded, his hands steepled in front of his face. He had the look of a man who would be surprised by nothing.

Cyrus thanked him and then walked to the door. Turning there, he said, "It's too bad about Tina."

Dean leaned back, his hands clasped behind his head. "It's tough, but they're young. They'll get it together eventually. One thing I've learned, people are resilient. They bounce back from stuff you think would kill them. It's the only thing that makes this job bearable at all."

Cyrus nodded and went back to his bench. A big manila envelope for Tina was making the rounds. When it was his turn, he signed the card and quietly placed half his savings inside. He went to the washroom then, and sat in one of the cubicles, hoping Dean was right.

After work that night, he called Janice and told her he had rented a car and was driving to Wilbury. He planned to surprise Hank and stay at Lake Isabel. "Good idea," she said.

When he arrived just before midnight, the marsh was bathed in the waxy glow of moonlight. The air was warm and humid, the lake churning in the distance. Somewhere on the marsh a flock of geese complained. As he came around to the screen door of the trailer, he saw his brother in his recliner, half asleep. Po sat beside him on the wooden chair, transfixed by the blue flicker of the TV. It was such an odd and private scene that Cyrus immediately backed away. He walked over to the bench on the stone patio and sat down to wait for the end of their program. He was in no hurry. It was a glorious night to be outside, the kind of evening when he used to sit on the veranda with his guitar after Clarence and Ruby had gone to bed.

A few minutes later Po shuffled outside and headed over to the other trailer, with Hank shouting instructions through the open door. "What's happening tomorrow, Po? Izzy's big party, right? So I'm not going to be back until late. And what are you going to do? Stay home, right? Take your medicine like you're supposed to? And I'll be back as soon as I can."

Cyrus stayed at the pond another few minutes. When he approached Hank's door again, his brother had one of the armrests of his wheelchair folded down and was holding the acoustic guitar in his lap. As Cyrus watched, Hank played the five-note theme of "The Bridge." It was out of tune, without vibrato or finesse of any kind, the phrasing only approximately right, but it was unmistakably Cyrus's music, his forgotten masterpiece. And the sound of it on that summer night, in the place that had once been their home but was now his brother's new beginning, was too much for him to take in. It conjured his mother's sweet face and his father's sad defeat, and all the people he had ever known, all the things he had ever done, all of it coming back, all of it flowing out of the night and into his aching heart, all of it. And not knowing what else to do, he backed up, his face covered with his hands, and ran as fast as he could to the rented car where he lay across the hood and wept.

When he straightened up again, Hank's lights were off, so he drove to Orchard Knoll. Though it was late, Janice was working in the shed, still fiddling with her father's monument. When she looked up and saw him, he said, "It's better, I think, if Hank gets some rest tonight."

She nodded her understanding and set down the electric drill she'd been using to etch letters and texture into the surface of the stone. Then she slowly and methodically removed her work gloves, safety glasses and the kerchief she had tied around her head. She stepped out of her coveralls and was wearing a pair of shorts and a sweat-stained T-shirt that was ripped on the shoulder. Instead of moving into his arms, she circled him, as though appraising a statue. She stopped in front of him and said, "I miss you like crazy, you know that?"

"Yeah," he said, "me too."

She nodded again, satisfied they could agree on that much. She reached out and fooled a moment with the top button of his shirt, then let her arm drop to her side. Retreating a few steps, as if she needed to take a running jump, she said, "Maybe we could do something about that."

NEXT MORNING, CYRUS left Orchard Knoll before Janice was awake and drove over to Lake Isabel. Hank was sitting out by the pond with toast and coffee. The minute he saw Cyrus he called out to him. "I was starting to think you weren't coming."

Cyrus walked over to the pond, took a bite of Hank's toast and, while he was chewing, said, "Your lights were off when I got in, so I stayed with Janice last night. What's the plan?"

Hank did something vaguely Elvis with his upper lip. "I thought we could have the party out here. Lots of room, that's for sure. But nobody was too thrilled by the notion. We're at the rec centre, instead." Ruby and her church group were providing the food. Drinks were BYOB. Bobby Nash and the Ramblers would keep everyone hopping. Best of all, he said, Izzy didn't have a clue.

"What do you want *me* to do?" Cyrus asked, feeling like an outsider.

"Stay out of sight," Hank said. "And be on time. Other than that, I don't know, stand around and look pretty or something."

Cyrus followed Hank into the trailer and, while his brother showered, made sure everything was arranged just so. Ten minutes later Hank left the bathroom and wheeled himself toward the kitchen. Cyrus said, "Brought you a present." He pointed to the corner where the hula dancer sat beside the chrome magnificence of the National.

"You're joking, right?"

"I never use this one, anyway. You might as well have it."

Hank rolled his chair across the room, lowered the right-hand armrest and picked up the instrument. After running his hands along the brilliant chrome contours, he tentatively strummed the strings.

Cyrus said, "Maybe you'll be able to keep this one in tune."

"Right. Like I'd know the difference." Then, carefully, his head bowed, he picked out the theme to "The Bridge." When Cyrus stiffened, Hank looked up, confused. "I thought you'd get a kick out of it."

"I do. I just—" He covered his face with both hands and waited until he was back under control. Looking straight at his brother, he said, "It's great you figured that out. Play it again."

Hank bent over the guitar one more time, his face taut with concentration.

When he'd played the figure a second time, he laughed and said, "That about right?"

"Perfect. Let me show you the next part." He grabbed Hank's old acoustic, sat at his brother's feet and tuned the guitar as best he could. His first attempt to finger the strings sent a fiery pain from his knuckles to his shoulder. "Christ," he said through gritted teeth, "you'd have to be Hercules to play this fucking thing."

Hank grabbed the neck of the acoustic and held out the National with his other hand. "Let's switch for now," he said. "I'm used to that brute. And let's face it, it's not going to hurt my technique any."

The National was only slightly less painful, but enough so that the two brothers could fool around a few minutes. Hank would never be considered a natural, but neither was he a quitter. He didn't seem discouraged at how little he could do.

"One last lesson," Cyrus said, when his hand could take no more punishment. "If you only know how to play a few notes, you'd better make them sound good." To demonstrate, he played a note with and without vibrato. Then he showed his brother the position of the hand, the fulcrum points and how to "worry" the string back and forth to create a shiver. "You'll sound like B. B. King in no time," he said.

Hank tried it for a few minutes, then looked up and smiled. "Look at me," he said, "getting private lessons from a rock star."

Ruby arrived soon after that and made a fuss over Cyrus, noting his bloodshot eyes, the bags, the scarred hand, muttering all the while, "My Lord, my Lord." She might have spent the whole day that way if Hank hadn't reminded her it was time to go. When she invited Cyrus to help them decorate the hall, he begged off. "I told Janice I'd be back soon," he lied.

After he watched the two of them drive off, he sat in his rental car and tried to place some of the old landmarks—the pond, for instance, and the willow trees where he and Blackie used to sit. It struck him how many changes this one piece of landscape had lived through: marshland, farm, oil field, trailer park. Did it make sense to ask which incarnation was the right one? Had the Owens used the land any more wisely than Benny Driscoll or the natives who roamed these marshes centuries before the white man ever set foot in these parts?

When he drove back to Orchard Knoll, Janice was on the front porch with a book. "Hey there, lazybones," he said. "I got tired of waiting for you to wake up."

"That's convenient. I was tired of pretending to sleep. How's Hank?"

"All right, I guess. Seems pretty excited. You got plans today?"

She closed the book. "I'm under strict orders to keep you hidden."

AS INSTRUCTED, Izzy arrived at Hank's trailer at about six o'clock. He'd told her that he was taking her to dinner somewhere, his treat. After she stowed his wheelchair in the trunk, she slid behind the wheel and asked for directions.

"A little surprise first," he said, rubbing his hands together. "I made you something in Janice's art class I'd like to show you."

As they drove downtown, Izzy bantered about the prestige of owning a Hank Owen original. She parked in the lot and helped wheel him up the wide ramp of the recreation centre. Stopping just shy of the front door, she said, "It's probably locked, Hank."

He held up a key ring, and when he unlocked the door, everyone jumped out of the shadows, blowing noisemakers and shouting. It took her a moment to gather her wits—she really was surprised. Then she laughed, a high girlish squeal that Hank was sure he'd never heard before. "Oh my God," she said, pounding his shoulders. "I'll get you for this."

The stream of faces flowed toward her and enveloped her, people she saw at the office every day and those from town she hadn't spoken to in years; her students, some of whom had careers of their own; clients who'd stuck with her through two or three home purchases and now were more friends than business; Ross Pettigrew and Janice Young; Ruby, of course, and the ladies from her church group; and lastly, standing off to the side and waiting until everyone else had given her a hug, her baby brother, Cyrus. She ran to him and hugged him tight and whispered so that no one else could hear, "You son of a bitch." Tears were running down her cheeks and smudging her mascara, but she didn't give a damn because it was her birthday, her fortieth, and people could call her a sentimental old fool if they wanted. It was true.

The Ramblers chose that moment to kick into their first number of the night, "Let the Good Times Roll," and people easily slid into the groove. The wine and beer began to flow. The food came out from under wraps. The volume and temperature and energy rose in equal measure, and the night moved inexorably into memory.

At the end of the party, Hank was so drunk it took both Cyrus and Izzy to get him back to the trailer and into bed. When they were sure he was safely tucked away, they walked to the pond and sat on the bench there. Cyrus clasped his hands behind his head and stared up at the stars. Izzy watched a pair of mallards cruising the water's edge.

"How's the job?" she asked without inflection.

"You know, shitty."

"Did the doctors tell you when you'll be able to play again?"

For the first time, he gave full voice to the dark knowledge that had been shifting around his head for months. "I'll never play again, Iz. Not professionally. They've done all they can, I think. The guy in physio said I should get used to the idea that it's downhill from here. Considering the damage done and the operations, he figures that arthritis could kick in any time." He shook his head. "It already hurts like hell most days."

Izzy thought a moment, then began to talk to him about money, about Ruby's generosity with Hank and the likelihood she would help Cyrus. She mentioned the rental money from Orchard Knoll, how half was going to Hank and the other into a bank account for Cyrus. "I can give you a cheque tomorrow, if you like, or whatever you want to do."

He nodded his head, feeling both embarrassed and appreciative. Desperate to change the mood, he said, "Now that you mention the orchard, I can't believe you'd let the place go that way. You know how Clarence was. It'd kill him to see it."

She looked down at her lap and tried her best to explain. Lack of time, she said. Lack of knowledge. In the end, thinking of the damage that could be done, she had felt it was better that no one work the place.

Cyrus knew his uncle had felt the same, and was sorry he'd darkened Izzy's mood with his complaints. Hoping to make up for it, he told her he would take on the responsibility of finding the right person to manage the farm. He had booked time off work, he said. He could spend the next few days talking to people. The longer they let it go wild, the harder it would be to get someone interested.

Izzy got to her feet and tossed her keys in the air. "Want me to drive you over there?"

He shook his head. "I told Janice I'd stay here tonight. I've got a feeling Hank might need a little help tomorrow." Isabel laughed and touched his arm. Then he watched her drive away. But the moment she was gone, he wished he had asked her to stay longer. They hadn't talked for ages.

The air was warm, and the heady smell of the lake was like a drug. Aside from the stars and moon, there were no lights anywhere that he could see, no sounds other than the tremulous shudder of a screech owl in the distance.

Full of nervous energy, he got to his feet and strolled out to the Marsh Road. There, he could hear things stirring in the ditch, a raccoon, maybe, or a skunk. And without thinking, putting one foot in front of the other, he moved smoothly into his recurring dream and began to run down the middle of the road. It took no effort at all to imagine his father there with him, the soundless strides as though his feet didn't touch the ground, the way he seldom seemed out of breath or even really trying. And just the way it happened in all the dreams, Cyrus left his father behind, or rather, his father stopped running and let him disappear down the road on his own. He passed the Van Vessens', the Wiebes', and ran down to the bend where it joined the Lake Road. He cruised by the "Gold Coast," ticky-tacky cottages on postage stamp lots, and across Roxy Beach where the sand was as fine and white as sugar. He ran without breaking his stride, even when he hit the water, the sand there so hard and rippled you could drive a car on it. He ran through the shallows, almost losing his balance but not quite, on and on into deeper water, sending up a fountain of spray until he was up to his waist. And without pausing to think, he leaned forward into a crawl and swam out beyond the breakwater to bob in the larger waves.

JANICE WOKE WITH A START, knowing something had just happened but not knowing what it might be. She clutched the blankets under her chin and tried to slow down her heart. Listening carefully, she could just make out the drip of water. Then one of the shadows in the room moved toward her and touched her with an ice-cold hand. "It's me," Cyrus said. "Rise and shine."

The horizon had begun to colour. It would be an hour at least until sunrise. The room smelled of lake. "Come to bed," she complained. "It's too early." But when he knelt beside her and hugged her, she pushed him angrily away. "Rotten thing to do," she muttered, drying her face on the blankets.

"Just water," he said. "It won't kill you." He hugged her again, and this time she didn't recoil but relaxed into it, sought further contact with his cool wet skin. "It's taken me a while to figure it out," he said. "I'm slow. I'm stupid. But it's finally starting to sink in that we should get married."

Janice grew still, the silence deepening with each beat of her heart. She untangled herself and sat back. She looked out the window, then up into his eyes. "And then what?" she asked.

He folded his arms, suddenly on the defensive. "I don't know. That's the only part I'm clear about. I think we should get married."

She pulled on her housecoat and dragged him to the front steps where they leaned together, the world around them gradually taking form. "This is what I know," she said. "I've lived here and in Toronto, and maybe someday I'll live somewhere else again. I've been single and I've had a relationship I thought would last my whole life. I've had periods when I've been surrounded by friends, and times when it seemed I had no friends at all. And you know what? When I think about what's important to me, when I think of the line that runs through my life, it really comes down to one thing—my work. So when you come to me all of a sudden talking about marriage, and you're dripping wet like you've just been baptized in some new religion, I get worried. I've seen you get carried away before."

Cyrus nodded soberly. He knew he deserved as much, but that didn't make it less hurtful. He also knew from bitter experience that few dreams last a lifetime. She was looking at heartache if she thought this career she loved so well would carry her to her final days. He had lessons to teach her on that score. Without looking up, he said, "Is that your answer?"

Janice thought about her time with Jonathan, about the few disastrous affairs she'd had since then, about the many nights she had crawled into an empty bed and wished she had Cyrus in her arms. Then she looked at him and said, "My answer is this: I don't want you to go back to Toronto. I want you to stay here in Wilbury. And maybe, I don't know, maybe I want you to stay here with me. But I don't want to marry you—not right now at least. I think we should take it one step at a time."

She squeezed his hand. He sat in stony silence, looking at the horizon. Finally he said, "I'm cold," and walked into the house. When she followed a few moments later, he was already in the shower. She tried the door, but it was locked.

DURING THE NEXT TWO DAYS Cyrus met with as many farmers as he could. Men like Ernie Bell, who had no apple experience, were eager enough to take on Orchard Knoll but were just too clueless. Those who knew about apples expressed no interest at all. Wade Dobbins over at D&B Orchard put it down to a sign of the times.

"Wouldn't make much sense our taking on your acreage," he said, pushing back the brim of his peaked cap. "We're pulling out half our trees as it is. Not worth our while. Now if the damn bureaucrats up in Ottawa would do something about these cheap imports, we might stand a chance. But the way it is, it's hopeless. We're putting in cherries instead. You might want to go that route, too, Cy."

As much sense as that might make from a business perspective, the thought of pulling out a single tree seemed a crime. He would, he realized, just as soon chop off his own hand as cut down one of them.

His other dilemma, Janice's refusal to marry him, was much more troubling. They had continued to sleep together but, by tacit agreement, there was little contact. On the third night after his proposal, however, their unspoken pact broke down and they made love almost desperately, as though they both feared it might be their last chance.

The next morning he awoke alone, after his first solid sleep in weeks. The sun was up and he stumbled out to the kitchen. There was a half pot of coffee. A clean cup, saucer and small breakfast plate were on the table. Janice's dirty dishes were in the sink. Her car was still in the driveway.

Peering out the low windows of the laundry room, he could just make out her silhouette in the shed. She was already hard at work.

While he dawdled through breakfast, his thoughts bounced back and forth through time: wondering about his future with or without Janice, remembering the smell of Ruby's *kuchen* and the sound of Clarence's tuneless humming, probing the aches and bruises from his life with Eura, occasionally pausing in the present to contemplate the luxury of a day off from Dominion Optical. His thoughts were interrupted by the telephone.

"Is this Cyrus?"

"Yes."

"This is Billy Maddux. I was phoning about guitar lessons?"

Cyrus looked at the receiver with disbelief. Then he said, "No lessons here, kid. Bother somebody else. Where'd you get this number anyway?"

"Was on the ad. Maybe I dialled wrong. I'm sorry . . ."

"Ad? What are you talking about? What ad?"

"At McCready's. On the bulletin board there."

McCready's was the new music store in town, the kind of place that Cyrus could only dream of when he was a kid. But he knew just the sort of ad the boy was referring to: a small typed notice with a phone number repeated on several detachable tags. It would be tacked on a corkboard with a thousand other notices announcing lessons, equipment for sale, musicians at liberty.

The boy continued. "Said to call Cyrus at 555–2134."

"Well that's the number, all right, and my name is Cyrus—"

"'Lessons from a rock star' is what it said . . ."

Suddenly it all made sense. It was Hank's doing. He'd gone downtown and put an ad in McCready's, the idiot. Cyrus clucked his tongue. "Sorry, kid. Somebody's practical joke."

A few minutes later he wandered out to the shed. When Janice saw him in the doorway, he said, "I can't believe how good I feel."

"Me too. It's a beautiful morning."

He jammed his hands in his pockets and half-turned so he could see the sunlight and blue sky and acres of trees. Without looking at her, he said, "I wish I could always feel this way."

"You can try."

He wandered idly around the shed, picking up tools and putting them down again. "Need any help?"

"Well, there is one thing you could do for me. You could get lost, Cyrus. I'm trying to work."

"Yeah, I know."

She hugged him with all her might and pushed him toward the door. "Call me for lunch. You keep telling me what a great cook you are, maybe you could show me a little more proof."

He drifted back across the yard. Before he went inside, he inspected the apple tree near the corner of the house, the one on which he and Izzy and Clarence had grafted three new buds to symbolize the union of the two families. It was in no worse shape than the other trees he'd inspected, but this one was special, so he returned to the shed for Clarence's bow saw and his heavy-duty shears.

Clarence didn't follow a lot of the common wisdom about apple trees. He thought it was wrong to prune only in late winter. Nor did he think topping trees was a good idea. It made them bolt and waste a lot of energy. In most ways, he said, an apple tree was like a person. It needed space and light. It needed to be protected, and when it got sick, it needed someone to care for it. It needed grooming and could not be expected to carry the full weight of its burden without some kind of help. "You can always trust a nice-looking tree," he liked to say.

Cyrus circled the tree a few times to confirm his first impression. Then, angling in to the trunk (both Frank and Clarence had advised him to prune from the inside out), he searched for a place to begin. It wasn't easy. He had always found it difficult to make that first cut, to limit growth and creativity however undisciplined.

Start with the obvious, Clarence had told him. Broken branches, split branches, branches that are causing damage to others. And so he did, one cut leading to the next with surprising ease until the tree began to open up, creating corridors of light and air where fruit could flourish. It was pleasant work. His muscles were humming. His mind was clear and focused. When he finished, he returned the tools to the workbench, then gathered the pruned branches together, three big bunches, and carried them over to the woodpile behind the shed, amazed at how much a tree could do without. As he walked back to the house, he stopped to admire his work one last time. To the untrained eye, the tree would now appear stunted and unnatural, but Cyrus knew it was a better tree than it was before, stronger and healthier and more likely to express its genius.

When Janice came in for lunch, he made grilled cheddar-and-tomato sandwiches (one of Sophie's specialties), which they ate outside on the front porch. After that they made love once again, then went for a long walk along the Marsh Road. Around five o'clock, he drove downtown to Izzy's office, where he found her alone doing paperwork. Without a word of greeting, she said, "How's the search going for a hired hand?"

He slumped in the chair opposite. "Haven't found anyone who knows even half as much as I do."

"Well, the job's yours if you want it." She scribbled something on a document and then looked at him over the rims of her reading glasses.

"That's not what I meant," he said.

"Well, no, neither did I. I was joking. Or maybe not. Why don't you think about it—at least until you know about your hand."

"I know about my hand. Besides, I already have a job."

But even as he said the words, he knew something was changing. During the past few days there'd been a feeling of suspension in the air, like those old spider chords Sonny used to play that stretched out in every direction and acted as a bridge to another key or groove. He got to his feet and said, "I'll keep looking." At the door he turned and added, "It's great, you know, what you've done for Hank."

She removed her glasses and rubbed her weary eyes. "Po Mosely, for Christ's sake. That was all his doing." Then leaning back in her chair, she shook her head and smiled. "Ever think your life would end up like this?"

He looked out at the main street of Wilbury, over to his middle-aged sister, streaks of grey beginning to colour her hair, then down to his mangled hand. "I guess I never thought about anything much at all, Iz. But I was always afraid I'd wind up back here sooner or later, burned out or washed up."

"You're not a failure, Cy."

He took a step back inside the room and leaned heavily against the door jamb. "I don't know what to think about any of that. Maybe I am, maybe I'm not. Maybe I'm about to find out." He thought about Clarence and how clear and unified his life had been. He thought about Jim and his many transformations. Then he said, "Let's you and me do something. Go to Hounslow maybe. I'll buy you dinner and tell you my whole sad story."

Instead they ate pickerel at the golf club and talked until midnight, filling in the blanks of the past twelve years. Afterwards, he dropped her at the office where she'd left her car. Then he drove on alone to Lake Isabel, believing that the two of them had established a connection at last, that after a lifetime of awkward negotiation, they had finally found a groove.

Hank was sitting alone at the pond with the National cradled in his lap. Cyrus walked up beside him and stood admiring the full moon. A jet soared high overhead. Nearby there were crickets, and out on the water the same two mallards. Hank plucked an open string—*pling, pling, pling*—then let his arm hang limp at his side as the final note rang out. Staring straight ahead at the pond, he said, "I did it, you know."

Cyrus was confused by the bleak tone of voice. He said, "I know, Hank. You should be proud of yourself. You've got a great set-up here."

"I mean a long time ago. That guy. At the gas station. I did it. I killed him. I told you I didn't do it, but I did. I killed him. I'm guilty."

Cyrus swallowed hard, tempted to tell his brother that no one had ever believed he was innocent. Instead, he took a deep breath and said, "That was all a long time ago, Hank. You're not guilty anymore."

His brother looked straight at him now. "I'll always be guilty, kid. Always. And I'm not complaining. I deserve that. It's the way it should be. I just wanted you to know."

"Well, Hank . . ."

"I mean, I wanted you to know, I guess, that I'm sorry."

Another jet passed over them. A car drove along the Marsh Road, stopped briefly and then moved on again. In a different voice, pitched a little higher, Hank said, "I love this place. It keeps me from thinking too much about all that. I got my plans, right? And when I come outside this way, I kind of get lost. Maybe it's spending all that time in prison, but I almost get stoned when I'm out here. There's the birds and the flowers and the bugs. Had a praying mantis here the other day, weird as fuck. And this pond, I could sit here forever and watch it. It kills me how it came up the way it did. Water's a tricky thing, right? I mean they built that dike over there to hold back the lake, and it works all right—we drive every day on top of it—but the lake, I guess, is just waiting. The minute you make a space for it, it flows right under the dike. That's what we did here. That's what this is, I guess, a bit of lake that managed to escape."

Hank struck a few more notes on the guitar, not really playing so much as keeping time. Then he looked at Cyrus and said, "You ever think of giving lessons?"

Cyrus closed one eye as though he'd been poked. "Funny you should say that. Billy Maddux called me this afternoon asking the same thing."

"No kidding. Word gets around, I guess."

They fell into a companionable silence, a space so calm and carefree it seemed to predate them and any of the troubles that had twisted their lives out of shape, before Portland and Burwash, before anything dark and dismal and disfiguring, back when two brothers could sit and say nothing and do nothing and just be together.

As Cyrus looked out across the pond, some part of the night detached itself and began to flutter toward them. It hovered above the water as if trying to make a choice, dipping down to the surface of the pond and then fluttering up again, dipping down and then up, before it finally continued in their direction. A moment later, he could make out a large summer moth, a cecropia, it appeared to be, lavish and unlikely. The closer it came to them, the more directly it flew, until it was almost within arm's reach. It seemed to hang there a moment, as though it had been mesmerized by the moon's bright reflection in the polished metal of the guitar. And before either brother could say a word, the moth moved on again, tremulous and fragile. The night was opening like a flower.

ACKNOWLEDGEMENTS

In writing this book I relied on information from a number of sources, including: *Music, The Arts, and Ideas,* by Leonard B. Meyer; *The Singer of Tales,* by Alfred Lord; and in particular, Larry J. Solomon's essay, "Sounds of Silence." The Rilke epigraph is from a translation of *The Duino Elegies* by Stephen Garmey and Jay Wilson.

Many thanks to my editor, Anne Collins, for all her help; to copy editor Stacey Cameron; to my agent, Bruce Westwood who, among other things, prunes apple trees like a poet; to friends and family far and wide who allowed me to gibber about a work in progress; and most of all to Christine, Claire and Anna.